PRAISE
WHAT REMAINS OF

"Prepare to be captivated by *What Remains of Teague House*, the kind of slow-burn suspense that hooks you with every twist while drawing you deep into its aching exploration of family bonds and secrets. With gorgeous writing and characters so vividly drawn that you'll feel like you've known them your whole life, this mystery is impossible to put down."

—Jess Lourey, Edgar-nominated author

"An impressive first novel from Stacy Johns, *What Remains of Teague House* is a sinister mystery wrapped within layers of secrets harbored by the members of the dysfunctional Rawlins family. Effectively told from multiple points of view, the story follows a sombre gathering of three siblings for their mother's funeral at their gloomy childhood home. The home has enough sordid history—including the father's suicide—but nothing that compares to the chance unearthing of multiple corpses in the woods located on residence grounds. Every character is delightfully gray, each with their own secrets, and it's up to private detective Maddie Reed to solve a dark mystery decades in the making. A powerful debut, and one that will keep you guessing."

—Carter Wilson, *USA Today* bestselling author of *The Father She Went to Find*

"A thrilling story of murder, betrayal, and a family home that hides dark secrets. I couldn't put it down!"

—Stacie Grey, author of *She Left*

"Who doesn't love a dark and twisty family saga with literal bodies buried in the backyard? In *What Remains of Teague House*, Johns give us the ominous mystery of the Rawlins family, where shocking sibling secrets are revealed in the wake of their matriarch's death. Set against the foreboding Teague House, Johns slowly builds a delicious tapestry of murder, betrayal, and a twist ending that had me guessing until the final pages. A compulsively readable debut."

—Kali White, author of *The Monsters We Make*

"Part murder mystery, part family saga, a dash of gothic horror—and totally gripping! *What Remains of Teague House* had me hooked from the first atmospheric page to the last chilling twist. Don't miss it!"

—Andrew DeYoung, author of
The Day He Never Came Home

WHAT REMAINS OF TEAGUE HOUSE

STACY JOHNS

Poisoned Pen
PRESS

Published by Poisoned Pen Press, an imprint of Sourcebooks
P.O. Box 4410, Naperville, Illinois 60567-4410
(630) 961-3900
sourcebooks.com

Cataloging-in-Publication Data is on file with the Library of Congress.

Printed and bound in Canada.
MBP 10 9 8 7 6 5 4 3 2 1

For my family.

1

VAL

....

FRIDAY

Val sways before the sliding door in her nightdress, tiles cool on the cracked soles of her feet. Through the glass, mist hovers above the long reach of the lawn, from the back patio to the edge of Teague Wood. Val grasps the smooth finial of her nearby rocking chair with a shaking hand. A snatch of bright birdsong reaches her, and she peers out at the feeder, but it's too early even for early birds to breakfast.

Last night she pretended to swallow her medicine but spit the capsule into her hand as soon as Phyllis left the room. The pills make her sleep right through the morning, and the half hour her bossy sister spends in the shower is the safest time for Val to steal a little privacy. She's been worried about her secret treasures in this damp spring, even though they're wrapped in plastic.

An ache in her left hip invades her lower back. She

grimaces, steps forward, and puts all her weight into sliding the door open. The morning air smells fresh, like evergreens and damp earth, and the boards of the patio feel alive and uneven under her bare feet. A zing of joy shoots through her chest, and for a moment, it's as if she's a girl again, sneaking out before dawn.

She kneels at the edge of the patio, and her knees crackle painfully. If she tumbles off the low platform into the long wet grass missed by the lawnmower, she'll never get back up. Reaching cautiously, blindly, into the gap under the boards, she cringes at the cling of a spiderweb, but when nothing crawls over her hand, she keeps going. Her stomach tightens when her fingers grab emptiness. She forces her hand in further, and is rewarded, finally, by the smooth edge of the lockbox.

She drags it out, brushes off the dirt, and spins the dial to her sister's birthday. Tension drains from her shoulders when the lid rises easily, and she runs her finger over the freezer bag enclosing the contents. Condensation clings to the outside, but no moisture appears to have seeped in.

Tempted by proximity, her fingers twitch at the top of the bag. Is there time to revisit her treasures? No. Dawn is coming soon, and her sister will be down any minute. It's best to wait. Perhaps tomorrow she can wake earlier, if she skips her pill again. Her heart races at the thought of bucking Phil's wishes. But she needs to. She will.

She maneuvers the box back under the patio and ruffles

the weeds along the edge to hide all traces. Using the support beam, she climbs to her feet in stages. There will be a day when she can no longer do this, when it's too much, and she wonders what will happen then. Will she tell Phil, trust Phil to fetch her treasures? Or will she keep her secrets and let them molder where they lie, like the others she can no longer reach?

Before going inside, she scans for birds again. Her movement must be keeping them away, though she hears a crow cawing in the wood. The mist twists like ghosts, as if someone is out there, disturbing the air currents. It could be a hunter. They trespass in all seasons, even though Russ posts signs along the property line.

She catches herself. Not Russ, of course. It's Robby now, her son Robby, who posts the signs, mows the lawn, chops wood for the pile by the shed. Her eyes seek the little building in the corner of the yard, and the overhanging maple where Russ took his life. She looks quickly away. Someone should destroy those awful white clapboard sides and green shutters, and turn that tree into kindling. Didn't she say that to Phil? But wait. She steals another glance. This shed is a prefab metal box on a concrete slab, tan with a red roof. Russ's studio was farther back, too far to see from the patio. That's why he liked it. Out of sight, out of mind, he'd say, slinking out to his liquor and his weed. As if she didn't know what he was up to, didn't smell the funk when he came in for dinner.

Val goes inside and slides the heavy door closed. Her

damp feet leave tracks on the tile. Phyllis will be down soon, fussing at her about slippers.

Movement outside catches Val's eye. Something emerges from behind the shed. There are hunters here, as she suspected, sneaking into Teague Wood before sunrise to avoid being seen. But why the lawn cart?

Two distant figures struggle over the tree roots of the path along the edge of the wood. The cart sways with its awkward, uneven burden; it's covered with a tarp, but a yellow pendulum swings from the side, almost brushing the ground, a beige blob at the end. Val squints.

It's blurry…but she thinks it's a hand.

Val's own hand jumps to her throat to quell the leap in her pulse. Her eyes are playing tricks. Unless—could that be Russ pushing the cart? He must be furious. She sucks in a breath, squeezing the loose skin at the base of her neck.

No. Russ is dead. Phil says he's dead. But Phil must be wrong. That must be him, with the lawn cart, with the body.

Valerie prays with breath held, but she's not sure whether she prays for Russ not to be dead or for that not to be Russ. She squints harder. The man in front wears a plaid jacket, dark jeans, and a ball cap. He's stocky, not gangly enough to be her husband. The one in back though, he's tall, with dark pants and big work boots, and a knit cap pulled down over his hair. He wrestles with the heavy cart, putting his back into it. That one, that could be Russ.

She's in trouble. She swore on her life, on her love for him. Her heart hammers and her vision darkens around the edges. Dizzily, she reaches for the arm of the rocker and lowers herself. Her hip hits the sharp wooden edge, hard, and pain shoots up her side and down her leg. She falls into the seat and sits gasping. Tears fill her eyes.

She gets so confused. But there it is, that yellow arm, swinging plain as day.

Not plain as day, old woman. A calm voice interrupts from the back of her mind—her wiser self that usually emerges when the kids need her. Like when Sandra, barely old enough to walk, fell from the window and broke her arm, or when Jon had a fever of a 102 and Russ was at work with their only vehicle.

The calm voice has a point. Here she is, eyes straining, seeing the cart, seeing Russ, and that yellow shape… Her old eyes cannot be trusted, especially in this early light. Maybe it's a dangling cord, a tool he needs for the trail, to keep it clear and wide so she can push the stroller to the swimming hole with baby Robby.

But—the kids are grown, aren't they? Why, Robby came for dinner last night, looking as though he hadn't shaved for a week.

Pain drums behind her eye like a migraine is coming on. That's definitely an arm. The sleeve swings hypnotically as the pair trundles closer, nearing the turn where the path veers into the woods. Valerie leans forward, ignoring the ache in her back, the throbbing in her head. She has to know. The men pause. The shorter one turns toward the house, the bill of his cap hiding his face in shadow.

She leans closer. The rocker tilts forward. His shape rings a bell in her mind. The way he moves, his stocky power. The face is unclear, but she pictures deep-set eyes meeting hers.

Above her left eye, the pain grows teeth. She tries to rise, to call out to Russ, to beg forgiveness and say she loves him.

The rocking chair tips her off and the floor hammers her face. Agony envelopes her head, her whole being, like fire. The world disappears in a white flash.

When she can see again, the view is sideways. A blurry patio and lawn stretch to a dense dark ladder of trees. A man swims toward her, his face washing close to her own, his eyes pained and shining. Her mouth struggles to form his name. A little robin redbreast lands nearby, so pretty in the light of dawn, and she strains to see.

The pain in her head bursts like bubbles into sweet relief and darkness.

2

ROBBY

....

Robby sheds his sweats and T-shirt and slips back into bed. Elly's breath is soft and even against his shoulder, but all else is silent. The tension that thrums through his body only increases, and he lies staring into the thick gloom. Elly grunts, rolling toward Christine's side of the bed. Her long brown hair is a stain across Christine's pillow. He'll have to change the sheets, vacuum, wipe everything down. If Chrissy finds a single strand, she'll know, and this time she won't bother with questions.

Giving up, he slides away from Elly's warmth again and sets his feet on the floor. He shouldn't look at his phone, but he does. Four thirty in the morning. Since Christine left with the girls, his nights are deserts of wasted time where he's too tired to do anything useful but too wired to relax. If only he could rewrite his life from where it went to shit, which in his darkest hours seems to be before birth. Or more likely, when he was ten, when Dad—he stops. That's a pointless road to go down.

He rubs his temples and the bridge of his nose, attempting to relieve the pressure behind his eyes. His muscles twitch. For a second, he wishes Christine could see him suffering; then she'd be sorry. But he takes it back immediately. She can't see him like this. If she finds out about his recent affairs, there will be no point going on.

He steps back into his sweats, pulls on the crumpled T-shirt. Elly doesn't stir. Robby sticks to beer these days after too many two-day hangovers, but Elly helped herself to Chrissy's fancy gin last night. Knowing her, she'll call in sick today. Add to the list of housekeeping chores: buy another bottle of the good stuff for Christine and level it off.

His whole body is parched, so he pads to the kitchen, where the window above the sink reveals his father staring at him with bloodshot eyes, stubbled cheeks hollow. Robby jerks away before realizing it's him mirrored there, not Russ. He swallows. No. Christ, they don't even look alike. It's the exhaustion. He needs to force himself back to bed, and stay there.

On the way back down the hallway, he pauses at the door of the twins' empty bedroom and his heart twinges. Checking on his sleeping daughters at the end of the day is the best thing about being a dad. His father hung himself, thirty years ago now, without a second thought for Robby or his siblings, and it still reverberates through every single day. Robby's nothing like that. He loves his girls more than life.

Easing their door open, he takes in their deserted bunks, dimly lit by a motion-sensitive night-light. Chelsey's artwork, big-eyed cartoons sketched in blue ink on notebook paper, surrounds the top bunk. The pages curl like relics from an ancient era. Around Lottie's bunk, horse posters crowd the walls, and a mountain of wrinkled clothes hides her comforter.

The night-light flickers off as he breathes in the musty smell: laundry detergent, girl sweat, and something fruity. He shuts the door with a hollow thump, then freezes, listening, but all is silent.

At the threshold of his bedroom, he hesitates. A couple days ago, he crawled into bed at 5 a.m. and slept through the morning, missing his chance to hide the car in the garage to make it look like he'd left for work. The one person who gives a crap right now, Aunt Phil, noticed it on her grocery run and interrogated him at dinner. "Why did you take a day off? Did you use vacation time? Are you sick?" Mom, chasing peas with the end of her fork, stared at him more morosely than usual, and he had the eerie feeling that she understood every word.

He has to fix this, has to rejoin the daytime world. Support his family. He placated Aunt Phil with a lame excuse about leaving work to hunt down his forgotten wallet, but that was a one-off. Aunt Phil is Mom's round-the-clock caregiver. All the sibs help support them—Robby with less money, more chores—but Aunt Phil expects him to remain employed, and she has an unerring instinct for when he's hiding something.

Technically, he's got a new job lined up online, but he keeps hoping something else will come through. Like his former boss, Cromley, begging on his knees for him to return.

He imagines snuggling into bed beside Elly, the static behind his eyes darkening into sleep. His muscles could warm and finally relax… The thought makes him feel trapped instead of tempted. He turns away, dons his jacket and shoes in the living room, and heads outside.

Brisk air shocks his bare face and soothes his gritty eyes. Just like when he was little, fishing with Dad before dawn, being out while the world sleeps makes him feel special, like he's part of the magic behind the everyday. Robby hasn't thought of fishing with Dad in years. Tilting his head back, he takes in the vast field of stars and a lung-stretching breath of night. Damned if he'll continue like this: The insomnia, the self-recrimination, the loneliness. The lies. But damned too, if he'll sit at the computer staring at hours of video about the customer always being right. There has to be a better way to win Christine's trust and keep his family, without selling his soul.

At the edge of the lawn, he peers up and down the empty highway. Giant Douglas firs loom on both sides, and some brisk animal, maybe a fox, trots along the centerline before veering into the shadowy woods. The sky might be a shade lighter than it was before.

He'll walk the property, he decides, from one side to the other, through the wood over to Teague House. A patrol, to make sure all is safe and well. He'll make a mental list of chores for the weekend and pop in to tell Aunt Phil. If he judges the timing right, she'll offer him a cooked breakfast. Then, he can walk home, hide the car in the garage, kick out Elly—for good, this time—and come up with a plan.

The half mile of winding path from the cottage to the big house dates from when Mom and Dad were young hippies with a cheap piece of land, nothing but state forest and logging roads for miles. They lived in the cottage, which was more of a rustic log cabin back then, while Dad learned his skills and built what the locals dubbed Teague House, after the old-timer who used to own the patch of woods it was nestled in.

Robby turns on his phone light, aims it near his feet where tree roots conspire to trip him, and thinks about Dad bush-whacking this path, forging ahead while singing "Stand By Me" at the top of his lungs, Robby skipping behind, joining in when the refrain came around. The ghost of fatherhood past. Another tune slips into his head, a made-up lullaby Dad used to sing, his calloused fingers brushing back Robby's hair…

Maybe we should move… For a moment, the idea of leaving everything and everyone behind—his father's ghost, his mother, Aunt Phil, Elly, and goddamn Gayle—seems so tempting, so perfect and easy and right, he starts spinning the words in his head to make Christine see it too.

A spiderweb breaks across his mouth, and he spits, brushing madly at his head and shoulders. Just like that, the fantasy evaporates. There's no leaving all this. This is what he has, like it or not, and whatever crumbs of self-respect are left will fall away if he forces his wife and kids to move just so he can start fresh.

Blackberry vines catch at his pants and thorns pierce his skin. He swears and tugs them free. He'd neglected to cut them back last fall, which means they should be on his list for the weekend. Upkeep of the grounds is his responsibility, but he does the bare minimum to keep Aunt Phil off his back. Mostly he fixes what she can see out the window and that's enough. There aren't enough hours in the day, with the twins enrolled in every sport and extracurricular activity in a three-county area.

Between the predawn darkness and the trail's poor condition, it takes a quarter hour to draw close to Teague House. He steps into the back corner of the yard. The horizon glows with the promise of dawn under a purple sky, the stars fading to a few bright spots. Mist shrouds the lawn. The walk settled him in some indefinable way, but as he nears the big oak where the tire swing hung when he was a kid, his heart rate jumps out of habit: anticipation or fear. He stretches up to reach the hollow where he kept his pipe and pot back in high school, and snags a cheap phone encased in a zipped sandwich bag.

In the house, a light flicks on in the upstairs bath. Aunt

Phil always rises early. The window's frosted, but Robby turns his back as he powers up the phone. He hasn't checked it or charged it for a couple of weeks, hoping Gayle would understand his complete silence as a final breaking of ties. In this temporary moment of strength, with the breaking dawn bolstering his resolution to be a better man, he needs to know the mess of his previous affair is no longer clinging.

The screen flickers behind the cracks radiating from the bottom right corner. The battery has a chunk of charge left, but it doesn't do well living outside, even wrapped in plastic.

The phone flickers again and stays on. He traces his lock-pattern, then glances at the bathroom window, still lit. The lock screen clears, revealing notifications in the upper corner. He bites his lips as he swipes to show a long list of texts.

Spam, spam, and more spam. He deletes, then pauses. The second to last is from Gayle.

We need to talk ASAP. I'm scared, Rob.

He checks the timestamp. It was from late last night, around the time Elly was grinning naked with the duvet around her shoulders, demonstrating how she could clench the gin bottle between her breasts without using her hands. A noise escapes him, a strangled bark carrying the taste of bile.

When he scrolls backward, there's nothing besides that exchange three weeks prior that ended with his "I can't help you. Don't come near me again." He'd started caring too much—loving her, even—and she'd started coming to him with every little problem.

He'd hoped Gayle had finally given up on him after that refusal, but he doesn't like that "scared."

A high-pitched shriek jerks him from the phone screen. He jumps, looks around guiltily, but sees nothing. It was probably a fox in the woods, but he shudders, feeling he's been standing here too long. It's the cold getting to him, that and Gayle's message putting him on edge. He hesitates, then powers down the phone and tucks it in its hiding spot, out of sight and reach of everyone else who lives here.

Still uneasy, Robby glances at the still-lit upstairs bathroom window, and then down to the sliding door that leads into the family room from the covered patio abutting the lawn. He squints. Something doesn't look right, a darkness against the inside of the glass. He frowns, stepping closer. In his old running shoes, his feet sink through the silver lace of dew, soaking his socks and the cuffs of his sweatpants. He's fixated on the oddity, stepping more quickly, jogging by the time he nears the door. A trick of the increasing light shoots his reflection back at him, but as he mounts the wooden patio, he discerns the dark splotch is a figure sprawled on the floor.

His mother is crumpled in front of the rocking chair where she likes to sketch the birds. There's an awful stillness about her, and her eyes are rolled back under half-open lids.

He knows instantly that she's gone, and stops short. Caught in her silence, he turns to take in her last view of Teague Wood, but his gaze is drawn lower. Across the porch, next to his own, a line of fading boot prints leads up to, then away from, the glass.

3

SANDRA

....

A knock wakes her, and Sandra blinks away a clinging dream as Jon's shape appears through the sliver of open door.

"Sis? It's almost eight. Denny had Cheerios. Gotta go. I'll be home late."

She rolls over with a groan. Teague Wood was in her dreams again. It's been years since she's thought about the pet cemetery. Now, night after night, she wakes clammy with sweat, the image of her father scrabbling in the dirt lodged in her mind. In the dream, tears run down his narrow face and into his dark mustache, infecting her with a miasma of sorrow that clings through the day.

Living with Jon's grief over his wife's death must have unearthed old memories. That's all it is. But Jill's passing was nothing like Dad's; hers had been slow and painful while his was swift and chosen. Considering Sandra's unsentimental nature, the dreams are more likely the result of fluctuating hormones, a warning sign of approaching menopause. Tragedy happens. Dad's death was not her fault.

A beat later, Sandra blearily asks, "Jon?" but he's no longer there. The clunk of the solid front door echoes in her ears over the shush and splash of rain outside. She sits up amid tangled sheets and blinks in dismay at the time on her phone. Today is her older brother's forty-seventh birthday. "Shit. Shit." She'd planned to make him waffles, but she hadn't even managed a "Happy birthday."

Jill's cancer destroyed Jon, and no matter the impact on her life, Sandra tries to be there for her brother. Though she's starting to wonder if she's enabling Jon to avoid his own son.

When she hurries into the living room, tugging her fingers through her tangled gray bangs—the rest cut pixie-short—Denny is perched on the edge of the couch staring at the muted television, where a grinning cartoon dog bounces up and down in a shower of alphabet letters. Denny's shoulders are rigid and tight tendons form hollows around his knees beneath baggy basketball shorts.

"Mornin', Den," she says, hugging his shoulders gently.

"We're late," he informs her.

"I'm ready." No one will see her ratty pajama pants when he jumps out in the school's drop-off zone. Unless they're truly late and she has to walk him to the office and sign him in. She checks her watch. They can still make it.

"I brushed my hair," he points out. "You have a rats' nest."

"Well, I'm not the one going to school," she says, but tugs her fingers through her bangs again. "Come on. Grab a jacket, it's chilly out there."

"Mom says I know best if I'm cold or not." His lower lip trembles. Thinking about Jill is enough to do that, sometimes. If he's tired, hungry, stressed. Awake.

Sandra summons a smile. "Your mom was a wise woman. But what if you're warm until recess time? And then you can't play because you're too cold to have fun? You might change your mind."

Outside, the rain has stopped. As she climbs into the driver's seat, her phone rings within her bag. Denny narrows his eyes in the rearview mirror. "I'll take it on the car speaker," she promises. "We're going, we're going." She pulls into the road and manages to tap the speakerphone button on the dash before her voicemail kicks in. "Sandra Rawlins speaking."

"Sandy!" Her aunt's voice. "So glad I caught you."

Sandra frowns. Aunt Phil is a strictly Sunday evening caller. "Hi, Auntie. What's up?"

"Are you at home? It sounds like a wind tunnel."

"I'm driving Denny to school right now. Denny, say hi to Great-Aunt Phil."

"Hi, Great-Aunt," Denny mumbles.

"Hi, terrific Denny! Don't have too much fun at school!"

"We're late."

"I'll let you go then. Goodbye, Denny. Sandy, give me a call when you get home, okay?"

Sandra checks her watch again. She has a client at nine, and she'll get home at quarter of, and she needs coffee, not to mention a shower. "I could do ten thirty, will that work?"

"The sooner the better, dear," Aunt Phil says and hangs up.

In the drop-off zone, Sandra gives Denny's hand a squeeze. "Love you. Have a wild day."

He squeezes back, already opening the door with the other hand. "Bye!" he says, and she watches him become absorbed by the whirlpool of children. He looks smaller and more fragile than any of them, as if Jill's death shrunk him. Sandra's heart aches for all the pain he has yet to face.

Friggin' hormones. Denny will be fine. Jon's an excellent father, or he will be once he gets his shit together again, and she's doing everything she can.

Too bad she's such a terrible role model. If she'd been warned she'd have to parent, she'd have practiced being a kinder, gentler version of herself, who knew how to trust other people and didn't avoid most of humanity at all costs. Someone who could keep a romantic relationship going for longer than six months instead of switching girlfriends more often than she changed her water filter.

At least letting her brother and Denny live with her proves her family can count on her.

Speaking of which—instead of waiting, she finds a

parking spot along a neighborhood street a couple blocks from the school and returns Aunt Phil's call.

"Sandy, you dropped him off?"

"Yes. What's going on?"

"I have some sad news. I'm not sure how to tell you, so I'm just going to say it."

Sandra closes her eyes. Ridiculously, they're already hot and prickling with tears.

Aunt Phil clears her throat. "Val's gone, honey. Your mother's passed away."

Sandra breathes in deeply, opens her eyes. Next to the car, a guy with a short ponytail is on his knees, pulling weeds out of a raised bed. The image of Dad scrabbling in the dirt flashes in her mind. Her throat feels thick.

"Sandy?" Her aunt's voice is gentle.

"Yeah," Sandra manages. "Um. Okay. How? I mean, she seemed fine. I thought she was fine."

"Out of nowhere, early this morning. She had a stroke and tumbled out of that rocking chair by the downstairs window. Robby found her on the floor, poor dear. They've just come and taken her away."

"Robby found her?" Mom's not a morning person. Aunt Phil usually lures her out of bed with strong coffee. "Are you sure she wasn't there all night?"

"She was asleep when I went to bed, and I heard the stairs creak around five but I thought I imagined it and went back to sleep. I wish I'd checked on her, but I don't usually fuss unless she's still in bed at nine…"

"You couldn't have known," Sandra says, but the thought of Mom lying on the floor, all alone, disturbs her. "It's lucky Robby stopped by."

The ponytailed guy has a tin can next to one knee in which he's been gathering slugs, but it's on its side now and the slugs are escaping with excruciating slowness. Sandra fixes her eyes on them, trying to overwrite the thought of her mother's body. "Is Robby okay? That must have been awful."

"Oh, yes. He's shocked, of course, and me too. Val's just a year and a bit older than me, after all."

Anyone meeting the sisters would guess Mom was older by a decade, and it's not a matter of hair dye. Aunt Phil brims with energy and laughter, overflowing with projects and plans. Mom turned frail long before her time. The night Dad died, she retreated, as if despite all their fights, she would have preferred to go with him rather than be with Sandra and her brothers. And now, finally, she has her wish.

Sandra hardened herself to that pain a long time ago. It was a part of Mom that neither therapy nor pills touched, and whether that was a failure of modern medicine or Mom's stubborn rejection of every possible life preserver, Sandra doesn't know.

But now there's no hope of last minute redemption, no deathbed apologies.

"She's with Dad," Sandra says in as neutral a tone as she can manage. "Like she always wanted."

"Oh, honey, she loved us in her own way."

Probably true. After all, she stuck around—sort of—to see her kids grow up and have kids of their own. Which had been awfully fucking brave of Jon and Robby, all things considered, and something Sandra never dared.

After a moment of silence and waiting for the ache in her throat to subside, Sandra asks, "So, what do we do?"

Aunt Phil shifts into efficiency mode. "You and Jon should come down tomorrow. I'll make arrangements for the burial, early next week. You kids can pick out the stone to go next to your father's. Your mom was never a religious woman. A secular service followed by a gathering at the community center to say goodbye, I think, unless you want a religious ceremony?"

"I can't imagine that any of us would," Sandra says. "Does Christine come from a religious background? Maybe she and Robby…"

"They don't go to church on Sundays or Christmas, but I'll ask before I plan anything."

Aunt Phil's pen scratches on the other end of the line. Sandra pictures her at the corner of the kitchen where the phone is mounted on the wall, with a line drawn between her brows and one elbow on the counter as she takes notes in her ever-present day planner. Sandra wonders whether to interrupt, go back a step. Is there any point to a funeral? Mom barely left Teague House for decades. Who would gather, beyond the family? But she supposes they have to do something.

Dad's funeral was excruciating. Sandra can't remember who spoke or what words were said, only a blur of black clothes and offensively scented flowers. She'd been trapped in her head, reviewing her final encounter with her father over and over, certain her actions had killed him and trying to find a way to take them back.

"Got to go," she says abruptly to Aunt Phil.

"Would you like me to break the news to Jon?"

"No, I will. We'll see you tomorrow." She hangs up.

Pulling herself together before her client appointment sounds overwhelming. She peruses her coaching schedule. Two slots are online check-ins, including the 9 a.m., and the other two are in person. She can handle it, if she rallies. It's not like this is a shock. Mom left them long ago. She wipes brusquely at her face with one sleeve, then digs a napkin out of the glove compartment to blow her nose.

If she's honest, it's partly dread that's getting to her: going home to the tiny backwater town of Horace. When she returns for holidays, she stays at the house and avoids the town, but this visit is bound to be longer and more complicated.

She blinks her vision clear and forces herself back on task. Maybe she should cancel her appointments. Call Jon to share the news and take a mental health day. She'll have to take bereavement leave; why not start now?

Her gaze wanders to the pretty green yard outside her passenger window. The ponytailed man isn't there anymore. He left his trowel, and the cushion he knelt on, so perhaps he'll be back. She wonders if he noticed her, if he thought it odd that a stranger was parked on the side of his street with tears running down her face.

4

PHIL

....

1972

Phyllis leaned close to the bathroom mirror, tilting her head right and left. At the salon yesterday, the hair had curled perfectly over her ears, but overnight, the whole haircut shrank. Now it was too short, and her ears stuck out, and her nose looked big, and she hated it.

She stuck out her tongue at the hideous reflection, and a brilliant idea struck. If she trimmed the bangs, the rest would look longer. She rifled through the drawer next to the sink. The nail scissors had short blades, but from accidentally cutting the flesh of her big toe, she knew they were plenty sharp.

As Phil trapped a lock of hair tight between two fingers to make the first cut, someone beat on the bathroom door and yelled, "Get out of there, I gotta go!" Her big sister's not-so-dulcet tones.

"I'm not done," Phil called, narrowing her eyes

in the mirror. Val spent an hour in the bathroom every single morning, and Phil wasn't allowed to complain because Val was in high school. As if that were a reason. Well, Phil was starting high school next week. "I'm going to take as long as I damn well please!" she added, and Valerie huffed an audible sigh.

Phil's hand fell away from her bangs. She should have listened to Val about the haircut. It was already too short. Cutting more was probably a bad idea. She dropped the scissors in the sink and smoothed the bangs over her forehead. The hair would grow back. Maybe even by the first day of school. Mom said eating eggs made your hair grow faster. She could eat a lot of eggs.

The rumble of a boy's voice reached her, followed by a tinkle of laughter and a lighthearted "Be right there!" from Val, still right outside the bathroom door. Phil could see the toes of her shoes through the crack.

Mom and Dad said Val was the boss only in case of emergencies, which pissed Phil off because, if anything, it should be the opposite. Val might be older, but Phil was more mature. And whenever Mom and Dad were out, Val invited her boyfriend Russ over. He was covered with pimples and had the worst mustache ever. And they practically did it, right on the couch. And Val treated Phyllis like a little kid, if the little kid was in the hands of the Spanish Inquisition, and not the funny Monty Python one either.

Valerie dropped her voice two tones deeper so she sounded demonic. "Swear to god, Phil, I'm going to friggin' break down the door." Her mouth must be right up to the crack, because it sounded like she was standing at Phil's shoulder.

"All right, all right," Phil said. She looked around hastily. The house's one bathroom was so small the girls were supposed to keep their stuff in the bedroom, but Val left a trail wherever she went. Phil palmed a mascara and slid it deep into the pocket of her bell-bottoms. Served Val right for being such a douchebag.

Val rattled the doorknob.

"Stop, I'm opening it!" Phil rotated the flimsy lock.

Valerie got in her face. "You better not have touched my stuff," she warned. "I mean it, so help me god." She spoke in an undertone, probably not wanting the Fuss to hear her being a bitch.

Phyllis and her best friend, Maud, had christened Russ "the Fuss" because of how Val acted around him. "Oh, Russ, you look like you might possibly be hungry or thirsty sometime in the next month, let me bring you everything in the entire house!" "Oh, Russ, do you like my dress? I stole it from the Salvation Army and ran over it with the car six times, just for you!" Val always wore full-face war paint, from foundation to blush to enough eyeshadow to recreate the Mona Lisa, but ever since she met Russ, Dad said her clothes were getting more hippy-dippy by the day.

Phil hesitated. She really wanted that mascara. She didn't know how Val's pocket money stretched to get all the stuff she had, because supposedly they both got the same amount, but it was real CoverGirl, not cheapo Wet n Wild.

On the other hand, Val was psycho.

Phil met Val's eyes and tried to look scared. It wasn't hard. "I wouldn't touch your crap with a ten-foot pole. I swear to god." For a few seconds, she thought she'd gotten away with it. But Valerie's blue-lidded eyes dropped to Phil's hands, and Phil realized she'd clasped them in front of herself like her pocket was radioactive. She tried to step back but was trapped against the sink.

Then Val was on her, trying to reach into her jeans. Her sharp fingernails scraped Phil's arm. Phil shoved her and tore into the hallway. Val tackled her, and Phil crashed to the floor, hand trapped under her body. Her chin hit the shag carpet, releasing a whoosh of dust, and Valerie's hair, peroxide blond this summer and down past her shoulder blades, lashed against Phil's face in a cloud of apple-scented hairspray. Val shook her shoulders and Phil tried to curl up and roll away, but Valerie was taller, heavier, and meaner. Defeated, Phil collapsed to her stomach and gasped for air as Valerie slapped the back of her head.

"Do not touch my shit! Do not touch my shit, you fucking spoiled little brat!" Valerie yanked hard at her hair.

"Whoa, whoa!" came the Fuss's voice. Phil hadn't heard

his footsteps. She opened her eyes. His big feet, toenails curling long over the end of grimy toes, were inches from her face.

Valerie relaxed. "She's such a spoiled brat," she said, but her voice had changed again, with a wheedling tone in it.

She doesn't want him to realize she's nuts, Phil thought. Good luck with that.

"Little sisters, man," Russ said. Valerie shifted her weight, shoving a knee into Phil's ribs, and then she was up and away. Phil rolled over, noticing that Val's nails had broken the skin on her forearm. She looked up at them but neither paid her any attention. They gazed into each other's eyes, and Phil could tell they were about to start smooching while she lay here on the floor bleeding. Disgusting.

Phil pushed to her feet, rubbing her rug-burned chin and sore back. Her scalp smarted. She eased down the hall.

"Oh, no you don't!" Valerie pulled away from Russell and pointed at Phil. "You are not getting away with it. What did you steal?"

Phyllis glared. After that over-the-top attack, she should get to keep the mascara. It was only fair. But no. Val stood with her hand out. Phyllis turned to Russ's big dumb face. His eyes were crinkled, amused, like he didn't see anything wrong with his girlfriend beating her sister half to death over friggin' makeup that shouldn't have been in the bathroom in the first place.

Phil freed the mascara from her pocket and threw it at

Val. It glanced off her shoulder and fell to the floor. The Fuss's hand curled around Val's arm as if restraining her, but Val just narrowed her eyes.

Tears spilled down Phil's cheeks as she whirled and stomped down the hall. Her door slam shook the Bugs Bunny clock off the wall, but it didn't knock down a single one of Val's stupid horse figurines.

Phil twisted the doorknob lock, even though it could be opened with a butter knife. She knew Val wouldn't follow. Russ would keep her busy. She lay down, waiting to see if the tears would turn into a storm of sobs, but no. She sat up and blew her nose copiously into a handful of tissues, glaring at the top of her sister's dresser where her lockbox was.

Both Phil and Val owned lunch box–sized lockboxes, Phil's purple and Val's blue, with combination locks—their parents' effort to head off some of the fighting. Val could have easily kept her makeup in there instead of making death threats.

Maud said her big sister was mean too, but Maud's sister played Barbies with them for hours when Phil slept over, and she made them brownies with peanut butter and Fluff on top. And Val was worse than mean. Phil rubbed the line of blood off the scrape on her arm with a finger and stuck it in her mouth, blinking fresh tears away.

Laughter tinkled through the thin door, and Phil could picture her, giving the Fuss a playful punch on the shoulder and batting her eyelashes at him.

Everyone thought Val was so pretty and sweet. She got treated like a grown-up and got to do everything first.

Well, Phil knew what Val was really like. And she wasn't about to forget it.

5

JON

...........:........

Jon's four hour drive from Bend to Horace is a defensive driving challenge, with eighteen wheelers clogging all the lanes and impatient SUVs weaving through traffic. By the time he spots Teague House and slows to turn at the flowered mailbox, Jon's whole being vibrates with an unpleasant tension like the humming of power lines.

He forces it to the back of his consciousness and checks the rearview mirror to gauge Denny's expression. His son is still entranced by the PBS shows Jon loaded on the iPad, but as Jon parks to the side of the double garage, Denny looks up eagerly and shoves his headphones down around his neck.

"Are we here?"

"Yeah, big guy. We made it." Jon scans the drive, frowning a little. He would have expected to see Robby's car. His brother should be helping Aunt Phil or at least keeping her company the day after losing Mom.

Denny squirms to release the seatbelt on his booster. "I wanna see Aunt Phil and Gramma!"

Jon steps out into chilly air that carries a rich green scent. He inhales deeply, trying to appreciate the beautiful day and let the rural peace soothe the static of the drive, but his tension goes too deep. When he turns to face the house, his jaw clenches. It's objectively attractive, if simple, a big rectangular three-story stack, built into a slope so that only two levels show at the front. Colonial, he thinks it's called, with no frills except for the wide stilted deck in back. Between the square footage, the acreage, and the second dwelling on the property, it could be worth eight or nine hundred thousand. A developer has been contacting him periodically for years; an entire subdivision of McMansions could easily fit on this slice of land. With Mom no longer needing special care, that money could be put to good use. Bonus: when the property is sold, he'll never have to come back here again.

He pulls open Denny's door. "Got your stuff? Put the iPad away, okay?" He watches Denny struggle with the zipper on his backpack and belatedly registers what his son said. "Remember, Den, Gramma won't be here, right? We talked about this."

Denny freezes for a second, then mumbles, "She's in Heaven with Mommy."

"That's right. But we're going to see Great-Aunt Phil, and who else?"

"Aunt Christine."

"Yep, and?"

Denny starts to smile. "Cousin Chelsey and Uncle Robby and Cousin Lottie. And Aunt Sandy is coming too!"

The high-pitched squeal of bad brakes sounds behind them, and Jon turns to see Robby parking a dented gray Prius. He exits, then approaches with open arms. "Hey, big brother!"

Jon grips his shoulder, checking him out at arm's length. The baby of the family, Robby is eight years younger and both shorter and huskier than Jon. His hair has receded a bit but still has a cowlick up front. His normally shit-eating grin has low wattage today, and the skin under his eyes is so dark it looks bruised. Robby's a year older than their father was when he died, but he's dressed like a teenager in a fraying black hoodie over faded jeans. Jon's throat aches, deep down, and he pulls his brother in for a tight hug.

As they release each other, Denny scrambles out of the car with his backpack clutched in both arms. "Hi, Uncle Robby! I had to miss my T-ball game because Gramma died."

Robby stoops to hug him. "That's right. I'm glad you're here though, buddy."

"Where's Chelsey and Lottie?"

"Oh, they'll probably be around later."

"See if you can find Great-Aunt Phil," Jon tells the boy, and Denny runs to the stairs that lead up to the back deck and the kitchen door.

"You okay?" Jon asks Robby.

Robby raises his shoulders and shakes his head. "A little messed up. You?"

Jon nods. "Yeah. That's one way to put it." He gathers their bags from the trunk and slams it closed.

From up on the porch, they hear Aunt Phil. "Denny! Give your auntie a big hug!"

"She holding up okay?" Jon asks softly.

Robby gives him a wry look, and Jon notices his bloodshot eyes, his pasty face. Mom's death must be hitting him hard. "Auntie's doing better than me, as usual. She's bustling around, organizing everything and asking a million questions I don't know how to answer."

"Sounds about right."

At the top of the stairs, Aunt Phil waits, a sturdy figure with short steel-gray hair, wearing a purple T-shirt, baggy pants that end just below the knee, and purple Crocs. No mourning black for her. Jon finds a smile despite the tension that still vibrates through his core. He sets down one of the suitcases and hugs her one-armed. "How are you?"

"Oh, it's a hard thing, to lose her," she says. She reaches up to pat his cheek then releases him. "Go on in. You'll be in Robby's old room. I sent Denny downstairs to check out the

Xbox. Robby hooked up his old one in the family room for the girls to play when they're over."

She turns to hug Robby, and Jon moves into the kitchen, a large homey space with oak cabinets, built-in wine racks, and stenciled pineapples on the wallpaper. Mom should be here, hanging back without expression, waiting for her own greeting before drifting off to sketch or stare out a window. The stillness and silence is momentarily oppressive, and he pokes at this proof of absence to see if it will bring sadness. There's nothing but bleak irritation. Mom's half-life is over. They need to get business taken care of and go back to life as usual. End of story. He just needs to be patient while the others grieve.

Behind Jon, Robby mumbles something about Christine and the girls to Aunt Phil. Jon rallies and opens the door leading to the basement level. "You down there, Den?" No answer. He drops their bags at the top and descends enough to see that Denny's exchanged his light blue wireless headphones for a pair of big black wired ones, and some kind of Sonic the Hedgehog game is loading on the big screen TV mounted above the mantel.

Jon glances around. While the outside of the house is deceptively plain, Dad delighted in installing custom cabinetry and little built-in surprises on the inside. It could be a plus to the right buyer. A family with children. This room wasn't finished until Jon was ten or eleven. It has a bar area, a woodstove, and a built-in hutch with two secret cubbies. He remembers Dad's mustache twitching with amusement as Jon and Sandra raced to discover the hidden treasures.

His eyes catch on the rocking chair, poised in front of the sliding glass door of the patio as if waiting for Mom, and the brief moment of nostalgia curdles.

"Got it!" Denny announces as fireworks erupt in the game. Jon's intention to lay down the law about screen time fizzles. He and Denny need to get through the next few days, and there's going to be a lot of boring adult conversations and reminders of losing Jill. A little extra escapism might be just the thing. If only Jon had a way out too.

He squeezes Denny's shoulders and ruffles his hair, then climbs back to the kitchen, closing the door gently behind him. Robby's got a beer at the kitchen table, and Aunt Phil is adding cream to a mug of coffee. She says, "Did you and Denny stop for lunch, honey? Can I get you something?"

He waves her away and starts a coffee for himself. "We got fast food and brought a ton of snacks to get through the drive. We'll be fine until dinner."

He settles at the old scratched up kitchen table, avoiding the chair where Mom always sat. "It's hard to believe she's really gone."

Aunt Phil nods. "You never know, do you?"

Robby is picking at the label of his beer bottle and seems lost in thought. Jon clears his throat. "Well, what's the plan?"

Robby looks up, narrowing his eyes. "Plan for what?"

"The service is scheduled for Tuesday," Aunt Phil says. "And I reserved the Community Center for a reception afterwards."

Jon pauses, about to suggest they don't need a reception because who will come, but swallows it. The family will want their rituals. "That sounds perfect." In a way, it's better than he expected. Sandra had suggested it might take a week to get Mom's affairs in order, but if the funeral is Tuesday, he might make it back to the bank by Thursday, the loss of his only remaining parent a blip on his schedule. The prospect should lift his spirits, but it only sharpens his sense of bleakness. "We're here to help. Do we need to, I don't know, arrange a caterer or something? A florist? How are we paying for this?"

Robby snorts.

"What?" Jon glares at him, then takes a breath. "I'm not being insensitive. I just want to help with the arrangements if I can."

"Not everything is about money."

"It's fine, dears. I'm on top of it," Aunt Phil says. "I'm just so glad you'll all be here."

Robby mumbles something under his breath, then drops his head into his hands and rubs his temples.

"Do you have a headache?" Jon demands.

Robby straightens. "No. Sorry. Haven't been sleeping." His phone buzzes on the table in front of him, and he tilts it to check the screen. "Gotta take this; be right back." He pushes back his chair and heads toward the living room.

After a moment, Aunt Phil says, "Poor boy, I wish he hadn't found her like that."

Jon sighs. Poor Robby, always poor Robby.

She takes a sip of coffee, studying him. "How are you, honey? This can't be easy. And Denny, losing his Grandma so soon after Jill."

Anger flares up at Mom's death mentioned in the same breath as Jill's, as if Aunt Phil is equating them. His rational side tries to tamp it down; they were both mothers, after all, and one shouldn't think ill of the dead. But he does. And that ill has to go somewhere. Jon stands, his chair legs scraping against the wood floor. Sandra better arrive soon, to take over conversational duties before something slips out that he'll regret. "Excuse me. Restroom break."

In the hallway, he hears Robby's low murmur emanating from the closed living room door. Jon hesitates at the threshold of the bathroom when Robby's voice rises into distinct words.

"How many times do I have to say I'm sorry? My mother is dead, Chrissy. I need to see my girls. I need to see you."

Jon pauses, frozen by the desperation in his little brother's voice. The whole family knows Robby and Chrissy struggle with money, with twin girls they spoil like princesses and, in Jon's opinion, a taste for vacations and toys far outside their means. He'd had no idea they were having relationship issues though. Despite himself, he strains to hear more.

Robby's voice rises. "Yeah? Maybe you should look at yourself. You need to be right, all the time. You need to be the martyr. Isn't it convenient for you that I keep fucking up?"

Robby had been a partier, pre-Christine, and flunked right out of college. But since Chrissy and the twins, Jon would have pegged his brother as a family man. If that stupid bastard has been stepping out—

Robby spits, "They better be. If my girls aren't at their own grandmother's funeral, there will to be hell to pay."

Jon doesn't want to hear more. He slips into the bathroom, pulling the door shut and drowning out sound with the exhaust fan.

When he returns to the kitchen, Aunt Phil is at the sink. "I took Denny some cheese and crackers," she says. "He's a growing boy, after all. Robby was a bottomless pit all the way through high school."

"Okay. I'll run our suitcases upstairs."

"Lottie and Chelsey left a bit of a mess, but it's not too bad."

Knowing Aunt Phil, she'd tidied whatever they left and washed not only the sheets but the curtains just this morning. Jon walks through the dining room, which was seldom used when he was a kid but has housed all their holiday meals since. The built-in hutch holds a few fancy trays and plates for display, but also a collection of kids' trophies and artwork. He and Sandra were past that kind of thing by the time Aunt Phil moved in, but Robby and the twins are heavily represented, and he even sees a couple of Denny's soccer participation trophies that Jill must have contributed.

Jon heads upstairs. The bunks are made with hospital corners, and Lottie and Chelsey's "mess" consists of some nail polish and a shoebox full of different-colored string atop the narrow desk in front of the back window.

He unpacks Denny's clothes into a couple of lower drawers, then sinks into the desk chair, staring out at Teague Wood. He runs his hand over the top of the sparse stubble on his head and realizes he forgot to pack his electric shaver. Dropping his head, he squeezes the bridge of his nose and tries to gather himself.

There are all kinds of things that need to be done, although Aunt Phil is on top of the funeral, thankfully. But the house is on his mind, the property… They need to put wheels in motion. There was no will, of course. In practice, Mom had been a dependent, and he and Sandra and Robby and Aunt Phil were always able to work out her care for themselves. But now, that may get messy. Letting Mom stay in her own home had been the only reason to keep this accursed place, in Jon's opinion, but what if the others don't agree? Aunt Phil will need a housing allowance, and Robby—is Robby going to be able to swing a mortgage somewhere else? Maybe not until the sale goes through.

He knows no one else will want to talk about logistics yet but hopes that at least Sandra will see the need.

When he makes his way back downstairs, Aunt Phil is at the kitchen counter, alternately sprinkling confectioner's sugar into a bowl and stirring with a wooden spoon. Robby has traded his beer for a cup of coffee, which he curls around, shoulders slumped. "Christine and the girls got sidetracked at her mom's house," he says. "They're not going to make it for dinner."

Aunt Phil says, "I hope the girls aren't too upset about Valerie. Are they handling it okay?"

"Yeah," Robby says. "I mean, as well as you could expect. In a way, she's been sick all along, so it wasn't a total shock."

Jon grimaces. Aunt Phil has been more of a grandmother to Denny and the girls than Valerie ever was, just as she was more of a mother to Robby and even Sandra. Jon exempts himself from this. Aunt Phil saved him from having to parent his younger siblings, but it's a point of pride to him that he'd already raised himself, despite his parents' dysfunction, by the time she came along to pick up the pieces.

A knock sounds at the back door. Sandra's short figure is silhouetted behind the thin curtains. Thank god.

Jon makes her tea and himself a second cup of coffee, conscious of jealousy at the way she injects cheer into Robby's dissipated sulk and offers Aunt Phil as much comfort as she takes.

"I haven't seen Christine in a while, how's she doing?" Sandra asks. "Does she still like that job at the school?"

Color floods Robby's face. "Uh, no. I mean, it's okay."

Aunt Phil snorts and turns from her frosting to face Sandra. "She's hated it for the past year, but she's been trying to stick it out until the girls move on to high school."

"Oh, no," Sandra says. "What happened?"

Aunt Phil looks to Robby, who fiddles with his cup. "Maybe Robby mentioned it last year? There was an incident. The daughter of one of the teachers was bullying Lottie, and it wasn't handled well."

"Sounds like a mess," Jon says.

Robby looks up. "It's fine. Really. I don't think Chrissy hates it, Auntie. There were a tough few months, but things settled back down, especially since the bully isn't at the school anymore."

Sandra shakes her head. "The joys of parenthood. I don't know how you guys do it."

Jon snorts. If he's learned anything about his sister while living with her the past six months, it's that she'd make a great mom. She's been there for Denny since the day they moved in, not trying to take Jill's place but just folding an awareness of Denny's needs into her everyday life. She must have learned that from Aunt Phil.

"Were you planning something for dinner?" Sandra says. "Or should we go out tonight?"

"Or if you have something in mind, we can help cook," Jon adds.

Aunt Phil smiles. "No, no, I'll take care of that. Sit and catch up with each other for a while. Later, you can look around and get a head start thinking about your mother's things. That's what needs doing."

Jon nods, but Robby blinks as if blindsided. "I mean, you'll still need everything, it's just her clothes we need to go through, right?"

Aunt Phil takes a breath and smiles at each of them. "I didn't want to say anything until we were all together. But I've got some news. I'll be leaving after the funeral. I've already got my tickets."

Robby protests, "You can't just leave!" and Sandra demands, "Tickets? To where?"

Aunt Phil waves her hands. "Oh, everywhere! I've always wanted to travel the world, and you never know what tomorrow brings, do you?"

Even as his siblings' faces crumple in hurt and confusion, Jon feels a wave of relief and the first lightness since he learned of Mom's death. If Aunt Phil is moving on, that will make it that much easier to get all the Rawlinses away from Teague House.

6

SANDRA

....

Sandra groans as she bends to tie her shoe at the old table in the Teague House kitchen late Sunday morning. After too much birthday cake last night, she'd taken an ill-advised twilight run along the road, where a passing pickup nearly turned her to hamburger. It shot enough adrenaline into her bloodstream to keep her up all night and made her jerk a tendon that would ache for days.

She'd had to get out of the house though. Something's going on with Robby and Jon—grief, probably—but based on the way they keep sniping at each other, they've regressed to some adolescent peak of moodiness. She's not much better. Mom's death threw her, and now Aunt Phil's news has drained her. The thought of Teague House without either of them in it casts a cold shadow in her heart. Sandra grew up here feeling stifled by isolation. Her odd, gossip-worthy family and her slow-growing suspicion that she wasn't into boys meant she never fit in, but these are still the only roots she has.

When she finally dozed off last night, it was back into a familiar nightmare, as if the clearing in the wood knew she was close. She woke this morning with the realization that she doesn't have to keep passively re-experiencing the warping of memory. With Mom gone and Aunt Phil leaving, it could be her last chance to face her decades-old demons in Teague Wood, and the night she'd shamed her father into suicide.

She tightens her laces, then digs her fingers into the sore tendon, trying to loosen it. She thinks she can find her way back to the pet cemetery. The wood is bound to have changed, but a lot of it is old growth, for which three decades is the blink of an eye.

Jon slouches into the kitchen with a mug and sets up the coffee maker without acknowledging her.

"Good morning," she says.

He turns to face her, and she's startled to see how old he looks. He takes in her jogging tights and shoes. "Running again?"

"I thought I'd go for a walk. Get some air. When I get back, maybe we can grab Robby and start talking about Mom's stuff and the house." This is an olive branch. Jon pushed hard to discuss the house last night but she and Robby had turned him down flat.

Jon lifts his eyebrows. "Denny and Rob are on the Xbox

already. I guess the girls and Christine aren't going to make it over today. Maybe all four of us should go for a walk together."

Sandra tries not to grimace. "That's okay. Let them play. When does Denny get to spend one-on-one time with his uncle? And didn't you say you had some stuff from work you needed to get done? I'll be back in an hour or so."

Jon glances at the basement door, shrugs. "Yeah, okay, we'll leave them to it. But I need some air too. Just give me a couple minutes. Aunt Phil's still at the store, so Robby needs to know he's the only adult in the house."

He disappears downstairs. Sandra sighs, stretches. So much for facing her demons alone, but maybe the walk will snap Jon out of his edgy mood.

When he returns and they step outside, sunlight assaults her eyes. The morning is nearly warm, low sixties but with a bite to the breeze, and the sky is clear and robin's egg blue. Sandra's gaze goes straight to the tree line, a good forty yards away, where thick shadows congregate amid the tall old firs. She feels a tug in her chest, half fear, half anticipation.

As she cuts across the grass, Jon trails her, asking, "Where do you want to go? Should we head to the river? I haven't been there in years."

"I'm going into the woods," she says. "You can go to the river if you want."

He stops and stretches, vertebrae cracking audibly. "No, I'll stick with you." He looks across the lawn with a half smile on his face. "Hey, remember that year that Mom hid Easter eggs out here? We were so little, we were still living in the cottage, and all this lawn was just a big stumpy field. And I don't know what she used to color them, but they were purplish-gray inside and out and I refused to eat them."

Sandra smiles despite herself. "Did you steal mine? I sort of remember being mad…"

He catches up to her. "I did. They were disgusting, but I still didn't want you to win."

"Pretty sure I got back at you, eventually. Did you ever find your Darth Vader Lego kit?"

His eyes widen. "Wait, that was you? I thought I lost it at school."

She shakes her head. "I buried it. Somewhere near the plum tree. I made a treasure map I was going to give you if you were nice to me, but…I guess you weren't nice enough! I forgot all about it."

"Feels like there were a lot of summer days and school afternoons when we ran wild out here, no supervision. Mom in the house, Dad in his studio—when we were older, I used to chill out in the woods to be away from them. As a matter of fact…"

"What is it?"

He turns off course again, and she sighs but follows him toward the right-hand corner of the yard, near the trail that used to lead to Dad's studio. "You never knew about this, did you? All the hiding places through the house that we all knew about, and I still managed to keep a secret." He stops at the gnarled oak near the shed and shoots her a grin. "I was such a rebel."

He reaches up into a shadowed hollow that Sandra would need a stepladder to get to. She shudders, imagining a nasty nest of spiders inside. Jon seems unbothered and pulls out a crumpled object, too small to make out.

"What is it?"

"Huh. I thought it was my old smokes. I'd sneak out at night sometimes and smoke under the trees," he says, turning the bag over in his hand with a frown. His voice is puzzled. He unseals the dirty plastic bag, and they both stare down at the beat-up black cell phone inside.

"Weird. Someone else liked your hiding spot, I guess."

Random hikers used to wander onto the property from the adjoining state forest because the border wasn't well-marked when they were kids. Robby should have fixed that by now, but maybe not. Still, why would a stranger stash a phone? "Could it be Robby's from high school?"

"Robby didn't get a cell phone in high school. They were just starting to come out back then," Jon says. He's frowning at the phone as if suspicious, but as far as she can see, it's garbage, with a cracked screen and chipped plastic casing.

Sandra shrugs; she wants to keep moving, that night with her father haunting her even now in the bright daylight. "Whatever. Are you still coming?"

"Yeah, sure," Jon says and stuffs the thing in his pocket. "Where are we going, again?"

"Into the woods. I just…need to see it for myself."

He looks at her closely a moment, perhaps seeing her unease, understanding the weight of Teague Wood on them all. "All right then," he says, gesturing for her to lead the way.

They walk in silence. Under the trees it's chilly, sunlight dappling through the overstory. Sandra zips her fleece up to her chin and pulls her hands into her sleeves, but soon warms up from exertion. The air is alive with the clean scent of evergreen and fungus, cool and damp against her skin.

Jon's presence fades into a vague awareness of an occasionally scuffed footstep as she relives the night Dad died. She'd been coming from the other direction, where she and her date had parked in a pull-off by the river. They'd been drinking, making out in the damp grass along the river bank, and then she called a halt when another car went by and she realized they were nearly naked in plain sight of the road. Chris Bagley, the third to last boy she half-heartedly tried to date. She can still picture his aggrieved face. Rather than get back in his truck, she'd bushwhacked along the river, knowing that would lead her close enough to home to pick up the trail. It had been fine until she approached her father's studio, a tiny shack tucked into the woods out of sight of the house. Dad had been on his way out, looking distraught as he weaved his way into the dark of the woods. She, to her everlasting regret, followed him.

Sandra stops to check the shape of the land. They should be coming upon a fallen tree that marks a left turn. It had been a big old monster, five feet around, and something should be left of it even after all this time.

Jon catches up and says, "When we lost Dad—it felt different than losing Mom, don't you think?"

Startled—is he somehow in tune with her thoughts?—she looks up into his face, but he's staring into the trees. "Of course. Dad killed himself. Mom didn't mean to die."

A hard bark. "She was halfway gone already."

She'd said almost the same thing to Aunt Phil, but it raises her hackles. "That's not fair. Dad's suicide devastated her."

"She was more devastated than her kids? So devastated she couldn't pull it together enough to say a single word to us? In thirty years."

Sandra shakes her head. "It's not that simple, and you know it." She picks up her pace, pulling ahead of him, and finally sees the fallen tree. Where there was once a deep gouge in raw earth is a soft green depression filled with ferns and a few saplings. The thick trunk has settled and collected greenery and fungi along its length. This is the one, she's certain.

"Are you ready to head back?" Jon asks.

"Not yet." She looks up at him, wondering how much to say. She lets out a heavy breath. "Do you remember the pet cemetery?"

"You mean—Snowflake? We buried him under the plum tree in the front yard."

Sandra frowns. "No. The one out here. We didn't use it, it was old. You really don't remember?"

He shrugs. "I guess not."

"The old pet cemetery in the woods," she repeats. Voice rising, she says, "I told you what happened that night. How do you not remember?" She shakes her head and continues walking, irritation winding around her spine even as dread grows in the pit of her stomach. Silly. They'll find trees, brush, loamy earth. A few old crosses, if they're still standing. Nothing but memories.

Twigs crack as Jon scrambles after her. "What night? When Dad died? I remember he tried to search my room."

"No," Sandra repeats. "After that. I saw Dad in the woods." She looks back at him until he shrugs.

"Okay. I sort of remember. You'd decided his death was all your fault because you ran into him when he was drunk out here. It was bullshit then and it's still bullshit now. Dad and Mom had serious problems. We were kids, Sandra. It's hard not to blame myself, considering I was the oldest. But I don't, and you know why? We are not responsible for the actions of our parents."

She wants to shake him by the shoulders. He never listens. Maybe if knows it all, what she kept from him back then. Then he'll understand. She tries one more time.

"Dad left me a note."

"What?" Confusion crosses his face, turning to hurt.

"The morning after. I found a note on my floor."

"But you never said anything. Everyone kept asking—the cops, Aunt Phil—and you never said." His jaw tightens.

Sandra tamps down the guilt. "I didn't read it. And I didn't tell you because I couldn't stand the idea of any of us reading it. He didn't deserve to be heard. I got rid of it."

Jon frowns like he thinks he can argue her out of something she did thirty years ago, and abruptly she sees the ragged-haired stoner kid he used to be. She's dizzied by a sudden sense of the hours and days and years that have spun past, to change him into the man he is now—her pragmatic accountant brother, with his shaven head and clean, long-fingered hands and his high-end, barely used jeans and sneakers.

Quickly, before she chokes up, she changes the subject. She hasn't had a chance to ask Jon about yesterday's shocker. "So, what do you think of Aunt Phil's travel plans?"

"I hope she's not expecting us to pay for a trip around the world."

She sighs. Of course they have to talk through the money piece first. "We need to help though. If we sell, she gets a cut of the house."

Silence from behind. When she looks back, she can tell he's doing math in his head.

She asks, "Do you know what it would have cost to have Mom in some kind of assisted living home all this time?"

"I know. But there's a limit. I'm only saying, I'm surprised at the travel-around-the-world idea. It's—extravagant."

"I guess we'll have to talk about finances with her in the next few days. That should be fun."

"Not to mention Rob—"

"Hang on." The shape of a huge boulder sunken in the earth resonates in her memory. "This is it. I think." She climbs over another fallen tree. Barely perceptible among the brushy salal, a narrow deer trail winds deeper into the woods.

They're almost there, and she braces herself, almost as if she's going to face her father himself, the man who took them camping every summer and made sure homework got done. Who wrote a song just for her. Who built hutches for her short-lived 4-H rabbit project and volunteered as a coach for Jon's fifth-grade basketball team, then couldn't make it to most of the practices. There was tension, there were fights, there were nights Dad slept in his studio, but he'd been her Dad. She'd loved him. She feels sick.

She squeezes between a tree trunk and a mess of brambles. Jon says, "I still don't get why you brought us all the way out here."

"I tried to tell you." She wills him to shut up.

He swears, yanking a vine off of his jacket. "What do you think we're going to find? How will this help you?"

"We'll see," she says, looking around as he draws up beside her. She pushes past a rise and spots a shallow muddy creek, almost narrow enough to step across from bank to bank. She looks up and downstream, then turns and follows the edge of the water. Dead twigs pluck at her running tights as she stays close to the thick brush around the bend of the creek.

"What are we looking for?"

"This," she says. Rocks are gathered just past the bend, creating an easier way to step across. She sees a muddy smear on a protruding edge of stone, and her eyes go from that to the front curve of a boot print sunk into the moss on the other side. The damp earth shows a pair of bicycle tracks, and she marvels that some hardy soul took a mountain bike out here, amid all the brush and uneven ground.

She steps from a large flat rock to the facing bank and pulls herself up with a sturdy sapling.

"You know, we've been gone an hour. Everyone's going to think we got lost," he says.

"Just a few more minutes."

"Sandra—"

She ignores him and ducks under a fallen tree that forms an angle with two others. Jon is close on her heels.

They're in a small clearing, the ground covered by fallen fir needles, ferns, and white trillium. Old-growth trees and brambles surround them, creating a sense of enclosure. A few knee-high crosses made from bound sticks protrude from of the ground among the sparse greenery, rotting strips of leather that had once been pet collars drooping from their tops.

"What the fuck?" Jon says, but his voice has faded to the far away buzz of a mosquito.

At the far edge of the clearing, the earth looks freshly disturbed, and it feels like Dad just left. Like in the dream, he'd been digging, again. Soil and needles from the fir trees are heaped in a rough mound, and she forces herself to approach. A bad feeling in her gut spreads weakness through her, making her shake. She crouches and, with a stick, brushes at a bit of yellow cloth visible under the top layer of dirt.

Something small and pale and rounded becomes visible, tipped with a pearly sheen.

Sandra swallows hard. She drops her stick and tears the top off a fern to brush at it like a squeamish kid petting a toad. Her eyes want to wince away, but she forces them to stay open even as she holds her breath. Even as a delicate but insistent odor insinuates itself into her nasal cavity.

As she expected, the rounded grayish something takes on a more familiar shape as the soil moves away. "It's a finger," she says.

7

MADDIE

....

SUNDAY

'm driving south on I-5 in heavy Sunday traffic. Other cars pass my little Kia, and my engine periodically makes that rattle I can't afford to fix. Mentally, I'm rehearsing telling Rose that I've failed again, when my car rudely interrupts with "Call from—Lianne Dunlop." A ringing sound follows, in case I don't understand what "call" means.

It's about the dozenth time she's tried to get through over the weekend. I accept the call and bark, "What?" then regret my curtness. I know I haven't offended Lianne—she's my best friend, and I'd have to work harder than that to put her off—but my bad mood will clue her in that I not only went back on my word, but it didn't go well.

"Oh no," she says. "Where are you? Are you in Washington?"

"Just crossed the border. I'm almost home."

"Fuck, Maddie. I was worried to death. Next time you decide to take off after promising you won't, at least send me a text."

"Sorry," I offer, with all the grace I can muster. "For what it's worth, you were right. I shouldn't have bothered."

Instead of chiming in with "I told you so's," she hesitates then asks, "So, it's definite? None of those bodies were Davina's?"

"Nope."

"Did you tell Rose yet?"

Rose, Davina's daughter and my sort-of-niece, as Davina had been my unofficial foster sister, had also tried to talk me out of the trip to Washington. With her pregnancy seven months along, she's become nearly single-minded in her need to find out what happened to the mother who disappeared when Rose was just an infant, but even she recognized that I was jumping the gun this time.

I slow to let an eighteen-wheeler merge into my lane and let out a long sigh. "I will. She ordered me not to go, but I'm sure she got her hopes up."

Rose had also yelled at me not to use her mother as an excuse to let my own life fall apart, after I let slip that I'd lost another client, but I don't want to give Lianne any more ammunition.

"Yeah, of course she got her hopes up," Lianne says. "You're the investigator, and she wants to trust your judgment, even when you're clearly impaired."

I don't respond. Lianne nails it, every time. It's what makes her such a good journalist.

"You need to go home and get your shit together, you know that, right?" She pauses. "Do you want me to come down and help you with your mom's stuff?"

Again, I give her silence. I don't want to go through Mom's stuff. She died a couple months ago, after a long slow decline, and I can't bring myself to deal with what she's left behind: her medications and electrolytes and nutrient shakes. Her collection of dragons. Her ashes, sitting on the entryway table in a cardboard box inside a plastic bag. Me.

I also don't want to return to our tiny rundown house. Unfortunately, despite the ill-advised trip I just took, I can't afford to sleep, work, or eat anywhere else. My credit cards are maxed out, and I've screwed up my struggling PI business by being nearly unreachable for six weeks. Running off to Washington State just because city workers uncovered some bones during the demolition of an abandoned building was not smart by any metric.

I've just been desperate for a win. *The* win. I need to fill one of these aching holes in my heart before I implode. My hand rises from the steering wheel to my left ear, where a silver hoop dangles an onyx bead from a second piercing. Davina used one of her mother's sewing needles and an ice cube, and we hid my sore, red ear under a strange sideways ponytail until it healed. Then she'd threaded a slim silver hoop with a bead from her precious collection. I leave it in, always, to remind me that family is more than blood. And that I owe her for most of the warmth and cheer I remember in my childhood.

"Maddie?" Lianne says. Her voice on my car speaker sounds fuzzy and artificial. "We're going to get you through this, okay?"

"Yeah, of course. It's fine. I'm fine." My voice comes out flat, and I try to inject some life into it as I drop my hand back to the steering wheel. "I just wanted an excuse to get out of town. I'll get shit done when I get home. Cleaning up the house. Calling clients. All the things."

"You promise? And real promise, not lie-promise?"

"I promise."

"Okay." She takes a deep breath. I can tell she doesn't want to say whatever she's about to say. "There's something I need to tell you, because I don't want you to jump to conclusions when you hear it on the news, okay? I'm going to tell you, and then you're going to remember what you just promised, and you're going to go home, get shit done, and wait patiently for more information instead of going off half-cocked again."

One of the perks of being a reporter is that Lianne sometimes catches wind of the news before it goes public. But what she's implying—that there's another possible lead in Davina's case—can't be true. Not so soon after my last wild goose chase. Davina disappeared when I was eleven, and I'm forty-four. I've been searching for her since my very first access to the internet, refining my efforts as I trained as a private investigator. I've systematically eliminated all possible lines of inquiry, and all that's left is waiting for new information or new Jane Does in a realistic radius. Promising leads are few and far between, and definitely not twice in one week.

"What is it?" I swallow, mouth dry.

"A body was found in Horace, which—I checked the map—is a teensy town somewhere in Melakwa County. The cops are radio silent right now, zero sharing. Before they locked it down, there was buzz about additional skeletal remains discovered at the same site out in the woods. A secret graveyard."

Despite Lianne and Rose treating me like an erratic lunatic, and despite my one-woman PI firm trying to go belly-up, I am a professional, so I ignore the rush of adrenaline that permeates my bloodstream. "So, it's not some abandoned pioneer graveyard, or Native American burial ground? Are they thinking serial killer?"

"It almost definitely *is* an abandoned pioneer graveyard," she says. "That's what I'm trying to tell you. You're going to hear this on the news, but ignore it. Go home."

"Where was it again?"

"Melakwa County. It's in the northwest corner of the state."

"Between Astoria and Portland."

She doesn't bother to reply. When Davina disappeared

at age twenty-three, her last known location was Astoria, a tourist town on the northern Oregon coast. She called her mother from a pay phone there, saying she'd catch a ride home with a friend. My heart is beating in my throat, and I realize that I'm gripping the steering wheel with white knuckles and my speed's edging up to ninety.

"I know what you're thinking," Lianne says.

I breathe deep, ease off the gas and find myself a nice cruising spot in the middle lane before replying. "I'm thinking that if I remember right, one of the cops from the Portland Police Bureau moved down to Melakwa County a few years back. I may have an in on the case. You've heard nothing yet about dating the bones? Don't you know someone with a contact in the state forensic lab?"

She groans softly and mutters something. I catch only "… mumble mumble Birkenstocks…"

My ears sharpen. "What? Repeat please."

She huffs. "It's too early for anything from the lab yet," she says. "But…and don't overreact. This could be a complete coincidence. I've got a friend covering the story on location. She overheard a couple of the techs at the diner. They found Birkenstock buckles at the site."

I consider that. "Not too many pioneers rocking Birks." Davina wouldn't have been caught dead in Birks—she was a Chuck Taylor girl when she wasn't in combat boots—but this is still good news. At least one item in the area dates from the last fifty years. For all I know, a lone sandal fell out of a passing hot air balloon onto an ancient burial ground. But I'm a fan of simple explanations: a sandal buried at a gravesite probably arrived on someone's foot, and one modern-day skeleton may mean the others are too.

Lianne keeps talking, but I'm fingering the onyx bead on my earring and mentally outlining where to start.

8

ROBBY

....

I n the late afternoon, Robby stares toward the tree line from
the spot in the family room where Mom took her last breath.
There's nothing to see. The first cops parked in the driveway and met Sandra in the yard, so she could lead them into
Teague Wood, but now they've moved their vehicles to the
old logging road. Sandra and Jon are conferring in the den.
Shutting him out, as usual.

"See anything?"

Robby jerks. Aunt Phil has appeared on his right. She
pats his arm.

"Nothing to see, Auntie." A little murder won't derail her
to-do list, and he's sure she's internally tracking the time, waiting for Jon and Sandra to switch their focus back to plans for
the house and getting Mom's things squared away.

Denny's behind them, on the Xbox again. Or still. No,

again. He took a break for lunch, but as soon as all the kerfuffle started, Denny snatched his chance for unsupervised screen time, and Robby and Aunt Phil both let it go.

Robby would like to be invited into Jon and Sandra's conversation, and he's certain Aunt Phil would too. They have the right to know exactly what happened on their land. Hell, Sandra and Jon both live four hours away in Bend, and whatever's going on here in Horace will affect Robby and Aunt Phil more than either of them.

Or, no. His aunt is leaving. And Robby doesn't know if he'll get to keep the cottage. Jon, who's rolling in cash from his bank job and probably Jill's life insurance, seems intent on selling Teague House. If Sandra takes Jon's side…

Robby wants to lean his forehead on the cool glass and rest his eyes, but Aunt Phil is still there, her hand on his arm as if that's the support he needs right now. He forces himself to smile down at her, feeling something twist inside. Aunt Phil has been a mother to him. She provided hugs and encouragement, schoolwork help, home cooking, clothes shopping, haircuts, sports sign-up, taxi service, boundaries. How can she walk away when he needs her?

But Robby's thirty-nine years old. He hasn't left home, but he's sure as hell left the nest. Except for dinners a couple times a week, and their partnership in taking care of Mom. That's the key, he supposes. Aunt Phil has been a foundation of his life for so long, he forgot she was primarily there to support his mother.

Auntie isn't betraying him, isn't leaving him, isn't letting him down. She's just retiring more suddenly than expected. He stoops to give her a one-armed hug.

"Are you all right, Robby?" she says.

He grimaces. "I can't believe someone was killed out there, that's all."

"I'm still hoping Sandra was mistaken," Aunt Phil says. "Maybe it was a doll, or part of a costume, something like that. Your mother would be so upset. She hated strangers tramping around in the wood."

Robby shoots her a look. The odds of Sandra mistaking a doll's plastic hand for a human finger seem vanishingly slim.

The doorbell chimes. Footsteps sound above their heads—Jon and Sandra, heading for the front door. It must be the police, coming to update them. Robby follows Aunt Phil after a last glance at Denny, who has an open can of Pepsi on the coffee table next to him. Robby sighs. Jon will blame Robby, but what the hell? Wouldn't his brother rather the kid get hyped up on Minecraft and Pepsi than worry about a dead body in the woods or a killer on the loose?

As a kid, Robby used to imagine Dad's ghost hanging around trying to tell him something. Long after the studio was destroyed, he suffered nightmares about taking a wrong turn and finding it still there, door hanging open in invitation, the sound of his father's guitar coming from inside. Sometimes his father would be dangling from the big tree, smiling as if nothing was wrong. But worst were the times when Robby was already inside the studio, and muffled voices argued above him while he tried to hide under a blanket.

As he enters the kitchen, Sandra ushers in an attractive blond in a navy suit and a tall, bald Black man, probably ten years older than Robby, also in a suit. Jon follows on their heels. Sandra catches Robby's eye. Her face is puffy, her voice strained. "These are Detectives Boon and Simonson. They want to talk with us about the—about the woods."

Boon surveys the family quickly and Robby studies her. She's maybe early forties, with a bony, pretty face. Her platinum hair looks frizzy and flyaway, but Robby likes her lipsticked smile and the way her suit jacket frames her collarbones. Despite having ten years on Christine, she looks good.

In a loud voice, Boon says, "If everyone could please sit for a moment, we'll bring you up to speed."

The guy, Detective Simonson, stands to Robby's right, checking out the collection of fancy gravy bowls on the hutch with an expressionless face, rocking on his heels.

Robby sits next to Aunt Phil. Boon says, "The victim you found in the woods this morning has been identified as a local woman." She pauses, looking down at her phone.

Robby swallows. He knows it's not Christine, but irrational dread grasps his throat. His words come out clipped and insistent. "Who is it?"

He catches a concerned look from Sandra but keeps his

gaze fixed on Detective Boon. Simonson strolls up beside her as she says, "Gayle Bethested."

Sandra coughs—a funny, stifled sound—and Robby's brain stutters. Hearing her name in this context is surreal, and he replays it in his head. When he can comprehend again, Aunt Phil is speaking his name.

"—Robby's girls' teacher. Oh, dear. I know her mother too, she's worked at the post office forever, and she has pictures of Gayle's little girls taped to her register."

Aunt Phil is looking at him as if waiting for something. Robby nods dumbly. "Right," he manages. The pulse in his neck flutters like a moth, and his face feels hot. Aunt Phil's brows draw together in concern, but Robby's tongue is stuck to the roof of his mouth.

Sandra clears her throat. "I—uh. I also knew Gayle, I think. A long time ago. Was her maiden name Pierce?"

"Uh…" Detective Boon looks to Simonson.

Simonson flips open a little notebook and nods. "Her mother is Frederika Pierce."

In a tone of belated recognition, Jon says, "Oh, Christ, Patrick's little sister, right? I remember her when she was twelve, such a skinny, shy little thing. That's awful. She married someone from away?"

"Married and divorced," Aunt Phil confirms. "She brought her kids back a few years ago. They live in that cute neighborhood by the elementary school, not far from her mom's house. This is terrible. Oh, I'm glad Valerie's not here to see this."

"Sandra mentioned you'd had a death in the family. We're so sorry for your loss, and that you have to deal with this now," Detective Boon said.

"Yes, my sister passed on Friday morning," Aunt Phil says. "Thank you."

Silence falls. Robby shifts uncomfortably. The detectives seem to be waiting for something, but he doesn't know what. With a dry mouth, he asks, "Do you know what happened to her?"

Detective Simonson speaks in a gentle voice that belies his size. "I'm afraid she was killed."

Aunt Phil mutters, "Well, we didn't think she buried herself in our woods."

Sandra shoots her a quelling look.

Robby swallows. "When did Gayle die? Did her family report her missing? I mean, how long has she been out there?" His voice catches. For a moment, it's Friday morning again, and he's standing out in the grass reading her text. *We need to talk ASAP. I'm scared, Rob.* He'd gotten caught up in finding Mom, and then Aunt Phil's preparations for the family's arrival and the funeral… He hasn't given it a second thought. In a panic, he slides his eyes away from the detectives' faces as if they might read his mind.

"We'll know more tomorrow," Detective Boon says. "But

Ms. Bethested was meant to be at a conference with two other teachers, returning today. Her mother was babysitting. She was surprised her daughter hadn't called to say hi to the girls, but she assumed the conference was busy."

"Did Ms. Bethested ever visit any of you at this property?" the other detective says. He lowers himself into a chair next to Sandra with his notebook in front of him and looks from face to face expectantly.

Sandra says, "It's been so long, it probably doesn't matter, but for a year or two in high school, we were good friends. We hung out in my room though, not the woods. It would have been around the early nineties."

Jon says, "Sandra and I both live in Bend. We haven't been back except for Christmas or Thanksgiving in decades. I don't keep in touch with anyone here anymore."

Simonson nods. "How about Patrick, the brother you mentioned?"

"Patrick Pierce. Nah. He was part of my friend group in high school, but we only hung out at school, basketball games, that kind of thing. Then I went off to college, and man, I don't even do Facebook. I haven't thought of the guy in twenty years."

"Did he ever visit the property?"

"Oh, uh. No, I don't think so."

"And Mrs.…Rawlins, is it?"

Aunt Phil shakes her head. "It's Ms. Temple. And no,

honey. There was no reason for Gayle to come here. Like I said, I chat with her mom when I go to the post office. Admire the pictures of the grandkids. It's a small town, eventually you know a teeny bit about everyone."

Simonson turns to Robby. "And you? Is there anything you can add?"

Robby says, "No. I mean, I don't think so."

"And where do you live, sir?" Simonson asks with pen poised.

"It's Robby. I live in a small cottage on the other end of the property, where my parents lived while they were building this place. Me and my wife and kids." His heart is beating so hard, he can hear the reverberation in his voice.

"And you work in town?"

His lips feel chapped. Why are the detectives asking him all these details, when they didn't ask Jon or Sandra? Do they already know about the bullying? Or more? "At the mill," he says.

"Was your wife friends with Ms. Bethested?"

"I don't think so." *God, no.*

"And your wife, she's not around today?"

"Uh, no. She's at her mom's with my girls. They'll be back tomorrow." He keeps his gaze on the detective to avoid his family's eyes.

"Okay. We'll catch her then." Simonson sets his pen down and sits up straight in the high-backed chair, rolling his shoulders. He raises his eyebrows at Boon, who's still standing at the head of the table.

"There is something else," she says. "When the techs removed Ms. Bethested's body, they found additional remains."

Robby blinks. Sandra sucks in a hard breath across from him. Her face pales and the tendons in her neck stand out in sharp relief above her T-shirt.

Jon shakes his head dismissively. "That spot has been a pet cemetery forever, as long as our family has lived here. The locals must bury their dogs and cats there, even though the property is marked private."

Boon tilts her head. Robby thinks he sees sympathy in her eyes, but her voice is even and cool. "The team is still out there. So far, at least one set is definitely human."

"At least one?" Sandra asks, her voice high and constrained.

Boon says, "An expert will take a closer look tomorrow. There are signs of multiple burials in that clearing. I'm afraid we're going to be in your hair for a bit."

Simonson clears his throat. "Is there anything you four can tell us about those bones, before we go any further?"

Robby glances around at his family. Aunt Phil has one hand to her chest, her brows drawn in an expression of concern. Sandra looked pale, her widened eyes fixed on the detectives. Jon meets his gaze, and Robby wonders if he too looks like he's been walloped. The silence seems to be going on too long.

He forces words. "We have no idea."

9

SANDRA

....

SUNDAY

Sandra meets Jon's eyes as Aunt Phil closes the door behind the detectives. He looks drained, his slight stoop more pronounced than usual. He raises one eyebrow, a trick she's always envied, and she shrugs, trying to hide how much the discovery of old bones shook her. Is still shaking her.

Their brief talk in the den has been the only time they've had to speak since calling the police. He stayed with the body while she returned to the house to lead them back to the site. She'd been fixated on the image of Dad digging, the flash of a silvery chain with two rings dangling from it, relegated to the dirt of that same clearing—but Jon had reassured her. What could such a recent body, the finger pale and discolored but still intact, have to do with their long-dead father and his suicide?

Well, that line of reasoning is fucked, considering what they know now. Old bones, right where their father dug. And possibly more than one set. She swallows, feeling like her own bones are about to jump out of her skin.

Jon stands and opens the downstairs door. "You okay down there?" he calls, and a suspiciously gleeful "Okay, Dad!" travels up from Denny in the family room. Jon shuts the door gently and returns to his seat. Sandra meets his eyes, then follows his gaze to Robby.

Robby's not looking great, and he doesn't yet know about the incident with Dad. Maybe she shouldn't tell him. But wait, she's just been reminding herself that he's a grown man with two kids. He deserves to know the whole story. Sandra lowers her head into her arms and closes her eyes.

No one speaks until Aunt Phil returns and says, "Well, that was quite a shock. Anyone want coffee? Or maybe we need something stronger." Sandra opens her eyes. Auntie studies the three of them with a frown, dark eyes darting from face to face.

Sandra shakes her head, then reconsiders. If there's a time to break her clean living streak, this is it. "Yeah, I'd say that calls for a shot. What about you guys?"

Jon nods. "Sure. Coffee with a little something, whatever you've got."

Robby's head is cradled in his hands, fingers kneading his scalp as if he has a migraine. He looks up, hair sticking out in every direction. "Works for me. This is a lot. Christ. I don't know what to do."

Sandra rolls her eyes.

Jon's on the same page. "*You* don't know what to do?"

Robby sits up straighter. "Yeah, Jon. *I* don't know what the fuck to do. This is all kinds of crazy, but I don't know if you noticed? I'm the one who's been living here with corpses in the woods, and I'm the one who doesn't know where he's going to be living next month because you want to sell my house out from under me!"

There's a brief pause.

"Robby, there's something—" Sandra starts.

Aunt Phil speaks over her. "No one's selling your house out from under you, Robby; don't be melodramatic." She's always been best at calming him down, although when they were kids, Sandra considered it spoiling. But the gentle tone works instantly.

Robby's head falls back into his hands. His voice is muffled. "Okay. I'm sorry. I know."

Aunt Phil pats his shoulder briskly on her way past. "We're all stressed, I think." She pours a shot of whiskey into each of the four mugs lined up on the counter, followed by freshly brewed coffee.

Sandra watches, her mind scrambling for purchase. All these years, she thought Dad was burying evidence of infidelity, something of sentimental value that he didn't want Mom to see but couldn't throw away. And Sandra witnessing it meant everyone would know. He killed himself because he couldn't bear the thought of shame and separation and divorce.

But with the bones out there—her muscles tighten, and when Aunt Phil sets the steaming mug in front of her, she slurps so quickly she burns the roof of her mouth. Liquid sloshes as she sets the mug down hard.

"Excuse me," she says, and ignoring their surprised faces, limps to the bathroom.

After locking the door with shaking fingers, she drinks from the tap and splashes her face with cool water. Patting her cheeks with a hand towel, she stares into the mirror, hearing the big cop say, "If there's anything we should know—"

But she doesn't *know* anything. All she has is one weird and terrible incident thirty years in the past, poorly remembered thanks to the alcohol she had consumed. Since then, she's cringed away from what she'd seen in the pet cemetery, except in dreams: her father, on his knees, digging with his hands in the light of a flashlight, the whites of his eyes gleaming as they opened wide when he spotted Sandra. The shine of the necklace, dropped into the hole as he lurched up toward her.

On some level, has she always suspected he wasn't merely burying a necklace, wasn't only hiding an illicit relationship? She's told herself her brain is playing fast and loose with that deeply etched memory—rearranging it, mixing and matching it with movies she's seen and fears she's repressed and other random crap. Her father was a sweet, music-loving hippie and a somewhat whimsical carpenter, not a killer. Prone to melancholy, probably alcoholic, and growing moodier and more distant through each year of her childhood as her mother continuously pinged between euphoria and doom, but not a killer.

The location has to be coincidence. He buried the necklace there because it was sheltered, hidden by trees and the shape of the land, and the ground was loose. He couldn't have known what was underneath. Surely, the police will find the bones are historic. Someone buried Gayle there recently, that's undeniable and terrible and sad, but it will turn out to be some local, familiar with the old logging road.

Hopefully the cops will put most of their energy into solving *Gayle's* murder and not waste time distracted by an imaginary serial killer. Sandra envisions Gayle as a teenager: serious gray eyes, wavy light brown hair, a dense constellation of freckles across her nose and cheeks that Gayle hated but Sandra thought were so much cooler than her own scattered dots.

Christ. Sandra must be as narcissistic as Robby, to focus on the discovery of a probably ancient skeleton when someone who was once special to her has been killed.

In the den, when they returned to the house, she'd told Jon everything she could remember about that night, including Dad burying a necklace in the woods. She'll have to ask him not to share that with the cops, to avoid confusing things.

Teague Wood is Rawlins property, after all. Dad had every right to be out there.

As for the note Dad left—Sandra told Jon it was long gone, but that's not entirely true. The evening following her father's suicide, she discovered it on her bedroom floor under some dirty clothes. She didn't want it. She couldn't look at it without thinking *suicide note*, and it took her years before she could use that term without falling into a mental abyss.

At the time, she unfolded the paper, identified her father's writing, and crammed it into the nook under her windowsill where she hid her diary from her little brother. In retrospect, she changed her whole personality, from introspective and bookish to driven and athletic, to avoid having to face that note again.

Now she sweats out her emotions rather than picking them apart. But maybe it's time. Sober, mature, and no longer in a position where the contents have the power to devastate her, she can read it and either share it or let it go. She's had years to heal, years of becoming inured to the fact that sometimes, things go to shit because people are in the wrong place at the wrong time. Some people get blown up on airplanes. Some people get taken out by drunk drivers. And some people are the last straw that causes the camel to hang itself from a tree.

Facing the note could be a milestone. Maybe she'll stop having the dreams.

With one last glance in the mirror—she looks more like

sixty than forty-five—she fluffs her bangs and slaps her cheeks for color, smiling experimentally. Time to face the family.

When she returns to the kitchen, she feels them assessing her mood with quick glances, then looking away as if all is normal.

"I'm fine," she says as she takes her seat and wraps a hand around the warm mug. "Just burned my tongue." Realizing her reddened eyes betray her tears, she admits, "I guess everything got to me for a sec."

"Oh, honey," Aunt Phil says and reaches to squeeze Sandra's hand.

Everyone sips, Sandra more cautiously than before. She closes her eyes and feels the whiskey burn all the way down. "It's really good, thanks, Auntie," she says.

"Well, you know the not-so-secret ingredient. Hard to go wrong, really. So tell me, did you know about that spot in the woods from when you were kids? I'm sure I never heard anything about a pet cemetery." She shudders. "I wouldn't have thought they were real, except in Stephen King."

Sandra eyes Jon in warning as she says, "Yeah. It was a ways off the river path, you have to bushwhack a bit to get there."

Jon adds, "I didn't remember until Sandra reminded me."

Aunt Phil shakes her head. "How strange. And strange that Gayle was left there, of all places. Poor girl."

Sandra forces a sickly laugh. "I still don't believe it. Let's wait for the expert opinion. People mistake animal bones for human bones all the time. Our local cops might be overeager."

"Oh, those weren't local police, dear. Those were Melakwa County sheriff's deputies," Aunt Phil says.

"Still. Our entire county is like a small town somewhere else."

"I'm with Sandra," Robby throws in. "Let's not jump to conclusions. Isn't Gayle's death bad enough?"

Aunt Phil says, "And however sad it is that poor Gayle was buried in our woods, and perhaps someone else as well, we have our own troubles to deal with. In a couple days we'll have the memorial service, and then I've got my tickets for the next day."

"You're not still going?" Jon says.

Aunt Phil shrugs. "The police didn't give us that old line about not leaving the country, did they? And none of this has anything to do with us. If I cancelled, it would just be a whole lot of hassle and fees for no reason."

Sandra swigs the rest of her cooling drink and stares at the table. She'd hoped perhaps Aunt Phil would change her mind, and Teague House could stay the same for a little while longer. She can feel Jon looking at her, daring her to tell Aunt Phil and Robby about the note, about following Dad to the pet cemetery the night he died. She opens her mouth but can't bring herself to say it. The whiskey is sapping her energy, and her brief moment of feeling centered is over.

Abruptly, she stands, making her sore tendon protest. "I need to stretch my legs. We can talk more later, okay?"

They look at her with varying degrees of surprise and disappointment. Sandra doesn't make waves, Sandra does what needs to be done without complaint. Sandra keeps confidences and loans money and tracks everyone's birthday.

Well, she's had enough. It's time to get the hell away from Teague House.

10

PHIL

....

1975

Mom elbowed her in the ribs. Phil startled out of a day-dream where she was living alone in New York City, modern and independent and, most importantly, baby-free, like one of the women in the *Cosmopolitan* magazines she and Maud giggled over.

When Mom elbowed her again, Phil spat out the end of her French braid and snapped, "What?"

Mom stage-whispered, "Can you believe it? He really brought her! That dickhead!"

Embarrassed, Phil darted a look behind to see if anyone had heard. Val and Russ's guests, seated on rows of scratchy hay bales in the faded jeans and flowy skirts that passed for their wedding finery, were absorbed in their own chatter. She turned back to her mother. "You knew Lucy would be here. Like it or not, she's Dad's wife now."

"Yeah—for five minutes! What does she care about Valerie? She's barely met her!"

Phil gave her father and stepmother a discreet wave as they took seats at the very end of the row. Good, Lucy was as far as humanly possible from Mom. "It's Val's day and she invited them. Ignore them."

She shifted and faced front, trying to catch a breeze. The front row had folding chairs instead of hay bales, but it was still hot and sticky. She prayed the moisture in her cotton underwear was the vanguard for "Aunt Flo" but suspected it was sweat. Phil had started counting and recounting the days since her last cycle, although it was too soon to worry. Or that had been her attitude before she and Mom got off the plane and got an eyeful of Val.

"I wanted it to be a surprise!" her very pregnant sister had exclaimed when Mom's eyes rounded. Phil had reeled too, but not with shock. The sight had crystallized Phil's slow-growing anxiety into decisiveness. The girls talked at school. There was a doctor at the free clinic who would do a test without telling your parents. When she returned home, Phil would go, and, if necessary, take "further steps," a euphemism that made her vagina clench. Nevertheless, she was determined to avert Val's brand of marital bliss for herself.

Last night, privately, in their cheap motel, Mom railed about Val repeating her mistakes: married too young, kids too young, a fast track to poverty and divorce, blah blah blah.

Russ was rushing her little girl into a life she wasn't ready for, isolating her far from home and family. All Phil could do was cringe at the truth of it. She'd never thought flower child Val would turn out just like their mother, tied down with kids before the age of twenty. If that happened to Phil, she'd—well, it wouldn't happen. It just wouldn't.

She shifted on the folding chair and stifled a sneeze brought on by hay dust. A few off-key notes rang out as a long-haired guy in a tuxedo T-shirt tuned his guitar. He began to strum the wedding march and Mom clutched Phil's hand. Val, who'd been primping in a borrowed Winnebago for the past hour, emerged and moved toward the arbor with measured steps. She looked like an angel, with her white cotton dress gathered above her burgeoning belly, her sun-streaked hair crowned with a wreath of pink roses and baby's breath, and a bouquet clasped in her hands.

"Oh my god," Mom murmured as Valerie passed them, beaming. Phil's heart lifted despite herself. This wedding might not be the greatest idea, but maybe it would work out. Russ was as bright as a box of rocks, but his steadiness balanced Val's mercurial moods. Paying the bills and caring for an infant might be good for them. Russ had a real job now, apprenticed to a carpenter, and they were saving to buy a cabin in the woods. That thought brought another twinge of unease. It sounded more like Russ's dream than Val's—but she pushed it away.

Under the canopy of silk flowers, Russ's eyes gleamed as Val approached. Phil retrieved her hand from Mom's sweaty grip to rub her crampy middle and admitted to herself that the old Russ the Fuss had grown up nicely. He was ridiculously handsome in an old-fashioned tuxedo with long tails and a frilly shirt. A top hat kept his unruly hair under wraps, and the waxed points of his long mustache bracketed his mouth. He looked awed by Valerie's beauty, and Phil, who'd rolled her eyes at her sister's attempts to hide from her groom in the middle of this nontraditional, ultra-casual wedding, was abashed. This was it for Russ and Val. All they saw, all they cared about, was each other.

In voices rough with emotion, Valerie and Russ exchanged their vows. Russ set his hands on his new wife's belly while he leaned in for a deep kiss, and wolf whistles flew from the crowd when it lasted a full minute. As the couple moved down the aisle, Phil and Mom and the other guests cheered.

The priest—actually some kind of mail-order minister and a Deadhead himself—announced that food and drink could be had under the tent next to the parking lot, and added that the five-alarm chili was meat-free and totally groovy, especially with Russ's mom's corn bread.

Phil's mother stiffened at that. Valerie hadn't told them to bring anything. But then Mom grabbed Phil's hand. "Come on. Looks like your father and his little girlfriend are snuffling around the booze. Let's say congrats to Val and Russ while we have a chance."

They weaved through the mingling hippies and found

Russ in the parking lot, one black Converse All Star up on the curb, smoking a hand-rolled cigarette. His top hat had disappeared, and the old-fashioned bow tie hung loose around his unbuttoned collar.

Mom pulled him in for a hug. "Congratulations! Oh my goodness. I'm so happy for the two of you."

He grinned at Phil over Mom's shoulder. "You look beautiful, Mama Darlene."

Mom pulled back and smoothed her sundress. "Why, thank you, you handsome devil. And what have you done with my daughter?"

Russ's face sobered. "I didn't do nothing with her, but she got a little upset. Maybe you can go talk to her. My friend Tracy is going to take pictures; he's a little late is all."

Mom narrowed her eyes and Phil's stomach roiled above the crampy ache. Valerie's version of "a little upset" could be anything from a quick sulk to a rip-up, smash-down tantrum. Six months pregnant on her wedding day might push the needle toward the latter. The Winnebago just sat there though, still and quiet.

Phil trailed Mom to the narrow metal stairs leading to the door, wondering if she'd ever be able to stop tiptoeing around Val's moods. And if, despite their years together, Russ knew her sister at all.

Mom called out gaily, "Knock knock!" Phil crowded behind to listen for a response.

The trailer was silent. Phil exchanged a glance with Mom, who tested the door handle, then eased it open. With one last look at Russ, who gave them an encouraging thumbs-up, Phil followed Mom inside.

The cramped space reeked of cigarettes and pot and the flowery perfume Val had worn all through high school. Val sat cross-legged in the middle of a bed, not currently crying but with her mascara smeared so much she looked like the soldiers on magazine covers with jungle camouflage on their faces. Her arms hugged her belly, and she'd pulled the cheap nylon coverlet around her bare shoulders like a cape.

Mom sat to one side of her, and after assessing Val's state of mind, Phil sat on the other. There were goose bumps on Val's forearms, and Phil could feel her trembling. With a wail, Val collapsed against Mom, sobbing and sniffling. Phil stroked her back as they waited her out, déjà vu all over again. A thousand dramas during middle school and high school, and none of them starring Phil. She bit the inside of her cheek. What would Val do if Phil announced right now that she might be pregnant? Mom would flip. She might pay more attention to Phil than Val for five minutes.

In a wistful voice, as if the ceremony had happened decades ago, Val said, "It was really beautiful, don't you think? Russ looked so handsome."

Mom squeezed Val's hand. "Such a beautiful wedding," she agreed. "And the start of a wonderful life. Look at you, with that baby growing inside you. Why, I can hardly believe it. It seems like you were my little baby just yesterday." Her voice was gentle. Mom never sounded like that with anyone else. Phil found her patience with Val admirable, because it worked, and also deeply annoying. Whenever Phil sounded self-pitying, Mom might—*might*—give her a quick hug and then she'd say, "For heaven's sake, pull yourself together, you think you're the only one with problems?"

Valerie let out another sob. "I don't know if I want to do this, Mama. I wanted to go places, go to Paris. Or Hollywood! Now I'm fat, and married, and all I do is eat and sleep. And cry."

"Oh, honey," Mom said.

Despite herself, Phil felt a surge of sympathy for her sister. If it was yesterday, if she hadn't seen the way Russ and Val gazed at each other during the ceremony, if she didn't know about the baby, she would have cheered at the idea that they might split up. But now, what would it mean for Val to back out? Whether she stuck with it or not, life was going to be full of complications.

Mom said, "You know, you don't have to do this. If you want, you can come home with me, and we'll figure everything out, okay?"

Valerie smiled through her tears. Phil's spine lost some of its stiffness. Valerie said, "Oh, Mom, I don't want to do that."

"But you could," Mom said firmly. "You feel trapped, but remember you have choices. You get to pick which one you like best. Stay married to Russ, be a mommy, break up with Russ, put the baby up for adoption. Mix and match, whatever you want. You can even live with me and we can take care of the baby together."

Valerie jerked away, face darkening. "You'd like that, wouldn't you? You never liked Russ and now you want to take our baby away. I knew you would, I knew it!"

"Now, that's not true," Mom said, the pleasant tone fraying around the edges. She'd misstepped, and Phil wasn't sure she could save it. "Russ is a fine boy. You have choices. That's all. And I'll help however I can, and so will Phil. Right, Phil?"

They both turned to her, Mom with a beseeching look, Val with a glare. Phil held her hands up. "Babies aren't my thing," she said. "I guess I could babysit a little, if you lived close enough?" She had a sudden flash of a future that would never happen: Val's towheaded child playing with the dark-haired cousin who could be growing in her own womb right now.

Val's storm rolled out as quickly as it had rolled in. She snickered. "Like I'd let you babysit," she said. "Phil the Pill. You'd probably forget to feed the baby, with your nose stuck so far in your books. That's how you got so smart, after all." She elbowed Phil, not too hard.

Phil rolled her eyes but couldn't repress a smile. Val had her sweet moments. Phil nudged her back and said, "At least I don't look like a raccoon." She cast a glance at Mom, hoping for a cue. Finding none, she decided to push everything along.

"Can we get some food and check out the dancing now?" She edged off the bed and stood. Her gut cramped hard enough to make her knees feel weak. Warmth trickled down her leg. She tugged up the hem of her maxi-skirt and saw a crimson droplet reach the top of her sandal. A wave of lightheaded relief passed through her even as she pressed her thighs together. An almost hysterical smile fought for control of her face as she calculated the distance to the porta potty.

Valerie scooted awkwardly to her feet. "Oh god, I must look awful!"

"You're lovely," Mom said. "Go fix your face and we'll see you outside, okay, honey?"

Phil opened her mouth to ask for the bathroom first, but Val spoke over her.

"Wait!" She opened her arms to Mom, who moved in and hugged her hard. To Phil's surprise, Val reached out and pulled her in too, and the three women stood together, baby bump cradled between them.

11

MADDIE

....

MONDAY

The door to the living room, also known as Mom's bedroom and a toxic waste dump of procrastinated tasks and despair, is firmly shut to keep it from sapping my will. The headquarters of Maddie Reed, PI, a.k.a. the kitchen table, is scattered with incoming and outgoing invoices, my laptop, various scraps of paper, and a pizza box. Nothing like cold pizza and lukewarm news feeds for breakfast.

The house is too quiet, the clicking of my keyboard and the humming of the fridge the only sounds until my phone buzzes on the tabletop. I check caller ID then swallow my mouthful of cold pizza. Melakwa County Sheriff's Office, returning my message. I clear my throat and accept the call.

"Madeline Reed Investigations."

"Maddie?" The voice is deep, friendly, and familiar.

I close my eyes in gratitude to an occasionally benevolent

universe. "Hey, Eb! I thought it might be you. Wasn't sure though. They call you Donald over there?" When I pulled up the sheriff's website this morning, Donald Simonson had been one of only two names in the detective division, and I'd squinted at it for a good minute, wondering if Melakwa's Donald Simonson was really the Eb Simonson who used to work out of the PPB.

"Oh no, you blew my cover! Just kidding. The sheriff insisted on full names on the website." He chuckles. "I thought things might be a little more peaceful out here. Turns out, not so much. So you're not working for P&Q anymore?" We'd met when I was working for P&Q Investigations, racking up the required work-experience hours for my license.

"Trying it on my own," I say. "Long story. Listen, Eb, I've got a journalist friend who says there were unidentified skeletal remains buried with your murder victim in Horace."

The warmth cools a little. "A journalist friend."

"I'm reaching out because I've got a possible ID for you, a missing person from around thirty years ago. Is that a likely time frame for your bones?" I hold my breath.

He draws out his words. "Well, that depends." I can tell he's delaying, trying to decide how much to tell me. How much he can trust me.

"It's my foster sister," I say. "She disappeared when I was a kid. It's important, Eb. I promise I won't share a word with anyone."

"Not even your journalist friend?"

"Not even my girl's family." My fingers are crossed. Of course I'm going to tell Rose, but it will be in complete confidence. I bite my lip, willing him to talk.

"Okay. Here's what I can tell you. While disinterring our more recent victim, we did find additional, older remains."

"How many? All female? Are there signs of foul play?"

"Five full skeletons. We think. Some are in pretty bad shape, so we're going to wait for the report to tell us more."

Darn. "Fair enough. Sorry, go on."

"There's only one forensic anthropologist for the whole state, so this could take some time."

"I'm aware."

"She'll be receiving the bones today. Until we hear back, I hesitate to guess when the burials occurred."

I hear some equivocation in his voice. "But?"

"But, there are indications that lead me to believe the nineteen-eighties or -nineties wouldn't be unrealistic."

I let out a shaky breath. "Great. So can I tell you more?"

"Why not. Hang on, I'll grab a pen. Okay, shoot."

"Her name is Davina Hempel. Twenty-three when she disappeared. She was five foot ten inches tall, with long light brown hair, probably in cornrows." My throat's closed up, and I swallow hard. Saying it aloud makes it more real. "And she had given birth only two months before."

His pen is still scratching, but I continue anyway. "No

dental records, unfortunately. Her dentist's office was in one of those old wooden duplexes, and it burned down in the nineties. No electronic records. I've got photos of her though. And she always carried her grandad's gold pocket watch, so that should be with her if she wasn't robbed."

"When did she disappear?"

"June fifth, 1989."

"Do we know what happened?"

"She was supposed to be hitching home from the beach in Astoria. Astoria to Portland—Horace is sort of along the way, if you stick to back roads and rural highways." There's a pleading note in my voice. I force it steady as I go on. "She'd run off with a sleazy ex-boyfriend who promised to take her to LA. One of her friends told her mom later that he was pressuring her hard to go with him, telling her she had nothing to offer a kid and it would be better off if she left it alone, that she could make it big in L.A."

"What a guy," Eb says.

"I know. Mrs. Hempel didn't want to believe Davina would fall for that kind of line anymore. They'd worked through a lot during the pregnancy, gone to counseling. Davina loved the baby, she wanted to be a good mom. But she had a hard time, with the birth, and after."

"Okay." There's another voice in the background, a thump as if he's covered the microphone, then he's back. "Go on."

I wrap up. "So, Davina took off with this guy, Axel, but she came to her senses in just a couple days. She called her mom in tears, saying she was sorry, she wasn't sure she could be a mom, but she still wanted to try. Axel was a prick and a liar; she'd left him; she was coming home."

"And did you ever track down this Axel?"

I nod before I can remember he can't see. "Real name Adam Baxter. He's a mechanic in Redmond, California, now, says he's sorry he led her astray, but she broke up with him in Astoria. She threw a dead crab at him and he never saw her again. I've talked to him myself. I can give you his contact info if you end up wanting it."

"Okay."

"So on the phone, she told her mom not to pick her up, to take care of Rose—that was the baby—and Davina would get a friend to drive her home. But she never arrived. I think she hitchhiked and her ride killed her along the way. And, like I said—Horace is along the way."

Eb digests this. Finally he says, "Her mom reported her missing?"

"Yes, but no one paid attention. Davina was an adult with a history of drug abuse who left with a known sleazebag under her own steam."

"Yep," Eb says. He sounds uncomfortable.

"You don't think it sounds like a good match anymore?"

"I didn't say that."

"But?"

"Addiction is tough to beat."

I roll my eyes. "The original case, the cops basically told her mom that Davina was an adult and addict. They'd keep an eye out but she shouldn't hold her breath. As if she'd had a bicycle stolen, or a TV. End of story."

"I'm sorry about that. But—listen. Who was this woman to you again?"

I close my eyes, feeling my stomach sink. "My foster sister. Her parents took me in for a few years when my mom was having issues, after my dad left." I pause, letting the memories fold over me. "They were kind, but stern. Strict. Davina was—" I swallow. Davina had glowed with warmth and playfulness and made a bereft little girl feel welcome and loved. "Special," I finish lamely around the lump in my throat.

He softens his voice. "I understand. And I don't want to be harsh. But thirty years on, I have to say the same thing. You shouldn't hold your breath on this. It's a long shot."

"Not impossible though. The location is a good fit." My words come out sounding combative, and I bite my tongue.

Eb lets it lie. "I'll send this info along to the state lab, special attention to the doc. If she thinks we may have a match, I'll get back to you."

"Thanks. I really appreciate this. I can't tell you how much."

"There's going to be a press release in a couple hours, so I'll give you an early news flash. But, Maddie. Don't make me regret it. Do not get in the way of the investigation."

"Of course not. One hundred percent professional, one hundred percent of the time, that's my motto." He doesn't have to know I'm in my baggy, worn-out pajamas and there are two, no—three empty wine boxes among the detritus on my kitchen/office counter. I reach out and tip a pizza box closed.

"The graves were in a little forest called Teague Wood on the outskirts of town. Belongs to the Rawlins family, the folks who found the schoolteacher. Okay? They got a funeral tomorrow, so don't even try to talk to them until Wednesday. I gotta go, Maddie. Thanks for the tip. Nice talking to you."

"Wait, schoolteacher?" I say. But the line's gone dead.

12

ROBBY

MONDAY

Robby stands inside the front door of the big house, staring out at the hollow oak and arguing with himself. The phone inside the tree, with Gayle's final text, has been burning a hole in his awareness since the cops came by yesterday. He can't decide if he should do anything about it or just sit tight, and the fog from the double dose of sleeping pills last night isn't helping.

If he doesn't figure things out, he's going to lose everything.

He blinks heat out of his gritty eyes and shifts to watch Denny kick clumps of grass along the driveway. The boy's mouth moves as if he's singing or telling himself a story, his brows drawn down in seriousness. Jill, who Robby met at family get-togethers, had been Chinese-American, short and sturdy with big round glasses and a turned-up nose. Denny is long-nosed and bony, like his dad, except for Jill's black hair and dark eyes. He's tall and gangly, with calves so thin the muscles sit on the bone like football pads. Robby remembers standing behind this very door, watching Jon and Sandra playing on the front lawn, the little brother yearning to be included—but now Jon's son is the lonesome one.

Taken with some whim, Denny runs to the plum tree and snatches a fallen branch, still in bloom. He carries it back to the driveway and starts hitting clumps of grass with the stick instead of his feet.

Jon pulled the plug on the Xbox when he discovered three empty Diet Pepsi cans under the couch. Sandra is out running or, more likely, limping. Aunt Phil is buzzing around straightening and packing, and Jon's on his laptop doing something with spreadsheets. Christine is at work, his girls at school. Robby should be looking at want ads, or cleaning up the cottage, but he can't. He just can't.

Get the phone…or leave it alone?

He steps outside. Denny looks up, then goes back to hitting clumps of grass without a change of expression.

"Hey," Robby calls. "You like basketball? You want to shoot some hoops?"

Denny drops his stick and runs to him. "I like basketball. Will you play with me?"

"Yeah. Let's do it. I'll get the ball, just a sec."

Robby ducks into the garage. He'd noticed his old ball there before, tucked between boxes, but now it eludes him.

Did he take it back to the cottage? Or maybe it rotted and he threw it away. He can't remember.

Denny's face falls when Robby comes out empty-handed. "No worries!" Robby says quickly. "I'll get your cousins' ball from my house."

"Can I come?" Denny asks eagerly. "I like your house. I like the logs on it."

Robby summons a grin. "All right, buddy. Let's tell your dad. We'll swing over there and come right back. I can only play for a while, then I have to go back to boring grown-up things."

Denny nods seriously. "Okay," he said. "Because Gramma died, right?"

"Right, kiddo. She died, and we'll miss her, and we have to figure some things out." For a little while yesterday, playing Minecraft, he and Denny discussed how Gramma was Jon and Robby and Sandra's mom just like Jill was Denny's mom, and how sad it is for moms to die. Robby holds his breath, wondering if they're heading down that road again. He's not sure he can take it. Gayle's kids, motherless. His twins—soon to be fatherless?

Denny nods, and rushes to tell Jon where he's going. Such a great age. His girls are at a good age too, still playful and energetic and getting smarter every day, but they're mixing in angsty teenager moments. Robby was a little bastard in his teen years, but his girls haven't had the kind of trauma he had, or the dark dreams that seem like memories. They'll have a better time. Unless—His eyes go back toward the hollow tree, and he bites his lip.

Jon appears at the front door, Denny clinging to his waist like a monkey. "Hey, Rob, let's walk over together. Stretch our legs. I need a break."

"Shouldn't we stay out of the woods today?" Robby says. "They've got their experts out there."

"Nah, that's the other direction," Jon says. "We'll be fine. Come on. We all need some exercise. Right, Den?"

A frown crosses Denny's face. "We're gonna walk? Do we still get to play basketball?"

Robby runs a hand through his hair, which feels unkempt and greasy. Walking with Jon is not what he had in mind, but he can't let his nephew down. He smiles weakly. "You bet, buddy. We'll make it work."

Denny races ahead, grabbing his dropped stick on the way and pumping it back and forth in one hand.

"He'll poke his eye out," Jon says as they follow across the grass.

"He'll be fine," Robby says. "He's a great kid."

"And I'm a crap dad."

Robby shakes his head. If anything, he'd expected Jon to hit him with more talk of money and selling the property, not parenting stuff. "Where did that come from? That's not true."

Jon's looking down at his feet instead of meeting his eyes. "Before Jill was gone, I thought I had it down. But it turns out, she was doing the heavy lifting. I should have been better. Done more."

Robby hesitates. His big brother wants parenting advice? Or maybe it's a warning, like he thinks Robby's not doing enough for Christine. Like he thinks it's weird that Christine hasn't been around and has figured out that Robby blew it.

Jon says, "If it wasn't for Sandra, I'd be screwed right now. But she's got her own issues she should be focusing on."

"I'm sure she's happy to help," Robby says awkwardly, still not sure what his brother's getting at. As far as he's concerned, Sandra has the perfect life doing what she loves, without any family responsibility to hold her back. It might be lonely, he guesses, but it sounds pretty sweet to him, even if he wouldn't give up his girls for the world.

"Ow!" Denny yells from ahead. Jon stiffens, but "I'm okay!" comes a moment later.

Jon smiles faintly. "I wanted to apologize for shutting you out yesterday. When me and Sandra were talking in the den."

Robby shrugs uncomfortably. Jon and Sandra always shut him out. They think he grew up in a different world, because he had less Mom and Dad and more Aunt Phil. But it's not true. He was ten when it happened. He remembers everything, kind of.

He casts for something to say. "It must have been terrible, finding Gayle's body like that." Her name almost chokes him.

Jon nods. Sunlight gleams on his narrow skull, and Robby

runs his hand through his hair. They pass the shed, enter the path. Denny's yellow T-shirt flashes through the trees ahead.

Abruptly, Jon says, "Sandra had a bad dream about that spot in the woods. That's why she wanted to walk that way yesterday."

"She dreamed about the murder?" Robby doesn't believe in ghosts or psychic bullshit. He can't imagine his sensible sister does either.

"Ah." Jon rubs his chin. "I feel weird telling you something that's hers to tell."

"Don't then," Robby says.

"You have the right to know. This mess, it affects all of us."

If only you knew. Robby grimaces and manages a nod.

"Sandra saw Dad there the night before he, you know…"

"Offed himself?"

"She followed him because she thought he was cheating on Mom. And he saw her. So she's been thinking she caused the suicide ever since."

"Oh, man," Robby says. A flash of anger startles him. Of course she thinks Dad's death was all about her, even though it was Robby Dad had promised to watch over that night. Dad's weakness had killed him, but sometimes it felt like a personal fuck you, aimed at the son who'd wanted to grow up to be just like his daddy.

"So she saw him out there," Robby says. "And now that we know there are bodies out there…"

Jon nods. "She's not sure what to think. Dad slid a note under her door, that night. Saying she shouldn't feel bad, I guess."

A worm of jealousy twists in Robby's stomach. *Gee, Dad, Sandy got a suicide note, why didn't I get one too?* A grotesque kind of envy. But at least Dad wished her goodbye, instead of promising to watch over her and then fucking killing himself.

"She got rid of it," Jon says. "If you're thinking about asking to see it. She said it freaked her out so much she tossed it."

"Huh." Robby turns it over in his head. "Do you think Dad knew there were bones out there?"

"Sandra's scared he did, but I can't see it. He was depressed, him and Mom, they were a mess, couldn't deal with their problems, couldn't deal with us kids—so he took himself out of the equation. We don't need to add anything else for his suicide to make sense. I'd give a lot not to have taken that walk though."

"Yeah." *I wish that too…* Gayle's face, flushed with emotion, flashes into his mind, juxtaposed with an image of her cold and gray and covered with dirt. Acid rises in his throat. In the big picture, their little fling meant nothing. But now she's dead, and his whole life is about to crumble.

His feverish, exhausted brain jumps to the other bodies. Multiple bodies. The words *serial killer* flash through his mind, but he thrusts them away.

"You okay, man?" Jon asks.

Robby nods. "Yeah. It's just freaky as fuck."

Jon stops to detach a bramble from the leg of his jeans. "So that's why Sandra's so upset. But don't say anything to her, okay? She doesn't want you and Aunt Phil sucked into it."

"Right," Robby says. This is the longest Jon's talked with him in a long time. Robby would be enjoying the sense of getting along with his brother, if the world wasn't falling apart.

"Oh, hey, do you have your phone?" Jon asks.

"Umm, sure." Robby pulls his new Galaxy out of his back pocket. "Did you forget yours?" There's an email notification, and he quickly traces his unlock pattern on the screen to see who it's from. Spam.

"Nah, I've got it. Yesterday I found an old phone in the hollow of the oak tree. Just wanted to make sure it wasn't yours. Sandra thought it might be your old one from high school, and I said kids didn't have cell phones when Robby was in high school. Unless they were incredibly rich." He laughs.

Robby has stopped breathing. He imagines saying, "That *is* my phone," but his mind is bleached like an overexposed photo and he can't imagine what words would come next. He can't tell his brother about the secret calls, about the phone he used to think of gleefully as his "adventure phone" until it morphed into a talisman of shame. Now, it's become something else too. The last trace of Gayle.

Jon says, "Probably just some crazy hiker stashing their stuff. Anyway, it was trashed."

Robby forces words out. "You threw it away?"

"Yeah. I mean, I will."

Robby nods numbly. *That's good.*

But should he try to get it out of the trash? He could wait until nightfall and—no. He swallows. It's fine. It's better this way. Garbage service is early Wednesday morning. He pictures it buried under tons of trash, and his mind slides again to Gayle in the dirt.

Ahead, Denny flits in and out of sight, running with one arm out and snatching his hand back whenever it gets too close to the thorny brambles. Then, slivers of the house and driveway appear. Robby squeezes his eyes shut and opens them hoping to see something different. Under his breath, he says, "Fuck me."

"What?" Jon says.

Robby forces jollity into his voice, in case the kid can hear him. "Aunt Chrissy's home!"

Her car is empty, which means he'll have to confront her inside, not knowing whether she's seen anything incriminating. He turns to Jon. "Could you hang outside with Denny? I need to talk to her for a minute; then we'll grab the basketball and head back."

"Everything okay?"

"Frigging fabulous."

Jon calls to Denny, something about checking out the swing set, as Robby climbs the steps to the front door.

Christine turns from the sink as he enters. She looks puffy and pale, like she hasn't been sleeping well either.

"What are you doing here?" Robby asks, and could kick himself for sounding so accusatory. He wants her here, that's not the problem.

"Getting my funeral dress and the black heels," she says. "And something for the girls to wear tomorrow." She waves toward the couch, where her dress is draped next to a grocery bag full of clothes. She's been in the bedroom, but she doesn't seem enraged. It must be free of signs of Elly.

His tension eases, just a little.

Gesturing broadly, to the house, to him, she says, "You kind of—you're not doing so great, Robby."

"Yeah, well, my mother died. And you must have heard, our kids' old teacher was murdered and found in the woods near the house."

Her eyes fill with tears, and he's immediately sorry for his harshness. "Oh my god, Robby. The girls are so upset. I wasn't going to tell them the part about—about her being killed by someone—but they heard from their friends."

He wants to go to her, but something about the stiffness of her posture holds him back even as she represses a sob.

"It's going to be okay," he says lamely, picturing Lottie and Chelsey living in terror of a murderer who'd buried a body on their land. Lottie had nightmares after watching *Home Alone*. A real-life killer is going to mess with her head.

"It's not going to be okay until the cops catch someone, Robby! Even then, they're going to need counseling. The whole school is. Everyone knew Gayle."

Robby nods, acknowledging her point. "When are you coming home?"

She takes a deep breath. "Let's talk. After the funeral. Maybe Wednesday we can get together?"

He nods. "I really need you back."

The undeniable truth reverberates into silence as she stares at the floor, arms still wrapped around herself. "I'll see you tomorrow," she says finally and starts past him.

"Wait. Could you say hi to Jon? I haven't—I mean, I haven't told the family anything about us. I just said you were visiting your mom."

She shoots an exasperated look over her shoulder. "I'm not sure what you think is going to happen at the funeral. I'm not going to tell the girls to lie about where we've been staying."

He opens his mouth to respond but hears an approaching engine and moves to the kitchen window. A charcoal gray SUV pulls into the driveway. Christine frowns at Robby, who shrugs. "No idea. I'm not expecting anyone."

The big detective from yesterday climbs out and Jon walks toward him, leaving Denny on the swing. Robby can't remember his name. He only recalls the woman, Detective Boon, and her frizzy blond hair. But the guy is alone this time, shooting glances around Robby's yard like he's gathering intel for a report.

Robby's stomach flips. He hears Gayle's voice in head. *I'm scared, Rob.* But no, it can't be anything to do with that. It's what he'd told them yesterday. He should never have said he worked at the mill. They must have checked. He's getting busted for lying, but he can argue it was only an exaggeration, that he's going to get his job back.

He swallows, dry-mouthed. Horace has been largely white for Robby's entire life; to the best of his knowledge, there are only two Black families with kids in the elementary school right now, although there were a few young Black guys who worked with him at the mill. Polallie, the county seat, isn't much more diverse. The detective probably assumes Robby is a racist hick, so why not a liar? Why not a killer?

Robby fights down the surge of paranoid defensiveness and tries to focus. He can fix this. "I'll handle it," he tells Christine as he opens the door. "You were just about to leave."

"This is my house too," she says, gathering her dress and the bag of clothes. "I want to know what's going on."

He catches up and grabs her arm. She shrugs him off and meets his eyes impatiently.

"Chrissy, please. Leave this to me? It's got to be about the murder, okay? You've got enough to deal with. I'll tell you what he says."

Something in his voice must convince her. Slowly, she nods. "Okay. Text me."

"I will," Robby agrees and continues toward Jon and the detective.

Jon asks, "What can we do for you?" as Robby moves up beside him.

The big man holds out a hand. "Detective Simonson. We met yesterday."

They all shake and the detective says, "We're speaking briefly to everyone who knew Gayle Bethested. I understand she taught your daughter?"

Jon says, "Oh, that would be one of Robby's girls. My son and I live in Bend." Denny sidles under Jon's arm, peering shyly at Simonson.

A surge of relief makes Robby almost giddy. It wasn't the phone; it wasn't the lie. He babbles, "Uh, yeah, this is my house. Wow, that's a lot of parents to talk to. And I mean, it was last year. A while ago now."

The detective shrugs genially. "Still gotta collect the information." His deep smile lines bracket a wide mouth and expressive brown eyes in which Robby reads cool amusement.

"My wife is just leaving. If you want to talk to us together, we could try Wednesday. After my mother's funeral," he says pointedly. His heart hammers, and he hopes he doesn't look nervous. He inhales, trying to relax.

"That's okay. Let's start with you and go from there. Where can we talk?"

Robby's answer sounds too quick to his own ears. "Is this

going to take long? I mean, my mom just died. We have family staying."

Jon says, "It's okay, Robby. You can meet us back at the house when you're done."

Robby sees Denny's eyes beseeching him. "At least take the basketball from the garage. I'll open the door for you."

Inside, he cringes as if the empty beer cans, dirty dishes, and piles of laundry reveal his sins. "The place isn't in the best shape, sorry."

Simonson shrugs meaty shoulders. "I've seen worse. Hell, I live in worse. So, your wife's been out of town?"

Robby hesitates. The guy sounds casual and like he might be fun to bullshit with, but he's not here as a buddy. Some of Robby's friends would recommend a lawyer in any cop-talking circumstance, but that costs money. He'll have to make do with keeping his answers short. "Yeah," he says. "Hey, go ahead, sit down. I'll get you a drink. Coke? Coffee?"

The cop accepts a can of Coke, shaking his head at an offered glass. "Nice place though. You can tell someone put work into it. Look at those built-in bookshelves."

"My dad," Robby says grudgingly, sitting across from the man. "It was falling down when he and Mom bought it. They fixed it up and rented it out when we were kids."

"Oh, right, and you guys lived in that big house over on Teague Road. Nice place. He built that from scratch, right? So, does the property connect?"

"Yeah. My brother and I just walked from there. There's a trail through the woods, about half a mile."

The cops must already know that. Robby flushes, not sure what Simonson is playing at. Silence gathers again. Robby wonders if the detective is testing to see if he'll start babbling. He wants to. He could talk about Christine, about lying to her. About Elly. Give the cop that, to divert the conversation away from Gayle.

Robby keeps his mouth shut.

Simonson takes another sip, sets down the can. "So, tell me about Ms. Bethested. She was your daughter's teacher last year?"

Robby swallows. "I have twins. Chelsey had her for fifth grade science; Lottie had her for homeroom."

"And that's how you met?"

"Yes."

"Such a small town," Simonson comments. "You'd think everybody would know everybody."

"I sort of remember her from when I was little, but she's Sandra's age. I mean, she was. Back then, I didn't pay attention to older kids. And she moved away."

Simonson nods. "Right, right. Came back after her divorce."

"Are you going to, um, write things down?"

Simonson pats the pocket of his suit jacket, where a rectangular device is clipped, almost camouflaged against the charcoal fabric. "Just going over some background. But yeah, I was going to let you know. I should tape this, okay?"

Robby shrugs, feeling like an idiot for not noticing the camera.

A tiny red light turns on. "Interview of Robert Rawlins, Monday, May sixteenth," Simonson says. "Okay. So you met her last year; tell me about that."

"It would have been at the online parent-teacher conferences in the fall, about a year and a half ago. At that point, Chelsey really liked her and Ms. Bethested was enthusiastic about Chelsey's work."

"What about your other daughter? How did she feel?"

"Lottie? It was just homeroom. We didn't talk about it during the conference."

"Did Lottie say anything about Gayle outside of the conference?"

"Not then, no."

"Meaning what?"

Robby winced. "You already know, don't you?"

"I'm hoping you'll tell me in your own words."

Robby's face heats. "Gayle has two daughters, Elizabeth— Liz—and Zoey. Liz is a year older than my girls, and she's... well, she's got behavioral issues."

Simonson nods sympathetically.

"Well, Lottie started struggling with anxiety toward the beginning of the year. She'd been placed in some advanced classes, with older kids, away from her best friends. It got so bad she had a panic attack at school. She was trying to catch her breath on the stairs, clinging to the railing. Liz knocked into her, and Lottie fell."

"Whoa," the detective says. "Was she okay?"

"Yes and no. She bruised her calf pretty good on the edge of a stair, but she mostly rolled down. And she blacked out, like, fainted." Robby still hates thinking about this. "The worst part, to her, was she wet herself. EMTs cleared the crowd and carried her out on a stretcher, but a bunch of kids saw. Lottie was utterly humiliated. She didn't want to go back to school. One of her friends had switched to online homeschool through the school district, and she tried to convince us that would be the best thing for her too."

"And Liz Bethested?"

"Denied that she even knocked into her. Lottie swears Liz pushed her on purpose, but no one saw it. Eventually the school decided it was an accident."

"No camera?"

"They have a camera on the stairwell, but the angle is bad."

The detective nods. "So what happened?"

"Well, in hindsight, I'm not sure we were right about this. But at the time, me and Christine made her stick it out. We told her that real friends would understand she'd had no control when she fell. And we were right. But Liz wouldn't leave her alone. Every time she saw her, she wrinkled her nose, like

Lottie stank, and made a 'dead' face with her eyes crossed and her tongue sticking out. She kept cornering her in the hallways, saying Lottie shouldn't have tried to get her in trouble. She got other kids to join in too."

"What a bunch of jerks."

Robby flashes a tired smile. "We didn't find most of this out for a while. Lottie kept begging to homeschool, but she didn't explain what was going on."

"And when she finally told you?"

"She didn't. Her sister spilled the beans. So we arranged to talk to Ms. Bethested, but as a parent, not a teacher."

"Okay. How did that go?"

Robby closes his eyes, tries to remember what he'd thought before Gayle let him see past her brittle facade to the vulnerable woman underneath.

"Um. It wasn't great. We met in her classroom, which felt weird. Like she wanted to hold her position of authority over us, even though we were talking to her parent to parent. We explained what was going on, and she sat there and nodded, and said, 'I see.' And finally she said Liz didn't mean to make Lottie feel bad, and she had issues expressing her feelings appropriately, and that she, Gayle I mean, would see that Liz apologized to Lottie. The whole time, she had this half smile on her face. She asked if we'd gotten therapy for Lottie, and when we said no, she implied that Lottie must be very troubled, if Liz's behavior bothered her this much."

"Wow. But you said Lottie does have an anxiety problem?"

"Well, yes. But we thought it was related to switching to advanced classes. She was fine when she was with her old friend group. Anyway. So Lottie didn't love Ms. Bethested, or her daughter, and neither did Chris and I. It was just one of those things," he finishes lamely.

"Was that the end of it?"

"Yeah. Pretty much. Liz Bethested was moved into a special program for a while, so that helped." Reluctantly, he adds, "We did talk with Gayle at Chelsey's parent-teacher conferences in the spring. We'd planned not to bring up Lottie, but Gayle said something about the girls having 'settled their differences.' And I couldn't help snorting, and I said we're just thankful Liz had moved to a different class. And Ms. Bethested snapped that had nothing to do with Lottie, and that she hoped we had her in counseling for her over-sensitivity. Fortunately, she didn't hold any of this against Chelsey," he adds, hurrying past the part where he'd looked up her address after the conference and slipped out that night to pound on the door, still boiling with righteous anger.

She'd opened the door in sweatpants, her makeup off, her girls, like his, freshly put to bed. The shadows under her eyes, the way her pale face looked both older and more delicate in the dim light, had melted his rage. When he'd left, after half an hour of awkward conversation in which, carefully, no child's perspective was treated with less than full consideration, she'd said, "You can come again," and he'd known what she meant, just as he always knows. It's his one superpower, and, he supposes, his Kryptonite.

Simonson's voice is impatient. "And Liz?"

"Right. Liz. I heard she's moved to a private school this year. Ms. Bethested must have recognized she needed special help. So that was a relief." Gayle had agonized over that decision. They hadn't talked much about their families during their stolen moments, trying to keep what they had in a separate space, but it was hard for both of them to filter out real-world problems about their kids.

Simonson regards him steadily. "So that's it?"

"Yeah." Robby has the urge to cross his heart or cross his fingers behind his back.

With both hands on the table, the detective leans forward as if to stand, but then settles back. "Oh, one last thing. Are you familiar with Gayle Bethested's vehicle?"

"I… What?" Robby blinks.

"Probably unrelated, but she reported a theft out of her vehicle in the school parking lot last year. Jewelry. You know which car is hers?"

Robby's mind goes blank. "Um…I think so. Yes. I dropped Christine off at school when her car was in the shop, and Gayle pulled in with another Prius. Gold, right? Ours is gray. I didn't know about the theft though," he adds quickly.

"Well…" The detective taps the camera to stop recording.

"I thank you. One down, dozens to go." He stands and looks around the house again before giving Robby a crisp nod and letting himself out.

Robby stays in his seat. The kitchen now seems gloomy, full of shadows and dust, as if everything here has passed its sell-by date. One down, the cop said. It probably doesn't mean anything that Robby was first. His hands have been fisted in his lap; he lifts and unclenches them to watch them shake.

13

SANDRA

....

MONDAY

Sandra surveys her old bedroom, which Aunt Phil uses during her occasional bouts of sewing fever. She used to make costumes for Robby's school plays and crafts for the church bazaar, and now, she quilts. Sandra received a beautiful quilt for Christmas last year, which she keeps meaning to mount on her living room wall.

Despite the tubs of fabric and the digital Singer sewing machine, the bed's in the same spot, her childhood books fill the bookcase, and the same worn rag rug stretches across the oak floor. If Sandra summons up the posters she had in high school—U2, REM, the Smiths—she can almost believe she's slipped back in time. Not an attractive proposition. Before Dad's death, she'd ignored how bad things were as much as she could, while she and Jon tried to protect Robby from the side effects of parental fighting and neglect. She cringes to realize how easy it would have been to ask for help, but at the time, she'd been terrified that "help" would shatter her family.

Biting her lip, Sandra turns to the window. Jon and Denny are shooting hoops down in the driveway, and their laughter wafts up with the thump of the ball against pavement and a warm breeze of green-smelling air. She's ambivalent about facing the note, despite examining her rationale during a long walk. Whatever Dad had to say could shed light on the bones in Teague Wood and let Sandra off the hook for killing her father. She knows she *shouldn't* blame herself. But, on top of shutting out all the signs that something in her family was terribly wrong, she'd followed him that night, and shamed him, and that was the last thing that happened before he died.

Her lunch, leftover stew from Aunt Phil's Crock-Pot, sits heavily in her stomach. She and Jon plan to take Aunt Phil out to eat tonight, but that hasn't slowed Auntie down at all; she's working on dishes for tomorrow's reception and filling the freezer with meals for after she leaves. Sandra rubs her belly, gazing out at the jagged green line of the wood, then lowers her eyes to the warped windowsill, where the white paint has dulled and peeled away in narrow spurs.

The first time she pried it up as a kid, she was wary. Dad built nooks and crannies all over the house, like the hidden panel inside of each of the kids' closets, but he also took short-cuts. The pink fiberglass innards of the house used to poke out of the unfinished laundry room walls, and rough edges still gape in hidden places, under the sink or behind the stove. Spiders and rats and earwigs scuttle in and out. As a teenager, Sandra wanted a clever, truly secret hiding spot because Robby was a nosy little brat, and he knew about the closet panel because he had one too.

So she'd wiggled the windowsill free, pulling up where it was beginning to warp, the nail loose in a widening crack, and discovered a cavity underneath where raw two-by-fours framed the window. There were gaps between the boards, so she couldn't trust anything too small in there, but all she really cared about was hiding her diary.

When she found Dad's note—a full day after his death— she hadn't pulled up the whole sill, but stuffed the folded paper straight into the narrow gap underneath, feeling like she was consigning it to a black hole of spiders and insulation where she'd never have to look at it again.

She swallows, wincing half from dread of finding the note, half from certainty that a black widow will be revealed when she lifts the wood.

The nightstand is in the way, so she slides it aside, then pries, first gently and then harder. The old board resists, but a final swift yank does the trick and it comes away in her hands. She yelps, holding it by thumb and forefinger as she scans for spiders, then drops it on the rug as a dime-sized specimen scuttles across the surface, its hiding place exposed.

In the revealed space, where the slender hardbound

notebook that served as her diary once was, is a blank square of paper with rough edges. She blinks at it. Dad's note had been on a sheet of the staff paper he used for composing songs, folded roughly into quarters. She remembers the edges hadn't lined up, but it hadn't been torn or heavy with visible fibers, like this. This scrap is more like something ripped out of Mom's sketchbook.

There's nothing else. The space is empty.

Disappointment seems to thin the oxygen in the room, but when she lifts the paper out and flips it over, one of Mom's bird sketches becomes visible, a messy scribble in ballpoint that captures the jaunty hop of a chickadee. She runs her finger over it, marveling. Her mother had been talented. And the jagged lines underneath aren't random. The words are almost illegible, the letters dashed hastily as if in anger. "ALL TOGETHER MERCY," Sandra deciphers, although the edges of the final letters of the last two words are missing.

In the bad years before Dad's death, Mom had been impatient with his playfulness, annoyed by his music and his attempts to banter with the kids and his hidey-hole treasure hunts. Funny to picture her in her older incarnation, poking around the house for the hidden places she'd once disdained. Sandra hadn't noticed on her rare visits, but Aunt Phil had mentioned that Mom seemed to enjoy squirrelling things away.

Is the bird, or the words, or both, a message from Mom to

Sandra? And what was so important about these three words that Mom broke her silence, if only on paper? Maybe stealing Sandra's journal was a mercy in Mom's confused mind. Sandra wonders how long the notebook's been gone and her face heats in embarrassment, wondering if anyone read it: Mom? Aunt Phil? Surely Aunt Phil would have returned it to her if she'd realized what Mom had discovered. Not that there was anything too humiliating in there. Except maybe some awkward sexy stuff. Oh god. Now that she thinks of it, there had been *a lot* of awkward sexy stuff. And sketches. Many, many sketches of curvy, pouty girls.

Is that the real reason Aunt Phil hadn't been shocked when Sandra came out to her?

Half laughing at the thought, she drops the paper on the bed and returns to the window, hoping to find Dad's note somehow slipped into one of the cracks along the edges. She then flips the sill on the floor over with her toe, as if the note could be stuck to it.

She remembers the moment of confusion as she recognized Dad's handwriting on the paper half-hidden under her discarded bathrobe. After she stuffed it away, it pulsed at her night after night as she lay in bed with her back to the window, longing for his words yet enraged that Dad had the nerve to expect her attention after what he did. She couldn't afford to care what he had to say. It hurt too much.

Her attention is caught by a pause in the game outside.

No more voices, no more ball pounding the pavement or the backstop or the garage door. When she leans to look out the window, she sees a police cruiser rolling up the driveway, Jon standing to one side of the parking area with his arm over Denny's shoulder.

With a quick glance back at the disassembled window, she slips out of the room and trots down two flights of stairs to join her brother outside. She ignores the twinge in her tendon, aware that anxiety is increasing her heart rate. There must be news. Maybe they've already figured out who killed Gayle.

A uniformed deputy, a pudgy young man only a little taller than Sandra, is exiting his cruiser when she breathlessly reaches the drive.

"Afternoon," he says with a smile. "This is Teague House, right? You the residents?"

Sandra shoots an anxious glance at Jon, who shrugs imperceptibly and says, "You're in the right place, deputy."

"Nice big house, but I expected Teague House to be a mansion." His eyes crinkle.

"It's not a formal title. First house out here back in the day."

"Got it, got it," the young man says. He shifts from foot to foot, and his duty belt creaks under the weight of a half dozen holstered items.

"Did you have news for us?" Sandra breaks in impatiently.

"Just a preliminary finding." He glances toward Denny, who's now leaning into Sandra's side. "Should I go ahead?"

"If it's not PG, I can take Denny up to the kitchen," Sandra says.

"Oh, no, no, it's PG all right. Anyway, we found some bones back there in your woods, well, the detectives told you about that, right?"

"Right," Jon says.

"Well, Detective Simonson wanted me to tell you there were five sets of human remains, and that they've been in the ground considerably less than a century." He makes air quotes, as if to demonstrate he's only passing along what he's been told. "And he's going to stop by with some more questions, so he wanted to make sure you all weren't planning on leaving anytime soon."

"Our mother's funeral is tomorrow," Sandra says curtly, not amused by the cop's ingenuous air.

"Sorry to hear that, ma'am," he says politely.

"Aside from that, we'll be around," Jon says.

The cop shrugs and smiles. "Very good. Very well. I'll leave you to it then."

When he's gone, Denny tugs at Jon's shirt. "C'mon! Let's keep playing!"

Sandra climbs back to the top floor. On some level, she'd guessed if the bones were human, they couldn't be historic— because who would have bothered to disguise them as pet burials?—but hearing it confirmed has crushed some remnant of hope. It also makes it more important than ever that she find the note.

Back in her room, she crouches and aims her cell phone's flashlight into the hollowed out windowsill. Maybe the paper slid along the interior of the wallboard, down into the wall, where neither her sight nor her fingers can follow. The cracks don't look wide enough though, and there's no sign of paper sticking up.

After a moment, she gives up and sits back on her heels. She knows better anyway, since the diary is missing. Most likely, Mom took them both and stashed them somewhere. Sandra will double-check with Aunt Phil to make sure she doesn't know where they've gone, but she's already certain; somewhere among all the nooks and crannies of Teague House are her father's final words to her, and she's going to hunt them down.

14

JON

....

TUESDAY

Jon greets the guests in the church vestibule, his expression a mask. At his heels, Denny, wearing his too-short funeral suit, hovers like an anxious satellite. Jon doesn't trust himself to reassure the boy, not with his heart pounding against his ribs like a prisoner in a burning building.

It's the burner phone. He came across it in his jacket pocket as he was changing for the funeral while Denny was in the shower, and on a whim, plugged it in with the micro-USB from his old headphones. When the screen resolved into the nine-dot grid of a lock screen, he'd tried an "X" pattern for the hell of it and then a plus sign that connected on a diagonal. The phone warned him he had one more chance, and he'd shrugged, thinking he'd been foolish to try, and what good would it do anyway? He wasn't going to track down the owner.

Nevertheless, he'd taken his last shot, tracing the outside

of the square as he'd seen Robby do a half dozen times when checking his texts this weekend. And boom. He was in, amazed that people still use pattern locks.

A disbelieving smile had spread across his face as he pulled down the notifications and the first non-spam text referred to "Rob." It was a common enough name, but what a strange coincidence. Then a chill went through him. The sender was Gayle. There was no way Rob and Gayle together could be coincidence, not on this land where Robby lived and Gayle had died, not on this phone that used the same lock pattern as Robby's.

He'd barely had time to blink at the bombshell in his hand before Denny barreled into their room, water droplets flying out of his hair and his shirt misbuttoned. But it had been long enough to reread her short text, this time with his brother in mind. With a dead woman in mind.

We need to talk ASAP. I'm scared, Rob.

When Aunt Phil called up the stairs, somehow he'd set down the phone, helped Denny dress, nodded and fetched and responded when spoken to, until he found himself here. With his muscles clenched against the tremors of panic running through him, Jon shakes the hand of one complete stranger after another, in a blur of dark clothes and soft words. It's all surreal, unimportant, compared to what he suspects.

Jon breathes. He needs to calm down and make it through the funeral and the reception. Robby's not a killer, he knows that. Not a cold-blooded killer, anyway. Jon needs to get back to the phone, arm himself by reading through every frigging text and then confront Robby. Or, better, talk to Sandra and then confront Robby.

Jon's muscles relax, just a little. He likes plans. With executable steps to hang on to, he'll be okay.

He breathes, blinks, and looks over the shoulder of the elderly man gripping his hand tightly with icy fingers. The last guest. Good.

Step one, get through the funeral.

When Aunt Phil beckons, he trails her to the front pew. Denny slides in next to him and clutches his arm like a toddler, thumb creeping toward his mouth. Jon pulls him close. Jill's funeral must be in the forefront of the boy's mind. This is just too hard.

The minister clears her throat and begins to speak. Jon tries to focus, aware that he's letting Mom down too, that no matter how complicated his feelings are, no matter what's going on, he needs to hold her in his heart at her own goddamn funeral. But all he can think about is how he wants to shake Robby until he understands everything he stands to lose.

At Aunt Phil's urgent nudge, Jon realizes it's time to speak. He gently disengages from Denny's grip and slides out of the pew to climb to the lectern, where he finds himself gazing over the heads of his few family members and the many strangers that fill the church. His eyes catch on Sandra's, reddened and hollow, then on Denny's hopeful face. His throat thickens. Deliberately, he reaches for a rare good memory of Mom, rubbed smooth by time: the river on a summer day. Mom, youthful and grinning, with jeans rolled up and her hair in twin braids, swooping him from chill water to the muddy bank, Jon shrieking in protest and glee. He must have been five.

The brief eulogy he'd written, about how a simple life in the woods had been Mom's dream, had turned sour with the gravesites in Teague Wood hitting the news and the whispers spreading through Horace like a disease. Sandra had helped him find a poem to read this morning instead. He forces it past the lump in his throat. At the end, he can't recall any of the words, and when he steps down, he's startled to find Sandra waiting next to the lectern clutching a poem of her own.

After, at the community center, he keeps blinking his eyes, which are stinging and gritty though he doesn't remember crying. Sitting at one of the round tables, he feels someone squeeze his shoulder from behind and twists to find a middle-aged woman in a dark suit. The room has the acoustic quality of an elementary school gym, and she repeats herself, leaning in close. "I knew your mother when you were very small. I'm so sorry for your loss."

Summoning a smile, he thanks her and is relieved when she moves on. Across from him, Sandra taps on her phone, ignoring him, and beside her, Robby has struck up a conversation with an elderly gentleman whose hearing aid doesn't seem to work. With a start, Jon realizes Denny has slipped away, leaving his suitcoat crumpled on a chair. He's probably in the restroom or grabbing a plate of food, but he should have asked first. Jon stares at the coat, the sleeves of which no longer cover Denny's wristbones. He imagines Jill next to him, commiserating at how quickly their boy has grown, her cool fingers entwined with his.

He casts a sideways glance at Robby, whose wife and daughters have already left the reception. He remembers the argument he overhead that first night, and wonders—what does Christine know about Robby and Gayle? Are they not only on the rocks, but separated? He can imagine Robby not wanting to admit that, in the midst of Mom's death and then the murders. What a bastard though, what a creep—a burner phone stashed in the yard, so he could pretend to be taking care of his duties at Mom's house and actually be communicating behind Christine's back.

It could be something other than, or in addition to, adultery. Robby's red-rimmed, bruised-looking eyes, his air of dissipation, and the lag before he responds to simple questions—it could be drugs.

And then, he finishes the thought he's been avoiding since he saw the name Gayle on his brother's phone. *What if it's murder?*

He orders himself to stop catastrophizing. Feeling

nauseous, he pushes away from the table and stands. Despite Mom's long self-imposed isolation, the community center is crowded. Aunt Phil sails from table to table in her maroon dress. These are her friends, not Mom's, the relationships forged when Mom could be left alone with less anxiety. When Jon was in college, Aunt Phil attended Robby's school events, volunteered in town, and went to church. All that fell away as Robby grew up, but Aunt Phil must have kept in touch. Nevertheless, Jon senses unfriendly eyes on him. Everyone here knows about the bodies found in Teague Wood. They must wonder about the whole Rawlins family.

Looking again at Robby still making nice with the old gent, Jon wonders if there could be something poisonous in their genes. What if Dad killed those people, then killed himself, and Robby is following in his footsteps? Hell, Gayle may not even have been the first. Nobody's said yet how long each body was in the ground or if they were all buried at once. What if some of the other victims were Robby's too?

Jon's close to hyperventilating again. Sharply, he reprimands himself for melodrama. Whatever the gossips want to think, the remains may be human, and they may be modern, but that doesn't mean they were murdered. There's still a chance, however slim, that they were natural deaths, buried in the woods due to frugality or a desire to avoid bureaucratic processes and fees.

He makes his way to the restroom, keeping an eye out for

Denny, but the boy's chair is still empty when he returns. He asks, "Anyone know where Denny is?"

Sandra looks up from her conversation with a woman at the next table. "He went to the playground with another kid."

"How long ago?"

She shrugs. "He's fine," she says. "Aunt Phil knows everyone here. The kids will come in when they get hungry."

"I'll check on him."

"You're a helicopter parent all of a sudden?" Sandra sounds annoyed. The woman she's been talking to looks from Sandra to Jon with open curiosity. Jon shakes his head and turns away. She's managed to put the fact that there's a killer in town out of her mind, while he can think of nothing else.

He is probably being overprotective. Sandra's right; small town rules. With all the adults keeping an eye out, there's nothing to worry about. But still, he needs to make sure Denny's safe.

He catches snatches of chatter which shift to discussions of the weather as he passes. Mom's "troubles," Dad's suicide, Gayle's death, and the bones in Teague Wood. He wonders if Aunt Phil and the others hear it too. Jon had doubts about this gathering even before the bodies were found, but Aunt Phil said they all needed closure.

Ha. So much for that.

Aunt Phil catches his eye with a smile from within a cluster of people.

"Jon! Do you remember Tom? He went to school with you before he moved away."

She gestures to a tall, gaunt man in a button-down shirt and slacks, slightly stooped at the shoulders. Jon smiles and shakes his head. "Doesn't ring a bell. Nice to meet you though." He offers his hand, a little impatiently.

Tom gives him an enthusiastic two-handed shake. "No, man! We were buds! You'd remember if you saw of picture of me about three feet shorter and with, you know, hair! You and me, we were besties for years!"

Jon squints at the guy. The voice is different, but the cadence and the energy are weirdly familiar. "Holy shit. I mean, sorry, Aunt Phil. But wow—Tommy?"

"Yeah, man! I generally go by Tom, now, but yeah, it's me!" He pulls Jon into a shoulder-thumping hug.

"Wow," Jon says again. His own laugh surprises him. "What a complete blast from the past." He and Tommy became friends before his parents got so tense and strange that he stopped inviting friends over. He hasn't thought of him in ages. "Sixth grade? Your dad got a job somewhere else, all of a sudden. I was so bummed when you left. I can't believe I didn't recognize you!" He can see it clearly now, in the deep-set eyes and the wide grin, half hidden behind a close gray beard. Self-consciously, he pats his own bald head. "I guess we've both changed a bit."

"How wonderful," Aunt Phil says. "You two should catch up."

"Definitely. I've got to check on my son though," he tells Tom. "He's out at the playground. Give me your cell number, I'll give you a call."

"I'll come outside with you," Tom says. "My daughter's there too, last I knew."

Jon nods. He's not sure he's capable of letting go of the Robby situation, but he gamely tries to be social. "How old's your daughter?"

"My youngest just turned seven," Tom says. "I've got a teenager too, but she's living with her mom this year."

They push out the wide double doors into the warm spring afternoon, and there's Robby in the parking lot, striding head down toward his car. Suspicion leaps in Jon's blood. What's so important he can't stay to the end of his own mother's funeral reception? He tamps it down. Christine left earlier too—maybe they have something kid-related.

He turns back to Tom. "She's visiting her mom?" Jon asks as they turn down the sidewalk. "Are you, um, together?"

"Nah. We split up a few years ago. Me and the girls didn't go with her when she was offered a position in Spain." He shrugs. "My older girl's there right now, but the three of us moved back to Horace to live with my gran so she can help out."

Jon's gaze is caught by an old guy in an oversized pickup truck idling at the curb, staring at Jon through his open passenger side window. Jon nods to him, wondering if he's waiting for someone paying their respects inside. "Wow," he says to Tom. "It must have been a tough decision, to stay."

Tom's jaw tightens. "Let's say, leaving was not a tough decision for my wife."

Jon nods, curious but not wanting to pry. "Ah."

They round the corner of the building. Jon spots Denny immediately, hopping on one foot in a straight line along the railroad ties delineating the playground, one of the tails of his white shirt untucked. He shoots Jon an open grin that loosens the invisible vise around Jon's temples.

Close behind, also hopping, is a girl about Denny's size with curly pigtails bouncing above each ear. She wears an oversized rugby shirt over a frilly skirt and looks every bit as intent on the game as Denny. A couple of older girls sit on the swings, idly swaying as they chat and ignore the smaller children.

"That's your girl?" Jon asks.

"Dana. She's a character. I told her most people dress up to show respect at a funeral, and she decided that was her most respectful outfit. My wife would have found a way to talk her out of it, but…" He shrugs.

Jon laughs. "Once upon a time, my mother would have applauded her free spirit. Denny's not stubborn about clothes, but he has lines that will not be crossed without bloodshed." They settle on a bench. A pickup navigates slowly along the chain link fence; Jon thinks it might be the same one from out front.

"So, how about your wife?" Tom asks. "Is she still in the picture?"

He must be the only person Jon's talked to in months who doesn't know. "She passed away. About seven months ago."

"Oh man, I'm sorry."

"Cancer," Jon says.

"That's rough. My mom went that way."

"I'm sorry." Jon conjures a vague memory of a woman with a loud laugh and a poodle perm.

"She hung on by the skin of her teeth to see her first grand-child. It's been over a decade though. How's your boy taking it?"

"Hard to say," Jon says. Denny rounds a corner, then stops, teetering on a railroad tie. He and Dana confer, then beeline toward the climbing structure and duck underneath to sit cross-legged in the bark mulch "He's a self-contained little guy. We've been living with my sister. I put in long hours sometimes, and she works partly from home, and we just— we're making it work."

In an effort to lift the mood, he asks, "So, what do you do? Pretty sure you were thinking fireman or video game designer last I knew."

Tom grins. "Nothing as exciting as all that. I work over in Polallie, in the county clerk's office." He lowers his voice. "Everyone's in a tizzy over there with the news of Gayle's death. Not sure what it will do to the election. I mean, Belter will be a shoo-in now. It just doesn't seem right, is all."

Jon's heart skips a beat at Gayle's name. "Gayle was in politics? What was she running for?"

Tom grins. "Sometimes I forget our tiny county doesn't make headlines in the national news, especially with the race being so contentious around these parts. But yea, we've got three county commissioners. Dustin Miller's term is up and he's not running again. Marcus Belter and Gayle Bethested were the only folks who put their hats in the ring."

Contentious. The word echoes in his mind. More contentious than an affair with a student's father? Contentious enough for murder? Jon's nerves kick up as his mind spins. He tempers his voice, trying not to show too much interest.

"Huh. Everything I've heard so far was about her being a teacher. Had she held other positions?"

Tom waves to Dana, who ignores him in favor of spinning Denny even faster on the merry-go-round. "Ah, yeah. Gayle. She'd been on the Planning Commission for three years, not quite one full term yet. Very outspoken on the topic of the unhoused, shelters, affordable housing. Got into it because of the students, you know. So many families living in cars or sleeping on other people's floors. Even here. Especially here!"

All that sounds…respectable. Good for the community. What's the catch? Jon pushes. "And her opponent?"

"Ah, that guy. Pretty similar level of experience, Belter. On the Horace City Council for a while."

"Was the campaigning heating up? Getting negative?"

Tom's brows draw together. "Wait. You're not thinking the election had something to do with her murder?"

A little abashed, Jon asks, "Well…could it? Would this Belter have killed her for the win?" God help him, this thought gives him hope.

Tom snorts. "Marcus Belter is one of the ten most harmless guys on the planet. That's got to be the most ridiculous theory I've heard yet. No way, man, sorry if I gave you the wrong idea. I'm just bummed because—I mean, on top of the tragedy of her dying—Marcus's dad rubs me the wrong way. He's got a hand in almost every club or organization in town, throwing his weight around like that makes him a big cheese. He's got a junkyard that's basically a toxic waste dump in the middle of an agricultural area, but he keeps managing to avoid fines and rezoning fees. Guy works the system like nobody's business, and I don't like the idea of him having a son in position to affect zoning and planning policies. No matter how nice Marcus is."

Jon nods. "Got it." His eyes are caught by the truck driving by again. Some creep scoping out the playground or just a guy who's too impatient to park while waiting to pick up a friend? He notes the bumper sticker. It's torn in the same place, definitely the same truck.

Tom laughs, oblivious. "You got me on my soapbox. Over at County, I'm neck-deep in it every day, so I have opinions.

Gayle would have been such a good voice for the commissioner's office."

"Huh." Could advocating for housing solutions be enough to get someone killed?

Jon hears his name and twists to see Aunt Phil gesturing from the corner near the front of the building for him to come inside, and he holds up one finger.

"I've got to help clean up," he tells Tom. "I better get Denny."

Tom stands and stretches. "Sounds good. Me and Dana can lend a hand as well. Hey, listen. I'm not sure how long you're staying in Horace, but it would be great to get together for coffee. Let me give you my number real quick."

Jon pulls out his phone. "I'm not sure either," he says. "Maybe the rest of the week." Denny barrels into him from behind with a bear hug. Jon lets out an "Oof!" and the knot of tension in his chest loosens. As they pass the same pickup, now idling in front of the double doors, his smile fades.

Aunt Phil turns to him as they enter. "Have you seen Robby? He promised he'd take leftovers to the cottage for the girls, but I can't find him."

"I saw him leave a while ago, Auntie. Hey, did you see that pickup truck?" Jon gestures outside. "The driver's been circling the block for a while. I saw him checking out the playground."

She puts a hand over her eyes as she squints through the windows, then *pfft*s dismissively. "Oh, yes. It's just an old crank who knew your parents. He knows he's not welcome here."

15

MADDIE

TUESDAY

At the funeral reception, I hover around the edges of the too-warm room, first contemplating the youthful photo of Valerie Rawlins and then visiting and revisiting the bounty of potluck dishes. My black slacks are uncomfortably tight across the hips from weeks of grief-eating, and my black blazer had a strange pale stain on the lapel this morning, so I'm wearing a slightly pilled navy cardigan, but I blend in with the general somber tone. No one points and accuses me of crashing the party, and I congratulate myself on ignoring Eb's directive not to come. Cops need to be respectful and by the book—it's in their job description. For me, it generally pays to poke my nose where it doesn't belong.

As I scoop another round of carby comfort foods onto my plate, I keep my eyes peeled for the best opportunity to approach the Rawlinses even as I pretend not to eavesdrop on the hushed gossip all around me about them and the bodies discovered on their land.

When the crowd thins, I make my way to an empty seat at a table adjacent to the Rawlins siblings and wait for a chance to strike up a conversation. The dead woman's sister, "poor Phil," has been a social butterfly, visiting at one table and then another through the whole event. Connecting with her in any useful way seems like a long shot. Based on what little information I found in last night's web trawl—the family doesn't share much online—the sons are, respectively, a banker and a dad. As my dad's been out of the picture since I was three and my bank account is perpetually dipping into the red, I'm more comfortable targeting the daughter. We're about the same age, we've both lost our mothers, and she's a runner as well, although far more hardcore than me. We should have enough in common to get a conversation started.

When Sandra's brothers are away from the table, I turn in my chair and say, "Sorry to interrupt. We haven't met, but you're Sandra, right? Just wanted to say, I'm so sorry for your loss."

Sandra has been scrolling on her phone, but she sets it down and gives me a perfunctory smile. "Thank you."

Her gaze, behind tortoiseshell glasses, is cool and measuring. Next to her well-muscled form in a sleeveless black sheath, I feel squishy and disheveled in comparison, but I soldier on. "I lost my mother recently too. It's surprisingly difficult, even when you expect it." My throat closes up a little and my eyes tear, as they still do when I talk about Mom. It's underhanded to use my grief this way, but the sentiment is sincere. "It's been over six weeks, and I'm still a mess. You should see my house. I mean—well, you don't need my life story. Anyway. I'm sorry."

Sandra relaxes a little, nodding. "I appreciate that. We lost my dad when I was a kid, but this—"

An urgent male voice interrupts from above. "Anyone know where Denny is?"

Jonathan Rawlins is looming above the table, six feet plus of bony agitation. At the funeral, he'd looked glassy-eyed and dazed to the point of sedation. Now there's color high in his cheeks and his words are clipped. I'd guessed the dark-haired child clinging to him earlier must be his son, and based on the thread of anxiety in his voice, that's who he's looking for. Politely I pretend to study my phone as the siblings bicker, only to notice a voicemail notification. I tap to play it with the phone held to my ear.

"Maddie, this is Eb. There have been some developments. I'd like to speak with you in person. Can we meet Wednesday morning? Give me a call back and we'll figure something out."

My heart gallops as my hand with the phone falls to my lap. Developments. There aren't too many things that would require a face-to-face. He's found a tie to Davina. This is really, finally, it.

Sandra's voice, high-pitched with annoyance, cuts through my bubble. "You're a helicopter parent all of a sudden?"

I look up and see Jon stride away without responding.

Sandra stares after him, lips pressed together, then rises abruptly. "Will you excuse me?" she murmurs without meeting my eyes, and maneuvers around tables, chairs, and people toward the hallway where the restrooms are. I look down at my phone, heart still galloping.

When she returns, she begins to fuss with the food on the buffet tables, rearranging the dishes and gathering some picked-over casseroles into a group. With a deep breath, I shake off Eb's message and focus on this moment and this connection, which has just become more important.

I go up to the tables and consider the array of cookies, then mime a double take as I notice Sandra stacking dishes in her arms. "Oh," I say, "let me help you with those."

"No need," she says, but I grab some anyway and follow her through a door to the commercial kitchen area. It's twice the size of my kitchen at home, with two refrigerators, stainless steel counters, a deep double sink, and a couple of ovens set into the wall. The counters are jammed with more foil-wrapped dishes, as yet unopened.

"Wow! So much food!"

Sandra shakes her head. "It's ridiculous. Really kind, but ridiculous. Especially considering we don't know these people…"

She's not looking at me, but down at the counter, and I don't think she's talking to me. At least she's not angry that I followed her. I pile my armload near the dishwasher.

"Are you okay?" I ask tentatively.

Startled, she meets my eyes. "No, not at all. This sucks. This whole thing. Everyone out there thinks my family are killers. I'm guessing that's why most of them are here."

"Well," I say lamely, "small town entertainment."

She checks my face to see if I'm joking, then snorts in mild amusement. "You're not from here, are you?" There's a ghost of a challenge in her voice.

I have a lie prepared, but I gamble at the last second that honesty will take me farther with this woman.

"I'm not." I look her in the face. "And I don't know your family. I'm really am sorry for your loss, but I'm looking for answers about a missing woman, and this seemed like my best chance to talk to you in person."

She pales under her tan. "Are you a reporter?"

"No, absolutely not." I slip my hand into my cardigan pocket and extend a business card. "I'm a licensed private investigator, based in Portland."

Sandra takes the card and studies it, leaning against the stainless steel countertop. She lowers her voice although we're alone in here, doors shut. "You're a private detective?"

"I am. The woman who's missing, she's been gone for decades. She was my foster sister. I heard about the bones found on your property, and I'm hoping…well, maybe I can finally find some answers."

Sandra's eyes are wide behind her glasses, her composure

rattled. Her arms are clasped tightly and she rubs them as if she's freezing, then looks up at me.

"What would make you think she's one of them?"

"Right place, right time." I shrug, not wanting to confide any connection to the police that might spook her.

She hesitates, then nods. "Okay. We can talk. I doubt it will help you, but we can talk. Come to Teague House tomorrow afternoon, two o'clock."

16

SANDRA

....

TUESDAY

Sandra cranes her neck from the passenger seat as Aunt Phil maneuvers the minivan into the driveway. The sun is setting over the trees, and the sky is streaked with pink contrails. Jon's SUV pulls in behind them. The only car here is her Leaf.

"Huh, I wonder if Robby's at the cottage," Sandra says. "I was hoping we could all have a drink together, decompress a little." And maybe discuss the private investigator. Sandra agreed to meet with her on impulse, maybe because of the woman's bold honesty, maybe because she asked Sandra if she was okay, but she wonders already if it was a mistake.

"He needs to take at least half of these leftovers," Aunt Phil says. "He promised he would. Those girls eat them out of house and home, and we can't fit it all in the fridge here anyway."

Jon and Denny join them in carting the food containers upstairs. Aunt Phil had planned the reception as a potluck, but still cooked enough for an army, and whatever Horace's attitude to the Rawlinses, the community had not stinted on their contributions either. Sandra trots up and down the stairs several times, her sore tendon twinging but the exercise feeling necessary after a sedentary day.

"I'm texting Robby," she decides after the last trip.

"Let him be," Jon says darkly. Denny is whizzing around the kitchen with a truck in his hand, running it along the edges of cabinets and counters. "Denny, put on your pj's, then go downstairs. You can have an hour of Xbox before reading time."

"Aww," Denny says. "Only one hour?"

Sandra thinks Jon's going to snap, but his expression lightens. "Well…sixty-two minutes. If you're extra good."

"Dad!" He's grinning as he races toward the stairs. Aunt Phil chuckles then goes back to dividing the food into piles based on some algorithm only she understands.

Sandra hits send on a text that reads, "Where r u? Get over here." Changing clothes sounds great, but she's hooked by something in Jon's expression and hovers in the doorway. "What is it? Is something going on with Robby?"

He darts a meaningful glance at Aunt Phil. "No, just thought maybe he'd had enough for the day."

Sandra rolls her eyes. More of the boys being prickly with

each other. "Well, I for one think we all could use an adult beverage and a family debrief. Robby should be here. I'm going to change."

Jon follows her up the stairs, and Denny jumps out at them from the open doorway of the bathroom, wearing footsie pajamas with soccer-playing hippos all over them. "Boo!"

"Oh no, a cow! Catch it!" Sandra cries and grabs for Denny's belly.

He evades her easily, giggling. "I said *boo*, not *moo*! Start my sixty-three minutes now," he directs them, and gallops down the stairs.

Jon says, "I need to talk to you."

Sandra sighs. "What's so important that Aunt Phil shouldn't hear?"

"That phone that was in the tree. I unlocked it right before we left this morning. It belongs to Robby."

She raises her eyebrows. "So what? Isn't that what I said, and you told me I was an idiot?"

"Not Robby in high school. Robby now. It's a burner phone. With texts from Gayle on it."

The smile dies. "Are you sure? I mean, how is that possible? How could you even—I mean, wasn't the phone dead?"

Jon lowers his voice. "I'm sure. I didn't have much time to look at it. But in the recent folder was a message from Gayle spelled with a 'y,' which isn't that common. And she called him Rob."

"He hates to be called Rob." It's a weak protest. She bites the inside of her cheek. "What did the text say?"

"Uh—'Rob, we need to talk, I'm scared. Something like that."

Sandra's stomach plummets. "Show me."

He leads the way to the room he's sharing with Denny. Jon's laptop is charging on the desk, and he frowns down at it and then the bare top of the dresser. "It's—what the hell, it's gone? Where did it go?" He walks to the bunk bed and starts patting down the blankets, then opens and closes the drawer on the nightstand next to the lower bunk.

"Where did you leave it?" Sandra asks.

"Next to my laptop. I left it plugged in; I know I did. The charging cord from my old headphones fit okay, but it was a slow charge." He gestures to a wire lying across the desktop.

Sandra raises her eyebrows. "Denny?"

"I doubt it. I can see him thinking he could sneak some game time, but he'd realize pretty quick he couldn't unlock it and put it back."

The only alternative she can think of is that Robby had come himself to steal it back, which implies too much desperation. Not to mention guilt. Sandra swallows. They shouldn't jump to conclusions. She suggests, "Denny could have gotten distracted. Or it's a practical joke?"

"I'll talk to him, but—"

"Did anyone else know it was here?"

"Robby knows I found it. I mentioned it, and he claimed he had no idea who it could belong to." Jon looks down at the empty charging cord, his fists clenching. His heavy breaths are loud in the silent room.

Robby with Gayle. Sandra's heart pounds. "When was the text from?"

"I didn't notice."

"Why would Robby be so stupid? Risk his marriage. And now—hide it from the cops."

"Because he's Robby." He turns to her, jaw tight, and she hears fear and frustration in his voice.

"Right." It comes out in a breath of surrender. They'd had similar conversations when Robby got suspended during high school, when he flunked out of college, when he lost or quit his first several jobs, when he got a DUI the week after the twins were born. There was something in him that was slow to mature, but she'd thought he was finally past that.

This would be extreme idiocy, even for him. She says, "I still don't see him just taking it off your desk though. He'd have to realize that you'd know who did it."

Jon grits his teeth. "I'll check with Denny first, just in case. But it was Robby."

Still no response to her text. Sandra calls him before she follows Jon downstairs. It rings straight to voicemail. "Get over here. Now," she says, with no humor in her voice.

Back in the kitchen, Aunt Phil has most of the food put

away. Jon opens the family room door. "Hey, Den, could you come up here for a sec?"

"Just a minute!" Tinny music and beeping floats up the stairs.

"Pause the game, buddy. Now."

"Okay." They hear Denny's footsteps slapping on the tiles and then "Ow!" followed by a moment of silence. A wail of absolute despair reaches them. Jon flies down the stairs, Sandra right behind him.

Denny's pretzeled on the floor next to the rocking chair where Mom died, cradling one foot to his chest and looking shell-shocked.

"Hey, hey, hey!" Jon says and wraps himself around the boy. "Hey, it's okay, let Daddy see, okay? Let Daddy see."

Sandra stands nearby, wondering if Denny stubbed his toe. An oddly cold, fresh breeze hits her bare shoulders, and she rubs her arms, frowning. Aunt Phil's footsteps trot down the stairs behind her.

Jon gently grasps the pajama'd foot. A spike of glass half an inch long protrudes from a spreading red stain on the white fabric, and Sandra cringes. "Okay, okay, we're gonna fix this," he says.

Denny's words are almost lost in his shriek of protest. "Don't pull it!"

"I'll get Band-Aids," Aunt Phil says, and hurries into the small half bath.

Sandra crouches to take Denny's hand, projecting calm.

"It's okay. Daddy's got to get it out. Squeeze my hand as hard as you can, ready? One, two, three!"

Jon uses a shirttail to grasp and remove the shard, handing it to Sandra, then applies pressure and rocks Denny back and forth as his sobs subside.

Sandra drops the bloody thing in the wastebasket next to the bar, then scans the floor to see what broke. More glass is scattered near the bottom of the drapes, which cover the sliding door, and the drape itself moves slightly with a breeze. She steps carefully closer—she has no shoes on either—and yanks the cord to open the drapes.

The door is ajar, but the source of the breeze is probably the spiky ham-sized hole in the spiderwebbed glass.

Sandra turns to Jon, her mind jumping to the conversation about Robby. Someone took the phone, and if it was Robby… But it doesn't make any sense. Robby wouldn't smash his way in. He has a key. Unless he was trying to make it look like someone else had. So if not him…who?

Denny's sucking his thumb, face smeared with tears and snot. Aunt Phil sets a little bundle wrapped in a hand towel next to Jon and calmly says, "I'll call the police."

Behind them, the stairs creak. Robby's loafers appear and then his jeans. He's the only one of them besides Denny no longer in funeral clothes, but he looks worn and disheveled as he scans their faces. Sandra can't imagine what he sees. Shock? Suspicion? "What's going on?" he asks.

Sandra and Jon exchange a look over Denny's head. Jon's eyes are narrowed, his anger glowing through. She frowns back, hoping he'll bite his tongue until they can talk privately.

Aunt Phil answers. "Robby, honey! Your poor nephew has stepped on some glass. And we've had a bit of vandalism while we were at the funeral. Come on down here and give us a hand."

Robby's face drains of color. His gaze darts around the room anxiously, as if Aunt Phil's "vandals" might still be present. Sandra follows his eyes with a jolt of panic; until this moment she'd assumed whoever it was must be long gone. The family has been home for nearly an hour, and they were loud on their way in, going up and down the wooden porch stairs over and over.

"I think it's more of a break-in, Auntie. Burglary," Sandra says, her voice soft. Jon is keeping up a steady stream of mumbled comfort in Denny's ear as he rolls the boy's pajama bottoms off his skinny legs and doctors the wounded foot with ointment and a bandage, but she doesn't want to scare the boy with the idea of burglars.

"Oh, dear. Is anything missing?" Aunt Phil asks. "I just assumed, since they didn't touch the TV and Xbox..."

Sandra can't help looking to Jon again, thinking of the missing phone, although she'd seen it when he took it from the tree. An old cracked thing that no one would want. Except Robby. A burglar would have found themselves disappointed by the lack of valuables.

Jon shakes his head nearly imperceptibly. She interprets it to mean he won't bring up the phone right now, and she agrees.

"We need to look around," Sandra says. "Should we call the police first? Wait in the driveway?"

"We should check to see if anything's missing first," Aunt Phil says sensibly.

"First thing is, let's get this guy into some fresh pjs," Jon says, climbing to his feet with Denny cradled in his arms. He walks past Robby without a glance of acknowledgment. "And then some bedtime snack! What do you think, Denster? Some of that apple pie you liked so much?"

"With Cool Whip!" Denny says, a small smile finally breaking over his face.

Jon carries Denny upstairs, Aunt Phil trailing, and Sandra avoids Robby's eyes. She wants to strangle him, yell, demand answers and explanations—but she doesn't want him to storm out. Robby needs to be handled, tiptoed around, cajoled, or he'll disappear, and next thing you know, he's—what? Arrested for murder?

She tries to fake a smile, but her face won't do it. "I better get this glass up before someone else gets hurt."

Robby pulls the drape back, looks at the damage to the window, and lets it fall back into place. "Holy shit," he whispers.

"Why did you leave, earlier?" Sandra asks abruptly. "We

were all looking for you." *And where did you go?* she adds silently.

He shrugs without looking at her. "Sorry. Just got overwhelmed. I headed home for a bit to get away from the crowd. I didn't think anyone would mind."

"We had to clean up without you," she points out, and bites her tongue. She wants to avoid an argument, and here she is, picking a fight over something stupid when an intruder just broke through their home. She shakes the dustpan into the wastebasket next to the bar.

"Sorry," he repeats, finally turning to meet her eyes. "I figured I'd make it up to you later." He pauses, gestures to the door at the bottom of the stairs, leading to the unfinished half of the basement that contains the laundry room and garage. "Hey, did you leave that open?"

The door is barely ajar, as if closed by someone who didn't know to push until it latched. Sandra's eyes had been on Denny as she raced down the stairs and she hadn't noticed. Her heart skips a beat. "No. We came in through the kitchen." Someone could still be hiding back there. There's a killer, somewhere. A murder and then a break-in, if it was a break-in...

"Robby, wait!"

It's too late. Robby nudges the door and it swings fully wide. He flips the light switch as she joins him, brandishing the broom as if it's a weapon.

"Oh, fuck," Robby says.

She peers past him. The narrow storage area, lined with rough shelving, leads to the laundry room on the left and to the garage through another door to the right. The shelves on the inner wall, the one facing the family room, have been full of jars of canned food for as long as Sandra can remember. Now those jars have been swept off the shelves as if by an angry hand, and a miasma of tomato and rotten green bean rises from the mess on the floor, which is topped by a broken Hungry Hungry Hippos game and a rusted TV tray bent nearly in half.

Her eyes circle the disaster in front of them. Why would anyone come in here? What could they imagine would be hidden…?

And then she remembers. She pushes past Robby and skirts the mess to check out the laundry nook at the far end, where Dad hid a tiny niche behind the back panel of the tall cupboard next to the washer. He showed her ages ago, proud of the hidey-hole for stashing treasures found in their pockets while doing laundry. She'd meant to check it to see if Mom might have cached her diary and the note down here, but someone else has gotten there first. Detergent pods, bleach bottles, cleaning supplies, and rags have been tossed out and the hidden panel is askew, the shadowy space inside empty.

"Did you know this was here?" she demands when she turns around. Robby looks clueless, but he's good at that.

He shakes his head. She marches to the inside door to the garage and flings it open. When she flicks the light on, the whole area is bare. All the cars are parked outside, and the overhead lights penetrate every corner.

She glares at Robby once more for good measure and returns upstairs to find Aunt Phil with Denny at the table. Denny has a huge bowl of pie and ice cream.

"We were out of Cool Whip," Denny announces. He seems no worse for wear, and Sandra acknowledges him with a quick squeeze around his shoulders even though her chest is burning with helpless anger.

"Is everything okay?" Aunt Phil asks behind her. She can't make out Robby's answer, as she follows the sounds of Jon's footsteps from the kitchen and into the living room.

"No sign of anything missing up here," Jon says grimly. "Except…"

"Right. Well, the storage area is a mess. Someone was looking for something. And they knew where the hidey-hole was next to the washer." She needs to scream at someone, to protest that it's too much. The suicide note, Gayle, Robby… She just lost her mother, for fuck's sake!

Jon's brows draw together. "Nobody but family knows about those—all those secret compartments." He goes to the mantel and checks the tiny niche disguised in the woodwork to one side. "This one's empty, but it's also dusty. No one looked in here."

They stare at each other. Sandra thinks of Dad's missing note, her missing high school diary, and a hysterical giggle tries to rise from her throat. Imagine what those would fetch on the open market.

Her mind jumps to what else Mom might have squirreled away, and what would be worth faking a burglary to acquire. Who, except for the family—except for Robby—could have known about the hidey-hole? None of it makes sense.

"I don't understand," Sandra says.

Jon looks past her. Robby enters the room. He stares back at them both, looking worried, but she'd give almost anything to know what's in his head.

17

PHIL

....

1977

The incubator was a science fiction machine, cold and alien, and the tiny bluish baby inside looked abandoned and unloved. Phil blinked back tears of exhaustion and wished she could collapse on the linoleum floor of this hallway, curl up around the dread in her chest, and sleep while doctors and nurses strode purposefully past her.

Russ was on his way. Supposedly. He'd been nearly impossible to reach at a multiproject jobsite outside of Seattle, where no one seemed to know how to find him. When he'd first left, months ago, Valerie had sounded so excited. It was a big job and the money was great. They might be able to finish the house. But commuting back and forth was expensive, so Russ camped at the site during the week. Sometime during the third trimester, Val started to complain.

Phil didn't know the details, having been a little busy.

Since her boyfriend left her with a pile of bills when he'd "rediscovered" his love for his ex, she'd had to drop her classes and pick up a third part-time job. Apparently, weeks ago, Mom had gone to stay with Val and little Jonboy, nicknamed after the handsome farmer on *The Waltons* TV show.

Despite her help, here they were, with the new baby delivered by emergency caesarean a month early, and Val recovering in the ICU from an overdose of Valium and alcohol. Ironically, the doctors had sedated Mom too, whose shock had uncharacteristically taken the form of hysteria. A kind neighbor was at the cottage, watching Jonboy while Mom slept. And that left Phil to witness the first lonely hours of another miraculous life created by her fucked-up sister and friggin' Russ the Fuss.

The baby's mouth worked, forming a cry muted by the glass, and the little arms and legs kicked as she turned from blue to purple. Phil's heart broke. *Welcome to the world, baby girl. You weren't quite cooked but here you are anyway, and now it's too bright, too cold, and you're a specimen in a tank instead of a treasure lovingly welcomed.*

A stout nurse hurried to the incubator, blocking Phil's view. Phil shifted anxiously.

"Miss Temple?" a woman said behind her.

Phil turned, and a nurse with brown curls showing around the edges of her white cap gave her a smile. She looked Phil's age, but much perkier. "Your sister's asking for you," she said.

With a last glance toward the incubator, Phil followed, wishing she could refuse. Until this "family emergency," Phil had thought she was going to survive her boyfriend's betrayal with only emotional scars. She was going to keep her apartment. She was going to return to the nursing program next term. But no. Val had ruined all that. Mom couldn't handle two babies with Val in this state, so Phil would have to step in, at least for a while. Phil could kill Val, just wrap her fingers around her white throat and squeeze.

Curtained partitions surrounded the ICU beds. Phil steeled herself before entering. She flashed to her mom on the phone last week, saying, "Poor Valerie, she's really struggling. Do you think you could come give a hand?" and herself, unable to suppress a skeptical huff. Mom had said, "You should be more patient. Remember how sweet she was to you when you were little? Remember that time the dog ate all your birthday cupcakes, and she went right up to you and gave you hers?"

"Mom, I was five years old. And the cupcake wasn't hers. She wasn't supposed to have one until the party. And you made her give it to me because she was taunting me with it! Is that really the last time you can remember her being nice? Because, honestly, that's about it for me too, and I'm pretty sure it doesn't count."

"Oh, honey." Mom had sighed enormously.

It wasn't completely true. Phil could remember lots of

times her sister had been nice, just not without an ulterior motive. Kissing up to get something she wanted, that was Valerie.

But Val and Russ were living on government cheese and peanut butter, despite Russ's job. They'd sunk their money into a property they'd bought out in the sticks, Val spent all day every day alone with a toddler, and what little time Russ had at home, he put into the new house. Mom had hoped the new baby would make it better—a sweet diversion for Val, and then when the new one got older, the kids could play together and give Val a break. Russ would find a job without so much traveling. Everything would work out in the end, Mom insisted. And Phil couldn't say no to Mom.

Having shored up her stores of sympathy as much as possible, or at least tamped down the anger, Phil breached the hanging curtains. "Val?" she whispered. The cubicle was eerily lit by the dashboard of a machine behind Valerie's bed. Medication dripped into her veins through an IV line in her hand, which lay on the covers with nails bitten to the quick. Valerie never used to bite her nails. That had been Phil's vice, until she gave it up senior year of high school. After Valerie left.

"Come in, Phil," Valerie whispered back. Her eyes fluttered open. She sounded woozy, high from whatever the doctors had her on, hopefully, rather than the crap she'd taken herself. An entire bottle of vodka and a bunch of Valium, Phil had gathered from Mom's panicked description.

Phil lowered herself into a plastic chair next to the bed. Her sister smiled slowly. Where the hard basketball of baby belly had been was a soft mound of blankets. Phil clenched her jaw. She didn't want the anger to go away. Then she might just cry. "Are you okay?" she asked, dredging up something a loving sister might say.

"I'm not not okay," Val said. "I'm good right now. Very good. The baby's good too, right? They said she was fine. She's a happy baby. I didn't think she would be."

The fact that she asked had to be a good sign. "Are you still going to call her Alexandra?" The name sounded pretentious, but Mom liked it because it continued the tradition of girl's names with boyish nicknames, which she found endearing. Val, Phil, Alex.

"I'm going to call her Sandra," Val said. "She's too little to be an Alexandra, don't you think? She can just be Sandy." She giggled. "But maybe I should ask Russ. It was his idea. His Pop-pops's name was Alexander, did you know that? Russ loved him best because his stupid parents abandoned him." She stumbled over the word *abandoned* and giggled again.

"You may have mentioned it," Phil said. She sat back. Valerie was too wasted to talk. Phil supposed she should keep her company, but she'd rather watch over the baby. Or sleep. Sleep sounded awfully good, but until Mom made it out of bed and back to the hospital, that wasn't in the cards unless

Phil commandeered the slick vinyl couch in the waiting room where that bearded guy had been drooling.

"Phil. Phyllis. Fill-er-up. Phil," Val said.

"What."

"Phil's kind of a funny name, don't you think? I mean, it sounds like fill, with an F. Like, everyone's always telling you to fill something, but they don't tell you what to fill it with or how to fill it."

"Hilarious," Phil said. She closed her eyes. Was it possible to sleep in one of these chairs? Or maybe, in this mood, Val would let her lie down next to her on the bed. No, that wouldn't work. Because Valerie would not shut up.

"Phil. I want to talk to you," Val said in a singsong voice.

"Okay."

"I did it on purpose, you know."

Phil opened her eyes, stared at the ceiling panels with their odd pattern of dots and lines and brownish stains, then closed them.

"The pills," Val said. "The booze."

"I know," Phil said.

"Me and Sandra were going to go away together," she said. "Just the two of us."

Phil should say something. Like, "Hey, don't say that. You belong in the world, with your family. We love you. I love you." But she couldn't form the words. All she could think of was that tiny bluish scrap of humanity up in the incubator.

What she whispered, finally, was inadequate to convey the immensity of her roiling grief and pain and anger and pity.

"Fuck off, Val," she whispered.

But Val had fallen asleep, a soft smile on her face.

18

JON

....

Wednesday morning, Robby's old room. Jon stands amid a scattering of Legos, eyes on the unplugged charge cord on top of the desk. He's revisiting the moment when he first mentioned the phone to Robby as they walked toward the cottage. Had his brother's face slackened into shock, or is this an artifact of memory now that Jon knows it was his?

Knocking interrupts him, and the door eases open to reveal Sandra. "You ready?" she asks.

Jon pats his back pocket to make sure his own phone is in his jeans. The household had a late start this morning; the police hadn't shown up for more than an hour after Aunt Phil called about the break-in last night. Denny, hyped up on too much excitement and sugar, popped out of bed several times before finally falling asleep, and Robby slipped away before Jon and Sandra could pin him down with any hard questions.

"Let's go," Jon says. On the way past the kitchen, he waves to Denny, who's engrossed in a drawing project that has the table covered with works of art.

When they pull up to the cottage, Robby's Prius is alone in the driveway. Drapes are still drawn across the living room and kitchen windows. Jon feels almost sick about the coming confrontation. He wonders if there's a better way to do this. He'd floated the idea of consulting a lawyer about Robby's options before they talk, but Sandra insisted that they first need to allow for an innocent or semi-innocent explanation. If he confesses, to murder—they'll turn him in. Their little brother.

His stomach churns, and for an instant he feels Robby's ten-year-old weight against him, lanky legs dangling, as Jon struggled away from the studio in a panic. The musty old quilt, reeking of stale cigarettes, pulled up around Robby's face to shield his brother from the awful shape in the tree. Jon wishes he could forget the hard, ugly lines among the dapples of light, but it still hangs in his mind waiting for the right trigger.

Sandra knocks politely on the door, but her knuckles make only a muted tapping on the thick hardwood. She switches to pounding with the side of her fist. Jon presses the doorbell, and the chime rings loud and clear through the quiet morning.

"Just a minute!" they hear from inside. Then, "Who is it?" Cranky.

Jon leans in. "It's us. Open up. It's ten-thirty, for chrissakes."

The door opens surprisingly quickly. "'It's ten-thirty, for chrissakes,'" Robby mocks. He's barefoot, wearing sagging sweatpants and a worn Metallica T-shirt. His hair stands straight up on the left side of his head. "What are you, the sleep police? Sorry, Officer. I stayed up past my bedtime, I promise I won't do it again."

"Nice hair," Sandra says, pushing past them both. Jon follows her in. The place is dim and stuffy, the sink full of dishes, a pan of congealed mac and cheese on the stovetop.

"Yeah, well, I just woke up. You guys have news? Wait—give me a sec. I need coffee."

Jon settles on the sectional sofa across from Sandra, pushing a laptop and a TV remote aside. His brother flicks on the kitchen light and slides open the curtain over the sink. He seems to flinch back from the bright spring day before starting the coffeemaker.

The machine starts to gurgle. "One more minute," Robby says and disappears down the hall. A door slams behind him, and they hear the high-pitched hum of a fan.

"Is he taking a shower?" Sandra says in disbelief.

Jon shrugs, sitting back. He closes his eyes experimentally, and his eyelids spasm. There's a burning sensation in his esophagus. He would give almost anything to be anywhere else. *I'm scared, Rob.* He forces calm into his voice. "It's okay. One minute, ten minutes, it's not going to make any difference."

Five minutes tick away on the wall clock. Sandra's tapping at her phone, but Jon just breathes, his gaze skipping from photos of the twins on the wall to a pair of misshapen vases they must have made to someone's seashell collection and a pair of blue ribbons on a hook. Robby comes out still barefoot and unshaven, but smelling of some piney soap or deodorant, in faded jeans and a Blazers hoodie. He grabs a mug. "You guys want?"

"No, thanks," Sandra says curtly. Jon says nothing. He's got his hands on his knees, braced.

Robby flips another switch and an overhead light illuminates the living room. He sits across from them and slurps at his mug before setting it on the coffee table. "I'm not going to like this, am I? Is this—what? Did the police bring you some news this morning? Or—the house? Is this about the house? I mean, everyone's okay, right? Is everyone okay?"

Jon studies him. Robby's eyes go from Sandra to Jon and back to Sandra again. Sandra is uncharacteristically silent, and Jon clears his throat. "I got into your phone, Robby. I told Sandra. We know."

Robby gives an unconvincing hiccup of laughter. "My phone? It's right here." He pulls a shiny oversized cell from the front pocket of his hoodie.

"Stop," Sandra says. "We know. Jon saw the text from Gayle."

Robby shrinks back into his chair cushion. "It's not what you think," he says, but it comes out weak.

"She was murdered, Robby!" Sandra says sharply. "Were you fucking her?"

Robby's jaw clenches. Jon shoots a look at his sister. They'd talked about this, about not barraging Robby into shutting down, but he guesses she can't help herself. He gentles his voice as if he's cajoling Denny, not a grown man. "We're here to help you. But you have to be honest. Whatever happened, we'll figure it out."

Robby's eyes widen. He stares at Jon. "'Whatever happened?' What are you saying? You think—you think I killed her?" His voice pitches high, a disbelieving smirk on his face, but his eyes dart between them and he seems to collapse in on himself. "Oh god. Oh god. The cops will too; they will, won't they?"

"Did you?" Sandra, ice cold.

"No, no, no. God, I wouldn't. I didn't."

Jon hesitates. Yesterday's fury has cooled into a sticky mess of anger and, somehow, compassion. He wonders if he should sit next to Robby, put his arm around him, but he needs to remember, this is an adult, a stranger. His little brother whom he loves, but also a grown man, with impulse control issues and emotional scars. Robby's got to pull himself together.

Jon hardens his voice. "Tell us what happened. We need to hear it. You were having an affair?"

"It was over! Long over. I hadn't heard from her in months, a month and a half, at least."

"Wait," Sandra says. "Just to be clear. So you hid this phone in our yard? Mom's yard? Why?"

Robby's shaking his head, rubbing his temples. "I couldn't have Christine finding it. Or the girls. And they're everywhere. Every square inch of this house, every square inch of my car... I have no private place, you know that? Nothing to myself."

Jon had never felt that way, with Jill and Denny. He'd even been lonely, sometimes. Isolated in the midst of what had been, overall, a good marriage. But they'd had only one child, and twice the square footage. And, he guessed, very different communication styles than Robby and Christine.

Sandra doesn't stop. "And then, last night—you took it? You snuck away from your own mother's funeral to steal it out of Jon's room?"

Robby looks up and swallows, entreating Jon with his eyes. "You said you'd throw it away. I didn't think you could unlock it, and I told myself it would be fine, that it would end up in a landfill somewhere, no connection to me. But I couldn't stop thinking about it. I wanted to read through it, one more time. Because she's dead!" His voice hardens. "And it wasn't yours. I wasn't stealing."

Jon and Sandra exchange a glance. This time Sandra

speaks softly. "Robby, did you try to make it look like a robbery? Did you break in through the downstairs sliding door so we would think someone else took it?"

He shakes his head adamantly. "*No.* I was pissed off. I left the reception and went to a bar for a few shots. Maybe I was a little drunk when I decided to—But I was clear-headed. I swear to god. I didn't give a fuck if you figured out it was me who stole the phone. I was going to make up some bullshit story. I didn't know you actually hacked into it. I didn't think you knew what it meant, what it said…"

Jon wants to believe him. It makes sense, and in a way, it's better, but it's also worse. "So you didn't go into the laundry room? You didn't go into that cubby by the washer?"

Robby appeals to Sandra. "I told you last night. I didn't even know that was there! I swear to god!" He's starting to sound whiny, put upon.

Jon changes tack. "Okay. Tell us about Gayle. What was going on with you two?"

Robby sucks in a breath of air through his nose, lets it out in a whoosh. "Nothing. Not anymore. We had an affair—well, I mean, I had an affair. She wasn't married or anything. But she liked knowing I'd sneak around for the privilege of being with her. She got off on it."

Jon can see Sandra rolling her eyes, but Robby doesn't notice, staring down at his own hands. Jon says, "When did it end? Why was she contacting you again?"

Sandra interrupts before Robby can answer. "Can we see the phone? See the texts?"

Robby says, "It ended—mostly ended—in September. The school year gets busier for both of us, and it had been fun, but we'd come close to blowing it a time or two. Christine started asking awkward questions. Every once in a while, Gayle would text me again, and once or twice, I answered and we'd hook up…"

"Is that what was going on with that last text? A booty call?" Jon says.

Robby shakes his head. "No. That was something else." He swallows. "She'd cornered me during the Spring Concert at the school a few weeks before and demanded to know if I was stalking her. She seemed rattled. I should have asked more questions. I should have told her to go to the cops." His voice drops. "But she likes…she liked to play games. I thought she might be trying to pull me into to some macho role-play, that I'd show concern, and next thing you know, we'd be fucking again."

"But you were too pure for that," Sandra says, sarcasm dripping from her voice.

"I'm not. You saw." His eyes meet Jon's with a kind of shame-faced pride. "If you looked through my messages. She wasn't the first. She wasn't the last. But I did care for her. Even loved her, in a way."

Jon sees Sandra open her mouth with what's bound to be

174

a cutting retort and pats the air surreptitiously, to get her to hold. "Listen, Robby," he says gently. "Why didn't you tell the police this? They need to know. Whoever it was—whoever was stalking her—is probably the one who killed her."

"Killed her and buried her in *my* woods?" Robby says. "After she sent *me* a desperate text? Oh yeah, and if by some chance the cops believe me, you think they're going to put my sorry life ahead of getting kudos for solving the case? No! Fuck no. They're going to blow up my marriage and ruin the lives of my girls without a second thought. They need to figure things out without my help."

There's an off-putting note of self-pity in Robby's voice, considering that Gayle is dead and her girls are now mother-less, but neither Jon nor Sandra responds. Jon's mind is spin-ning, caught back on "buried her in *my* woods."

Had someone framed his brother? Someone who knew about the affair? Someone who'd been watching her and had their own reasons for making her gone?

Sandra must be thinking along the same lines. "Robby, you said Christine was asking awkward questions. Is there any way...?"

Robby stares at her and then at Jon. He lets out a high bark of laughter. "Christine? No! No! You're asking if *she* killed Gayle? No! She didn't even know about her. She never knew."

Sandra doesn't look entirely convinced, but she nods slightly.

Jon waits a moment for Robby to relax, then says, "Maybe we can keep you out of it."

Sandra looks at him with almost as much surprise as Robby does.

"It's a burner phone," Jon says. "No connection to you, right? Did you pay in cash? Did you have to use your name anywhere?"

Robby shakes his head. "I got one for Gayle too. Her cell phone was paid for through the school district where Christine works, and I didn't want there to be any possible link."

"And you two must have been careful. You were highly motivated to keep it from Christine, and you said Gayle got off on being secretive."

Robby nods, relaxing a little. "It wasn't just that. Her mother's a nosy bitch. She helps with the girls, but she's always in Gayle's business, trying to fix her life and get her married off again. Since it worked out so well the first time."

"Okay. Where's the phone now?"

"And can we please see it?" Sandra asks again. "Not that I don't believe you about how things were, and I love you and all—but you are a greasy lying scumbag."

Robby winces, but doesn't protest. "It's gone. I smashed it on the rocks, then threw it in the river last night."

Jon exchanges a look with Sandra. Everything Robby has said will have to be accepted on faith—but Jon believes him. Ninety-eight percent.

WHAT REMAINS OF TEAGUE HOUSE

"So what do we do?" Sandra chews her lip.

"I think…we wait and see what happens," Jon says. Some of the tension eases from his core. His brother is a cheating bastard but not a killer. If only Jon could be equally certain that he was telling the whole story.

"What if the police ask me about Gayle?" Robby says. "I told them she was just the girls' teacher. If they come back asking again, it means they know something."

Jon knows innocence isn't enough, not if things go really bad. "Don't tell them anything. If they come back to you, we'll find you a lawyer. But maybe they won't. Remember, the police are poking into all the corners of her life. Someone else must know she thought she was being watched."

Robby nods slowly. "Thank you. Thank you both for believing in me."

Jon's throat tightens. He looks at Sandra. Her face is somber, worried, and she shakes her head. "You may not have killed her, but Gayle was still buried on our land. With all those others. Whatever's going on, there's worse to come for us, I know it."

19

MADDIE

....

B y Wednesday the route to Horace is becoming auto-
matic, and I navigate the interstate late in the morning
with gritty eyes, clutching a homemade black coffee strong
enough to dissolve the enamel off my teeth. A stew of adrenaline kept me tossing and turning through the night, counting down the hours before meeting Eb. He's agreed to show
me the burial site at Teague Wood, but he was pressed for
time and offered no details when I returned his voicemail
last night.

We're supposed to meet at a pull-off on Teague Road just
before mile marker seven, which must be where I noticed the
police vehicle as I drove by yesterday. I slow a mile ahead of
time, after I spot the number eight on its narrow metal spike
among the weeds of the ditch. Another minute or so goes by
before the wide gravel neck of a gated logging road appears

on the left. I swerve quickly into it. There's no indication of law enforcement, but I'm pretty sure I'm in the right place.

"I'm here," I text and lean to smooth my dark ponytail in the rearview mirror. There are more streaks of gray showing than I remember and more lines around my hazel eyes. Vanity pinches me for the first time in months. When Eb pulls up a couple minutes later in a dark gray SUV with the Melakwa County Sheriff's logo on the door, I climb out and suck in my gut, aware of the extra pounds collected in the years since I've seen him. Not too noticeable on my tall frame, and Eb and I were never romantically involved—but I can't help being aware of him as a good-looking man.

He climbs out: short black boots, long legs in gray slacks, a button-down shirt with no tie. The smile lines around his mouth are deeper, the crow's feet more pronounced, but his crooked smile is the same as ever, as if he just thought of a joke to share. "Maddie. Nice to see you. It's been a long time."

"Eb." I hold out my hand and he grasps it warmly, clapping me on the other shoulder. I step back. "Great to see you," I say heartily, to cover my awkwardness.

"You're looking good."

"You too." In his case, it's true. Despite a bit of a belly, he looks fit, like he's been climbing mountains and chopping wood. Surreptitiously, I glance at his finger. No ring, but that doesn't mean much.

He shrugs. "Not much to do around here but get outside.

Usually." His face falls into more somber lines. "Come on. I'll take you back to the site. We can walk and talk."

We traipse around the old metal gate, chained and pad-locked at one end, with a sign prohibiting motor vehicles. The gravel road continues straight into the woods with an explosion of soft green ferns along its edges, backed by tall stands of brambles leafing out and just beginning to flower. I sneeze and dig deep into my pocket for a crumpled tissue.

He's silent for several moments. I probe. "So, you must have learned something, to want to meet."

He meets my eyes, then returns his gaze to the road ahead. "Yeah. We have some tentative identifications at this point. One of them looks like a match for your girl. I'm sorry."

My feet continue navigating the uneven gravel, but inside, I freeze. Even though I'd guessed this must be his news, part of me hadn't believed it. Part of me had believed Davina would never be found.

I swallow hard. "But it's not definite?"

"Right. There's no intact ID, no personal belongings. But based on her pelvic bone configuration, the doc believes she gave birth within six months of her death."

"Davina had braids in her hair when she left. Cornrows, with beads and bells."

He shakes his head. "No sign of braids or beads, or hair of any kind."

"Maybe it's not her then." But the pregnancy. "She's tall?"

"Like you said. Tall and fine-boned. But really long feet, maybe size eleven, the doc said."

Unexpectedly, tears spring to my eyes. "She had giant feet. For a while she would only wear ballet slippers. She thought they made her feet look smaller. I insisted on copying her, and it drove my mother crazy."

Eb veers off the road when we reach a length of yellow crime scene tape knotted around a sapling, next to a rough path of trampled underbrush. I follow him, the low scrub brushing against my jeans. I hadn't known what to wear, considering the interview with Sandra later, so it's hiking boots on the bottom, office casual on top. The woods around me are hushed, the huge evergreens soaring to old-growth heights.

After a few moments, I manage to ask, "Is it time to tell the family?"

"I think so. They're in Portland, right? You should break the news. And then I'll give them a call, arrange a DNA test."

"Davina's mother is in her late seventies, and this will—I don't even know. She never gave up hope, but this will be a shock. Davina's dad passed away a while ago. But her daughter, Rose. If this is Davina, it will change her life. She'll need to come here, to see the woods. She'll need the whole story." For that matter, I want the whole story. If it was someone in the Rawlins house, why? And how?

"One step at a time."

I'm trying to wrap my head around the call I'll have to

make when my toe catches on a tree root. He reaches out and grasps my arm to steady me. My cheeks warm. "Are we almost there?" I've been sticking with him automatically, not paying much attention to the trail.

"Nearly."

After more tramping through underbrush, breathing in the cool, piney air, I break the silence again. "You said identifications, plural. You have names for the other remains?"

"Tentative IDs only. Well, one we're pretty sure about. An elderly woman who used to live in her car around here. She'd park at various spots around the county, get food bank stuff, shower at the Y in Polallie. She was well-known at the time. A bit of a character. But back in '86 she stopped coming around. The only reason I heard of her is the retired sheriff came in to flip through the info we got on the bones. He saw this one with the false teeth, real short older lady, and he was sure. Guess he was always worried about how she suddenly dropped off the radar. We're trying to trace descendants of her younger brother so we can confirm."

"Lucky the sheriff remembered her." She was vulnerable, living in her car, like Davina with her hitchhiking, trying to get home. "And the others?"

"We got one of the males via dental records, a Michael Cable. He'd failed to return from a solo bicycle camping trip. It was considered a likely suicide at the time. The two other males have no match so far. We're spreading our net wider."

"All the bodies date from approximately the same time?"

"Plus or minus, with disclaimers on the part of the doc. But basically, yes."

I wonder how much traffic there is in these woods. The parking area looked pretty well used, with trash scattered in the surrounding bushes, and we'd followed an established footpath around the gate. But right about now, in the hush of the trees with no human sign anywhere, I'm willing to bet no one comes this far back regularly. "Can you tell me anything about cause of death?" I want to fill in the blanks of Davina's story, but I almost choke on the question. If she died out here, the victim of a serial killer, her last moments must have been terrifying. The thought of Rose's stubborn determination stiffens my spine. Rose, who grew up with her mother's absence front and center in her life, will want to face every detail. She won't flinch and neither can I.

Eb shakes his head. "No details yet."

"You don't have information yet, or you can't tell me yet?"

"Yep." He flashes me a grin and I roll my eyes. He's a hard guy not to like, but I need to remember—he's only sharing now because it suits him.

When we come to another length of crime scene tape tied around a tree, he leaves the path to step up an embankment of fir-needle-covered ground that sinks under our feet and shows older tracks of something heavy and wheeled. I sling one leg and then the other over the massive girth of a downed tree, stabbing my thigh with a sharp stub of broken branch in the process. "Ouch. How did all the techs get their stuff past this?"

"They didn't. I didn't think you'd want to go the easy way. Jeez, Maddie, you getting old?"

I shoot him a look. "Seriously?"

He shrugs. "Nah. It was a pain in the ass for the techs too. Our killer didn't make it easy. Probably had a hard time themselves, but it's so isolated out here, they could take their time."

Just ahead, a stand of cedars huddles together, and Eb pushes through the swooping lower branches, then stops abruptly. I join him at the brink of a hollow, where an old-growth giant with a warped double trunk rules over a misshapen rectangle of raw earth, dotted with wooden stakes and fluttering pink flags. Here's my sign of human interference, and I feel sick.

"This is it," Eb says, stating the obvious after a moment of silence.

I sweep the clearing with a glance. Everything is hushed. Sunlight arrows through the canopy, and goose bumps rise on my arms. All those people, killed and hidden beneath the dirt. But it's not them I sense. They didn't choose this place. It's the killer who dug the graves, who dumped the remains here. Like garbage? Or possibly, a private memorial for him to savor.

I roll the little onyx bead in my earring. "I'm guessing after all this time you can't tell if this was more than a burial site? If the victims died here?"

"Gayle Bethested definitely did not die here. She lost a lot of blood, and it wasn't here. The others…my gut says no. But it's hard to prove a negative, after all this time."

"Right." I gaze into the clearing, trying to picture it as it would have been before the police tore everything up. Maybe Eb has photos that I can share with Mama Hempel and Rose. Maybe, unlike me, they'll appreciate the peace and the greenery, rather than focusing on the machinations of the killer and this remote site that allowed him to get away with it for so long.

If the DNA is confirmed, Rose will stand where I'm standing, and I'll come with her. This is no place to be without support. If anything of Davina remains, perhaps her spirit will be comforted to know that her baby grew up well. Perhaps it will matter to her that I still care.

"The remains we think were Davina's were on that side, if it matters," Eb offers. He points across. I follow the line of his finger to a patch of bare soil adjacent to the outside edge of the roped-off area, then imagine the line continuing out of the woods.

"The Rawlins house is that way, right? Or did I get turned around?"

"Um, not directly that way." His finger swings toward the right. "More that way. West."

"How long does it take to walk here from their place?"

"Depends. The woman who discovered Gayle Bethested's

body showed me the trail she followed. Without her help, I wouldn't have known it was there. Fallen logs and brambles block it at multiple points, so you lose it, and then when you find it again, it's barely a deer trail. She had to backtrack a couple of times, and she'd just walked it twice."

"So you have to know what you're looking for."

"At least from that direction."

"You're looking at the family then?"

He narrows his eyes at me. "Don't start puzzling at my case. If the bones belong to your young woman, you've done your duty. Leave the rest to me. And stay away from the Rawlinses," he adds. "There are multiple connections between those people, the Bethested case, and the older cases. Could just be the small town effect, but that's an awful lot of smoke for no fire."

I shrug. No way I'm telling him I've already made a connection. "It's got to be tough, trying to figure out who knew what over thirty years ago. Who used the logging road back then. When it was even made."

He nods. "We're on it. Looking at old topo maps. Talking to the company that had the timber rights back here and would have been in charge of the gate. Uniforms are checking with old-timers who might have fished or swum in the river."

"Great." I wonder if he'll keep me updated. "Thanks for showing me this. I'll call Rose and her mom right away and let you know once I get in touch."

"Maddie. Despite everything, there may not be a match. Don't get their hopes up too far."

An impossible piece of advice. The location and the similarities with the skeletal remains have me mostly convinced, and it will be difficult to keep that from coming through. Plus, to Rose, the timing will seem meant to be; her mother returning to her just as she's about to give birth herself.

I linger to take a last look at the clearing, then hurry to catch up with Eb as he retraces our steps. He asks, "You heading back to Portland then?"

I check my phone for the time. "Pretty soon. I have an appointment." As I hoped, he asks no follow-up questions, just nods as if satisfied.

....

After Eb pulls away, I sit in the gravel pull-off, jotting our conversation into my notebook. Last night I outlined what I need to cover with Sandra today, and I'm grateful I did, because the trip to the gravesites left me reeling. Until we get DNA results it will be unofficial, but I know. I've finally found what remains of Davina. All that's left is to gather up what I can—her bones, her final story—and bring them home.

And the story starts with learning everything I can from the Rawlins family.

Out on the road, a vehicle with a souped-up engine whizzes

by, trailing a pounding bass beat that dopplers away. I set my notebook down and check my phone. It's close enough to two o'clock, and I navigate the short distance to Teague House.

The parking area at the end of the gravel drive is paved and contains three other vehicles, arranged to allow access to a basketball hoop mounted above the double garage doors. When I climb out, the air smells of cut grass and manure. I wonder whether to walk up the stairs to the porch where I can see a modest side door or go around to the front.

Before I can choose, Sandra appears on the walkway. She's less polished today, with her curly graying bangs frizzing in every direction, wearing torn jeans and a stained gray sweatshirt. She peels off yellow rubber gloves and offers a perfunctory smile.

I hold out my hand. "Thanks for letting me come by."

She gives my fingers a brief squeeze, her hand moist and unpleasant from the glove. "Like I said, I'm not sure how I can help. But I'm willing to give you a few minutes." She sounds more harried and unfriendly than yesterday. I wonder if something has happened, or maybe her brothers were against this meeting.

"I appreciate that. You must be busy. So, this is your mother's house?" I know the answer, of course, but I'm hoping to warm her up and get her chatting on something easy.

She nods. "The family home. Let's go back to the kitchen. I could use a cup of tea. You?"

"Sure."

I follow Sandra up a short set of concrete steps and through the gray-painted door. We're in a high-ceilinged foyer with a stairway leading up, rooms to the left and right, and a wide hallway ahead. Everything looks worn, with dated wallpaper and paneled skirting on the walls. Despite that, it's clean and homey and smells like lemon furniture polish, except for a faint vinegary taint to the air. I sniff, then hope Sandra didn't notice, as the odor seems to be coming off her.

She stumbles over a pair of blue hard-shell suitcases next to the stairs and curses under her breath. "You can leave your shoes on," she says as I pause next to a mat where a dozen pairs of boots and shoes are scattered.

"Thanks."

On the landing above, Jon Rawlins appears in dark blue jeans and a button-down shirt with the tails out, his cell phone to his ear. "Hang on," he says into the phone. To Sandra: "This is the private detective? Are you sure—"

"She's asking about someone who disappeared decades ago," Sandra says with the air of someone repeating herself for the umpteenth time.

"Should I come down?" he asks.

"No, it's fine. I can't imagine how we can help, but she says it will just take a few minutes."

I nod and try to look harmless.

He still looks concerned, but he retreats from the landing, murmuring into his phone.

"It's kind of crazy around here," Sandra says over her shoulder as she continues toward the kitchen. "We had a break-in yesterday. The police say it was probably a thief drawn by the obituary, but whatever it was, it was upsetting. Plus, my aunt is leaving today. She was Mom's caregiver. I'm not sure what we're going to do without her." She gestures toward a large oak table half covered in a drift of childish artwork. All the figures have long curving limbs like cooked noodles. "Have a seat. So, coffee, tea, diet cola, water…"

"Coffee would be great if it's no trouble." I lick my teeth. What I really need is food, as my stomach burns with acid, but coffee will do for now.

"All right, just a sec. Hi, Auntie," Sandra adds, as the older woman I identified at the funeral as Valerie Rawlins's sister beelines to a tall corner cupboard. "We have a guest."

"Oh?" the shorter woman asks with her back to us as she rifles around.

"She's a private detective. She thinks the bones found in the wood could be a missing person from, what did you say, 1985?"

"1989," I say. "Nice to meet you. I'm Maddie Reed."

She turns from the cupboard balancing a stack of tea tins. "Oh my, a private detective? What an exciting job! Someone missing almost forty years. Imagine that."

"Auntie, can I get you something? Would you like to sit with us?" Sandra says.

The older woman shakes her head with a smile, hugging her tins close. "Busy, busy! The glazier will be here in a few minutes, dear, to fix the sliding door. I'm going to remind the boys after I put these away."

"Did you live here in 1989?" I ask quickly.

"Oh, no, dear, I think it was '93 when I came to stay. Yes, that's right. 1993. Well, nice to meet you, good luck!" She bustles out, balancing the tins precariously against her chest.

"Did you say she's leaving?" I ask Sandra.

"She's going on a cruise." Sandra frowns after her. "It's too late to cancel without a huge fee, but… Anyway." She sets a coffee down in front of me, and puts another pod in the Keurig for herself. Through the door across from the table comes a man's voice: "Booyah!" followed by a child's laughter.

"I was my mother's primary caregiver until she passed," I offer. "I loved her, of course, but I would have jumped at the opportunity to travel when she died."

Sandra snorts as she sits down with her mug. "It's been less than a week. I don't begrudge my aunt…but there's so much going on right now."

That's an understatement. "Maybe that's it. She needs space, and she's put her own needs second for how many years?" I catch myself sounding like I'm taking sides and grimace in apology. "Don't mind me. It's a topic that hits close to home."

Sandra laughs a little, studying me. "No, I can imagine.

And I'm in awe of caregivers. I don't think I'd be capable of more than about a week. Good thing I never had kids, right?"

"I'm told that's different," I say.

"Yeah. I'm told that too." She rolls her eyes.

I laugh, guessing that as two childless women, we've probably heard the same comments.

She sips her tea, seeming more relaxed. "Honestly, I still don't see how I can help you. In 1989—Christ, I was twelve years old."

I reach into my shoulder bag and shuffle through the contents for a print of Davina, copied from a candid shot Mama Hempel keeps on her fridge. I look down at it, then slide the picture toward Sandra. "This is her. Take a look, see if it rings any bells." Senior year of high school, Davina made up and mugging for the camera. Her head is thrown back as she sings into a handheld microphone, the fringe on her leather jacket blurring as she dances. Her striking features are apparent, even with too much blue eyeshadow. "When she disappeared, she was a few years older than this, with her hair in beaded cornrows."

I watch Sandra's face carefully. Her eyes linger, and I see pity but no flicker of recognition. She looks back at me and shakes her head before sliding the picture back to me. "I don't recognize her, but I doubt I would even if I'd seen her. It was just too long ago. Do you know—are they sure yet? That it was her?"

"It looks likely. They're testing DNA."

"What was she doing here?"

I give her my well-practiced rundown of Davina's downward spiral, hard-won recovery, and final error. Sandra nods and asks, "So you've been looking for her ever since?"

I shake my head and laugh. "Sort of. I was only a kid when it happened. I helped her mother put up flyers, but that was it. As an adult, when I leaned into investigation as a career, I started looking into it more seriously. I've gotten my hopes up before, but nothing like this. I'm so grateful you found the burial site."

Sandra looks uncomfortable but smiles gamely. "The whole experience has been rough, but I hope it provides some answers to people who've lost loved ones. It must be tough, looking for missing people. Heartbreaking."

I shake my head. "I'm sure it is. Davina's a special case for me though. I generally do insurance fraud cases, sometimes infidelity. Boring, for the most part. Looking for Davina is more of a personal quest. She was like a sister, and her daughter's a friend of mine, grown up now. For her to know why her mother disappeared and left her with a hole in her life—it would mean everything to her. To me as well." My eyes sting, and I realize I've crossed the line from professional to personal again. I clear my throat. "Can we talk about the history of the property? When did your parents move here?"

Sandra nods. "Mom and Dad bought the land around

1975. It's a large plot, around ten acres, and it came with an old run-down cottage, no electricity, no plumbing. My dad did carpentry, worked for a contractor, and he built most of this house himself, over the years as they could afford it. I heard the story so many times when I was a kid. He and Mom were very proud of it." A wistful smile crosses her face.

"So you don't know who owned it before that?"

"I think it was the Teagues. They owned a lot of the land in Horace."

"And what about the woods and the trails?"

"What about them?"

"Did your parents have plans for them? Were they going to sell them or develop them, or did they hunt? Why did they want such a big piece of land?"

"They were back-to-nature types. They grabbed up as much forest as they could afford, and imagined they were going to live as hunter-gatherers or something. The way the property abuts the state forest, there's some kind of legal issue. I don't think we're allowed to develop the land in certain ways. But my parents never would have, anyway. They said we were 'on the porch of the wilderness,' and they loved that."

I scribble more notes. "Your dad was a carpenter, you said. What about your mom?"

"She was a homemaker. She gardened, she liked to draw… and way back, when Jon and I were at school, she used to work in a shop downtown. At least before Robby was born."

"Your younger brother?" I'd seen him at the funeral and reception but hadn't interacted at all.

"Yes, he was born in, let's see, 1983."

"And your father was Russell Rawlins?" His name had been in Valerie's brief obituary. I look up from my notes when she doesn't respond.

She picks at the cuticle of one of her fingers and answers reluctantly. "He went by Russ."

"What was he like?"

"He was a musician. A carpenter, like I said. A good father." Each phrase comes out as if she's being charged by the word, and I know by the resistance that I'm pushing in the right direction.

"When did he pass away?"

"That was 1993," Sandra says, and it clicks. The same year her aunt started caregiving for her mother.

I open my mouth for a follow-up question, but before I can speak she adds, "He killed himself."

I hadn't turned that up online, but it makes sense of the rumbling I heard at the reception. In the eyes of the community, Valerie was a shut-in and her husband a suicide. The town must be wondering if the mental illness in the family extended to murder—and if the same proclivities had passed on to the children.

Quickly, I school my expression. "I'm sorry," I say. "That must have been awful for all of you."

"It was."

My pulse has quickened. "Did something happen that pushed him over the edge? Job loss, financial issues?"

Even before her face shutters, I sense that I've pushed too much, too fast. "I haven't put a lot of thought into it," she says. "I was too pissed off at him for leaving us that way. Reasons didn't matter at the time."

"And now? Don't you want to know? Especially in light of the bodies that were found?"

She looks down at her hands and then back to me, shaking her head. "Listen," she says. "I don't remember much about those days. My parents had their problems, but they weren't psychopaths. There's no way they had anything to do with the bodies in the woods." She pushes out her chair and stands up. "Sorry I can't be of more help."

For a moment, I remain where I am, calculating the best way to get her to open up. Softening my voice, I say, "There's a lot at stake. You were just saying you hoped the families would get answers. Can you at least help rule out your parents' involvement?"

"Rule them out? When were they ruled in?" she demands. Then her brother Jon speaks from the doorway. I'm not sure how long he's been standing there.

"I think it's time for you to leave," he says firmly.

I look to Sandra. She nods, freckles standing out on her pale face.

Damn it. I should have softballed. Standing, I dig in my pocket for another card, which I pass to Sandra as I move to follow Jon.

"Think of the victims' families," I say. "Please. Call me if you reconsider."

20

SANDRA

....

Sandra stands at the kitchen table, eyes pointed toward Teague Wood out the window but unseeing, her breath coming in short hitches. When Jon returns to the kitchen, she turns on him.

"What the fuck was that?" she demands.

"What?"

"I'm in the middle of a conversation with someone and you come barging in and tell them to leave?"

He holds up his hands. "You told her you were done! I was backing you up!"

"I had it under control."

"Did you? Because it sounded like she was looking for whatever she could twist to make it sound like Dad was a killer. Did you actually check her out? Even if she's not a reporter, she could be writing a book or doing a podcast or something. I don't know why you agreed to talk to her." He walks past her, fills a water glass at the sink, then drinks it down. His motions are clipped, and she realizes how pissed off he is. He'd barely spoken since coming back from Robby's. He's on edge, just like her.

Sandra presses her fingertips against the edge of the table and takes a breath. She had checked Maddie out, briefly. There was a dated but professional-looking website with quotes from supposedly satisfied customers, and she was listed as licensed and in good standing on the Oregon.gov website. But Jon was right. That didn't preclude her from collecting information for a self-serving narrative that she could share with the world in a dozen different ways.

Sandra swallows. She needs the truth, but not at the cost of leaving all the Rawlinses open to the kind of vitriol spewed at the families of suspected killers. And yet—Maddie's story of the missing girl had moved her. For all the difficulties Sandra, Jon, and Robby had growing up under the shadow of her parents' dysfunction, each one of those graves represented another family wounded by loss.

As Maddie had said, all she wanted to do was rule out her family's involvement.

"Right. You're right," she tells him. "It's fine."

He sets the glass down in the sink and turns to her with tired eyes. "I've got to get out of here for a while, clear my head. And Denny needs to get away from the Xbox. We'll be back by dinner."

He doesn't ask her to come. A plan takes shape in her mind at the realization that she'll have the house to herself, except for Aunt Phil, who's been buzzing around packing and organizing all day. "Good idea." Her adrenaline jumps. She'd been chipping away at the utility room mess downstairs before the private detective came, but now...

When Jon and Denny leave, she rushes to Mom's room, only to stop short because Aunt Phil's already there, humming as she smoothes a stack of shirts piled on the faded bedspread.

Aunt Phil smiles, pulling an earbud out of her ear and slipping it into her pocket. "Oh, hello, dear. Are you finished with that private detective?"

"For now. I need a break from the basement. I was thinking I might work on Mom's room for a bit. Are you done packing?"

"Oh, yes, I packed light. I'm putting my other things into boxes though, and setting some aside for Goodwill. You three may decide to sell the place, after all, and I don't want you to have to pack for me. I got sidetracked when I realized a lot of Val's clothes will go to Goodwill too."

Sandra scans the room. Her aunt hasn't gotten far. "You go back to your packing, Auntie. I'll worry about this stuff."

Aunt Phil steps back and casts a look around. "Well," she says. "I suppose I should focus on my own things. Are you sure though? There's a lot in here, not just clothes. I was going to bring up the recycling bin too. Your mother seems to have decided every little cubby in the bureau and vanity should be packed with pictures of birds, torn from her sketchbooks!" Aunt Phil sighs. "Maybe you'll want to choose a few of the nicer ones to frame. But most are just scribbles."

"I'll take care of it," Sandra says, her pulse quickening at the thought of all those papers. Maybe Dad's note had found its way into one of the same stashes. "You've done so much already."

"Oh, honey. That's okay. I'm happy to do it."

"No, no, I want to."

Aunt Phil shrugs. "Well, if you insist. But, honey—" She breaks off, searching Sandra's face. "Don't let it upset you, all right? Your mother was as happy as we could make her, wasn't she?"

Sandra nods, but a chill works its way up Sandra's spine as she watches Aunt Phil replace the earbud in her ear and bop out of the room.

In the early days after Dad's death, Aunt Phil's presence seemed to soften the worst of Mom's moods, and once Sandra and Jon moved on to their own lives, Mom had seemed okay during holiday visits, in her mute and distant way. Aunt Phil had typically responded to inquiries about Mom's health and behavior with things like, "Oh, as well as could be expected," and, "She's getting along just fine," and Sandra had been more than happy to leave it at that. She thinks of the odd note she'd discovered in her windowsill. Maybe she shouldn't have.

With a deep breath, she gently clicks the door shut and turns to face the room. Filled with dark massive furniture made by her father, and with the light filtering through the same faded lilac curtains her mother had sewn when Sandra and Jon were small, it feels like a sepia photograph. She remembers rolling under the bed, giggling, to hide from Jon, then her mother yelling that her room was off-limits and slamming the door. She remembers Mom standing in front of the big mirror over the bureau, frowning as she fingered gray streaks in her hair. She remembers sneaking in during high school to steal half-full liquor bottles as the entry fee to parties, and the way everything in here had been infused with the scent of flowery perfumes married to ashtrays and booze.

Aunt Phil left the windows open, and those odors are lost to history anyway, overtaken by decades of lemony furniture polish. Crumpled papers on the top of the long narrow desk flutter in the breeze, and Sandra goes to push the window shut. She's surprised to see a large bird feeder, half full of seed, right outside the high window; Robby must have installed that for their mother. At the thought of him, she slams the window down with a thunk and gathers herself.

Robby and her father, her father and Robby. Her suspicion that Dad was cheating on Mom has always been tangled with what she saw that night, and now there are the bodies and Robby's adultery and Gayle's death. It's a terrifying suggestion of a pattern. She's entrenched in this torturous, horrifying mess because of her family—and she can't stand the thought of people losing their lives here, on her land. Land that Dad and then Robby were supposed to keep safe: men betraying their home as well as their families.

She shakes it off. Stupid patriarchal bullshit, fucking with her emotions. Grimly, she gathers the loose papers from the desk into a heap on the old braided rug, then stacks the sketchbooks there too. She adds several more drawers' worth from the dresser, desk, and nightstand. Her parents' room has been the least explored for secret areas, and she spends an extra few minutes searching. Knowing her father's tricks, she easily locates the false bottom in a couple of drawers and a hidden panel near the closet. She finds only papers, except in the closet, where Mom had hidden an entire outfit, from undergarments to stockings, shoes, and a jacket. She tosses them on the bed with the rest of the clothes.

Sandra avoids the temptation to look too closely at anything until she sits in the middle of the mess. Her mouth goes dry, looking at mounds of her mother's papers, understanding for the first time how disordered Mom's mind must have been to do this, to secrete all these things away. What had she believed she was doing? Or was it no more than a simple hoarding impulse, an inability to throw things away and move on?

She tries the sketchbooks first, turning them upside down to see if the note falls out. Nothing, but she flips through quickly anyway, to find mostly scribbles and sketches. She notices her mother's penciled block letters here and there, random words, as if Mom was trying to shake something loose from her head. Over and over, the word "CLEVER" across the sketch of a crow whose dark beady eye is incised like a solid thing among the messy blur of graphite and "EVERLASTING BLISS" on the corner of a drawing of a squirrel. "MERCY" shows up a lot, and Sandra starts to wonder if it's someone's name or a plea for forgiveness.

Uncomfortable with this nonsensical voice from the grave, she adds the papers to the recycling pile. It's not until she's worked her way through all the sketchbooks and most of the crumpled pages, her speed increasing with frustration as she goes, that she hits on a trove of concentrated writing.

Aunt Phil has subscribed to craft and cooking magazines through the years, and Mom must have torn out every advertisement and article having to do with pets and animals. The slick paper is easy to sort straight into the recycling, and Sandra's making great headway when she finds a folded wad of Mom's midweight sketch paper in the midst of it. She unfolds it carefully, thinking Dad's note could be inside—but it's not. It's more of Mom's writing, inked in blue, applied with great pressure to the fronts and back of several pages. The words waver in uneven lines across the page, misspelled and unpunctuated, as if Mom's mind were spilling over far too quickly for her hand to keep up. "I'M SORRY I LOVE YOU I LOVE YOU IM SOORY I WONT I wONT IM SRRY"

Aunt Phil's sideways comment about her mother's happiness comes back as Sandra's stomach curdles. Whatever had been going on in Mom's head the day she wrote this was less than pleasant. Sandra would love to know who she'd been addressing, Dad or Aunt Phil or one of her kids.

She sets those aside and pushes onward, jaw clenched, to find two more stashes like the "I'm sorry" page, along with a childish-looking skull and crossbones, and one that says "GO AWAY I HATE YOU" over and over.

Nothing else. No note. She regards the mess, half wishing she hadn't bothered. Is this what she wants to remember of her mother? But it's the truth of her. She remembers all too well Val's roller-coaster emotions, her dark days. The silence that she refused to break once her husband died. Better not to look away now, surely.

The "Sorry" pages bother her the most, and she slides them into her pocket, then rises and glances out the window. Outside, it's bright and sunny, and her stomach is beginning to rumble, but she's heard no sign of Jon and Denny returning. She's gotten this far. She needs to continue.

She hauls the recycling bin downstairs and finds Aunt Phil having a cup of tea and reading a book at the dining room table.

"Just taking a break, dear! I may as well finish up the

broken glass in the basement after this. I really don't like to leave it. What if Denny goes in there?"

"I promise I'll work on it more later, Auntie. I just got through the papers in Mom's room, and I wanted to ask you about this."

Sandra takes the scribblings out of her pocket and watches her aunt carefully. Aunt Phil closes her book over a bookmark with a sigh. "Oh, dear. My poor sister." She smoothes the papers out and pages through them one by one, smiling a little at the skull and crossbones. When she gets to the end, she lays her hand on top and shakes her head.

Sandra asks, "Do you know what she was sorry about? Was it something about Dad?" *Like his homicidal impulses, for example?* But she can't say that to her aunt. She won't.

Auntie raises her shoulders. "It's hard to say." Her aunt's pleasant, vaguely sorrowful expression stays the same.

"If she was wracked with guilt about something, maybe we could have helped. Did you ever ask her?"

"She would have been furious if she thought any of us were prying into her things," Aunt Phil says. "And you know, I tried everything in the early days, I really did. It came down to a choice between institutionalizing her or letting her live the way she wanted, at home with us. Maybe I made the wrong choice." Her tone is starting to sound defensive.

"I wasn't suggesting that," Sandra says evenly. "And *we,*" she stresses, "made the right choice. Mom wasn't able to be happy, but we did the best we could for her. No one could have asked for more." The words sound rote to her ear with the proof of Mom's mental agitation so fresh in her mind, but Aunt Phil nods, seemingly mollified.

"Yes, that's true. We did the best we could." She climbs to her feet, giving Sandra a quick squeeze, and leaves the room. Sandra frowns after her. Auntie has taken the bundle of scribbles with her. And Sandra's question about the source of Mom's guilt is still unanswered.

Grimly, she begins to check the house's other hidey-holes for the note, starting with the easy ones. The three kids' bedrooms each have a built-in secret cubby in the closet. She slips into Aunt Phil's/Jon's old room, wondering what she'll say if her aunt finds her there, but it's been stripped of all belongings, with a stack of cardboard boxes to one side. That cubby and the other two are completely empty.

Under the floorboards in the upstairs linen closet, she gets confirmation that her mother has been using the house's hidey-holes to stash her things away. There's a pile of bird sketches and what must be a portrait of Robby's girls, but Mom was never good with faces.

In the bookshelf in the living room, she finds her diary, not in the secret niche under the bottom shelf but behind a row of dusty old Foxfire books about old-fashioned homesteading skills. She flips through it for the note, biting her lip, but it's not there, so she trots the journal upstairs to hide at the bottom of her suitcase for later perusal.

Aunt Phil pokes her head in while she's continuing to explore the bookshelf, but withdraws quickly. Sandra feels the weight of her disapproval and wants to dispel it. If she confides in Auntie about Dad's note, maybe she'll understand.

But at the same time…Auntie hasn't been open with her, about the extent of Mom's mental deterioration. She's shielding Sandra as if Sandra is still seventeen. If Aunt Phil won't share, Sandra has no recourse except to search out the truth herself.

The kids had never discovered any nooks in the kitchen or the main floor bathroom. Sandra descends to the basement level. Many of Dad's secret places relied on camouflaging openings in corners or in the shadows of overhanging decorations, but here on the bar, there are two decorative portholes, and one of them swings out with a twist of the third spoke.

Inside, there's another crumpled stash. It looks just like the rest at first. But she carries it to the couch to smooth it out and finds what look at first like religious flyers for some kind of long ago event. A dark-haired man with low brows and a seething gaze is pictured above an amateur-looking illustration of a walled city and the words "Community of Love." Mom has two copies, twisted together as if she'd tried to strangle them. The fronts are glossy and colored, but the backs are of plain matte card that may once had a description and location but now are overwritten in black ink so densely it's hard to make out the words until Sandra holds it directly under a bulb and slants it so the light falls just right.

"MERCY FOR THE LOST," she reads. "CUT AWAY THE DROSS AND WE SHALL MOURN AND THRIVE."

Sandra turns it over in her hands. The blue-eyed man looks unfamiliar. The sentence is more complex than what she's seen on Mom's other papers. Perhaps it's a quote from a book or even the Bible, but it's not familiar to her. It could be a line from a song. She can't imagine what it has to do with this man and his "Community of Love."

Sandra smooths the second twisted sheet. It's the same flyer, but the back reads, "ONE HARD CUT THEN BLISS FOREVER." Over and over and over.

She shudders. Mom was preoccupied with forgiveness, with mercy and violence. The fears in Sandra's mind, growing since the police broke the news of the old bones, take a harder shape. Dad must have killed those people. And Mom must have known, all these years. Maybe she stopped talking, not because he killed himself, but because she couldn't bear to speak the truth.

21

ROBBY

....

Robby's eyes snap open to bright afternoon light. After Jon and Sandra left, he meant to clean up the house before Christine arrived on her lunch break for their discussion, but his siblings' accusations and suspicions exhausted him, and the bed tempted him with its promise of oblivion. Now some internal alarm has woken him. A glance at his phone tells him Christine will be here in minutes, but Robby's as sweaty as if he's been running from a pack of dogs, his heart beating double time. He thinks he's been dreaming about the man Gayle was afraid of, a faceless person… He'd been thinking about him while dropping off into sleep, wondering if the man really existed or if Gayle made it up. Somehow that had morphed into nightmare.

In the bathroom he turns the tap to cold and splashes his face until his skull feels numb. There's a heavy ache deep in his gut. He keeps trying to convince himself that Jon and Sandra's support—and their ability to pay a lawyer—is going to make all the difference, but he keeps seeing the doubt in their faces. If his own brother and sister, who've known him longer than anyone, believe he could be a killer, what would Christine think if she knew everything?

He's barely spared his father a thought since the police showed up on Sunday. The mess with the old bones and Sandra's suicide note has less urgency for him. But for the first time he wonders if, when he decided to die, Dad was trying to save his family from something worse than abandonment.

Christine's car pulls in as he's getting out of the shower, and the car door slams while he's pulling on his jeans. He runs his fingers through damp hair and puts on a smile as he exits the bedroom. He really should have forced himself to clean up instead giving in to the urge to sleep.

Everything—his good intentions to get his job back, to scrub Elly's presence out of the house, to show Christine that she and the twins are his entire world and nothing else matters…everything got slammed out of the way by Gayle's murder.

When the door opens, he's standing ready with a welcoming yet sober smile. Christine is silhouetted by golden sunlight, looking beautiful but harried, her blond hair frizzing around her face. Robby's stretching for the right words when Chelsey pushes past her and launches herself at him with full force.

"Whoa! What are you doing here, pumpkin? Shouldn't you be at school?"

"I'm sick so I got to go home," Chelsey says into his shoulder. "Mom and me are going back to Grandma's after this, and Lottie's getting a ride to practice with her friend."

"Oh." He looks helplessly at Christine over Chelsey's shoulder.

"Chelsey needs some things from her bedroom," Christine says. "Right, honey? So me and Daddy can talk in private?"

Reluctantly, Robby lets Chelsey go and she scampers to her room and slams the door.

Christine remains in the doorway. "Let's talk outside. That one's probably got her ear glued to her door by now."

Robby looks down at his bare feet. "Give me a second."

When he joins her, Christine is leaning against her car, arms crossed over her chest. Despite the May sunshine, her windbreaker is zipped nearly to her chin.

"What did you want to talk about?" He waits, looking at her. Her face is pale, eyes bloodshot and puffy. Maybe she can be his insomnia buddy.

Christine looks at the ground. "Robby, this is really hard for me."

He flinches, then braces himself. She must have found out. She must know.

She says, "I didn't mean for this to happen, not when we're having so much trouble. It's too much."

Robby holds himself still, confused, then parses it out. It's another man. Of course she found someone else, because Robby is a loser, a sniveling, cheating piece of shit.

Raising her eyes to him, she says, "I'm pregnant."

He can't speak for a moment. Then he says, "Is it mine?" The words pop out unfiltered, attached to his previous chain of thought.

He regrets them before they've left his mouth, but it's too late. She slaps him. Her wedding ring scrapes his nose, hurting far more than it should, and he's left cupping his face as she marches to the front door.

"Wait, wait! I didn't mean that!" he calls.

Christine slams the door. She can't be pregnant. Oh shit. Oh fuck. He blew it.

He lopes to the door, leans in. "Hang on Chrissy," he says with a false, desperate brightness, trying to hide his tension from his daughter.

Silence.

"Chrissy?"

Chelsey sticks her head into the hall. "Mom's in your bathroom," she says.

"Thanks!" Robby pastes a smile on his face, eases the front door shut behind him, and forces himself to stroll down the hallway.

As he sets his hand on the doorknob, Chelsey asks, "Are you and Mom breaking up?"

Robby backs up to look Chelsey in the face. "No, honey. We're going to be okay. It's just grown-up stuff, that's all."

"Mom keeps saying Grandma needs our help, but I don't think Grandma even wants us there." Chelsey's gaze is serious.

"We'll figure it out," he promises, knowing he can't promise any such thing. "Don't worry."

She looks at him sadly, like she doesn't quite believe him, then disappears back into her room. He hears drawers opening and slamming shut, and returns to the master bedroom door. With the word "pregnant," ringing through his head, the room's dishevelment seems worse than it had been just minutes ago.

The bathroom door is closed with the sound of water running at full force beyond. She's probably crying with the taps on, a sign that she doesn't want to be disturbed. He sits on the bed to wait, then starts collecting empties in the wastebasket, which is too small. He transfers them into a pillowcase, then stuffs it under the bed. Now the naked pillow looks weird, and he starts stripping the whole bed.

The water stops. He looks up and sees Christine, silent, in the bathroom doorway.

Robby blurts, "I didn't mean what I said! I trust you. I was just—I didn't know what you were going to say to me, and I was scared that you were going to leave me. I'm sorry."

She looks to one side, her face a stubborn mask.

"Are you sure? You're definitely…" he asks. His throat

closes on all the things he can't say. Technically, they'd decided they couldn't afford another kid. Without Robby's job, they can't even afford the kids they have.

Not to mention, he may need a lawyer.

"I'm sure," she says.

"Are you—I mean, do you want to—" The words feel like a fishhook tearing loose from his flesh. "Will you keep it?"

She hides her face in her hands and a sob escapes her.

"Oh, Chrissy," he says. "It's going to be okay. I love you." His eyes overflow. He approaches, and when she doesn't pull away, he wraps his arms around her. She grabs on as if he's a life raft. Her body feels so good, so familiar, against his, and for a second, everything really is okay.

She pulls back, wiping at her eyes, then disappears into the bathroom again to blow her nose. When she comes out and sits on the end of the bare mattress, he sits next to her.

"Robby," she says and clears her throat.

He swallows.

"You're all messed up. I don't know if you can be a dad right now. I don't know if we should have this baby." Her voice breaks.

"What? No!" he protests. "We can make it work. We always do. I swear, I'll do better."

She searches his face. "I want to believe that, but you look like hell. Have you been sleeping, at all?"

"Chrissy, my mom just died, okay? I know, I've been

fucking up. But trust me. I can do this. *We* can do this." He wills her to believe in him the way she used to.

"Have you been seeing *her*?"

Robby looks away.

"Have you?"

She means Elly. In all these years, she never found out about any of the others. He pictures Gayle's wry smile, her hazel eyes obscured by a layer of dirt, and swallows down a bolt of terror. The investigation could ruin him, tomorrow or the next day or the day after that. *Don't borrow trouble*, Aunt Phil says in his head.

"I'm not doing that anymore," he says firmly.

"Doing *that*?" Christine's eyes flash dangerously.

"I'm not cheating on you. I'm not seeing anyone else. I'm not lying to you. I'm so sorry, I was such an idiot. All I want is for you to come home, and I want us to have our baby, and I want the girls here. I want to be a good dad."

"God, I want to believe you."

"You should! You can believe me. It's one hundred percent true, one hundred ten percent. All I want is you and the girls and our baby, all together in our home. I'll do anything."

She sniffles and blows her nose on a wad of tissue still clutched in her hand. For a long moment, she says nothing.

"Mom?" Chelsey calls. Her voice sounds muffled. She's calling from her room, not right outside the door, thank god. He rolls his eyes at Chrissy.

Chrissy almost smiles. "I'll be there in a few minutes, sweetheart." She looks at Robby. "This is how it's going to be. You're going to call Mr. Cromley. If you can't get your job back, you're signing up with the unemployment office and the temp agency, and if you don't have a steady income in four weeks, we're done. Four weeks. If I can't rely on you, that's it."

Robby nods eagerly.

"And we're not coming back to this." She gestures to the chaos. "I'll call you tomorrow during my lunch break, and you tell me the truth. This whole house is cleaned, top to bottom, all the booze and empties out of the house and out of the garage, I don't want the girls seeing any more of it. The bathrooms are scrubbed, the kitchen is scrubbed. Everything."

"Everything," he says. "You got it."

"Okay," she says. "I'll call you at lunch. If you're on track, I'll bring the girls home tomorrow night. We'll get pizza. The girls will be ecstatic, and everyone will sleep in their own beds."

"But you'll come to dinner at the big house tonight?" he asks, suddenly panicking. "Aunt Phil won't want to miss saying goodbye to the girls." And she'll know who to blame, he adds to himself.

She shakes her head regretfully. "I told her at the reception yesterday. I'd promised to take the twins to see their friend's recital tonight, so we said goodbye already."

"Oh." She told Aunt Phil, but not him. He swallows his irritation. "How far along is the pregnancy?"

"Two months. I've been sick as a dog the whole time I've been at Mom's. I think she knows. She keeps shaking her head when she looks at me."

"Twins?" he asks with a lump in his throat. With Chelsey and Lottie, she vomited twenty-four seven for weeks, and they joked that it must be twins, but it turned out not to be a joke.

"Don't go there," she says.

He pictures two little boys in matching baseball uniforms. Then he remembers the eighteen months of hell it took to get the girls to sleep at the same time and knocks on the wooden top of the dresser. She smiles, and he puts his arm around her. She tilts her face toward him and they kiss. It tastes like love and forgiveness and home, and it's so good he can hardly bear it.

"Mom! I can't find my library books! I'm going to be in trouble!" Chelsey's voice is sharp this time.

Christine pulls away and stands up. She looks down at him. "I'm serious, Robby. This family needs you to have your shit together. No lies. No women. You get your job back, and you pull your weight."

"Chris—Elly was just a stupid flirtation," he says. It's true, in a way, though he feels bad for saying it. Elly deserves something real. Someone who can be loyal to her. Something like he and Christine had, before he fucked it up.

"I know she wasn't the first," Christine says, voice suddenly hard. "Don't pretend. I knew about Gayle too. I'm not an idiot, Robby. I'm not blind."

The bottom drops out of his stomach. She sounds so certain he doesn't try to protest. "How?" he manages.

"Gayle? She told me," she says simply and stands, rezipping her jacket, patting her pockets.

Robby stands automatically. He has too many questions fighting to reach his mouth. He wants to know when, and how. And why Christine never said anything. "Why didn't you—"

"Just leave you? I don't know, Robby; why didn't I?"

"Wait!" he says, but she's already moving down the hall, knocking on the twins' door. The conversation is over.

Chelsey appears with an armload of clothes. "I found my library books," she announces.

"Good job, honey," Christine says. "Let's go."

Robby follows them to the entryway.

"Bye, Daddy!" Chelsey says.

Christine says, "I'll call you tomorrow at lunch." It sounds like a threat.

He waves to them both, weakly, then closes the door behind them and collapses on the couch, wondering if his wife killed Gayle Bethested.

And if she secretly hates him enough to set him up for it.

22

SANDRA

....

Wednesday evening, Sandra pauses on the stairs on the way to dinner, hand wrapped around the smooth banister. The family's voices reach her from the kitchen, not in word but tone: Denny chattering, Auntie chuckling, Jon and Robby contributing the occasional lower-pitched counterpoint.

Sandra takes a breath, feeling shaky. It's Aunt Phil's farewell feast, and she needs to pull herself together to give a heartfelt send-off to the woman who's held their family together through force of will. But between the morning's revelations about Robby and Gayle, and an afternoon spent wrestling with suspicions of her father and a growing understanding of her mother's mindset, Sandra would rather shake her aunt—and maybe Robby too—until some unvarnished truths come out.

"Sandra!" Jon calls, impatient. "You coming?"

Grimly, she pastes a smile on her face and continues the rest of the way into the dining room. "I'm right here, keep your shirt on."

Auntie had insisted on making a feast despite all the funeral leftovers, saying it would be a while before she could cook for them again. The dining room table is lit by flickering candles and is almost invisible under all the dishes: baked salmon, mashed potatoes and gravy, roasted asparagus, and butternut squash.

Sandra slides next to Robby, feeling the flyer in her pocket crinkle. Jon and Denny are across from them, Denny bouncing and pointing at what he wants Jon to load onto his plate. Robby's face is dark and closed off, and he barely acknowledges Sandra when she nudges him. He probably wants to be here as little as she does, but if he doesn't pull himself together, Auntie will notice something is wrong and wheedle it out of him. Maybe that would be a good thing.

As they dig in, Auntie chats about her cruise, seeming not to notice how subdued the table is. Sandra manages a few polite questions, but her heart isn't in it. Jon steps on her foot under the table and frowns a question at her, and Sandra shakes her head slightly—no, there's nothing terribly wrong that wasn't wrong before. She tilts her head toward Aunt Phil, opening her eyes wide, and Jon reluctantly picks up the conversational thread, making an effort to include Robby.

When silence at last overtakes the table, Auntie switches gears, looking at them curiously as she helps herself to more salmon. "So, have you all decided how to handle the property?"

Jon shrugs with an apologetic glance toward his brother. "I think we have to prepare to sell," he says. "We still need to talk through the details. But Sandra and I will stay through the weekend. The three of us will have time to figure it out. We'll keep you posted."

Robby grimaces and pushes asparagus around with his fork but doesn't offer an opinion.

"I wish I had more time to spend with you," Aunt Phil says. "This old house is full of energy when you're all around." She beams. "Your mother would have loved it."

With a prickle of irritation, Sandra raises her eyebrows. Auntie's rewriting history again. Mom was overwhelmed by her children. Even before Robby was born, Sandra and Jon relied more on each other than on their mother, at least the way Sandra remembers it. She's aware again of the shape of the flyer in her pocket, her mother's disturbing words. *One hard cut then bliss forever.* Sandra looked it up online but hadn't discovered its source. Just Mom trying to come to terms with Dad's suicide? There was no blade involved, but it could be a metaphor. Or had she been coming to terms with something worse?

Robby clears his throat and manages to sound almost like his usual bantering self. "Auntie is trying to distract us from the fact that she's going to be partying while we're sorting through the house."

"That's just like you, Aunt Phil. Lazing around while everyone else works," Jon says.

Denny chimes in with an indignant protest. "No, she doesn't!"

"We're teasing, bud," Jon says from behind his hand and winks at Aunt Phil.

"We know Aunt Phil has done more than her share of the work already. Looking after the house, looking after all of us," Sandra says. She tries to smile.

"Looking after Mom," Jon adds. "That was never easy." There's a dark undertone to the comment, and Sandra recalls what he'd been saying on their walk the other day. He'd been so angry, wrestling with Mom's death. Still angry, she thinks. Wait until she catches him up on all the strange papers she found.

Aunt Phil is oblivious. "Oh, pshaw. Val was my sister, and you kids are the best family anyone could have asked for. Teague House has been a wonderful home to all of us."

Jon snorts. "We're lucky you didn't throw your hands up and leave in the early days. Remember that Christmas Mom wandered off? I was in college and staying with a friend over winter break, but you called Christmas night sounding so upset I almost bought plane tickets home."

"I remember," Sandra says. "I was still in high school."

"What happened?" Robby looks interested. She can't believe he hasn't heard the story before, but then again, they've never made a habit of talking about the tough spots in their childhood. There are too many of them, and it had seemed disrespectful somehow to the living specter of Mom. Maybe her death has freed them to share more.

Sandra glances at Denny, who has gravy smeared from ear to ear and is swirling his fork in his milk glass. Not paying much attention, but she gives the short version anyway. "Aunt Phil woke me up in the middle of the night saying Mom wasn't in bed. We traipsed all over the yard in the freezing cold before she called the police."

Aunt Phil chimes in. "Oh, yes. Your mother wandered a fair amount back then, around the yard and the house and back toward where the studio used to be. But that night truly scared me. She turned up in the cottage, in the end. The tenants had moved out after your dad died, but your mother knew where the spare key was hidden."

"I don't remember that part. I mostly remember being pissed off at you, Auntie, for calling the cops," Sandra puts in.

"You were furious. You said we would have found her ourselves if I hadn't panicked, and you didn't speak to me for a week afterward. But every time she wandered, I worried about the road, and the river—I had no choice! I'd already searched every inch of the big house five times." She shakes her head, smiling. "When I found her, she was in the attic crawl space, sitting cross-legged like she was meditating. I poked my head up through the trapdoor and she followed me back to the car, pretty as you please."

Robby makes a face. "I don't remember any of this. Where was I?"

"You slept right through, dear." Aunt Phil chuckles and pats Robby's hand. "You had a real gift for sleeping through anything in those days."

"Those days? Isn't that every day?" Jon says, eyeing their brother.

Robby says, "Ha. Ha."

Aunt Phil clears her throat. "You know, speaking of your mother wandering around the house. There was something that I was hoping to find as I was packing that didn't turn up. It's an old lockbox that Valerie took from my room years ago and hid away. I had some photos in it, predigital. Val and me as kids with your grandparents, me and my ex-husband, that kind of thing."

"Mom stole it from you?" Jon sounds shocked.

Sandra's ears perk up. A lockbox must have been irresistible to someone as fond of hiding things as their mother. And maybe a good place to hide something extra special.

"Not stole," Aunt Phil clarifies quickly. "Val probably thought it was hers. Our parents gave one to each of us when we were kids, because we shared a room, and we were always arguing and getting into each other's things. Metal boxes, a little bigger than a lunch box. Mine was purple and hers was blue. I don't know where hers went, she may have gotten rid of it or lost it over the years, but mine had faded and some of the paint chipped away. It probably looked blue to her."

How like Aunt Phil to make excuses for Mom. "No idea where she would have stashed it?"

Aunt Phil shrugs. "It's a big house. Just set it aside if you find it. It would be nice to look through those old photos again."

Feeling reckless, Sandra pulls the flyer out of her pocket. "Earlier today, I found something else Mom had hidden away. Will you take a look, Auntie? I wonder where she got it. And what she's written all over it." She passes it to Aunt Phil.

Her aunt makes a face but takes the paper amiably enough, smoothing the wrinkles against the tablecloth next to her plate. "No…doesn't look familiar," she says. "Your mother would scribble on anything. Usually sketching, yes, but some-times, she'd get the oddest phrases stuck in her head. Probably songs from when she used to be so into music. Did I tell you she followed the Grateful Dead for almost a year when she was a teenager?"

Sandra narrows her eyes, but Robby takes the bait. "I didn't know that. They're some kind of jam band, right?"

"Oh, I don't know, dear," Aunt Phil says. "It wasn't my thing. If she'd been born a decade earlier, your mother would have ended up in San Francisco with flowers in her hair."

"Can I see?" Jon reaches for the flyer, leaning past Denny.

Aunt Phil looks reluctant to let it go, but Sandra passes it to Jon, who studies it front and back. "'Mercy for the lost'? I can't even make out the dates," he says, sounding disappointed. "But this guy—he looks kind of familiar. Is he local, Auntie?"

"I don't think so," Aunt Phil says.

Robby reaches across to take the flyer from Jon, frowns at it briefly, then shrugs and hands it back to Sandra. "You never could tell what was going through Mom's head," he says, seeming undisturbed.

Aunt Phil sits up straight and pats her belly. "Well, has everyone had enough dinner? I have a cheesecake waiting! Let's have some decaf with it. Hot cocoa for you, my lovely nephew. Sandra, will you help me clear?"

Sandra narrows her eyes at her aunt, who's usually of the "you eat it, you clear it" school of thought, but she pockets the flyer and rises to take her brothers' plates.

"I'll help," Jon says, starting to get up.

"Me too!" says Denny.

"Oh, no, Jon and Robby will have dishwasher-loading duty after dinner, and Denny will assist," Aunt Phil says merrily. "Did you know Sandra's been cleaning that mess in the basement all by herself? We'll save the hard work for you fellas, don't you worry."

Sandra makes a couple trips to clear the table, while Aunt Phil busies herself with the Keurig, then rattles in the cupboards for more leftover containers. While Sandra's scraping food from the plates into the compost bin, Aunt Phil lays a hand on her arm and says softly, "Please don't worry about your mother's scribbling. That's all it is. Just her poor brain trying to untangle itself."

Sandra looks into her face. Aunt Phil has nothing but concern in her eyes, but Sandra is tired of evasiveness. The words on the flyer feel ominous, *one hard cut* rattling around in her mind. Had her mother been thinking of Dad's death—or the bodies in hidden graves? Her tongue sticks to the roof of her mouth, but she forces the words out. "Aunt Phil, did Dad kill those people? Is that what drove Mom over the edge?"

Aunt Phil stiffens, planting her feet as if claiming her position. "I don't know where you're getting that," she says. "Your parents were fine people, burdened with more troubles than most. You'd best leave the details of the past in the past, and move on, Sandra dear."

"Please, Auntie. Dad wrote me a note, the night he died. A suicide note. I was too angry to read it. Or scared. But I'm ready now. Mom must have taken it out of my room, and I need to find it."

Her aunt's face softens a bit. "Ah. I see. Still. You're best off leaving it, if you can." She squeezes Sandra's arm, then turns away to collect the mugs. "Could you grab the cheesecake and a spatula?"

Sandra tries one last time. "You don't know where the note went?"

"Your mother certainly never shared any of her little treasures with me," Aunt Phil says with finality as she parades into the dining room. Sandra hears her cry out, "Who wants whipped cream?"

"I do, I do!" Denny says. "Great-Auntie, did you say there's a treasure?"

Sandra slides back into her seat as Aunt Phil dispenses a tall cone of whipped cream on top of Denny's dessert.

"No, no, honey. Grandpa Russ made some hidey-holes your dad and Aunt Sandy used to hide things in when they were kids. But I don't think there's any treasure in them anymore."

Robby takes the whipped cream and squirts a massive pile onto his cheesecake but speaks when the hissing is over. "Do you remember, before the renovation downstairs, wasn't there a hidden cupboard at the bottom of the basement stairs?"

An odd look crosses Aunt Phil's face. Sandra knows about the cupboard. Apparently the ghosts of their past refuse to stay in the grave tonight. It was too much to expect a normal, cheery farewell dinner in this family.

"Your dad redid that whole wall," Aunt Phil agrees reluctantly. "You're right, there used to be treasure of a kind in there. Your parents used it as a safe. Your birth certificates, the title to the family car, the fancy jewelry your grandma Darlene left to Val in her will, all that kind of thing. It's in a safety deposit box at the bank now. The information is in that top drawer in the desk, in the den."

"I may have slept through a lot, but I remember the time Mom got so mad at you because you opened it, right?" Robby says. "And you fell down the stairs?"

Sandra exchanges a glance with Jon. The night Aunt Phil fell down the basement stairs is one of her worst memories from before Dad died, but she wouldn't have thought Robby remembered it. He was younger than Denny is now. Sandra and Jon had been up in their bedrooms, but when the shouting started, they ran down to find Mom jeering as Aunt Phil pleaded with her to call for help.

"Did Mom tell you about that?" Sandra remembers the ambulance, the paramedics rushing in, Jon racing to fetch Dad from the studio. She tried to distract Robby with a game of Candyland, but he kept getting up to watch the flashing lights in the driveway.

Robby shrugs. "I think so. She was telling me why she had to go away for a while. I don't know why the part that stuck with me was the part about that safe though. She said something about Auntie getting into her treasure, and I guess I was around Denny's age, so it stuck."

They fall silent. Sandra is thinking about her mom "going away" to an inpatient clinic. That first time, after Aunt Phil's accident, she was gone for about two months, and she'd come home noticeably happier and more energetic. The second time, after Dad died, hadn't done a thing.

By six-thirty, everyone is picking at second slices of chocolate cheesecake and sipping decaf. Aunt Phil pushes away from the table. "I should do a last walkthrough," she says. "I'm sure I've forgotten my phone charger or my reading glasses or something obvious like that. You always do, don't you?" She hurries upstairs.

Jon opens the door to the basement family room, where Denny has excused himself to play Xbox, and calls in a loud whisper, "Denny, it's time! Bring the surprise!"

Denny exclaims unintelligibly, and soon his footsteps pound up the carpeted stairs. He appears with a gift he and Jon wrapped in Christmas paper, all they'd been able to find without asking Aunt Phil for help. It's an odd occasion for a gift, but Robby suggested it, and it seems fitting.

Aunt Phil's footsteps approach the landing, and she looks down, a charging cord curled in her hand. "Is the Uber here already?" she asks.

"No, Auntie. But we want to make sure you open this before you leave," Robby says.

Aunt Phil's gaze alights on the package. "Oh, no, you shouldn't have."

"It's not much," Sandra assures her.

Aunt Phil descends and accepts the lumpy gift from Denny, who's jumping on his toes in anticipation. She squeezes it and frowns in a parody of concentration. "Hmmm. I think I know what this is," she says. "Could it be…a teddy bear?"

Denny giggles and shakes his head. "No way!"

"How about… a new sweater?"

"It's not soft, Auntie!"

Sandra smiles, wishing she'd thought to video this moment.

"Well, I just don't know then. I'm going to guess it's a sandwich. Peanut butter and jelly, my favorite."

She tears off the wrapping, and Denny gives an ecstatic hop. Aunt Phil's face is eager. She'd have felt the frame and known right from the first what it was. But when the wrapping comes off, her smile falters. Sandra can't name the expression that crosses her aunt's face, but the older woman pulls herself together quickly.

"Oh, isn't this beautiful?" she says.

"I made it!" Denny says proudly. He'd decorated the frame using a half-dried paint set from the old games cupboard.

"I can see that," Aunt Phil says. "What a wonderful job." She holds the photo, looking down at it thoughtfully.

"I always liked that picture," Robby says. "I found it tucked in a drawer a while back. You and Mom as girls. It's amazing, you're different in so many ways, but look at you here."

"That Temple look," Aunt Phil says. "That's what your Grandma used to say. The whole side of the family has something around the eyes that gives it away."

There's a silence. Sandra wonders if her own insistence on talking about Mom's troubles today has hurt Auntie's feelings somehow, or made her think of her sister's pain when she was most trying to honor her memory, and she feels a stab of guilt.

"Well, I better find a safe place for this!" Aunt Phil says. "Snug in my suitcase so I can put it next to my bunk on the ship. Now, give me a hug, everyone."

Sandra finds herself last in line and leans in. Aunt Phil gives her a squeeze then tut-tuts at her watch. "The Uber should be here by now. Walk out with me, my dear. You can carry one of my suitcases."

When they get to the painted mailbox, Aunt Phil arranges both cases upright in the gravel, then turns to Sandra and holds her at arm's length, looking into her face. Sandra notices gold flecks in her aunt's brown eyes. She doesn't know what Aunt Phil sees—maybe traces of Mom?—but where Sandra usually reads determination and optimism in her aunt's features, now she sees exhaustion.

"I'm sorry," Sandra starts to say, but the sound of a loud engine speeding up the road interrupts.

Aunt Phil looks past Sandra and sighs in relief. "I was beginning to think they'd gotten lost!" The car slows and turns carefully into the drive, halting beside them, and the trunk pops open.

Sandra tosses in the suitcases and her aunt closes the trunk, then turns to her. "I hope you know, I have always tried to do the right thing," she says. With a sad smile and one last kiss on the cheek, she closes Sandra's hand around a folded piece of paper before bustling to the passenger door.

The car door slams, and Sandra automatically moves away to let the Uber reverse out of the drive. She looks down at the paper revealed by her opening fingers. It's been folded into a small square, but she recognizes it. Her father's musical composition paper. Her father's handwriting.

Her father's note.

23

PHIL

....

1983

Lipstick looks terrible on me. I'm going bare," Phil told Carole, who was focused on her own reflection, blue eyes wide as the mascara wand stroked steady as an artist's paintbrush. The dressing room in the historic home Phil and Ned had rented for their wedding had six mirrored dressing tables and a series of screens for changing, but thanks to Val backing out at the last minute and Mom flying out to check on her, Carole and Phil were the only ones here.

Trying to make the best of things, Phil attempted a vivid smile in the mirror. The cloud of white netting set off her dark hair nicely. If only she could keep the veil over her face for the whole day.

"Just a sec." Carole holstered the wand and blinked several times. Pink and purple eyeshadow, dramatic behind thick black mascara, complemented her lavender bridesmaid's dress.

Critically, she eyed Phil's lips. "Mmm, too orange," Carole said. "Let's try something darker."

"I'll look like a clown."

"A gorgeous clown. Stay still, silly," Carole said, smiling as she wiped away the old and applied a layer of new. "Now close your eyes."

Phil squeezed her lids shut. The sweet scent of powder enveloped her as Carole's brush danced over her face. "Purse your lips, here comes the gloss. That's better. Take a look."

Carole backed off and Phil blinked. Her lips were red and shiny, her skin flawless, her eyes huge and doe-like. She could be on the cover of a magazine. "Holy shit," she said without moving her mouth. "How did you do that?"

Carole laughed. "You idiot. You look effing amazing, and you could do this every day if you took five extra minutes. Ned is going to faint when you come down the aisle."

"Ha! That's all we need!" Her face felt weird with the unaccustomed layers, but she wiggled her nose and eyebrows experimentally and nothing cracked. A tiny hope bloomed in her chest. Her wedding pictures might come out okay, and Carole was such a great friend, and Dad was downstairs waiting to give her away, and Ned—she couldn't believe they were really tying the knot. It was going to be the best day of her life, she decided, even without Mom there. She reached out and squeezed Carole's hand. "Thank you, so, so much."

"So your mom really can't make it?" Carole asked, settling

back onto the padded vanity seat to put another layer of gloss on her own lips.

The tentative bloom of joy shriveled a little. "Val's practically popping again, eight months along. She says she's double the size she was with the other two, so she backed out, and my mom got worried, so…"

"Oh yeah? Did Val change her mind about wanting help?"

Carole had heard the saga of Val's ups and downs and shared the soap opera–like adventures of her own family, but Phil didn't want to go into it, today of all days. "Mom flew out anyway, just in case. It's fine. I mean, I wish she was here, but it's better this way." It's true. Considering how unbalanced Val got at Sandra's birth, and how evasive she'd been lately, Phil understood why Mom decided to miss the wedding in favor of being ready to shore up Val. She didn't like it, but she understood it.

Carole leaned in for a side hug, smiling into the mirror. "Forget about it. Val will be fine and your mom must want you to enjoy every moment of your big day. I shouldn't have brought it up."

"I talked to her earlier and, like you said, she's so happy for me. She's really fond of Ned, but she's where she needs to be." Phil's eyes moistened, and she dabbed cautiously at the corner of her eyes to prevent spillage. "I'm just nervous."

"That proves you're taking marriage seriously. It's a good thing!" Carole said. "'Cause I gotta tell you, it's a friggin' pain if you change your mind."

Phil laughed and rolled her eyes, grateful for the change of subject. At twenty-six, Carole had been married and divorced twice, at six months and eleven months, respectively. And she was right that it had been a huge pain in the ass, especially the first time, which had included a tearful "rescue me" call to Phil during a midnight snowstorm.

A knock sounded on the door, followed by a voice. "Miss Temple? Phone for you!. You'll have to take it in the office, I'm afraid."

Phil stood, her dress rustling around her. "Who is it?" Her mind rushed to Mom. She wouldn't call back so soon, not unless something was wrong.

"It's your sister."

Val must be calling for last-minute congratulations and best wishes. Bad timing, but a sweet thought. Mom had probably reminded her to do it. Just when Phil had been thinking poorly of Val too. She turned to Carole. "What time is it?"

"We've got…about twenty minutes," Carole said. "And look at you, you're all ready! Go say hello, then come back here, and I'll touch you up one last time."

Phil peeked around the door. Mr. Villiers, the manager, smiled and gestured for her to follow.

"You look truly lovely," he said over his shoulder. "And I happen to know the groom-to-be is safely ensconced in the downstairs reception area, so no fears there. Right this way."

He left her alone in his office, which must once have been

a stately parlor, complete with a marble fireplace and a pair of antique sofas. Phil leaned over his desk and retrieved the handset of the phone, stretching the coiled cord so she could sit in one of the padded armchairs meant for clients. "Hi, Val!"

"Oh, thank god. I'm so glad I caught you!"

Val's voice was distraught. The smile faded from Phil's face and a familiar, aching fear formed in the pit of her stomach. This could be about anything from a stray dog Val had seen on the side of the road to something going wrong with the pregnancy. Phil modulated her tone to the sympathetic briskness she'd perfected as a nurse. "Is it an emergency, Val? The wedding starts in less than twenty minutes."

"That's why I called! You can't get married, Phil; you can't." Val broke down into gasping tears.

Phil bit her lip. What had she done to deserve this? Could she just—hang up? She eased the phone from her ear, but brought it back when Val started talking again.

"I loved him so much, Phil, you know I did but"—gasp— "now I think I hate him, he's never there, and"—gasp—"there's someone else, Phil. Someone much smarter. Someone who understands everything. But I'm stuck, I'm stuck."

"Hush," Phil said helplessly. "Calm down, Val, calm down." Her mind whirred. Val had been avoiding her calls and Mom's for a while, but before that, she'd been excited about new friends she and Russ had made, Phil had thought maybe through a church or a community group. And then she'd fallen off the radar, only popping up again a couple months ago to let them know she was expecting and fine and didn't want help.

Val wheezed her words out. "I can't calm down! I can't! Russ will guess. When he sees the baby!"

She sounded terrified. Heart sinking, Phil pulled the phone from her ear and stared at the black handset, stark against the satiny white folds of the dress's petticoated skirt. From the tiny speaker emitted more gasping sobs. Phil raised her eyes to the clock. The second hand stuttered through another minute. Phil took a breath and returned the handset to her ear.

"Honey, do you think you could give Mom a call? She's staying at the Downtown Inn in Corvallis. She's not that far from you, and she'd love to come and help. Do you think you could do that? Just call and ask for her at the hotel?"

Sniffles. Then a muffled nose blow, and Val's voice, surprisingly clear. "Don't make my mistakes, Phil. That's all I wanted to tell you. The world will be a better place without so many…mistakes."

Dial tone.

Phil swallowed. Her hand shook as she reached for the phone's cradle on the desk. The clock said 2:25. Five minutes to the time when she was supposed to descend the sweeping staircase with hope and loving intentions in her heart and a glowing smile on her face.

A cool female voice picked up after she dialed. "Directory assistance."

Phil wondered if she could pass the whole mess on to Mom and segue seamlessly back into her own happy day. Then the image of a tiny bluish infant in an incubator, almost six years ago, came to her. "Put me through to the police, please. Horace, Oregon. I need them to check on my sister and her husband."

24

JON

....

THURSDAY

Thursday morning, Jon lies in bed, wondering if it's worth trying to fall back to sleep. The silence is heavy, the normal sounds of Teague House stripped away with no one stumping down the stairs at the crack of dawn to fill the house with the smell of eggs and coffee, no wicked chuckle erupting here and there as Aunt Phil bustles through ceaseless tasks. He misses her already, but she is an odd duck. Taking off the way she did yesterday, after purporting to be overjoyed they're all home—and yet she must have bought her tickets before Mom's body was cold.

Jon rises and pads to the door of Robby's old room across the hall to peek in at Denny. His son is fast asleep, his face relaxed. He looks younger this way, still the chubby-cheeked toddler who snuggled in Jill's arms. Jon brushes a kiss across his forehead and pulls himself away.

Sandra's door is closed. She'd gone up to her room close-mouthed and pale after Aunt Phil's departure last night, and not come back down. It had been a stressful day for all of them. He steps across the squeaky board just like when he was in high school, hoping she can sleep longer than he did.

In the kitchen, he makes coffee, watching the sky lighten as the machine heats the water. He should check texts and email while he sips. Last night he'd reached out to colleagues for criminal attorney recommendations, and to Tom for info about Gayle. But Robby's issues fill him with dread, and he wants a few more minutes to get used to the new world order before facing the day. The house feels strange without Mom and Aunt Phil, as if his childhood is receding into myth. He carries the mug to the family room and gazes out at Teague Wood in the morning mist. Even that is changed now, its shadows hiding secrets beyond the ghost of his father.

Quick footsteps sound overhead, then Denny's voice, singing, floats from the kitchen. Jon climbs the stairs to make him breakfast and divert him from the Xbox. Afterwards Denny curls up with a book from Jon's old bookshelves, and Jon settles at the desk in the den with his laptop and phone.

No response from Tom yet, but one of his colleagues has a secondhand recommendation for an attorney based in Polallie, the county seat and nearest city to Horace. Jon sends a politely worded request for a consultation.

He moves onto reviewing news stories about the Teague

Wood bodies. There's still very little about the old bones, but Jon's eyes rest for a long time on the words "being treated as suspicious deaths" and "signs of foul play." Sandra's fears about their parents are getting to him.

His phone buzzes as he's skimming news articles for biographical detail on Gayle Bethested, and he glances down to see "Tommy!" on the screen.

"Hey!" Tom says. "Just noticed your text; glad you're still in town! Want to grab some coffee or a beer?"

"Yeah, sounds great," Jon says. "I'll have to double-check with my sister, find out when she'll be around to watch Denny."

"Or bring him! I'll bring Dana; it'll be a party."

"Maybe, I'll get back to you on that. Hey, do you have a minute now though? I wanted to pick your brain a little more on what you mentioned back at the playground. When you were talking about, was it, the county commissioner election? I'm interested in learning more about Gayle Bethested's campaign." He's thought a lot about how to couch his request and hasn't figure out a justification that doesn't skim the truth. He drops his voice. "Her body was found on our land. The police aren't telling us anything. It's driving me crazy, to be honest."

Tom is silent for a moment. Then he says, "I guess I don't see how it can hurt. But you're barking up the wrong tree if you think her death had anything to do with the campaign. I hope I didn't mislead you with my complaints about county politics. We're a fairly civilized crowd."

"Yeah, I bet." Jon laughs falsely. "It's just, all the information in the news is so bare bones."

"Sure, sure. I know the guy who was helping to organize her campaign. I'll give him your number, how's that?"

The doorbell rings. Jon walks toward the front door as he talks. "That's great. Is there any way you could hook me up with a conversation with Marcus Belter too? I could cold-call him, but you said you knew him, right?"

There's no one out there. It must be the side door. The bell rings again.

"Uh, yeah." Tom sounds uncomfortable. Jon wonders, crazily, if he thinks Jon might be the killer, trying to squash something Gayle knew. He's about to withdraw his request when Tom says, "Listen, the kids have a no-school day tomorrow, and it's Dana's birthday. We'll be at the water park in McMinnville. Marcus will be bringing his kid. You should bring Denny."

Jon's only half listening. Through the peephole on the kitchen door, he recognizes the Black detective who'd come over Sunday. The man is shading his eyes with one hand as he gazes over the porch rail toward Teague Wood. Jon's stomach tightens. Shouldn't they call first, if they have news?

"That sounds great; send me details. Listen, I got to go; someone's turned up at the door. I'll be in touch later." He hangs up and looks around to make sure Denny hasn't crept up to hear something not intended for children's ears, then opens the door and sticks out his hand. "Detective Simons, right?"

"Simonson," the man says. "Mind if I come in for a few minutes?"

"Sure. Come sit down. Is there news? Anything about our break-in?"

"Afraid not. Anyone else around?" The man follows him to the kitchen table, looking around curiously.

"Just my son. My sister's out running, and my aunt's left on her vacation."

The detective's eyebrows raise. "I'm not sure she mentioned she was going on vacation. I'd hoped to have a chance to talk with her."

Jon tries a smile. "I'll give you her cell number. She was so excited for that cruise, I think you would have had to handcuff her to keep her from going."

The detective nods and pulls out a small notebook. "Might as well get that from you now."

Jon dictates. He considers offering the man a drink, but doesn't want to extend the encounter longer than necessary. "How's the investigation going?"

Simonson rotates his neck with a disturbingly loud crack. "We're running two parallel investigations for the time being, looking into Gayle Bethested's death on the one hand, drilling down into the older bones on the other."

"Makes sense. Man, I've been trying to remember Gayle,

but I can barely picture Patrick, and he was my friend. She was just another little kid in the background." He braces himself, wondering if he's about to be bombarded with questions about his brother.

"It's the older bones I'm interested in today," Simonson says. "And if you don't mind, I need to record this conversation. Frees me to listen." He taps a small black box clipped over his dark tie. Jon had dismissed it as some kind of police radio, but now notices the central iris of the bodycam.

Uncomfortable but not sure how to protest, Jon shrugs. "I guess that's okay. But I don't know anything. It's technically our land, but the pet cemetery was just a random place when we were kids. Not on the way to anything, not interesting or notable. I'm surprised Sandra even found it." That sounds like he's implicating her. "Not that she knows anything about it."

The detective acknowledges with a small smile. "It's clear that 'pet cemetery' is a misnomer. We've identified some of the remains and narrowed down when they were buried. All five were very likely interred during the years when you and your siblings were growing up."

Jon's chest tightens. He recalls Sandra crouching in the woods, the way the blood drained from her face. Feeling the detective's eyes on him, he forces himself to speak. "I'm so sorry. I just can't—it's surreal to think we didn't sense it somehow. People being buried in our woods without us knowing. And it's definite…the deaths were not natural?" His voice goes up at the end, almost pleading.

Simonson says, "Forensic examination of the bones is incomplete, but there are significant indications of trauma."

"Awful," Jon murmurs. Sadness wells up, always close to the surface since Jill's loss. All those people, all those families, reaching for their loved ones and finding nothing. Then his mind goes to Dad's strange behavior before he killed himself and his mouth goes dry. He should tell the detective about that night and the note. But that's Sandra's story to tell. He says only, "We don't know anything about it, if that's what you're implying," his words shaky and belligerent in his own ears. Sounding like lies.

"Not implying anything," Simonson says, raising his hands in a show of deference. "But I'm sure you can see, we have to ask some questions." There's a glint in his eye, and Jon has the sense of being toyed with, poked and prodded so the detective can see what comes out.

"No, I get it," Jon says. "It's our land, after all. So what if we were kids? Sure. You have to ask."

The detective nods. "What do you remember? Anything weird? Any odd people hanging around your family?"

Jon shrugs. "Are we talking when I was five years old, or ten, or fifteen? My memory isn't that great. I couldn't tell you most of my teachers' names anymore, and I spent a year at a time with them. In general, my parents weren't that social.

Not a lot of visitors. Maybe more, when I was pretty small? I think I remember parties back then." He has a flash of the living room in the big house filled with adults, drinking coffee or beer and chatting with animation. He and Sandra sneaking into the kitchen to steal from plates of deviled eggs, spying and making fun of the grown-ups. There was one guy who'd go on and on, pacing in front of the fireplace and speechifying while the others listened.

Jon stiffens. That guy. That's why the flyer looked so familiar last night at dinner. That guy was the same guy that used to come to the house. Then he doubts himself. It's been decades. He's must be misremembering, conflating two dark-haired, intense-looking men.

The cop's watching him patiently. "Wouldn't that make visitors stand out?"

Jon blinks. "Well, Aunt Phil came once in a while; you met her. And Nana Darlene used to come a lot, before she died." When he was little, he and Sandra were encouraged to invite their friends over, and Mom would sit in the kitchen or on the porch with the friends' moms, laughing and talking. "There were random people around, the mothers of our friends. My dad played guitar, and he had a band for a while." He gets a flash of that too, Russ's curly hair soaked with sweat, laughing and singing with a couple of other mustached dudes.

Simonson waits quietly.

Jon wants this to be over. "I don't know," he says. "How

am I supposed to tell what was weird or suspicious? It was a long time ago, and kids don't notice the same things adults do."

"Keep thinking about it," Simonson says. "Maybe something will come to you." He glances at the wall clock and seems to gather himself.

Jon feels almost dizzy with relief. The scene his sister described, of Dad on his knees in the nighttime woods, hovers behind his eyes, and he feels irrationally like the detective will see it if he looks hard enough.

Simonson puts his hands flat on the tabletop and stands. "Well. We haven't been able to narrow down the dates much yet, but that will come. There's a chance all this happened after you left for college—that was, what, 1995?"

Jon's skin crawls. Why did the detective know that? "Ninety-four, actually." Nine months after Dad's suicide. His legs feel weak and he remains in his chair.

"Or it could have been before that, when you were an older teen, seventeen, eighteen," the detective says, looking down impassively. "Most people have a pretty good recollection of those years. Lots of changes, starting to feel like an adult. Any of your friends back then have issues: explosive temper, family stuff, drug problems, that kind of thing?"

Jon feels Dad push past him into his bedroom: the heat, the roughness, the ever-present smell of beer and cigarettes. The way he yanked Jon's closet door open, tossed books off the bookshelf, tilted up the mattress to peer underneath. "No! Nothing that would lead to murder. Just normal stuff."

"How about you? Before his death, your father must have been struggling with depression, mental health issues. That couldn't have been easy. Put a lot of pressure on you, as a young man."

Jon clenches his jaw. "I was just a kid," he says. Bile rises in his throat.

The detective nods slowly and reaches into a pocket. "Let me know if you think of anything. Here, I'll give you another card." He sets a business card down on the table and taps the camera on his shirt. "Thanks so much for speaking with me today. Have your sister call me to set up an interview time."

Jon nods. He follows him to the door and closes it behind him. On the table, his phone buzzes. The text is from Tom.

Sammy Krieg will call you. Gayle's friend/election help. Super upset but told him u were one who discovered her body, he wants 2 talk

Jon's heart falls. If he and the detective had been in a boxing ring, he would definitely be down for the count. When the phone rings, he lets it go to voicemail, staring into the distance, trying to picture his father's face but seeing only the shape in the tree.

25

MADDIE

....

L ast night I called Rose and told her we may have finally found her mother's remains.

She cried. Then she and I arranged to meet at Mama Hempel's assisted-living suite, and all three of us cried. I warned them not to get their hopes up, but Rose said, "Do as I say, not as I do?"

Sitting around the same table where Davina and I once struggled for control of the cow-shaped sugar bowl until it fell on the floor and broke, the two of them quizzed me about Horace, about the Rawlins family, about the Bethested case, and what it means that another woman was killed and buried in the same clearing just last week. I stayed too late and had to Uber home to be on the safe side after three glasses of Mama Hempel's cheap red wine.

That probably explains my poor sleep. I wake still stuck in

the tatters of a dream where I was building a house out of the cops' marker stakes at the burial site in Teague Wood. Rose was coming and I needed to convince her Davina had been living there in a little house, not moldering under the ground. Sandra was with me, digging with her bare hands. She kept approaching me, shaking her head. "Another one," she'd say and pass me a dog collar clotted with dirt.

My phone buzzes while I'm buttoning my jeans, and the cobwebs clear when the caller's name shows on-screen. Sandra Rawlins. I take a deep breath. I didn't expect she'd call me again, and I'm not sure what to expect, but I snatch up the phone. "Madeline Reed Investigations," I say crisply.

"This is Sandra Rawlins," she says. Her voice is subdued. "I'm sorry about yesterday. Would you be willing to meet and talk this afternoon?"

"Of course." I disconnect after setting a time, wondering what changed her mind, and if her brothers will be there.

Energized by the promise of progress, I focus on a batch of background checks for a while until Eb texts a thank-you for connecting him with the Hempels. He says a local officer will collect a DNA sample from each of them, and Eb will notify them when results are in, but it could take weeks. I text back that Rose and her mother are desperate to know what happened and who was responsible, and ask him to keep me in the loop. There's no response.

Thinking about the case, I stand and pace my kitchen.

Speculations about Davina's last days reverberate through my mind. Last night, Mama Hempel told Rose for the umpteenth time how sweet Davina had been with her as an infant, how she'd pop up at the faintest cry and walk her through the house. I told Rose how Davina had laid her tiny self in my arms as carefully as if she were allowing me to hold her heart. We'd all fallen silent at the bittersweet memories. Invisibly, Davina must have been riddled with self-doubt, afraid of a relapse. Ripe to be bullied or seduced away by Axel and the idea that Rose would be better off without her mother.

I shower, dress, and head out to meet Sandra, considering my approach. The Green River Killer had been active in the Washington/Oregon area during the time Davina disappeared, but had never been known to kill men, and Eb said three of the skeletons are male. It seems likely to me that the killer is someone with a connection to Horace, who knew Teague Wood, although any stranger could have used topo maps to find suitable terrain, or lucked into it while driving around. A killer with no connection to Teague Wood would be almost impossible to find after so long. On the other hand, the Rawlins family is at ground zero. Russ Rawlins's suicide makes him a good fit, whether Sandra likes it or not.

When I pull up, the little boy is crouched in the grass at the side of the driveway, poking at something with a stick. Sandra and Jon appear deep in discussion at the foot of the flight of wooden stairs that leading to the side porch. He rises as I climb out of the car, face unwelcoming. I nod politely, but he ignores me and moves to his son.

"Hi," Sandra says as I approach. "Don't worry about Jon; he's in a bad mood. And I apologize, I timed things wrong. Just got back from a run. Let's head in and I'll clean up really quick."

"No problem. I appreciate you seeing me."

She deserts me in the kitchen. I wander, checking out the magnets on the fridge and the children's trophies and projects on the hutch. Things look much the same as yesterday, in homey disarray. There's an open bag of bread on the counter next to a jar of peanut butter with a sticky knife balanced on top. A few dirty dishes and cups cluster next to the sink, and the dishwasher door is hanging open. There's a landline phone in the corner near the door with a small bulletin board, and I check out the postings. Mostly coupons and sale flyers, with some emergency numbers on an index card in the lower corner.

Sandra is back in minutes, pink-cheeked in jeans and a sweatshirt, smelling of soap with her bangs in ringlets. There's a small purse slung across her body. She starts talking as soon as she enters, heading to the coffee machine.

"Sorry about that. Honestly, Jon's still not happy about this. But I believe you, that you're not trying to sensationalize anything. You just want the truth. Like me."

I settle into a chair to be less threatening. "I can sign

something if you want. I'm not a reporter, I'm not going to post anything that I learn from you on social media or pass it along to anyone who will. All I want is the truth about Davina and the others."

She nods. "I called one of your clients from your website. They vouched for your professionalism."

"Great!" I hope my surprised relief doesn't show in my voice. Over Mom's last months, I let things slide so much there are quotes on the website that clients may no longer agree with.

Sandra pushes a mug of unasked-for black coffee at me. "Let's go into the den; I want some privacy."

I follow her quick steps to a cramped, windowless room with a desk against one wall, bookshelves, and an overstuffed couch. When she switches on the lamp, the warm glow transforms it into a cozy office.

I sit and cradle my coffee mug. Sandra turns the desk chair to face me and says, "I've been thinking about what you said, about the victims' families. If…if I did choose to cooperate with your investigation—if I share information with you, will you be able to be open with me? Will you share whatever you're able to put together about what happened back then?"

I blow on the coffee and take a sip, considering, then say, "With the exception of anything I'm told in confidence by the police or another interviewee." I wait.

Sandra swallows. She's much less composed than she

was the past times we met, her movements nervous and darting, and I can see that she's steeled herself for this conversation.

She says, "I don't want to believe that my parents knew anything about the murders, but…they changed. Something shifted during my childhood, and things that had been just a little bit off crossed a line. My worst fear is that they—knew something. Hid something." She's been looking straight at me, hazel eyes through tortoiseshell glasses, but now she slides her eyes away. "I'm worried that my father had something to do with the deaths," she says, then takes a breath and looks at me again. "And I want the truth. One way or the other."

My heart's beating fast. "Okay. I want to hear all about it. I hope for your sake that your parents weren't involved, but whoever buried those bodies probably had some link to your family or this land. Let's figure it out."

Sandra sticks out her hand. It's dry, calloused, slim. We shake. When she smiles, it's shaky but genuine. "Great. Where do we start?"

"Let's start with whatever brought you to me. What makes you think your father is involved in the deaths?"

She tosses back her head, stares at the ceiling, looks back at me. "Okay. It's been a tough week. There's stuff I haven't ever talked about, so forgive me if I'm not…I don't know. Making a lot of sense."

I laugh a little, and she chuckles too.

"Number one—my dad was in the woods, the place the bodies were found, the night he killed himself."

"What was he doing out there?"

"I'm not sure, really. It was really late. I was a little drunk. He was drunk—maybe a lot. I saw him disappearing into the woods and followed after him." Sandra shrugs. "He seemed to be burying a necklace. That's what I thought at the time. I thought it had something to do with a woman, an affair that he was trying to hide from Mom. He spotted me, came after me, but I ran away."

She stares down at the carpet. "So, naturally, when he turned up dead the next day, I thought he was so ashamed of what I'd seen that he had to kill himself. That my knowing tipped the scale between his living and his dying.

"And now that we know what was actually out there…it's so much worse! What am I supposed to think? Was he burying evidence? And this note—this stupid fucking note—is supposed to make me feel better because he killed himself to make it right?" She digs into the purse at her side, then shoves a manila envelope toward me.

I reach to set my coffee mug on the desk blotter and tug open the metal prongs. "What is this?"

"His suicide note. He slipped it under my bedroom door that night. When I found it, I was so pissed at him, I refused to read it. Last night, I read it for the first time."

I reach inside to find a folded paper. One sheet, lined as if for music composition, folded small enough to fit in the palm of my hand. I glance at Sandra, whose eyes are fixed on it as if it's dangerous. Carefully, I unfold it and smooth it over my knee.

Pumpkin—I'm sorry. Believe me, I'm making things right the only way I know how. I love you and your brothers so much. Take care of each other. You three are the center of my universe, no matter what. Love always—Dad.
PS—Make sure your aunt gets her letter. It's in the White Album. *I'm trusting you.*

Making things right. A confession to murder? Or adultery, like Sandra had once believed?

I look up at her. "Do you know, did she get her letter?"

"I'm not sure. My aunt gave me this yesterday without a word. I assume she read it, or how would she have known what it was? But she said nothing."

"Can't you ask her?"

"She left for her cruise. I might try her tonight or tomorrow, but for now…" She shrugs again.

"Would she have known where the *White Album* was?"

She tilts her head side to side—maybe. "Originally, it would have been in his studio, the little shack down by the woods where he practiced music. That's where he killed himself, hanging from the big tree right outside. Aunt Phil had the

tree cut down and the studio destroyed to spare us the sight
of it. That was long before she would have had a chance to see
this note; it was hidden in my bedroom until I went to college.
After that…I don't know when she found it."

"What happened to your dad's stuff?"

"At first I assumed it had gone to the dump or to charity.
I've been through the house top to bottom in the last few
days, and I didn't come across any of Dad's things. So I've
been wracking my brains, and something else occurred to
me this morning as I was dealing with the mess left by the
break-in."

I tuck the note back in its protective envelope and raise
my eyebrows.

Sandra looks pained. "Our house is full of hidden nooks
and crannies. Dad loved them. I looked through every secret
hiding place I could think of, but I completely missed the
cupboard under the stairs, because it wasn't secret, it was just
blocked by some shelving."

"And we're going to check it out?" I ask, eager at the prospect of hunting through the personal belongings of Davina's
possible killer.

Sandra nods. "Yes." She doesn't move though, and I wait
for the rest.

"I haven't told my brothers that I have the note. My aunt
gave it to me last night, and I wanted some time to think about
it. I also didn't tell them about these, not completely anyway."

260

She digs in her purse again, this time coming out with a handful of papers, which she sets on the desk. She fishes out two flyers, bent and wrinkled, and hands them to me, saying, "I showed my brothers the top one, because I wanted to see if they recognized the man in the photo. But these and the rest are all scribbles that my mother had squirreled away all over the house. Ramblings. She'd been voluntarily mute since my father died. And she never wrote to us. But apparently, she'd been scribbling the overflow from her head every once in a while." Her voice is bitter, but her face is stoic.

I look down at the flyers, taking in the number of times the words must have been traced for the ink to have soaked and carved the card stock like this. I squint and try to catch the depressions in the light to read the lettering.

Sandra says, "The first one is: 'Mercy for the lost, cut away the dross, and we shall mourn and thrive.' The other one is: 'One hard cut then bliss forever.' "

"Disturbing. And the other pages?"

"Not quite as poetic. Random words on a theme. *Mercy, hatred, apology.*" She begins to gather up the pages, lips pressed together.

"So, what are you thinking?" I ask. "What's so bad you haven't told your brothers?"

"This makes me think Mom knew something about Dad, something dark," Sandra says. "She knew, and she was too afraid to say." She shakes her head. "I don't know why that bothers me so much. I've just been angry with her for so long. But I can't be, now, can I?"

She leads me down the stairs to a large family room with a bar area, a massive slate fireplace, and a pair of sliding glass doors. Outside is a wooden deck overlooking the lawn sloping toward Teague Wood. My eye catches there, thinking that Davina had been out there, just beyond that tree line, for decades.

Sandra gestures to the glass doors. "I told you about the break-in, right? We were lucky enough to get someone to replace the glass right away. It still feels weirdly vulnerable, like we should install bars or a burglar alarm, but that was the first burglary since the house was built. I've just started locking the door at the top of these stairs when we go to bed."

Sandra turns and unlocks another door at the bottom of the stairs. A waft of rotting food, like a restaurant dumpster, hits me in the face and I cough. Sandra smiles apologetically. "Sorry. They got in here and broke a bunch of canning jars. That door was unlocked; we never used to lock it." She flips a switch and a concrete area lined with wooden shelves is revealed, with a pair of wheeled trash bins sitting in the middle next to the source of the smell. "This is the unfinished half of the basement. Garage ahead through the door, and as you can see, storage in this middle bit and the laundry room over to the left.

"And as you can see, I got distracted before I finished cleaning up this morning. Let's get these out of the way." She grabs one of the trash cans and starts rolling it toward another door, which leads to the garage.

I follow with the other. "Did they take anything valuable?"

"As far as we can tell, they didn't take anything. Although, aside from this mess, one of the hidden compartments I told you about was left hanging open, in the laundry nook. The police said they may have been interrupted by our arrival."

I look around, trying to understand what a thief would want back here. There's just a bunch of junk, more canning jars, a warped cardboard Scrabble box and another one for Hungry Hungry Hippos, a child's potty-training seat, a clear plastic bag full of yarn balls. Maybe fit for a yard sale, but not a haul for a thief.

"The thing that worries me," Sandra says, brushing off her hands, "is that the intruders found the hidden compartment. I have no idea what was in it, but no one outside of the family would have known where to look." She points out the sliding opening at the rear of the large cabinet next to the washing machine. "How would anyone know this was here, if they weren't familiar with our house? But my brothers and nephew and my aunt all say it wasn't them."

It also seems like too big of coincidence for the break-in to happen just after the discovery of the bodies, but it's hard to see how it could have anything to do with the bones or the schoolteacher's murder. "Definitely no liquor missing from the bar area out there?" I ask.

Sandra snorts. "Right, we wondered that too. But we had cleared the booze out because Jon's kid hangs out by himself down here all the time and keeps getting into the caffeine, which is bad enough."

"And did they go upstairs?"

"Doesn't look like it. The police are saying it was probably teenaged vandals, which is hard to believe because of the hidden compartment. I don't know what to think. We're being a lot more careful about locking up."

"Good plan." I nod toward the empty shelving against the area under the stairs. "So your dad's stuff is in there?"

She nods. "I peeked inside, but I was interrupted by Denny and not ready to share what I found. Dad's name is on at least one of the boxes." She laughs and says, "You must think I'm a coward."

I stand next to her and look at the door outlined beyond the wooden shelving. "You're talking to a woman who hasn't even scattered her mother's ashes, and it's been six weeks. I don't plan to take on her old boxes for a few years, at least."

She snorts and grasps the shelving unit in front of the door, yanking hard. A four-foot wide segment slides across concrete with a gritty, jaw-tensing sound. The revealed door is held shut with a hook and eye. Sandra pauses, obviously reluctant.

"Open it," I urge, feeling my heart beat faster.

She bites her lip. The door swings outward, revealing a

rectangular opening about three feet wide by four feet high. The smell of damp cardboard joins the odor of rotten vegetables and vinegar. The boxes are of regular size, like banker's boxes, and tightly wedged.

Sandra crouches to wrench at the front one until it slides forward and I can read the block writing along its side. "RUSS STUDIO." I can't imagine what she must be feeling, to be handling her father's things after so long. Her face is intent as she pulls open a flap to peek inside, and I glimpse yellowed newspaper. She thrusts the box back toward me and reaches for another.

If the storage space fills the interior of the stairwell, a dozen boxes belonging to a serial killer could be in there. I think almost guiltily of Eb and the police team, but push it away. They apparently haven't made this connection yet, and if there's anything to it, I'll tip them off.

"Maddie?" Sandra breaks into my racing thoughts.

"What?"

"Can you line these up along the other wall? I'm running out of space."

"Oh. Right." I bend down and put my back into it.

Eleven boxes emerge before the space empties. I've got them lined up in a row, but I don't want to open them until Sandra gives the go ahead. I feel like an archaeologist about to open an ancient tomb, but Sandra looks more like someone about to get a root canal.

One by one, we pull off the covers, revealing neatly packed interiors sometimes stuffed or topped with old newspapers. Several appear to hold record albums.

"How do you want to do this?" I ask.

She shrugs. "You start at one end, I start at the other, and we look for the The Beatles' *White Album*. It's just plain white, right?"

"I think so." I do a quick image search on my phone and hold it up for Sandra. "How many records did your father have?"

"Hundreds. I don't really remember." She settles cross-legged in front of the first box. "I've been thinking about the timing. I don't think there's any way Aunt Phil could have known about my dad's letter to her when she packed all these things away—she couldn't have seen the suicide note until after I left for college, I'm almost certain. And no one had moved that shelving for years and years. The bottoms of the crosspieces were caked in dust and grime; you can still see the outline on the floor."

It's true, an outline of each of the wooden supports from the shelving unit is etched into the concrete with grime. For me, although the letter Russ Rawlins wrote to his sister-in-law is interesting, it's not necessarily the most important part. Anything in these boxes could be evidence of what he'd done. Imagine if he kept trophies of his victims, and the aunt had packed them away, not knowing what she held in her hands.

My first box holds a rusting stapler, a stack of old *Playboy* magazines, and rolls of toilet paper and paper towels, grayed and warped by time. I sneeze, Russ was definitely a smoker. Everything emanates the stench of stale tobacco.

"Do you have any idea why your dad left the letter to your aunt and not your mother?" I ask.

Sandra looks over. "Mom had mental health issues even before he died. And she drank a lot. I'm guessing…he knew that she wouldn't be up to caring for us. Maybe it's an appeal to her to step in. Which, she did, anyway, so…"

"I'm sorry," I tell her, responding more to the pain in her voice than her words.

She looks back to her box. "No *White Album* yet," she reports tonelessly.

My second box is records, and I flip through quickly, finding nothing. My third has spiral-bound notebooks full of the same staff paper that Russ's suicide note was on, along with a stack of *Fine Woodworking* magazines. I riffle through, finding something of a slightly different shape mixed in—a calendar.

"Oh, wow," Sandra murmurs. I look over. She's surrounded by crumpled newspaper, cradling something small and shiny in her hands.

"What did you find?"

"Dad collected shot glasses. I'd forgotten. He had at least a hundred of them, from every bar he visited or played at. Once he built the studio, Mom made him take them out there. She said they were ugly." She holds one up for me, and the shamrock on the front catches the light.

"Nice." I look down at the calendar: 1992, the year before he died. The police will need to see this. I shouldn't even handle it. But if I weren't here, Sandra would be doing this on her own.

I show her. "This could be important. We know exactly when Davina disappeared, and the cops said they've got other IDs now, so they may be able to pin down a date for them as well. If your dad was in the habit of making notations in his calendar…"

Sandra jumps to her feet and hovers over my shoulder. I flip through quickly. "He marked some things. Jon's birthday, a dentist appointment…" There's nothing earth-shattering, but I set the calendar to one side. Sandra returns to her work.

"The *White Album's* not in this box," Sandra says and moves onto the next. "Must be the junk drawer. Huh, I thought my dad hated CDs."

I riffle through the magazines and notebooks more carefully, and find calendars from 1985 and 1986. Then 1989 is there, a dinged-up calendar from the Humane Society with puppies and kittens on the cover. I take a sharp intake of breath and Sandra looks over.

"What'd you find?"

"1989. When Davina disappeared." I flip through quickly, then lick my finger and start paging through month by month.

Sandra leaves her box to kneel down next to me. I flip impatiently to June. Russ's writing utensil of choice must have been a dull golf pencil, because I can't make out some of his notations unless shadows fall into the depressions of the letters. I hold the calendar six inches from my nose, squinting.

Russ Rawlins had doodled a daisy on the calendar four days before Davina's last call home. My mouth dries up.

"Oh my god," Sandra whispers.

I squint and turn the calendar this way and that to catch the light and make out some letters. "RIP" above the daisy, and below, "Pop-pop." In the next square, very lightly, it says, "Delta, 6:30."

"Look at this!" I tell her. "You see that, right?"

"'RIP Pop-pop'?" Sandra says blankly.

I pull the calendar back from her and scan ahead. Two weeks later, there's another nearly illegible notation, outlined in a scribbly cloud shape. "Delta, 12 p.m."

I stare at the calendar and bite my lip. "Your father may not have been here when Davina went missing."

Sandra looks hopeful for a second, but then frowns. "I don't remember Dad's parents at all. They never visited. I don't even know where they lived."

"It could have even been his grandfather," I suggest. "'Pop-pop.' Does that ring a bell? You don't remember him saying goodbye, he had to go to a funeral, anything like that?"

Sandra shakes her head. "He always had out-of-town jobs.

He'd take off for a week, sleep in his truck, or the guys would share hotel rooms. It was no big deal for him to be gone."

"Wouldn't your parents have talked about it though? Try to remember. Even if the airlines have ticket records from so far back, it will be hard to prove he was on the flights. Maybe there are other relatives you can call, who would have gone to the same funeral?" I'm almost begging.

"Maddie, I was *twelve*. And that side of the family wasn't in the picture even before Dad died. But this is still good, right? I mean, if Dad wasn't here, he couldn't have killed Davina, and if he didn't kill her, he probably didn't kill the others."

Her eyes shine hopefully behind her glasses. I hate to burst her bubble, especially since I'm thinking along the same lines. But one of us has to play the skeptic. "That's a lot of ifs. Your dad could have been picking someone up from the airport, rather than going out of town himself. Or, what if someone else did the kidnapping, and your father did the killing? As people keep telling me, don't get your hopes up."

She deflates a little. "It's something though."

"It is." I set the calendars carefully on top of the box they were found in, and we go back to work in silence. My next box is full of albums, mostly bands I listened to in high school: Red Hot Chili Peppers, Nirvana, Bon Jovi.

Sandra yelps. "I found it! I've got the *White Album*."

I hustle to crouch next to her. She's holding a cardboard sleeve gone cream-colored with age, still partially encased in plastic shrink-wrap. It looks less grimy than the ones I've been flipping through. Newer, or maybe handled with more reverence.

"Well?" I prompt her.

Sandra tilts the cover, and the inner sleeve containing the album slides free. I reach to catch it. It feels heavier than expected, but I haven't handled a record album in maybe twenty-five years.

Sandra shakes it. Nothing else comes out. There's no letter.

26

ROBBY

Robby pulls into his driveway and sits staring at the cottage. The car reeks of garbage after his trip to the dump, thanks to a trash bag spilling mysterious fermented liquid in the hatchback, but he should be happy. He's done it, and Christine and the girls will come home tonight. Once the police investigation is over, he'll be able to relax. Well, not relax. Ever since learning Christine knew about Gayle—for how long? And how much?—he's been in a hell of self-excoriation. All those times he thought he was being so smooth, and Christine was looking at him, thinking—what? That he was a bastard? That she was going to kill Gayle and poison Robby slowly?

It's ridiculous. Christine, the mother of his children, doesn't believe in the death penalty for convicted murderers. She wouldn't kill Gayle for sleeping with him.

And yet, his mind won't leave it alone.

Nothing he can do about it now, he reminds himself. And Christine said she wants to come home, wants him to be a good dad. She doesn't hate him. So, for now—*soldier on, Robby!* That's what Aunt Phil would say.

He gets out and draws in a giant breath of clean spring air, spreading his arms to stretch his tense back and shoulders, looking toward the green of the forest. The hairs on the back of his neck prickle, as if someone is watching him. He lowers his arms and rotates to face the house. The windows reflect in the spring sunshine. Maybe he'd caught the movement of a reflection in his peripheral vision?

He swallows, feeling paranoid, but he approaches the front door slowly, scanning for some sign of an intruder. Behind him, something crashes in the dense underbrush of the woods, and he whirls to face the thick trees bordering the driveway. A man breaks into the verge of weedy grass near the road and takes off running. Robby sees the back of a solid-looking guy dressed in a fitted black tracksuit and beanie, the pale line of his neck the most distinctive thing about him. He's out of sight, footsteps fading, before Robby reacts. Heart pounding down in his stomach, he jogs across the driveway to get a better look, but the man is gone.

A moment later, a car engine turns over and its low buzz soon fades too. A dog barks. He listens for another moment, but there's nothing to hear.

Robby feels woozy. He runs around the cottage and finds the impression of a large shoe in the soft dirt outside the garage window and then again, near the master bedroom window. He'd left both windows open; in fact he'd left almost every window in the house open to air out the stuffiness and cleaning products while he was out. But the screens seem intact and un-tampered with.

Had he arrived just in time? His luck finally changing, if it could be called luck.

He checks each room, closing and latching each window securely, then falls into a chair. Everything is almost shockingly clean after this morning's efforts, and there are no signs of intrusion.

He breathes and stares straight ahead until his heart slows. Call the police? He almost laughs. No way is he inviting the police to look any closer at him or his property unless he absolutely has to.

But his family will be home tonight. Will they be safe?

He thinks of the break-in at the big house. Someone is preying on this neighborhood. Someone who thinks his family has something valuable? If Robby could afford a security system, he'd buy one right now. As it is, he fetches a baseball bat from the garage and lines it up under the bed skirt on his side of the bed. Chances are, he'll barely sleep, but he's used to that.

He can't do anything else about it, and he tries to move on, going back to the living room and sitting down with his laptop. Aside from his brain's constant buzz of imminent doom, he feels okay. No drinking last night. He'd taken a single Tylenol PM and then the melatonin Christine swears by, and eventually, after hours of reassuring himself there's no way Christine would've killed Gayle, dropped off. This morning he guzzled enough caffeine to clear most of the fog and has been working like a machine all day.

He looks around again. Christine will flip. He's never pulled off anything like this before. She'll have to see how much he cares, how despite his slippages, he can be a good father and take care of her and the girls. And the new baby.

The thought of all those hungry mouths to feed gooses his memory. He's managed to shove the unpleasant task of calling Cromley out of his mind yet again, but he's gotta do it. The old man should still be in the office, and Chrissy and the girls won't arrive for at least ninety minutes. It's not too late.

Settling at the polished kitchen table, Robby pulls up Cromley's number then sits there looking at it, breathing. Maybe some of that doomed feeling is about this call, not just the almost intruder. And Gayle. And Christine. When it comes down to it, he's pissed at Cromley for letting him go, and when he opens his mouth, the anger will rush out. Unless he plans in advance. He can make notes, like Christine did for her job interviews. His heart beats faster, and he swallows. A little liquid courage might ease the anxiety, let him bluff his way through the tough stuff, but he dumped almost everything during the deep clean.

His habitual charm makes people assume he lies like a politician. His buddies tease him about his line of bullshit. But it's not true. Every word he says is sincere, especially the self-deprecation. Sure, he glosses over the occasional inconvenient truth, but if the past couple decades have proved anything, it's that people who know him pick up his lies from a mile away. Like Christine. Like Cromley.

What the fuck can he say to the man?

Deep, ragged breath. The scent of bleach grounds him, and he looks around at the vacuum lines in the carpet, the gleam of the wood floor, the shine of the window over the sink. His home, his family's home. He needs to figure this out.

Cromley warned him more than once that he couldn't look the other way anymore. There are good men without jobs, he said. But Robby never believed he'd go through with it. Cromley drinks at Lucky's every night of the week, never stops bitching about his lousy wife, and used to be amused by Robby's shenanigans—the late punch-ins, the long lunches. Envious, even.

Used to be. That's the key. Just like with Christine, Robby pushed it too far and didn't recognize the line when he crossed it. He's no better than the twins, constantly testing their limits. Except he's turning forty this year.

276

Maybe he needs to admit this to Cromley, show that he gets what he did wrong. Apologize, and not over the phone.

He showers, shaves and changes into the clothes he'd laid out: a button-down shirt that Christine got him last Christmas, with khakis and his better boots. He wishes there was time for a haircut, but it's too late.

At 4:35, he pulls into the yard. Cromley's niece is the receptionist this year, a high school senior getting work experience by staring at her cell phone here instead of at home. Beyond her, Cromley's door is closed, meaning he's in a meeting or dealing with the kind of paperwork that makes him short-tempered. When Robby asks to go back, the girl waves him through without looking up.

He's shaking, suddenly realizing this is it. He never had a real interview. On the day he walked into the office, they were so short they hired him on the spot. Back then, he didn't give a shit—would've ended up at McDonald's if they'd hired him first. But Robby cares now.

He steps in and stands in front of the same beat-up metal desk Cromley's been using for decades. Cromley meets Robby's eyes over the screen of a laptop as his fingers continue typing at a pace that belies his thick hands, like a boxer tap-dancing.

"Whaddaya want?" he grumbles.

Robby swallows, clears his throat. "Hi, Mr. Cromley, thanks for seeing me." The "Mister" feels strange in his mouth. Most of the guys go by their last name, or a nick-name, and Cromley's been Cromley since Robby's second day on the job.

"Rawlins," Cromley acknowledges. He lowers the laptop screen and raises grizzled eyebrows. "Surprised to see you. Taking a break from your supercharged new job to visit us losers, are you?"

Robby winces. He'd said some things on his way out. "Uh, yeah. Sorry about that. I didn't mean it."

Cromley leans back in his chair, eyelids lowered, hands clasped over his belly. "I know what you meant." No effort to make this any easier. Fair enough.

Robby says what he'd practiced on the way over. "I realize my behavior was problematic. I left you no choice but to let me go, and I apologize." He stops, stuck. He hadn't figured out a way to say the last part without sounding pathetic. He's just going to spit it out. "Please, give me another chance."

Cromley's already shaking his head mournfully. Laying his hands flat on the desk, he straightens. "I gave you more chances than I should have, Rawlins. When we got to the point of official warnings, I told you, it's in the books. Owner saw it. Owner knows about it. What am I going to tell him, Rawlins said please? Rawlins thinks maybe he can finally start showing up for work every day like a grown-ass man?"

Heat rushes to Robby's face. This is the possibility he'd avoided thinking about. If he stepped up, Cromley would find a way to take him back, he'd promised himself, suspecting the truth all the while. He's seen plenty of guys fired, for booze or no-shows or being an ornery asshole. No one's ever been rehired.

He falls into the chair in front of Cromley's desk and puts his head in his hands. "Are you sure there's nothing you can do? I mean, I can start from the bottom. Take a pay cut. Sweep floors, whatever."

"Aw, Rawlins. Short of changing your name, you're not getting back in."

Robby looks up, trying to find hope in that.

"No," Cromley says. "You can't fucking change your name. Listen, son. What you do now is go and get yourself some training. Look at this as an opportunity. Go back to school. Like you said, the money's in computers, right? Get yourself one of them IT jobs you said you wanted. Work from home."

"That sounds like a fucking nightmare," Robby says, rubbing at his temples.

Cromley shrugs. "I don't know. Be a truck driver, what do I care? You made your bed. You gotta make the best of it."

"Christine will leave me if I'm not bringing in a paycheck. We're having a baby."

Cromley's wide mouth stretches into a genuine grin, revealing too-bright veneers. "Ah. Congratulations. I wish you guys the best, I really do." His face falls. "But I swear to god, there's nothing I can do for you. You burned these bridges."

Robby stands. His face feels numb. "Can you—if I need a recommendation, will you say—"

Cromley says, "Robby, you're a pal. Of course I'm gonna give you a good recommendation. I trust you'll get your shit together and not make a liar of me."

"I will."

Cromley nods. "Yeah. You said that when those girls were born too, and you did, for a while, right? Do better this time."

Robby nods, cringing at the truth in that. He shakes Cromley's offered hand. "I appreciate everything," he says, forcing himself to meet Cromley's eyes and accept pity from the miserable alcoholic bastard who's been almost like a father to him, for lack of anyone else.

"Don't forget your locker. I left it alone, figured you'd come back for your stuff."

"Right," Robby says.

He turns to leave. Cromley says, "Eh, uh, Robby…"

"What?"

"I don't know how to say this, so I'll just spit it out. I saw you with that schoolteacher. The one who got herself killed."

Robbie turns around again. Gayle had picked him up at the gate at lunch time a few times. He'd known it was risky but had figured he'd talk his way out if one of the guys mentioned it. What were they going to do, call his wife? He's got a different perspective now, and fear runs through him as he says, "So what?"

Cromley ignores the belligerence, shrugs. "So, I'm sorry. I knew you knew her, that's all, so I'm saying sorry she's dead. And, you know. I know she got around."

"Got around?"

"Yeah. I saw her with some other guy around the same time. So, you know. Maybe not worth getting too messed up about."

"Who? Who was it"The guy she got scared of? But what's Robby going to do, confront him? "Never mind. Don't tell me. Tell the cops, okay?"

"I don't know the guy's name." Cromley sounds disgruntled. "It's not a police matter or anything. Just, don't take it so hard."

"Where were you?"

"That's the thing. I was"—and he blushes, an unhealthy dark red that bodes ill for his heart—"with a lady too. That hole-in-the-wall bar on 223 outta town."

Robby nods, understanding. The old bastard had finally stepped out on his wife. "Thanks, man," he says. "See you around."

At the lockers, he sees a couple of the guys still on shift. They wave from a distance, but he knows. They don't want to talk to him. He's bad luck, not part of the club anymore. He swears under his breath, shoving his extra deodorant, hair gel, toothbrush into the worn brown grocery bag that holds his spare clothes. There's a bunch of snacks in there too, and he goes to dump them on top of everything else in the bag when he notices a piece of black lace sticking up from under his shirt.

Automatically, he checks over his shoulders and reaches inside the bag. *I dare you,* Gayle said, grinning down at him. *Keep them, I don't care. I'll just go without the rest of the day. Your come dripping down my leg. No one will notice.*

Robby sucks in a breath. He hadn't forgotten, exactly. His taboo trophy from a lunchtime quicky. Knowing the panties were in there had given him a thrill every day for a while, and then he'd stopped noticing them. His spare clothes seldom came into play, and he'd meant to trade out the bag, drop the undies in the trash after he and Gayle broke up. But he never had.

Hurriedly, he tosses the rest of the locker's contents into the garbage, rolls the top of the brown bag until it's a sealed bundle, and fast walks out of the building, across the lot, toward his car. Maybe he can dump them in garbage bin at the park? He's breathing fast, panicking almost, the letters *DNA* bouncing around in his head, when he sees a black SUV pull up to the gated entrance. Detective Boon is inside; she lifts her badge to the security guy in the booth. Robby freezes, and he sees her clock him, standing there with his brown bag clutched to his chest like a stuffed animal.

282

27

MADDIE

....

THURSDAY

'm in my car, parked across from Downtown Grinders in Horace, scribbling down a few thoughts from my time with Sandra. She'd been disgruntled by our failure to find whatever letter her father had written to her Aunt Phil and had ushered me out pretty quickly. I'd warned her I'd have to notify the police about the presence and possible significance of Russ's boxes.

Sandra had perked up a little. "Tell them to come anytime. If they can match up any of the other dates, maybe it will help exonerate Dad."

I dial Eb, not expecting him to pick up, so of course he does. "Maddie! Just coming off an interview!" There's a zing in his voice. They must have learned something.

I force lightness into my tone. "Anything new about the bones?"

He bats it back to me. "You got anything for me besides questions? I've been on the go all day, and I missed lunch."

"I did learn one thing that may be of interest."

"Hmm. Well, you still in Horace? You want to grab an early dinner?"

Either he's got a one-track mind or he's willing to talk about the case. "I'm still in town. Sure, let's eat."

Out of the three non–fast food restaurants, we settle on Chinese. "See you in ten," he says.

"Hang on—" Dang. He's gone, but I'm still stinking from Sandra's basement. Russ's ancient tobacco stench is either stuck in my nose or it's glommed on to my clothes. Sighing, I retrieve my gym bag from the back seat and trudge toward a public restroom. Disposable wipes, a fresh layer of deodorant, and my emergency black sweatpants and top will have to do.

As I'm scrubbing with an "unscented" wipe that smells vaguely chemical, I hear myself humming and realize my thoughts may be a whirlwind but not a single one of them is about Mom's death or my struggling business. I smile into the mirror and give my earring a tug. "We're getting there," I tell Davina. "We're going to bring you home."

....

Eb's seated in a booth in the back corner, and I slide in across from him. A teenage server with chipped black nail polish and silver rings on every finger brings him a root beer, and I ask for water.

As soon as the waiter is out of earshot, I say, "Any news on my bones?"

Eb cracks his neck, then stretches each shoulder with a groan. He's rumpled but relaxed. As he shifts upright in his seat, he says, "Four out of the five remains identified, including your girl if those tests match up."

"Are you willing to specify cause of death?" I ask hopefully.

"For your ears only?"

I nod.

"Blunt force trauma to the head. Possible strangulation in one case."

Swallowing, I push away a vision of Davina's braids matted with blood and worse. "What about items found with the remains?" I ask, thinking of the Birkenstock buckles Lianne's friend had mentioned. "You said there were no belongings around Davina's bones, but what about the others? Can you tell me anything about that?"

"Not really," he says evasively. "But hey, I'm on your side. Seriously. The minute I find out anything I can share, I will."

The server returns, and I order lo mein with tofu and broccoli. Eb orders more extensively and hands back our menus.

When we're alone, I push a little. "It sounded like you had a good interview. Was that for my case?"

"No. I'm on the Bethested case too." He pulls a face.

"Honestly, I thought we'd have our answer on that by now. Local woman dumped in a nearby wood. I thought we'd get a boyfriend, or the father of her kids, and boom."

"Was there a history of domestic violence?"

"No. Her only brush with the law, ever, was reporting some jewelry stolen from her car last year. The kids' dad has a watertight alibi. He's so completely out of the picture that he lives in Australia. And the lady had a busy social life. Much more interested in playing the local dating scene than finding a second Mr. Right. She also dabbled in politics and enjoyed pissing off parents at her school."

"Oh." He's awfully willing to talk about the case that I'm only tangentially interested in, I note sourly.

"Including the Rawlins family, by the way. Mr. Robert Rawlins—say that three times fast—was one of several parents with a kid bullied by Bethested's daughter, and Bethested swept the complaints under the rug. Apparently made a habit of it."

"You can't be suggesting that's a motive for murder."

"Bullying? Oh, I definitely think it could be. Suicides and school shootings all over the news. You think parents might not get a wee bit frustrated when bullying isn't taken seriously?"

As a nonparent without kids in my life, I haven't dwelled too much on the issue. I backpedal. "You're right. I shouldn't have said that. It was reflex. When I was young, 'Kids will be kids' plastered over an awful lot of truly crappy behavior."

"Don't sugarcoat it. It was 'Boys will be boys,'" Eb says.

"Ha! Girls might be better at staying under the radar, but they're just as mean and twice as sneaky. 'Kids' is more accurate."

Silence falls as our food arrives. I'm remembering a girl in my sixth grade class who used to come to school in her big brother's worn-out hand-me-downs. I never joined in the name-calling, but I snubbed her like everyone else, and giggled with my friends when she raised her hand in class and revealed a yellow stain in the armpit of her wrinkled Ninja Turtles T-shirt. Shame flows through me as if it happened yesterday.

"Anyway," Eb says. "We interviewed this guy, Swannick. Bethested's daughter was taking his third-grader's lunch every day. She promised to buy the kid a video game he wanted at the end of the school year. It was a payment plan in the form of food."

I snort. "So this Swannick is a suspect now?"

"Nah, he's clear. But he and his wife finally got the kid to admit why he was so hungry every day after school, so Swannick called a meeting with Bethested, right? And her phone's buzzing away on the desk every two minutes. He's annoyed, asks why she doesn't turn it off, put it away. She got real flustered and said an ex-boyfriend is harassing her. Swannick saw the screen at one point, and he recognized the name. A local guy named Piper."

"So she had an ex who makes a good suspect, after all?"

Eb shrugs. "Let's say, he and I, we're getting to know one another. But she never reported it, and there's no corroboration with her phone records. Her older daughter says she saw her with a different phone sometimes, but we haven't found it, and everyone we talked to has only one number for her."

I look down at my plate and realize I haven't been eating. My bean sprouts have become slimy in the cooling sauce. Unlike Eb, I'm not used to talking murder over dinner. Maybe I'll ask for a doggy bag.

Eb's cleaning up his last bites. I guess it's my turn to share. "I visited the Rawlins house for the second time today."

"Oh yeah? Still think they're nice folks?"

"I didn't talk to your protective parent, he wasn't around."

"Huh. Guy lied to us about his employment. Wonder where he was at."

I shrug. "I was at Teague House. I think his sister said he lives in a cottage on the property."

"Mmm," Eb says noncommittally, forking up some shrimp and mushrooms.

"Anyway, I talked to Sandra for a while. Gave her a hand sorting through some stuff in the basement." I hesitate. "Can I ask you a hypothetical? This guy Russ Rawlins killed himself in ninety-three, right? If the five victims all died before that, and it was his land, is there going to be an assumption that he suicided out of guilt or to stop himself from killing again? And if that's the assumption, will you still investigate?"

I hold my breath. In my years of following missing persons cases, I've seen it happen before. A missing five-year-old's drug-addicted mother overdosed a couple years after the disappearance, and a doll the little girl had with her when she disappeared was discovered in the mother's belongings. Although no body was found, the case was quietly put to bed. The same thing could happen if the district attorney concludes Russ Rawlins is responsible for the older set of murders. If so, I'd be able to investigate Davina's last days and hours on my own, without worrying about stepping on law enforcement's tender toes. Or, to put it another way, the weight of uncovering the truth of what happened in Teague Wood would fall entirely on my shoulders.

Eb chews thoughtfully, then tilts his head from side to side in seeming fresh consideration, although he must have considered this as soon as he got estimated dates from the lab. Finally he says, "Good question. Can't prosecute a dead man, and the suicide is pretty telling. But so far, the window of death isn't that exact. Which may change as we nail down identities and times last seen. And Gayle Bethested's murder may point to a younger accomplice who knew where the bodies were buried. One of the older kids? Prosecutor may be interested in that."

I bite my lip, feeling dubious, but I'm not sure I can pin down why. "There's another weakness in the Russ-did-it theory," I tell him. "Sandra and I found probably a dozen boxes of Russ Rawlins's stuff. She was shocked, said the aunt got rid of the studio where he killed himself, and she'd thought all his belongings had gone too."

"So what's the problem?"

"There's a calendar in there from 1989. Looks like he may have been away at a funeral during the week Davina disappeared."

"Or…that could just be what he told his wife when he went out hunting."

I hadn't thought of that. I had the sense Valerie Rawlins didn't go out to the studio much, but even so, he could have made the note as a reminder to keep his story straight. I shrug. "Could be. Anyway. I figured you should know. Maybe you'll match up more dates or find something else in the boxes."

Eb wipes his mouth with a napkin, then studies me. "Thanks, Maddie. I'll see that someone deals with it. It's looking like a messy couple of cases. Leave the rest to us."

There's something annoyingly dismissive in his tone. Patronizing. "And if you don't pursue it?"

"We'll pursue it as far as we can."

"Davina's family needs to know what happened and how it happened. I'm sure the other families will too, when you find them all."

He smiles a little. "Good thing you're on it then."

I narrow my eyes at him. "Will you let me know if anything comes up? About Davina?"

One eyebrow goes up. "If I can."

Exiting the Chinese restaurant with a carton of tofu broccoli and two fortune cookies, I return to my car feeling thoughtful and pull out my notebook to untangle my ideas.

It is a messy case. Already, I'm torn three ways between wanting the truth about Davina, respecting the scope of the official investigation, and developing sympathy for the people involved. Gayle Bethested's death means the issues aren't buried. Like Eb said, someone knew the remains were there. The location can't be coincidental, but I'm not sure I buy it being one of the kids. Neither Sandra nor Jon live in the area, for one. How could they have gotten so embroiled in some issue with Gayle as to kill her—and then why would they pretend to "discover" her body, drawing attention to that clearing, if they knew the other bodies were there? And Robby had been, what, ten? Ten-ish, anyway, when his father died. Too young to have been an accomplice in the deaths and be reusing the clearing now, surely.

The next order of business has to be more research. Lianne told me the archives of the local paper aren't online, so I'll check whether the newspaper office or public library keeps them on microfiche, and look for more about Russell Rawlins's death and the surrounding time period. It's also worth asking around to see if there are old-timers who remember the family from back then and might be willing to talk. Eb mentioned the retired county sheriff had identified one of the victims, an older woman who'd lived in her car, but he'd been close-mouthed about her name and about leads on the others.

....

At the library, I splash my face with cold water in the bathroom after my first hour, then force myself back to the microfiche reader. Russ Rawlins's obituary was bare-bones, nothing about cause of death, no one "left behind" except for his wife and children. I scroll restlessly, hoping for more on the family. Barring that, it would be nice to find a possible motive for Davina to come to Horace on her way home, in case it was more than her driver's whim.

The Melakwa County Register microfiche I borrowed spans from January of '89, months before Davina disappeared, through August of '93, when Russell's death occurred. Eyeballing each issue page by page is killing me, but there's no keyword search.

My efforts are somewhat rewarded. Robby Rawlins's name jumps from the caption of a blurred action shot taken during a Little League game. He must have been six years old. There's no information about him or his parents in the accompanying article. Jonathan and Sandra appear in their respective middle school graduation photos and that's it. I don't find records of suspicious disappearances. Nothing portrays Russ Rawlins in a negative light prior to his suicide.

I tap my fingertips on the table top. Sandra mentioned he was in a band, and I request five more years of fiche from the librarian. What if Davina, always a huge music fan, diverted on her way home because of a show? Maybe she wanted one last night out before buckling down to parenthood again. That was plausible. And she could have met the man on whose land her bones were buried.

Of course, it wouldn't have to be Russ's band, they could have met at someone else's show, but it's worth checking. Davina's weakness was a yearning for fame and fortune. Someone she was impressed by, a professional musician, might have had the power to lure her from her intended path.

I work backward from 1989, hoping to find a story featuring Russ's band. As I'm about to give up, in 1983, I discover Russell and Valerie in a photo with a dozen others at the top of an article called "Vision 2000: the Future of Horace. Local Citizens Envision Horace's Future."

The City Council of Horace has formed a Vision 2000 Committee to strategize toward Horace's long-term goals.

Nathan Belter, well-known local preacher, businessman, and committee chairman, said, "More and more, our little town is buffeted by winds that already rock larger cities: changing economies, drugs, homelessness, violence, and a lack of family values.

We need to face these issues head-on as we design our
policies moving forward. The Vision 2000 group will
give all citizens the opportunity to share their opinions.
We will consider what has and hasn't worked in other
communities, and propose priorities for the Council to
shape the kind of town we want for our kids."

Volunteers from local neighborhoods and church
groups make up the committee. All local citizens will
have a chance to contribute in upcoming meetings
and mail-in surveys.

I study the black-and-white picture taken six years prior
to Davina's disappearance. The committee is posed in two
rows, with five seated in front and seven standing in back.
Valerie, obviously pregnant, sits in one of the chairs, and Russ
stands upright behind her with one hand on her shoulder, a
reluctant frown on his face. Sandra and Jon would have been
born closer to my own birth year of 1978, so that must be
Robby in the oven.

My eyes are drawn to the man standing on the far left,
identified in the caption as Nathan Belter. The photo is
blurry, the pixels enlarged on the microfiche reader's screen,
but there's something very familiar about the thick dark hair
and close-set eyes.

My breath catches. Sandra's flyer. *Cut away the dross.*

I pull out my phone and navigate to the snap I'd taken of

the flyer. It's more than just dark hair and similarly shaped eyes—it's the placement of the ears, the shape of the head, the angle of the neck.

I snap a picture of the newspaper article with my phone. This guy is worth spending some internet time on.

First though, I continue scrolling forward to see if future issues mention the Vision 2000 Committee. If I'm lucky, I'll find a deep dive into the committee members by some bored reporter. Or an interview with Russ: "So, Mr. Rawlins, what's your take on the committee's mission?" "Well, in the future, I'd really like to see a hidden graveyard in every backyard!"

No confessions spring to my attention, but in 1985, a press release from the office of the mayor announced that the Vision 2000 Committee had been dissolved due to "irreconcilable differences" between committee members, and would not be re-formed without outside funding.

Huh. Well, that's intriguing. Maybe it's time to track down someone who was on the city council thirty-five years ago.

I pack up the microfiche and pull out my laptop. The strings of words Valerie Rawlins had scrawled over the flyers for Nathan Belter's event don't bring up anything useful. I do an image search for the flyer itself and have no luck at all, but while I have the jpeg file open, I notice that the enlargement on my screen allows me to make out some of the type I hadn't been able to read under her overlapping scribbles. "Preacher Nate Presents: This IS Utopia. August 28, 1981."

"Preacher Nate" is also a dead end. Frustrated, I smack my table a little too hard and the teenager at the next table shoots me a dirty look. "Sorry," I mouth. I try a database search on Nathan Belter and winnow through dozens of false hits before I narrow it down to the right guy. Nathan Ian Belter, born 1950 in Horace, Oregon. Served in Vietnam 1968–1969. Married to Cherise Alice Belter nee Abner 1970–1981, Constance Belter nee Warner 1989–2010.

Mr. Belter has chaired more than one local government committee, was an active member of the Rotary Club, and owns Horace Antiques & Junk Shop. He still attends local Chamber of Commerce luncheons, although, based on last month's photo, his thick hair is now snow-white. Sounds like just the kind of community-minded guy who would be happy to enlighten me about the Rawlinses.

As directed by numerous signs around the library, I exit to use my cell phone.

28

SANDRA

....

THURSDAY

Sandra returns to the basement after Maddie leaves and tears the whole box that had contained the *White Album* apart. The album cover and liner rip open so she can make sure there's no secret pocket, no hidden lining. The other albums, she removes one by one, then slides out each disc and checks the sleeve. When the box is empty, she shakes it, gets up, kicks it, and glares at it. Then she sits down and silently loads the albums back in. The *White Album* gets to bunk with *Sgt. Pepper*.

After, she pushes all of Dad's boxes against the wall, planning to ask Jon and Robby if they want any of the records or shot glasses as keepsakes. Maddie left the calendars on top of the box she'd found them in; Sandra flips to her birthday, and sees Dad had scribbled her name and circled it. It doesn't seem to matter anymore, and she closes the calendar and sets it back where it was.

Upstairs, she showers to wash the stink of the canning jars off. Aunt Phil still hasn't returned any calls or texts, and Sandra hopes she's safely boarded her ship. Most likely, they won't hear from her for awhile. Auntie's gone to Hawaii for a week each year for the past fifteen years, and there was never a peep from her until she bustled in the door. This time should be different, with Auntie planning to travel "indefinitely," but she'll talk when she's ready and not before.

If she was planning to be easy to reach, she wouldn't have handed off Dad's note like that. She must have known Sandra would be full of questions, and she'd sidestepped all opportunity to be asked.

Sandra stands under the hot water, mind wandering. Jon had told her that the police came and interviewed him earlier while she was out running, and he wants to meet later to talk about it. She wonders if it was about the old bones or about Gayle, if the police are so desperate for leads that they're interviewing people who knew her thirty years ago.

But more likely it's the old bones. If Dad's calendar suggests he was on a trip when at least one of the victims was killed, someone used Teague Wood to hide an atrocity, but Dad's suicide could still be about depression. It was the horrible reality she'd hated only last week, but now it sounds like the lesser of all evils.

The soothing sound of water is interrupted by thumping, and she pokes her head out of the shower to listen. Someone is pounding on the bathroom door with a frequency and abandon that can only mean one thing.

"I'll be right out, Denny!" she calls. "Use the downstairs potty!"

"I need help with my popsicle!" he yells back.

She rinses one more time and turns off the shower. Through the door she says, "Okay, bud. Where's your dad?"

"He said ask you; he's busy with work."

"Okay. I'll be right down."

Sandra dresses quickly but pauses in the mirror as she finger-combs her bangs, checking out her tired eyes. Every step forward has a cost. If Dad was a killer, she'll feel less responsible for his death, but her whole family will be overshadowed by his inhuman acts. Chelsey and Lottie and Denny will suffer the way she and Jon and Robby had, Robby probably worst of all.

Robby's issues now, his inability to be faithful, to be truthful… Maybe if she and Jon and Aunt Phil had done more for him back then, he'd be more stable now. He'd been fast asleep on the studio couch when Jon found him, maybe a dozen feet from Dad's corpse in the tree outside. Sometimes Sandra wonders if Robby knows more than he's saying or if he's repressed some terrible memory.

"Aunt Sandy! Hurry up!"

"I'm coming!"

She pushes the thought away impatiently as she trots

down the stairs. All she can do right now is focus on learning the truth. Then they'll all deal with it. Unless Robby's in jail.

Denny's at the kitchen table, holding a book open with one hand, and a squished unopened popsicle with the other. He hands her the pop, already liquefying from the heat of his fingers. "I want this one, but I can't open it."

"Let's find you a more frozen one. What color do you like?"

"I like red but they're all gone," he says sulkily.

She shuffles through the pile in the freezer. "Guess what? There's a yellow one, and it tastes like bananas."

"Really?"

She slices the top off with a knife and pops the tiny piece into her mouth. "Mmm. Bananas."

"Hey!" Denny protests, but he grins.

"Popsicle tax." She hands him the rest and leans on the counter. "What have you been up to so far today, dear nephew?"

He shrugs, trying to get the pop to push up one-handed and finally flipping the book upside down on the table. "Dad made me breakfast and then talked to the policeman. And then went into his room to work. He told me I could read books or go outside."

"*Captain Underpants* is pretty good stuff," she says.

He nods. "I read it twice so far, and I read *Ricky Ricotta's Mighty Robot* too."

"Today?"

He nods.

"Well, that's a lot of reading. When you're done with your pop, maybe we can take a walk or something." She narrows her eyes. She'd planned to poke around for more places Aunt Phil's letter could be hiding, on the off chance that Auntie—or Mom—didn't find and destroy it. "Or we could go on a treasure hunt." Maybe Denny's childish eyes will find hidey-holes that she and Jon missed.

Denny eyes her suspiciously. "Where?"

"All around the house," she tells him. "Upstairs. Downstairs. Maybe the dining room?" She's always been suspicious of that built-in hutch.

"No one hides treasure in the dining room!" He giggles.

"No? You don't think pirates like dining rooms? I was thinking we could dig a hole right through the floor, see if there's any pirate gold."

"No! Great Aunt Phil will be super mad when she comes home!"

"Well, where then?"

"Outside!" Not quite what she had in mind, but he's fully into it now. The pop in his hand starts to drip, unnoticed, onto the table.

She lifts it upright. "Outside is pretty big. I'm not sure where to start."

"Well," he says with apparent sympathy for her lack of imagination. "We could just look around."

"Lead the way."

As they wander the yard, Sandra tells Denny how Grandpa Russ used to make her and Jon run circles around the outside of the house when they were very small and making too much of a ruckus inside. "Or sometimes he made us dig up dandelion roots. If we were lucky, we got a penny for each one," she says. "We could try that. Only problem, your Uncle Robby mowed all the dandelions."

"I know where there's some big ones!"

He pulls her to the backyard, where Robby had avoided swathes around the big ceramic planters of geraniums that Aunt Phil had arranged around the sides and edges of the wooden deck.

"Wow, look at all those dandelions," Sandra says. "If I dug those up when I was a kid, I might have got a whole dollar."

"One dollar? That's not very much money!"

"It's a hundred dandelions, buddy. But you're right. Treasure hunting probably pays more. Thing is, first you have to find the treasure."

Denny shrugs. "I'll look in the dandelions next to the porch. You can look in the birdhouse because you're tall." He points up the trunk of a slim maple tree.

"You think a pirate got all the way up there?" she says. "I guess it's a good spot for a very small treasure. Hmm, I'll need something to stand on."

Denny traipses around the porch, pushing bunches of

dandelions and long grass aside to look underneath. "It's pretty dark under there. Do we have a flashlight?"

"If there's treasure, it will be close to the edge," she says quickly, not wanting him to squirm underneath. If there's anything under there, it won't be treasure. More like black widow spiders and rusty old pop tops from Dad's beer cans.

She's dutifully stepping up onto a bench she borrowed from under a geranium pot to peer into the birdhouse when Denny says, "You're right, Aunt Sandy!"

He sounds so flabbergasted she grins. "Of course I'm right. What am I right about?"

"It's close to the edge. Really close!"

Startled, she turns too quickly and the bench tilts precariously into the soft earth. With a quick hop, she lands in the grass, ignoring the complaint from her sore leg. Her eyes are fixed on the metal box cradled proudly in her nephew's arms. He gives her a gap-toothed smile. "Treasure."

Phil's faded purple lockbox.

In the house, Sandra lays some newspaper on the dining room table and has Denny deposit the box on top. She's already brushed off loose soil, but it's remarkably clean for something that's been lying in the dirt for an unknown amount of time. The combination is four digits, and Sandra remembers her aunt saying she still remembered it. She tries Auntie's birthday and the latch clicks.

When the lid flips up, Denny grabs the bag inside like

it's the treat at the bottom of a box of cereal, his little hands tearing at the plastic.

"Wait!" Sandra half laughs.

He dumps it out, and a spray of loose papers and chunkier items fall, scattering in the box and across the table. Among them, a flash of silver and a thunk. Sandra scoops Denny back as she cries out, as if to keep him from something poisonous.

The necklace she once saw her father bury in the dirt, with two gold rings threaded on a serpentine silver chain, is nestled among her mother's drawings.

29

JON

....

Jon paces behind his closed bedroom door as if he's pre-
paring for a presentation at work. Finally, he taps the
number on his phone and holds it to his ear. When Sammy
called earlier, Jon stalled him, knowing he needed to think
through what he wanted from this conversation. Now he's got
privacy and some written questions, but it still feels wrong to
be hassling someone who's grieving.

He needs to do this for Robby. Jon takes a deep breath and
whooshes it out as the phone rings again.

"Hello?" comes Sammy Krieg's nervous voice. He
sounds younger than Jon expected. Jon googled him.
Sammy is a sociology teacher at Horace High, and he and
his husband run a house-painting business. Jon checked
out his social media too. Aside from photos of nice paint

jobs, Sammy loves growing, eating, and preserving organic vegetables, to the point of proselytizing. None of which help with Gayle.

"Hi, Sammy. It's Jon Rawlins. Thanks so much for talking with me."

"No problem. Tom said—" He swallows audibly. "Tom said you and your sister actually found—you found Gayle."

"We did, but—"

"I was one of the people she was supposed to be at a conference with," Sammy says. "I can't believe it. I knew something was wrong. Everyone said she probably had a kid thing and would drive up separately, but I knew."

"That must have been hard," Jon says, floundering. "Um, do you mind if—"

"The police have talked to me two times. Twice! But they won't tell me anything."

Jon makes a check mark next to his first question: Have the cops talked to you? He'd planned a whole preamble to convince Sammy to open up to him but skips to the next question. "Did Gayle have a boyfriend?"

"She was dating. She was always dating. I don't know who though. She was very private about her personal life. Didn't confide. I talk about my husband all day long. She was more like that about her mother. 'Mom did this, you wouldn't believe, Mom did that.'"

"So you don't know who she was seeing?"

"Not this time around." He laughs a little. "Why do you want to know all this, anyway? Tom didn't say."

"It's…complicated," Jon says, glancing at his notes and finding they don't help. "I—my family owns the land where she was found. I want to make sure the cops are covering all the bases. And Tom said you were helping with the election, so I figured you'd know about that part of Gayle's life."

"The boring part." He snorts, or maybe it's part sob. "I mean, neither of us really thought it was boring, but we joked that no one had any idea what the county commissioners do, so people's eyes just glaze over. She'd been great on the Planning Commission, a real voice for getting folks off the street and into transitional or affordable housing, so I talked her into running. I designed her signs and got her on community radio for an interview." Sadly, he says, "Her murder is causing more of a splash than putting her on the ballot ever did."

"But—there are people who didn't want her to win, right?" Jon collapses into the hard wooden chair at his old desk. "Like the guy she was running against? Or people who'd be affected by her policies?"

"Sure. You'd be surprised how heated people get about every little thing. I've seen people come to blows over the placement of a stop sign. But, if anything, she was getting some wining and dining. Not threats."

"Would she have told you if something scared her?" *I'm scared, Rob.* Jon shudders.

"I think so. She seemed really upset last year when her car was broken into, and we talked about that a lot. Her mom's heirloom brooch was stolen, right out of the school parking lot, and it really worried her. She campaigned the PTA to fundraise for new security cameras."

"Did they figure out who took the brooch?"

"I don't think so. Gayle would've said."

Jon tries a different tack. "What do you think of Marcus Belter?"

"Nice guy," Sammy says. "Sometimes we play pickleball."

Jon sighs and decides to be done. He's confirmed that the police aren't concentrating solely on his brother, which is helpful. "Thanks for talking to me."

"Before you go. I wanted to ask you—I know it's a stupid question, but I just keep thinking about it. Did she look peaceful, when you found her? I can't help picturing her—"

"We only saw her finger," Jon breaks in. "She was covered in dirt."

Sammy's silence is dense. Jon has time to realize he was too harsh, but he's not sure how to take it back. Of all people, Jon knows what a terrible game it is to fixate on someone's death. He's spent far more time reliving Jill's painful last days than she spent living them.

Sammy says, "That's right. They told me that. Right."

"Listen, I'm sorry. I didn't mean—"

"No, it's okay. I shouldn't have asked. I…wasn't thinking."

Jon thanks him again, awkwardly, and lets him go. Now he knows Gayle hid her relationship with Robby at least from this man, which makes it more probable that she hid it from others. One point for Robby.

Also, Sammy had been genuine in his grief and confusion. Jon would have liked to consider him a suspect, especially after the "interviewed twice" comment, but it seems unlikely.

Talking to Marcus Belter may be more worthwhile. He checks his phone again. Tom texted that he's planning to spend tomorrow at the waterpark with Dana, and he doesn't know exactly what time Belter's showing up. Jon RSVPs. He'll take Denny shopping in the morning for some kind of gift and a pair of swim trunks.

Meanwhile—time to finally get some of the house sorting done. With all the craziness this week, he and Sandra are going to have to pay someone to do the bulk of the cleaning and sorting unless they take even more time off, but he can get some done this evening.

A sudden flurry of noise comes from downstairs: Sandra yelling "No!" with an edge in her voice, and Denny letting loose a loud, jagged cry.

Jon throws the door open, races downstairs, and finds them in the dining room. Sandra is kneeling on the floor with her arms around Denny, whose crying is already subsiding as she murmurs, "I'm sorry, I'm sorry, buddy," and strokes his hair. Jon, heart steadying as he takes in the absence of bad guys or thieves, meets her eyes with a quizzical frown, and she tilts her chin toward an open metal box, maybe nine by twelve inches, on the dining room table. Dozens of scraps of paper are scattered around it, and he recognizes Mom's sketches of birds, some in colored pencil, some in charcoal or ballpoint pen, torn out of her little sketchbook.

The box itself holds more paper scraps, interspersed with other items. He registers the corner of a photo, a silver ring.

Still perplexed about the cause of upset, he pulls out the chair closest to Sandra and Denny, and puts his hand on Denny's shoulder. "Come sit with me," he says. The boy loosens his hold on Sandra, and Jon pulls him gently onto his lap, savoring his weight and warmth.

Sandra stands. Her cheeks are pink, and her hands shake as she corrals the sketches into a pile. She grabs a torn plastic bag by one corner and sets it aside.

"Gee, it looks like you guys found some of Gramma's drawings," Jon prompts.

Denny nods, thumb in his mouth.

Sandra pushes the box and the pile closer to the center of the table and collapses into a chair.

"Sorry I scared you, Denny," she says. "I must have scared your Daddy too, when I yelled!"

Jon feels Denny's head nod against his chest.

"Must have been some pretty ugly birds in there," Jon says.

"Well," Sandra says, and stops. Then she tries again. "It

WHAT REMAINS OF TEAGUE HOUSE

looks like Gramma put some valuable stuff in the box that maybe we shouldn't touch."

"You mean treasure?" Confused by what seems like a massive overreaction on Sandra's part, Jon can't suppress a chuckle.

She shoots him a tired glare. "I mean, grown-up stuff."

"Oh?" He cranes his neck to get a better view of the box's interior. Mom must have been collecting junk like a magpie. Maybe Sandra's stress is making her irrationally snappish.

Denny wiggles on his lap. "I want to go. Can I play Xbox now?"

"Sure," Jon says, releasing him. "I'm looking at the clock. One hour, and then it's bath time. We need to get some of that sticky stuff off of you."

Denny nods and flies out of the room.

Sandra collapses her head into her hands. "God, I can't believe it."

"What's going on?" he asks with concern. When she looks up, she looks angry, bright pink spots high on her cheeks.

"So, Aunt Phil gave me Dad's suicide note last night."

"What?"

"Don't look like that, we've barely had a minute to talk."

"You said it was gone. I thought you threw it away."

"No. I hid it. And somehow, Aunt Phil ended up with it." She reaches into her purse and hands him the note in its protective manila envelope.

He reads quickly, then again more slowly, letting his father's voice fill his mind. "Wow."

"'Wow' nothing. It doesn't say much at all."

"What did you expect?"

Sandra rolls her eyes. "I don't know. *But*—this morning I found Dad's copy of the *White Album* and there's nothing in there, no letter. So Denny and I went on a treasure hunt, and this is what we found." She gestures to the box.

Jon looks again. "I still don't get it."

"I'm looking for something to exonerate Dad," she enunciates slowly. "And instead this is what I found! Look at this!"

"Mom's junk," he says. "This must be the box Aunt Phil told us about. Are her photos in there?"

He stands and reaches to stir through the papers, but Sandra grabs his wrist.

"Don't! Look at the rings! On a chain?" She points more closely, her finger an inch away from a pale, gleaming ring.

"So?"

"Two rings on a chain. Which I saw Dad bury. And now they're in Mom's box."

He shakes his head. "Why do you think they're the same ones?"

"Because they are. Because I saw them up close when Denny dumped the stuff out. And see that photo?"

He reaches for it, but she lays her hand on his arm. "Don't touch anything in there. We may have to give it to the police."

Stubbornly, he slides the photo out anyway, holding it by the edges in compromise. It's an odd shape, carefully torn. Mom's at the rough edge, looking very young with her hair in a central part, pulled forward over her shoulders. She holds a baby, maybe a year old, with dark hair and a wide blue stare—Robby? Next to her, arm over her shoulder, is a young man who is not Russ. His hair curls over his collar and a generous mustache curls over his lip. He's beaming at the camera. Mom, gazing over the top of the baby's head, beams at him. Something in her expression makes Jon's heart skip a beat.

"Isn't this the guy from that flyer you showed us?"

"Looks like him."

"You know what's weird? For a second the other day, I thought I remembered him. From our house when we were little. Do you remember, Mom and Dad would have those parties with like, a dozen people over, and this one guy would talk and talk?"

Sandra's looking at him like he's crazy. "I barely remember anyone coming over. I don't think… Except I remember—did we steal party food out of the kitchen? I remember something about dropping a bunch of deviled eggs."

"Never mind. The baby is Robby?"

"Who else could it be?"

He sets the photo back in the box carefully. "Listen, whether it's the same guy I was thinking of or not, I bet it's one of Dad's friends. Look how the paper is torn. Dad was probably right there, and she ripped him out when she was pissed at him."

Sandra shakes her head. "Nice story. It doesn't explain the way she's looking at him. And doesn't it freak you out that the rings I saw Dad burying on top of a bunch of dead bodies are here, in this box that Mom took and hid from Aunt Phil?"

"Maybe a little," he admits. "I'm not sure what it proves though. You think we should call the police?"

"We should talk to Robby first. He has a right to know." Her voice is uneven.

He's almost afraid to ask. "What are you thinking?"

When she speaks, her words slice the scar tissue from his childhood, as Dad's suicide and Mom's retreat peel away to reveal a deeper hell. "I was right. Dad killed those people, and Mom stopped speaking because she couldn't bear to say it."

30

ROBBY

....

Robby pitches the brown bag with the underwear into the dumpster behind the take-and-bake pizza place. The dumpster is almost empty, and he prays that means his lonely package will soon be covered over with a layer of built-up restaurant trash.

Then, feeling slightly less sick, he walks around to the front, pops into the restroom to wash his hands, and goes to the pickup counter. "Rawlins, should be two large ready," he tells the plump blond woman working the cash register. She's short and curly-haired, with some kind of pink false eyelashes, and he gives her the patented Robby Rawlins grin. This one can be a firecracker, he remembers from past pickups. She's quiet tonight though, handing him the uncooked pies with just a quick "Thanks!" when he shoves a fiver into the tip jar.

His smile fades as soon as he's out the door. He glances

at his phone. A text from Christine: "Chelse says pepperoni pleez," and one from Sandra: "Found box of Mom&Dad might have to show cops call me." Later, he'll deal with that bullshit later, and he drives toward home in a daze, forcing himself to focus on what happens next. Christine will ask about work, and he needs a good answer, but they also need to talk about Gayle. The nausea returns even thinking about it, and the thud of that brown bag echoing in the near-empty dumpster keeps punctuating his thoughts. He needs to know what she knows. He needs to know what—if anything—she did. And he needs to get there without her eviscerating him. Knowing Christine, if she wanted to talk about it, they would have already, so she's not going to be happy if he insists.

Everything's fine though. Or at least better. No more phone. No more undies. Chrissy's coming home. He just needs to make her happy, make her stay. Gayle will be buried, and this will all be over, and in six months' time, he'll be a new daddy again.

The dark gray SUV is in his driveway. He recognizes its silhouette even before he sees Simonson's bulky form visible in the front window. Robby slows, parking his little Prius with care, then unwillingly steps out. Simonson follows suit, and they look at each other over the top of Robby's car.

"Detective. Hi," Robby says, his voice sounding odd in his ears. "I, um. My wife will be here any minute. With the girls."

He smiles hopefully. Maybe the detective will take the hint. Come back another time, or not at all.

Simonson doesn't smile. "This shouldn't take too long. But we can take it down to the station if you prefer."

Robby looks at his watch. Five thirty already. Soccer practice wraps up by six, but sometimes they're out early, sometimes late. "Uh, no. Let's get this over with. Let me get my pizzas, and we can talk at the table."

Inside, Robby sets the oven to preheat and gets himself a tumbler of water. "Can I get you a drink?"

Simonson has made himself comfortable, draping his suit jacket over the back of his chair, tracking Robby with an unsmiling yet amused mien. "No, thank you though. Place looks nice."

Robby pushes down a flicker of resentment that the man noticed how hard he's working to get his family back. "Thank you. How can I help?" His flailing mind comes up with Sandra's text. He should have called her back. Something about cops? "Is this about that box my sister found?"

"I'm not sure I heard about that."

Robby blinks. "Oh, it's nothing. They texted me they found something of Mom's, that's all. I haven't gotten back to them yet." Robby wipes his hands on his jeans under the surface of the table and tries to shrug nonchalantly.

Simonson nods. "Well, we have identification now on all but one of the remains, so we'll be talking to all of you about that. Four of the deceased have been matched to missing persons in the state of Oregon."

Robby swallows. "You must have some idea of dates then. Were they buried before my folks owned the land?"

"Unfortunately, no. We're going to have to keep bothering you three with more questions about times you barely remember."

"Well, at least someone will be happy." Realizing that sounds strange, he adds, "I mean, their families. Not happy, but—"

The detective nods. "Right. Some kind of relief, we hope. And perhaps, justice."

The word floats oddly in the air of the cottage, out of place among the gleaming surfaces and the sound of the clock ticking in the living room. Robby looks at the time on the oven, hoping Simonson gets to the point. And that the point isn't anything dangerous.

"Right. Justice."

"It's the other case I want to talk to you about this afternoon. A student has come forward with some video footage."

"A student. At the elementary school?" Robby's mouth goes dry.

"Right. The cameras on the teachers' lot behind the school are so old, they're pointless. We didn't have any usable footage, until now." He sets his cell phone on the table and fiddles with it.

Robby knows the cameras are useless. Christine has

complained about them more than once, grumbling about vandalism in the teacher's parking lot.

"Why would a kid be taking video back there?" he asks in a strange, high voice.

The detective smiles broadly. "I'd say they were probably up to no good. Somebody's parents dragged them into the station today to fess up. We let them off with a warning though, out of consideration for helping the police." He slides the phone across the table, screen up. "You were pretty unhappy about the bullying situation, I guess."

Robby watches the parking lot at the elementary school come into focus at an odd, low angle. There's a brief flash, ridiculously close up, of a burning cigarette right in front of the camera lens, a blur that ends in a sideways middle finger and tinny suppressed laughter. "Oh shit, duck!" someone says as a pair of knees in faded jeans comes into view and passes, receding until a whole man fits into the shot. Robby recognizes himself but continues staring in horrified fascination. Is he identifiable from this? The kids must have been down in the bushes, and he had been oblivious.

The guy in the video wears a denim jacket over a bright blue sweatshirt, the hood pulled up with the bill of a red ball cap protruding. A pair of sunglasses and a paper Covid mask cover his face as he strolls alongside a gold Prius with a "Bethested for County Commissioner" sticker in one corner of the rear window, a rainbow Oregon shape in the other.

He can't keep his eyes off the small screen. The man in the video lifts a crumpled plastic bag to the driver's side window, which is open two or three inches, and shoves it through.

Then he continues to the sidewalk that leads around to the front of the school, stopping momentarily when he gets to the corner. His face is turned toward the hidden camera, and Robby rallies. With the sunglasses over his eyes, the mask over his nose and chin, who could prove that was him? But then the man pulls off the sunglasses, polishes them on the hem of the sweatshirt, and sticks them in the pocket of the denim jacket. He pulls back the hood, crumples the hat in one hand, and runs his fingers through his hair. *You idiot*, Robby thinks, but he remembers that moment. He knew he'd passed the parking lot security camera and had decided to run into the school to give Christine a quick hello.

Robby lifts his eyes to see the detective's steady gaze on him.

"I didn't hurt Gayle," Robby blurts.

"What did you put in her car?"

"Nothing!" Shit. He needs to make up something. If he admits it was a phone, it opens the whole can of worms.

Simonson cocks an eyebrow.

Robby flounders. "You should have seen my daughter. She went from loving school to hating it, all because of Liz Bethested. Gayle wouldn't do shit. Just 'neuro-atypical' this and 'normative privilege' that, like Lottie was the one doing the bullying. She was steamrolling us."

He pauses, flashing to himself sitting in that undersized chair, feeling an echo of the heat that built slowly at the realization that he and Christine were being patronized and Lottie's pain dismissed. "I mean, I get it, Gayle was struggling with how to deal with Liz. Christine kept saying, 'There's got to be something we can do, someone else we can talk to,' but the principal pointed us to the school board and it felt like… too much. Lottie was so miserable."

The detective waits.

Robby takes a deep breath, but his words come out in a near whisper. "I needed Gayle to work with us."

Simonson nods. "This is all about the incident between her daughter Liz and your daughter Lottie?"

"Yeah. And the bullying that came after."

"Did you develop a more personal relationship with Gayle Bethested?"

"No!" Robby blurts, before his brain recovers from the shock of the question. There's no way they could know that. The sparks that had flown when Robby went to confront her on his own had taken them both by surprise. But the detective will ask again what he dropped into Gayle's car, and he still can't come up with an answer that won't make him even more of a suspect. Robby swallows, his tongue sticking to the roof of his mouth. "I'm done answering questions." He shoots the detective a quick look, then forces his gaze down to his hands on the table. His wedding ring gleams.

He and Gayle had been so careful. Except Gayle had told Christine. The cops must be guessing. Or what if Gayle had told someone else too? There's not enough air in the room, and the pulse on the side of Robby's neck flutters like the gills of a landed fish.

"Think about this carefully," Simonson says. "Right now, I'm just gathering information. You start refusing to answer, I might think you're hiding something."

Robby shakes his head. "I swear to you, you're wasting your time. But if there's anything else, you can talk to my lawyer." He looks past the detective at the shining kitchen, his home, his lifeboat. He's losing it. He's going to drown, just like Dad, sucked under by a riptide of his own weaknesses.

Simonson inclines his head with that half smile on his face. "In that case, Mr. Rawlins, you might want to give them a heads-up."

Christine walks in two minutes later. Robby, just sliding the unwrapped pizzas into the preheated oven, turns to her. Her smile is hopeful, but her eyes are reddened and she carries herself as if braced for a blow. He's done this to her with all his shit. How much she must love him, how much she loves the kids, to keep trying.

Robby feels sick.

31

PHIL

....

1988

When Phil's plane landed in Portland, Oregon, she rented a car and pulled up late to Val and Russ's house in Horace. Another argument with Ned had overshadowed her travel. Adoption versus giving up was what it came down to. He wanted to give up. Was she ready?

Not really. Except the self-centered belligerent man Ned had become would make a terrible father.

Phil shook it off. The windows of Teague House were all aglow, strange for a school night. She and Val hadn't been allowed to stay up past nine-thirty on weeknights until they were in high school, but their parents had been stricter than most. Maybe Val let the kids stay up to greet her.

With her suitcase she hurried to the door. The bell ding-donged and went silent. She hit it again and heard quick steps from inside. A pink-cheeked Sandra threw the door open and stared at Phil as if she were a ghost. The girl wore a Care Bears nightie that looked like it might have fit two or three years back, and her dark hair hung in two crooked braids.

"Auntie!" Sandra cried. "You're here! Mom, Auntie's here!"

An indistinct yell, then Jon was flying down the slippery wooden stairs in stocking feet, six inches taller than when she'd seen him at Mom's funeral a couple years back. He wore ripped jeans and a Metallica T-shirt. Where had her little Jonboy gone?

"Is it okay if I come in?" Phil asked, smiling despite her unease. Since Mom's death, she seesawed between worrying about Val and trying to convince herself Russ would tell her if something was really wrong. But would he? Or would he hide things to keep his wife's sister from prying into their lives?

Sandra threw her arms around her, holding on for a long moment until Jon tapped her on the shoulder. "Let her in."

Sandra stepped back, looking embarrassed. "We didn't know you were coming!"

Phil shut the door. The smell of burnt marshmallows and menthol cigarettes enveloped her. "Should we be quiet? Is your brother asleep?"

"Robby? Nah, he's in the living room with Mom. They're working on Legos," Jon said and exchanged a glance with Sandra. "Did Mom and Dad know you were coming?"

Phil set down her things next to the door and stepped out of her shoes. "Oh, I think so. Is your Dad around?"

"Out in his studio."

"A studio, that's new," Phil said. "Awesome."

"Yeah. It's over by the woods so he and the band can play as loud as they want."

Phil started down the hall toward the living room. Jon and Sandra fell in behind her. "How's your mom?" Phil asked casually.

Jon shrugged. "Fine."

"Yeah? Your dad too?"

"Yeah."

In the living room, Legos were scattered across the rug in all their pointy glory. In their midst sat Val, cigarette burning unheeded in the ashtray behind her as she peered at a block structure held in one hand. Robby lay on the flowered couch in Star Wars pajamas, thumb in his mouth, struggling to keep his eyes open. At Phil's entrance, he pushed up to his elbows.

"Hey, Phil," Val said lazily. "Oh my god, I thought you were coming tomorrow. I totally meant to clean up." She grimaced at the mess around her and reached back for her cigarette. When her loose sleeve pulled up, Phil spotted a hand-sized bruise yellowing on her sister's bony forearm, and her heart sank even as she waded in and dipped to give her sister half a hug and a kiss on the cheek. Val smelled of beer and sweat, her hair lank over her shoulders.

"No problem," Phil said. "You never have to clean for me. You're the one with three kids, right? I'm here to help you out."

She continued to the couch where she wrapped an arm around Robby and gave him a squeeze.

"Right," Val said agreeably. She set the cigarette down and squinted at the Legos in front of her. "I'm gonna get the kids to bed after I finish one last thing. Okay, Robby?" Her words were slurred. Phil's heart sank. She hoped it was just one beer too many and not something worse. At the funeral, Russ had mentioned she was on lithium for her moods, which meant she shouldn't drink. But Val avoided topics she didn't want to talk about, so Phil had no idea what current prescriptions she had, if any.

Lightly, she said, "Yeah? Well, you heard her, guys! Sounds like bedtime. We'll have to do our catching up tomorrow."

....

At 4:30 in the morning, from the uncomfortable foldout couch in the living room, Phil heard Russ come in and make coffee before his truck engine roared. She rose shortly after, getting the kids off to school while Val slept in. She cleaned up a little and then, curious, went to check out Russ's studio, where he'd apparently spent the night. What did he get up to out there? She found it just past the rear corner of the yard, on the outskirts of the wood—a large shed with two curtained windows, raised up on blocks with a concrete stoop in front. An overflowing can of butts sat on the stoop, a cardboard case of empty

Bud cans in easy reach. The door was locked, and the curtains blocked the windows well enough she could only make out slices: metal shelving on a plywood floor, Russ's guitar on a stand, an overstuffed couch covered with an old sheet. Hard to imagine a whole band in there—it must be a tight fit.

Phil chewed her lip. How much time did Val and Russ spend isolated from one another these days? That couldn't be good for her sister. Unless Russ had changed. She pictured the bruise on her sister's arm and thought, Russ? No. It must be something else. He'd never had a temper, and he'd had all the patience in the world for Val.

She wandered down a trail toward the river she remembered from a long-ago visit. In the quiet beauty of the morning, some of her anxiety fell away. The stark contrast between Russ and Val's messy life full of responsibility—three children, constant money issues, the sprawling property—Phil's relationship suddenly seemed simple and free of strings. She could leave Ned so easily. And she would. She didn't know where she would go or what she would do, but the horizon was open.

She sat and watched the water flow over and around a collection of skull-sized rocks midstream, then stuck her hand in and the chill sent a bracing shudder right up to her shoulder. Valerie should be up by now, and she walked faster on the way back.

....

Val left for a grocery run, saying she'd be back in an hour or so, and reminding Phil to meet Robby's early kindergarten bus. She'd dressed and put on lipstick, startlingly bright on her wan face, then disappeared out the front door with a list clutched in her hand.

Phil snooped upstairs in the empty house. It wasn't that she was spying, although there was a teeny thrill of breaking a taboo. She just needed to know Val was okay. Mom had always done it and updated Phil on her medicine cabinet and booze stash and sex toys in whispered phone calls that Phil had found both inappropriate and fascinating. Her sister's life was the opposite of hers. Sordid, while Phil's was vice-free. Messy, while Phil's was efficient. Gossip-worthy, while Phil's was tedious.

The bedroom was a large corner room, lit only by the glow of sunlight edging the heavy drapes still covering two sets of large windows. The drapes moved—one of the windows was open behind them, letting in fresh air, but not enough. The reek of menthol cigarettes blended in a sickly way with floral air freshener. The flowered quilt was tangled with dark sheets, and a finger of clear liquid in a water glass was on the nightstand next to the overflowing ashtray. A vodka bottle was tucked in the cubby under the nightstand drawer.

Russ's nightstand was clean and only Val's clothes were strewn on the floor. Phil peeked in the bathroom. Damp towels hung over the shower curtain rod and another full ashtray sat on the counter next to the open window, ashes scattering in the spring breeze. Val's perfumes and makeup crowded a small vanity table against one wall, her lipstick from this morning still uncapped on its surface.

The medicine cabinet was jammed, an army of amber prescription bottles dominating their over-the-counter compatriots. Too many to check them all. She randomly grabbed a few. Amoxicillin for Jon, dated 1983, and Russ, 1986. Prozac for Valerie, last year. Valium for Russ, last month. Lithium, dated two months ago. Phil peeked inside. Five pills left, whatever that meant.

She made it to the bus stop just in time to meet Robby, who chattered to her about his adventures at school. She fed him and they played together until the older children arrived. There was no sign of Valerie. Maybe she'd taken advantage of Phil's presence to stock up at a big discount store, but she'd said she'd be back in an hour or so.

Russ arrived after Jon and Sandra had gone upstairs to do their homework. Phil heard his truck and went out onto the side porch to greet him. He looked older, stooped even, as he climbed slowly from the cab. His jeans drooped low on his hips despite his belt. He glanced toward the house but didn't spot her. If he had any concept of the kids' schedule, he must know they were home, and that Valerie wasn't, since her car was gone. Instead of mounting the stairs though, he began to trudge across the back lawn.

Irritation tightened her shoulders. What was so important he couldn't even acknowledge her before running off to hide in the studio? Was he ashamed?

Phil called, "Russ! Hey, Russ! Aren't you going to say hello?"

For a second she thought he would ignore her. But when he turned, his smile looked genuine. His ponytail had receded an inch or so off his forehead, and with the weight loss, his face had become long and bony. Jon looked like him, with Val's hazel eyes in Russ's narrow face.

"Philly!" he said. "That your car?" He strode toward her with more energy in his step.

"Don't call me that! Please!"

On the porch, he wrapped her in a hug and smiled down at her. The shadows under his eyes were deep, and she wondered if he'd slept at all.

"I flew in from Chicago last night. Val went grocery shopping. I've been hanging out with the kids. Are you heading to your studio?"

"I was going to catch a nap before dinner," he said. "But I'll come in and chat for a few minutes."

"You knew I was coming, right?" she said. "You don't mind?"

"Oh, yeah. No, I think it's great. Glad you're here. Come on, I'll drink some coffee and we can catch up."

He started into the kitchen, but she caught at his sleeve. When he turned to her, she went tongue-tied for a moment.

"Before we go in. Is everything okay? I mean, is Val okay? Is she, you know, taking medication?" She wanted to ask if the two of them were fighting, but that felt like a question too far, especially when his expression closed up at her words.

"She might be struggling, a little." he said after a few moments. "It's good you're here."

He wasn't going to make this easy for her. "Is she doing okay with the kids?" she tried again. "I mean, sometimes it can be overwhelming—three kids."

"The kids are fine," he said firmly. "We're fine."

"I know. I'm just trying to figure out how I can help."

"Spend time with Val," he said. "That's all she needs. A little adult companionship. A bubble bath, once in a while. A little free time."

She wondered why, if Val needed companionship so badly, he wasn't the one giving it to her, but she bit her tongue. No doubt it was more complicated than that, as things always were with Val.

By four-thirty, when she still wasn't home, Phil considered concocting a soup out of a few mealy potatoes, a couple of sprouted onions, and some limp carrots and celery. She rummaged through the cupboards, looking for bouillon or canned tomatoes or beans, but all she found were two cans of SpaghettiOs. There had been pantry shelves in the basement last time she was here, she remembered.

Phil opened the door to a steep and narrow flight of stairs.

A switch lit a square of dingy concrete at the bottom with a sickly yellow glow. Even though the house was fairly new, the basement smelled dank under the corrosive stench of bleach, and as she descended, she noticed a rusty stain stretching across the floor as if they'd had flooding issues. She wrinkled her nose.

At the bottom, another light switch awaited, and fluorescent overheads dispelled the spookiness. The wooden pantry shelves ran alongside the stairs, sagging under a mix of store-bought and home-canned goods.

A stampede above her head, and cries of "Mom's home!" and "Did you get ice cream?" alerted her that Val had finally returned. Quickly, Phil grabbed canned tomatoes and black beans and corn, then shoved them back. She wouldn't need to make bottom-of-the-refrigerator soup after all.

Val's even footsteps were distinct from the kids'. As Phil started up, she heard grocery bags being dumped onto the counter. It would be interesting to hear what the excuse would be, but at least Val came through with the food.

Val's silhouette appeared at the top of the stairs.

"You made it!" Phil said.

"What are you doing down there?" Val asked testily.

Phil paused. "I was thinking of making soup for dinner. Checking out your canned goods."

"Where are they, then?"

Phil narrowed her eyes. She knew this Val, paranoid and

accusatory. When they'd scrapped in her teen years, she'd learned some tricks to derail the argument her sister wanted to pick. Now, her sister wanted to fight to call attention away from her lateness.

"Where have you been?" Phil said lightly, refusing to engage. "Did you go all the way to Portland for groceries?"

Val didn't move. "Why were you in the basement?" she said again.

"I was going to make soup, but we don't need it now, because you brought food, right? Boy, I thought you'd be back a while ago, did everything go okay?"

"I don't want you nosing around," Val said.

Phil had snooped as hard as she could and seen little of interest, so Val's resentment seemed misplaced. "I wasn't nosing around," she snapped, then mentally kicked herself. Sinking to Val's level fed into the negative spiral.

"I trusted you alone in my house."

Phil heard at least one kid in the kitchen behind Val. She raised her voice. "Me and Robby sure had a good time. And Jon and Sandra got right down to homework after a snack."

Val's arms were crossed in a belligerent pose one stair above her. Phil forced a smile. "Your kids are pretty great," she said. "Do you want help unpacking? What's for dinner?" She set her foot on Val's step, bracing to shove past. Beyond Val, Phil could see Sandra, worried eyes on the grown-ups while she removed food from brown paper bags on the kitchen table.

The door that led out to the side porch slammed loudly, and Robby's piping voice said, "Mama!" He flew across the kitchen and flung his arms around Val's waist. She turned to embrace him, and Phil slipped past into the kitchen. She still didn't know where Val had been for five hours, but for a minute there it had felt like her sister was planning to lock her in the basement. Just getting out was a victory.

After the groceries were put away, the kids disappeared back upstairs. "I'll make tea," Phil told Val. "Can we sit down for a minute?" She'd been studying Val. Her sister seemed sober but defensive.

"I'm not in the mood for tea," Val said. "I'm fine."

"Okay," Phil said. She put the kettle on anyway, then turned and lowered her voice, hoping Val would do the same. "Then where the hell were you?"

Val flinched, but she came closer to Phil, her body tightening. "I didn't realize when you came to visit you were going to be tracking my every move."

Phil let out a bark of stifled mirth. "Val, you said you were going to be gone for an hour and you disappeared for *five*! No phone call, no explanation. And then you try to pick a fight?"

Val huffed a sigh and ran her fingers through her hair. She jerked out a kitchen chair and sank into it. "I'm sorry," she said. "I just couldn't make myself come back."

Phil took a deep breath and sat across from her sister. "What do you mean?" she said more gently.

"I couldn't make myself turn around." She lowered her voice to a near whisper. "I didn't want to come home." Her eyes shone with tears, but she blinked them rapidly away.

Phil's eyes watered in sympathy for a split second before she caught herself. Classic Val. Taking off for five hours doing who knows what, then making a play for pity instead of apologizing and taking responsibility. Phil sucked in a breath and rose to busy herself getting mugs and tea bags ready, hands shaking. When the kettle finally boiled, she set one mug in front of Val and returned to her seat with a semblance of calm compassion. "You don't have to drink it," she said. The soothing scent of chamomile reached her nose. Val drew hers close and blew on the steaming surface.

"I love my kids," Val said.

"I know."

"I don't know what's wrong with me."

"Is it Russ? Is something going on with him?"

"What? No, of course not. Russ is fine. Russ is normal."

That sounded like too much protest. Phil bit her lip uneasily. "Are you still seeing that psychiatrist?"

Val shrugged. "I'm seeing someone, yeah. And I'm on medication. But sometimes it seems like I just feel worse and worse. Some days are hard. Some weeks are hard."

Phil looked at her helplessly. "What does the doctor say?"

"That it's normal. That I need to find healthy ways to cope. That everyone feels that way sometimes."

"Yeah, but." Phil tripped over her tongue, trying to figure out how to say it without giving offense. Val had had at least one affair, and though she'd shared that, she'd never shared how it resolved. What if Russ had turned on her sister? "Are you and Russ okay?"

Val stared down into the teacup. "Not what I used to call okay. But pretty okay for right now."

"He's not…hurting you?"

"What? No!" Val pushed away the mug, stood up, the chair scraping away from the table across the tiled floor. "Listen, I know you mean well. I'm sorry I was out for so long, okay? I promise I won't do it again. But I don't feel like the third degree right now."

Phil nodded. She'd lost her. For a second, it had felt like Val was going to trust her to help, the way she'd trusted Mom. Sometimes. Sometimes she'd pushed her away too. When Robby was born, Val hadn't let Mom, Dad, or Phil visit for months. They'd gotten all their updates about the baby over the phone.

Phil offered a smile. "I guess I'll go for a walk before it's time to eat. Do you want to come?"

"No, thanks," Val said. Her fingers massaged her scalp, knuckles white. She kept her back to Phil.

"I don't have to go now, if you want help with cooking," Phil tried.

"Even I can manage TV dinners."

"Okay. I'll be back in an hour."

"Wait a sec," Val said.

Phil turned.

"Would you mind grabbing these and stashing them in the pantry before you go?" She pointed to a single brown grocery bag that had been left on the end of the counter. "It's the stuff that belongs downstairs. I'm going to lie down for a few minutes while the kids are being quiet."

"Okay," Phil said. Val's voice was apologetic. She was making a point about trusting Phil with her canned goods, which Phil had to acknowledge, however silly the whole issue had been. "No problem."

The bag was heavy, with cans at the bottom and boxes of pasta on top. Phil cradled it in both arms down the narrow stairs, thinking of the silver lining. Val never used to apologize, not sincerely. This was progress. Val had as much as admitted her suspicion of Phil's presence in the basement was ridiculous. It was something.

Phil shelved the food. Her sister should check her stash next time she went shopping, because some of the cans were joining dozens of the same kind, but at least the family would be set in an emergency. She folded the bag and headed upstairs at a trot, chalking up the afternoon as semi-positive. The kids had a good time, got their homework done, spent a little time with Auntie. Valerie disappeared but managed to come back. They'd almost had a heart-to-heart discussion.

Smiling to herself, she looked up to see Val dart into the doorway, arms forward. Phil shrieked and tumbled back, feeling her leg twist under her.

32

MADDIE

....

FRIDAY

I reach Horace early Friday morning hoping to flesh out the Rawlinses' lives around the time of Davina's disappearance. My mind is preoccupied by the disturbing doggerel that Val scribbled on the backs of those flyers. *Mercy for the lost.* Was it Val who was lost? Russ, because of his suicide? Or the poor souls buried in the woods?

I'm also worried about what Sandra said about the break-in. She showed me the secret cubbyhole in the laundry room cupboard, and she's right; it would have been very hard to find without knowing it was already there. Either someone in the family is lying, or an outsider has inside knowledge of the house.

When I arrive downtown, I refill my travel mug at the café, then walk down Main Street to the Antique & Junk Shop, which I learned yesterday is owned by Nathan Belter, the guy on Valerie's flyers. If I'm lucky, he'll be able to offer a window into their lives closer to the time of the murder, from a nonfamily point of view. Maybe he can also lead me to others who knew them.

The shop is a narrow slice of a shingled building, with a large bay window. On display are a wooden calliope pony on a gold post, several musical instruments, a dressmaker's dummy, and a velvet jewelry tray full of silver rings and bangles. The website claimed this shop would open at nine, but it's completely dark inside, the door locked. I'm annoyed to see the clock hands on the sign are set to eleven.

There's a phone number for consignment appointments, and I take my phone out to dial but see that Sandra's just texted.

I've got something to show you. Come over as soon as you can.

Ten minutes later, I'm in her dining room looking down at an open metal box the size of a lunch box, but slimmer, and with a combination lock. A torn plastic bag lies to one side.

"I tried not to touch anything, once I figured out that the police will want to see, but Denny ripped open the bag before I realized, and Jon and I poked around a little," she says apologetically.

"So you haven't sifted through all the papers? What is all this stuff?"

"More of Mom's sketches, as far as I can tell. I was hoping for Aunt Phil's letter, but unless it's torn into pieces, there aren't any full sized sheets of paper in here. There could be more little poems or quotes or whatever too. I just don't know." Her voice sounds sad, and she points with a pencil. "This is what bothers me though."

She indicates a silver chain and nudges a piece of paper aside to reveal a pair of rings. "These are the rings Dad buried that night."

They look like wedding bands, sterling silver or possibly white gold but dull and grimy. When I bend over and squint at them, I can make out a partial engraving on the inside. "*MC—*" My heart stutters. Hardly unusual initials, but Eb said one of the victims was identified as Michael Cable.

"And this—" She points to a photo of Valerie with an infant on her lap and Nathan Belter by her side, as he'd been in the newspaper article.

"Do you have a sandwich bag I could use? I'd love to see if there's any writing on the back of that photo, but I don't want to touch, just in case."

Sandra hurries out of the room and comes back with a small plastic bag. I slip it over my hand and flip the photo over. "1984" is scrawled across the back.

As I go to set it down, I freeze. The inside corner of the box has been revealed, and a small bead nestles there: no more than a quarter inch in diameter, dark red Fimo with a wavy white line pinpricked with green dots in the curves. I recognize that bead. I was there the day Davina selected the red beads for her friend Grace to weave into her braids. Baby Rose had been sleeping in a playpen next to the couch, Davina and I had played gin rummy, and we'd all watched *Days of Our Lives* with the volume down low as Grace worked.

Someone here had touched Davina's hair. My stomach flips over.

"What is it?" Sandra asks.

I hesitate, then decide to trust her. "That's Davina's. The little bead, stuck in the corner. She had those red beads in her hair when she disappeared."

Her eyes grow wide. "God. What is going on? How did Mom get this stuff?"

I want to confiscate the box, but I stop myself. I'm not a cop, and Sandra already knew the rings might tie her father to the murders before she chose to show me anything. She can be trusted, but just in case, I snap a picture. I'll share it with Mama Hempel for confirmation about the bead. I tell Sandra, "No one should touch any of this, okay?"

"I promise," she whispers. "I'll keep Denny out of here, and we won't touch anything."

"No more thoughts about the letter your dad left for your aunt? Did you try again to reach her?"

Sandra shakes her head. "Auntie's still not picking up; only now her voicemail box is full."

I point at the photo. "I know who that is. It's the same guy as on the flyer, right?"

"That's what Jon and I thought. It's blurry though. What do you think?" Her purse is slung over one of the chairs, and she digs in it to pull out the flyer again. We both look from the flyer to the much sharper photograph.

"Hang on, I found a newspaper photo too." On my phone, I pull up the shot I'd taken from the microfiche reader yesterday. "Look at all three. The distance between the eyes. The shape of the overall head and face, the placement of the ears."

She nods slowly. "Yeah, it's him. The question is, does it help us?"

I shrug. "Well, from the newspaper, we have his name. It's Nathan Belter. And he knew your parents. They were all on the same committee. I'm going see if he'll talk to me. He may remember something about your parents' activities and state of mind back then."

"He may know more than that. This photo—it makes it look like they were in love."

We both look down at it. "Hard to say from a snapshot. Your brothers around?"

"No. Jon took Denny to a waterslide park, and I guess Robby's over at the cottage. I haven't seen him."

"Do you want to come with me?" I ask impulsively.

She looks excited for a second, then says, "I better not. I'm supposed to go back to work on Monday, and I've still got to sort through some of Mom's things. Who knows, maybe I'll get lucky and find the letter."

"Keep me posted. And keep the doors locked," I add.

Outside I climb into my purple Kia and drum my fingers on the steering wheel in Sandra's driveway.

Finally, I text Eb:

Pls txt asap. Important evidence @ rawlinses' place.

I set the phone on the passenger seat and stare at it unhappily. My stomach rumbles and the phone does nothing. However momentous it feels to have discovered what may be a serial killer's trophies, I need lunch, and Eb is too busy to check his phone every five minutes.

After a sandwich, I feel better, but Eb still hasn't gotten back to me. I bite my lip, then leave him a message through the nonemergency police number. Afterwards, I approach the junk shop again, silencing my phone before I go in to avoid interruption.

This time, the lights are on, and when I enter, a tiny bell tinkles and a smiling white-haired woman in a bright pink cardigan says, "Welcome!"

The shop smells of citrus and sandalwood, and it's cluttered with pieces of antique furniture mixed in with more modern kitsch. High price tags dangle tastefully on tiny brown tags. My mom, who used to drag me to every shop with the word "Junk" in the title within a hundred mile radius, would've hated it.

I look around hesitantly. There's no sign of Nathan Belter or any other customers in the store. Approaching the front counter, I say, "I was hoping to talk to Mr. Belter. Is he around?"

"No, I'm afraid not. He generally comes in, but he had some work to do over at the warehouse. Is there anything I can help you with?"

I haven't yet decided whether to approach Belter as a potential customer or a private investigator, as it depends on my sense of who he'll be more willing to chat with, so I can't be completely honest with this woman. She's old enough to have known the Rawlinses though. "I'm thinking of consigning some collectibles. Is that something he takes care of?"

"Oh, yes. You could either head out to the warehouse—it's on Route Twenty-Six, you can't miss it—or pop back in here tomorrow. We open at eleven on Saturdays."

I look for inspiration, and my eyes light on a row of half a dozen angel figurines on a glass shelf behind her head, each holding a different flower. "What days do you work?"

"Normally, Tuesday and Thursday."

"Oh? Maybe you helped my friend. Sandra Rawlins? She came in here looking for a gift a couple weeks ago."

The woman looks fascinated. "Really. I didn't think she'd come all the way up here for a gift! Doesn't she live down south somewhere?"

I kick myself mentally for forgetting how very small this town is. "Yes. I'm sure she meant the last time she was visiting. Do you know the Rawlinses?"

"Oh, not so much."

"It's so sad about her mother."

"I know. Hard to believe she died so young, after having so many troubles!"

"Sandra wanted to get one of those little angel thingies behind you," I say, "but she was hoping for one with a daffodil and you didn't have one. I'm not sure she saw that one with the other yellow flower though, can I see that?"

She hands it over to me, and I study it as I ask, "Did you live in Horace when Russ Rawlins was building Teague House?"

"Oh, yes! My husband was an electrician, you know. Russ insisted on doing all his own wiring and it passed inspection too, but my husband was always saying Teague House may sound grand and look grand, but someday it's going to burn right down." She giggles.

I blink, not finding the premise of an entire family burning up quite so funny, but I summon up a chuckle and hand her the angel. "Can I see the one with the pink rose? Thanks. So you didn't really know Valerie back then?"

"Well, she kept to herself even then. Although I do remember—do you know, she actually had this job at one time? She worked for the Belters and even joined Nathan's little church group, back when he used to preach. He had them all wearing robes and playing music... The whole town wondered if he was going to up and abandon the store to preach on the road, for a while, but he went the other way and settled into his businesses. Just as well, really. Some of the things he'd say. He's a good man, Nathan, but not a tolerant one."

I remember the words on the flyer—*Community of Love.* Even though I think I know the answer, I cross my fingers and ask, "I had no idea there'd been anything like that around here. Did you belong to this church group?"

"Oh, no. My husband and I didn't really do church; it just wasn't our thing. We brought up three lovely children who all went on to become doctors. One of them is Jewish now." She nods happily.

"Any other folks you can remember who were in Belter's church? I'd love to hear more about it. I'm an anthropologist. At the college. I study religions." I smile, hoping that sounds more believable to her than it does to me.

She doesn't seem to have a problem with it. "Let's see, I think Linda Atwater might have joined, but you know, she moved to New York City twenty years ago. Franklin, what was his name? Eric Franklin. But I heard he died last year. Stroke? Or maybe heart attack. No, I think Nate himself is probably the last one still around. And you'll be lucky if you get him to talk about it. He's become so respectable over the years, it's hard to imagine him going around in a homespun robe and bare feet with daisies in his hair, isn't it?"

"I suppose it is," I say. The angel has a price tag of $29.95. I hand it back to her feeling guilty for not buying anything after she's been so forthcoming. "I'm not really sure Sandra would like this. I'll have to double-check with her about the flowers. Thanks for the chat though."

She slides the angel back on the shelf and settles down to her crochet project again. "Lovely talking with you. Good luck."

33

SANDRA

Sandra groans into the silence after Maddie leaves. She'd decided last night to show the lockbox to the private detective, needing a nonfamily take on the contents, but Maddie's grim expression has shaken her. Despite everything she'd hoped, it's looking more and more like Dad killed those people, and kept trophies, which Mom saved and locked away.

Maybe Mom had been trying to protect her children.

The thought brings back an image from the nightmare the alarm dragged her out of this morning: Mom, young and beautiful in an extravagant white dress, standing within a deep grave and proffering a chain of wedding bands up to Sandra on the surface.

Sandra tilts her head back and sucks in a deep breath. This house, this situation, has not been conducive to good sleep. She wishes Jon hadn't left her alone today, but he seemed to think taking Denny to Tom's party might help Robby some-how. In the meantime, she's left with actually talking to Robby. No matter his own mess, he needs to be updated on the lock-box and its confirmed connection to one of the victims. He should be warned that behind the mask of affable yet moody carpenter/musician, Dad may have been a serial killer.

Unless Robby already knows. Unless that's how Gayle ended up buried in that clearing.

She stands so abruptly it sends pain zinging down from her injured tendon to her big toe. Bullshit. Her brother is not a killer. There's some other explanation, and she's not in denial; she just doesn't have the full picture. She grabs her phone and texts Robby for the fourth time.

I give up. If you won't come to me, I'll come to you.

....

She buzzes the cottage doorbell three times before the door finally swings open. Robby's standing there in unshaven in flannel pajama pants, a blanket around his shoulders.

"I don't care," he says and begins to close the door.

She pushes past him, then halts, wondering if she's in the wrong house. Everything shines, and instead of the smell of old pizza and a scattering of dirty socks and plates all over the place, there's the smell of waffles.

"Christine is back?" Sandra says. She remembers, belatedly, that it's a no-school day. "The girls?"

"They were. They left. Hey, did you know it's not a good idea to accuse your spouse of murder?"

Sandra stares at him. "Are you drunk?"

"No. Not at all. I've just lost everything. It feels kind of the same."

She pulls him to the couch. "Sit down."

He collapses obediently and leans his head back to stare at the ceiling. He says nothing.

"Well? What happened? Christine asked if you killed Gayle?"

He smirks but doesn't look at her. "Nope. Guess again."

"You're not saying…you asked Christine if she killed Gayle? You thought your wife murdered a woman because you slept with her?" Sandra's mind boggles. She stares at him.

He laughs a little. "Yeah! Right? Crazy." He sucks in a breath. "Christine told me that she knew I slept with Gayle, that Gayle told her. Like a sucker, I believed her. And I figured, you know. Teague Wood. It's right there."

"Your wife. You thought your wife, who asks for your help opening cranberry sauce cans every Thanksgiving because she can't manage the can opener, overpowered a grown woman and dragged her bodily into the woods. Because of you."

Robby sits up, rubs his face hard. "Okay! I'm a fucking idiot. I wasn't thinking straight. Forgive me, okay? I'm about to be arrested. I know I didn't do it, so I'm a little stressed about who did."

Sandra feels a tiny stirring of pity. He really is an idiot. What Christine ever saw in him, she can't imagine.

"She packed up and left?"

"We put the kids to bed. I accused her of murder. She made me sleep on the couch and bundled them out first thing in the morning. Some bullshit about her mother needing them again. She wouldn't even look at me."

"You've been sitting here feeling sorry for yourself ever since? Ignoring my texts?"

"I guess. Pretty much the only reason I ever do anything is Christine." His voice is colorless.

"Or Gayle? Or whoever else?"

He shrugs. "I tried to get through to Aunt Phil. Nothing. Oh, by the way, also in my shitty life, the police have a video of me slipping the phone into Gayle's car. That detective, Simonson, came by yesterday afternoon."

Sandra has called and texted Auntie a couple more times herself and is beginning to think she must be out of range, because she wouldn't ignore Robby being in trouble. "Why didn't you call me or Jon?"

He shrugs. "Last night I was too happy my wife was home, figured I'd deal with it today. And today—I didn't want to have this conversation. The one we're having right now. I think they're going to arrest me. Some kids were hiding in the bushes that day, messing around, and they got the whole thing on video."

A chill goes up her back. "What did you tell the detective?"

"Nothing! I told him he'd have to talk to my lawyer with any more questions."

"Jon left a message for that guy in Polallie. I'll see if he got back to him." She sends the text. "So, on the video, you're just putting the phone in her car?"

"It shows me stuffing a bag through the cracked window. I didn't tell Simonson what was in it. He's focused on the idea that I had a grudge and was harassing her, but if he knows it was an affair, won't that be worse?"

Sandra shakes her head. "I don't know. This is why you need a lawyer."

Robby stands and starts to pace. "I can't take this. How the fuck is this my life?"

Sandra watches him in silence. The silver lining of him blowing up his marriage is she finally fully believes in his innocence. She sighs. He may not care very much right this second, but he still deserves to know about their father.

He pauses in his pacing to stare out the window toward the woods.

"Robby."

"What?"

"I came over to tell you something else that's going to be hard to hear. Sit down."

"Fuck that. Just tell me. What is it?"

Briefly, she tells him about the rings and the beads in the lockbox, and her theory that Mom hid the trophies that proved Dad was a killer. She doesn't mention the calendar, which seems to suggest Dad was away during of the deaths—she doesn't want to raise false hope. "I think Mom was trying to protect us," she says, hoping that this will give Robby a measure of comfort the way it has her.

Robby's Adam's apple bobs. "No. No way. This is about a bead that some private detective saw? A frigging bead! How can she tell one bead from another?" His voice rises.

"I believe her. And I saw Dad with those rings, the same ones in the box. The night he died, he was burying them by the graves in Teague Wood. How do you explain that?"

His face crumples and he opens his mouth just as her phone vibrates. It's Jon getting back to her, and she holds up her finger. "Just a sec." She moves away from Robby to talk to Jon in the kitchen.

"What's up, sis?" Jon says over a raucous background.

"Did that lawyer get back to you?"

"Not yet."

"We need to talk to them as soon as possible." She starts to tell Jon about the video, but the shouting in the background gets louder and he interrupts.

"I can't hear you very well. I'll call them and give your number this time. Listen, I talked to Marcus—"

Through the kitchen window, Sandra sees a police car pull into Robby's driveway, followed by a dark gray SUV.

"Hang on, the cops are here. I'll call you back," she says, forcing calm into her voice as she turns to meet Robby's eyes.

Detectives Boon and Simonson approach with two uniformed officers.

Robby gets up as if in a dream and opens the door before they ring the bell. Sanda moves to hover by his shoulder. She feels her phone buzz as she puts it in her pocket and hopes Jon's letting her know he's calling the lawyer.

"Robert Rawlins, we have a warrant to search your home," Detective Boon says formally.

Sandra flicks her eyes across their stony faces.

Robby backs slightly away from the door. "You won't find anything," he says. "I didn't kill her." He turns entreating eyes to Sandra.

"He has to allow this?" She addresses Detective Boon, who seemed to be in charge last Sunday.

"He does. You'll have to wait outside. This shouldn't take long." She hands Sandra a packet of paper folded into thirds.

Robby and Sandra file out to the driveway, Robby still in his pajama bottoms and bare feet, with a blanket wrapped around his shoulders. One of the officers follows them and stands on the stoop. "Should we wait in the car?" Sandra asks Robby.

"I'm fine out here," he says, but walks toward the swing set and lowers himself onto a swing.

Sandra follows and perches on the bottom of the slide. She'd love to know what changed between the cops showing Robby the video yesterday and serving a warrant today. She skims the papers for details.

"They're looking for a cell phone with a specific number," she tells Robby. "And/or jewelry belonging to Gayle."

"They won't find anything," he repeats. "Gayle's never been here." His face is bloodless. Sandra reaches to squeeze one of his hands, and it's freezing.

Minutes pass. She pulls up the message on her phone and sees Jon asked the lawyer to call her as soon as possible. She responds with an update about the search warrant. She and Robby wait in silence until the front door opens and the officer on the stoop moves over to allow the blond detective to come out.

Sandra checks Robby's expression. He slowly rises so that he's standing by the time she reaches them, Detective Simonson on her heels.

Detective Boon holds a plastic bag in one latex-gloved hand. "This item was reported stolen by Gayle Bethested last year. Can you explain its presence in your home, Mr. Rawlins?" she asks.

Sandra stands and leans in, trying to make out the object through the shine of the plastic. It's an old-fashioned jeweled brooch in the shape of a preening peacock. Probably costume jewelry, with the tiny blue and green gems made of glass or crystal, but she's not an expert.

She looks to Robby's face, which has gone even paler.

"No," he says. "I can't explain that at all."

Detective Simonson moves up to flank him. "We're placing you under arrest, Mr. Rawlins," he says, almost gently.

34

MADDIE

....

After lunch, Google Maps directs me out of town along a rural highway, where signs for local honey, vegetables, and fresh eggs abound. A metal roof sporting "JUNK WAREHOUSE" in ten-foot-high letters looms over a chain link fence on my left, and through the plastic privacy slats I spy a yard full of rusted cars, washing machines, old bicycles, bathtubs, toilets, and more. A metal and concrete warehouse presides over the fenced area, followed by an empty gravel parking lot.

I park and sit for a minute, thinking about what the pink-sweatered woman in the downtown shop told me about Nathan Belter's so-called church group. Sandra made her parents sound like back-to-the-land granola types, hippies who'd been born just a little too late, but it sounds like, once they settled on their dream acreage in rural Oregon, they felt isolated and found a new group to join that superficially had some similar trappings.

And then…what? Nate's group was less "peace, love, and rock and roll," and more intolerance, to the point of murder? *One hard cut then bliss forever.* I think of the calendar I'd found in the Rawlinses' basement. What if Russ wasn't away at a funeral, but just pretending to be? He drove off, picked up the hitchhiking Davina—surely a lost lamb if there ever was one, probably tearful and full of regrets about leaving her baby. Cut away the dross. He could have killed her out of mercy, for the good of society, according to the teachings of Nate—if Valerie's ramblings on Nate's flyer are linked to him and not just random words scribbled in a random place.

But if Russ was away on construction jobs all the time, why would he bother with a false alibi?

If Russ really had been away at a funeral and hadn't killed Davina and the others, why would Val have the victims' possessions? Val herself could have been his accomplice who went solo while he was away. Or maybe someone else was involved. But then—why did Russ kill himself? Why did Val silence herself, for three decades?

Tired of thinking in circles, I climb out of the car. A guy who supposedly led a bizarre robe-wearing sect and then became a respectable community leader probably won't share much voluntarily with a private detective. Too much to lose. I'll have to stick with the potential consignment story. This place, Mom would have loved—a giant junk store literally in the middle of nowhere—and her collection will give me the verisimilitude I need.

Before I enter, I silence my phone again and check out the flyers and signs choking the glass storefront and door: "Belter for County Commissioner," "Touray for School Board," "Pancake Breakfast at the Lions Club." Through the gaps, I can see a mishmash of crowded shelving holding an eclectic mix of items.

The mouthwatering scent of chocolate chip cookies welcomes me as soon as I open the door. A baking rack is cooling on the countertop, and I realize my sandwich didn't quite fill me up.

"My grandson made those," a man's voice says, and I turn to see a wiry white-haired guy on a stool behind the counter. "They're terrific, but my daughter-in-law said to give 'em away before we eat 'em all. Please, help yourself." He's dapper in a button-down checked shirt, and his silver mustache bristles as he smiles. A gold watch chain dangles from the pocket of his jeans.

The hair has changed color, the face gained some wrinkles and pouches with age, but I'm pretty sure this is the man from the flyer and the newspaper, twenty-odd years later. Returning his smile, I take a cookie. Unbelievably delicious. "Thanks."

"You looking for anything in particular?" he asks.

"Are you Nathan Belter?"

"Call me Nate."

"I saw the sign about consignment on your store down-town." I allow a not-entirely-faked note of distress into my voice. "My mother passed away, and I'm thinking it's time to take care of her things."

"That's a hard thing, I know." He pauses for a respectful moment of silence, then says, "I see it all the time, people who aren't quite ready to let go of their loved one's treasures. And that's fine. There's no rush, no rush at all. Do you want to take a wander, look around for a bit? Ring the bell when you're ready." He gestures to an electronic doorbell button taped to the countertop.

As Maddie, the slightly overwrought customer,, I nod and offer a pained smile. "Sure, that sounds good."

I thread through miscellaneous wares until I reach the back wall. The aisles of pine shelving overflow with everything from stenciled coat hooks to old-style Crock-Pots to battered Chia Pet boxes. A twinkling Christmas tree sports handmade ornaments in a corner otherwise lined with scavenged road signs and license plates. Comic books in plastic sheaths hail back to five cent prices, and a dozen mirrors throw back my bedraggled reflection.

There's no sign of any particular social philosophy or religious belief, just a whole lot of junk.

I find a worn paperback mystery that I'd love to reread, decide I've given myself time to fake calm down, and return to the counter. No one's there, so I hit the electronic button he showed me. It makes no sound. Maybe it buzzes straight to his phone or a speaker in the back room.

I wait a few minutes, but no one comes. The anti-theft domed mirror in the upper corner of the store shows a warped reflection of most of the interior, but I can't see any movement. Sticking to the perimeter instead of weaving through the shelves, I walk through again and discover double swinging doors in a back corner marked "EXIT." They must lead into the warehouse. Nudging the doors open, I peer through and call, "Hello?"

No answer. An unevenly lit space lies beyond, metal roof far above. The volume of junk is overwhelming—some furniture, but lots of smaller stuff, like toilet seats, windshield wipers still in the package, a game of Parcheesi taped shut with curling masking tape. All piled haphazardly on the shelves, definitely not meant for public browsing.

I'm prepared to spout apologies if someone comes running, but no one is in sight, and for a minute or two, I look around, curiosity piqued by the sheer amount of crap. Before long, the looming shelves and silence start to feel eerie, as if I've been abandoned here.

Just when I'm starting to creep myself out, I hear voices. With a surge of irrational relief, I realize I've been clutching my phone like a security blanket, and slide it in my back pocket.

Following the muffled sounds, I spot a makeshift office in one rear corner next to the industrial garage door across the back wall. From the office's unsealed top, voices carry. They're low and intense, but I start making out words as I approach, soft-shoeing across the concrete floor.

"It was safe," Nate is saying. "Some things are unpredictable."

The answering voice is also male, and almost a hiss. "You bastard. That woman—"

I freeze, even as the voice drops low enough to be unintelligible. He can't be talking about me, can he? My ears strain, but all I get is a jumble of syllables. Discomfort tugs at me. I should leave—but I am a professional snoop, after all.

Nate breaks in. "It's a hard thing, I know," echoing what he said to me just a few minutes ago, in the same tone. Is he offering condolences?

I think I hear a sob, and I suddenly worry that I'm eavesdropping on grief, not anger. It's somehow less intriguing and more morally questionable to spy on.

Nate's voice again, still calm. "I'm sorry. We have to burn it down."

I catch my breath, wanting to hear more but sensing, whatever's going on, it's time to retreat. *Burn it down* could be a metaphor for something, a figure of speech—or they could be planning some kind of insurance scam, though I can't imagine how that fits in with someone's death. Unfortunately,

I've never been particularly lucky or graceful. As I turn, my heel hits a box lying next to one of the shelving units, and a high-pitched reverberation rings out like a bell.

The voices stop.

Quickly, I step into the middle of the aisle and call, "Hello?" again just as the door to the office opens. A rangy guy with broad shoulders and a full head of dark hair sticks his head out. He could be the doppelganger of the man on the old flyers. Heart pounding, I smile self-deprecatingly, holding my paperback up like a shield. "I'm so sorry, I rang up front, but no one came."

With a narrow-eyed gaze, he checks me out from head to foot, then pulls back. A moment later, Nate emerges. He shuts the office door firmly and approaches with an uneven gait, stiff in one knee. Now that he's out from behind the counter, I see I'm a full head taller than he is.

"Sorry, I wanted to buy this, and no one came when I rang the bell, and I also wanted to ask about the dragons, the consignment," I babble, aware my two-dollar paperback is not a great excuse to have come into a clearly nonpublic area.

His skeptical expression warms a little. "No problem, no problem. That darn bell, the batteries are always dying." He starts toward the door I came through. "I was just having a chat with my son DJ, got distracted. Sorry about that."

My words come a little too fast as I follow back into the store. "Do you have time to talk about a consignment? I'm not sure it's up your alley, I didn't see anything like Mom's collection. It's pretty large. Two hundred forty-two dragons, some metal, some glass, some ceramic."

He leads the way to the checkout counter and takes the paperback from my hands to ring up. "Huh. You know, we've had quite a few dragons come through recently. A shield painted with a Chinese dragon, a friend of mine bought it for his den. And then we had some glass knickknacks, delicate little things. I think Miriam Holsing bought them for her goddaughter. I sell quite a few things online, as well. This is going to be two dollars, it's three for five if you want to take another look, by the way."

I keep a few small bills in the front of my purse and hand him the cash. "No, thank you."

He passes me the book with a receipt tucked in the front. "Well, here's this. On the dragons, I might consider offering you an up-front price, instead of going consignment. It can be a lot of work to do all the individual pricing and tracking with a collection that large. Sometimes I prefer to buy bulk, but I still offer a fair price. When did your mother pass away?"

"A few weeks ago." Six weeks and two days. "I should be used to it by now, but somehow it keeps taking me by surprise."

"That's not uncommon." He offers a quick smile. "Now, let's see what you've got."

"Oh! Today? I didn't think you'd want them today. I didn't bring them with me. I just wanted to find out how it worked.

The consignment. Although if you want to buy them outright, I guess it will be straightforward."

I hear quick steps behind me and look over my shoulder. It's the other man, the son. Up close, he's handsome, if you like intense guys that spend a lot of time in the gym. Probably five or ten years younger than me. He smiles, revealing whitened teeth.

Nate says, "Well, stop by tomorrow and I'll take a look."

I turn back to him. "Um, here or at the downtown shop?"

He pulls out a spiral-bound calendar and flips it open. "I'm here 'til eleven, downtown after that. Whatever's easier. I have one appointment at two..."

"Is it okay if I come downtown around noon?"

He nods and makes a note in the calendar. The son is behind him, poking around as if looking for something, but obviously waiting for his father to be free. I've missed my chance to talk to Nate privately, but take a stab anyway.

Casually, I ask, "Did I hear you used to be a preacher?"

Nate's cool blue eyes flick to me, startled. He chuckles a millisecond late. "Oh, no. I help out at church some, that's all."

"Someone said it was a long time ago. In the eighties?"

He tilts his head with a smile. "I promise, I'm just a farm-boy who started a junk shop. I talk too much sometimes, but that's as close as I get."

"Oh, well." I shrug. "I'll see you tomorrow with a big box of dragons!" I look down at my bare wrist, where my watch would be if I wore one. "Do you know what time it is?"

He pulls the gold watch from his watch pocket, but before I get much of a look, DJ says, "Two thirty-four."

"Thanks." The spring sunlight is a shock to my eyes when I emerge onto the concrete walk leading to the parking area. Behind me, the bells on the door jingle again, and I turn to see DJ emerge behind me with a cell phone to his ear and a vape stick in his hand. He watches as I climb into my car. I pull away, waving, feeling the uneasy reverberation of Nate's lie.

35

SANDRA

....

Sandra watches her brother being driven away in the back of a police car with the sense that she must be dreaming, then climbs wearily into her own car and returns to the big house, where she reheats leftovers and numbly picks at the food. She supposes she should go up to Mom's room and start sorting through the items Aunt Phil started on the other day. She can fit in a drop-off to Goodwill before dinner.

Instead, she wanders down to the storage area where Dad's boxes are piled. No one's come yet to pick up the lockbox or the calendars yet, and it's shocking to realize that it's only been hours since Maddie was here, confirming Sandra's worst fears.

Sandra plops on the floor and starts emptying the boxes again. The letter that Dad wrote to Aunt Phil may have been lost or destroyed or hidden elsewhere…but there's still a chance it could be in his things. Even if not, Dad knew the answers that Sandra desperately needs, at least some of them, and she can't do anything for Robby right now…

She's much more methodical this time, working her way item by item and spreading everything across the floor, putting like with like. Every single album gets checked inside and out, then sorted alphabetically by band. Every CD case is checked, every notebook, magazine, and calendar riffled through.

As she's lifting the last of the magazines out of the box where Maddie found the calendars, her cell phone rings. A deputy who introduces himself as Deputy Yakowski arranges the collection of both the calendars and the lockbox in forty-five minutes, and instructs her not to touch either.

"I already have," she says. "These are things that were found in my house."

"Well, don't touch them anymore," the deputy says.

Sandra hangs up and sets down her stack of magazines on the concrete floor. In the now-empty box, a single bright bookmark is jammed in the reinforcing flap of cardboard at the bottom. On second thought, it's more likely a magazine subscription card, with rounded edges and a floral design, but it doesn't seem on-brand for the two magazines she's seen, *Fine Woodworking* and *Playboy*. With her fingernail, she tugs it loose. It's made of stiffer, more plasticized card stock than she expects.

Honoring the life of Alexander Everett Rawlins, April 29, 1910~ June 3, 1993. On the back is a prayer.

She's seen one of these before, at the funeral for a friend raised Catholic. It's a prayer card, and it must be in remembrance of her paternal great-grandfather—Dad's grandfather. Pop-pop. She and Maddie came up with a couple reasons her father might still have been in Horace despite the flight notations on his calendar, but unless someone had mailed him the prayer card…it seems likely that he went to the funeral, came back with this memento, and tucked it into one of his notebooks. He was there. He couldn't have been responsible for Davina's disappearance.

Excited, she snaps pictures of the card, front and back, and texts them to Maddie.

....

Denny and Jon arrive shortly before six, and all through dinner, Denny overflows with waterslide stories. His eyes shine as he tells her how many times he went down each slide and how many curves they had and how Dana said his present was the best. Sandra puts two plates of leftovers in front of him one after another, and he inhales them both without seeming to stop talking, then retreats downstairs to play on the Xbox.

Jon has been picking silently at his own plate throughout, and now he collects the dishes and starts rinsing them at the sink.

"You must be exhausted after a whole day of that!" Sandra says when the door shuts behind Denny. "Did you get a chance to talk to Gayle's opponent?"

"I did. Marcus Belter. Gayle's friend Sammy, who was helping her run for office, and my old friend Tommy both said he was the nicest guy in the world. And he was a super nice guy. I agree."

"But?"

"But he wouldn't talk about Gayle at all. He talked for about ten minutes about an initiative to support small business in Melakwa County, and then when I tried to shift the topic to his late opponent, he excused himself to go play in the pool with his son."

"Did he point you to someone else to talk to?"

Jon shrugs, drying his hands on the dish towel. "We should check with Robby's lawyer at this point. You guys went with the guy Tom recommended? He'll come up with a strategy and decide if we need to hire an investigator. I don't know. I can't believe Robby's actually in jail."

He leans on the sink, looking at her. The silence is thick, but she doesn't know how to comfort him, how either of them can be comforted. Aunt Phil would have suggested an adult beverage, she's certain, and almost smiles.

She says, "Yeah, David Grady. He finally got back to me this afternoon. He's going to visit Robby at the jail tomorrow and prepare for the arraignment on Monday. He said he'd talk to us after his conference with Robby. I told him you and I would take care of paying him."

Jon nods. "Yep. Sounds about right."

As he starts the dishwasher, she tells him about the prayer card and the collection of the lockbox and Dad's boxes, then they both go downstairs and convince Denny to switch to a car racing game they can all play together.

Shortly after Denny goes to bed, Sandra goes up to her room, but although she feels as wiped out as Jon looked, she can't sleep. The old curtains let in the too-bright moonlight. She curls up with her back to the window and wonders what Robby's cell is like, if he's alone and able to rest. She flips over, turns her pillow to the cool side, trying to think of anything else. The lockbox comes to mind, and the way Maddie's face hardened when she recognized the bead nestled into the corner. The way she'd reached up to touch the bead on her own earring, slowly. Disbelieving. Dad's scribbled notes on the calendar. Sandra rolls over again and sees the sparkling brooch, Robby's horrified face. Recognition?

The brooch, the bead, the rings… She drifts off for a while and finds herself in Teague Wood, flitting from tree to tree, breathless and afraid. Someone is following her, watching her, sneaking through nearby brush with unnatural speed. A figure crouches over a body in a clearing, which she knows is *the* clearing, although it is different. There are no small crosses topped with dog collars, no ferns and salal or other underbrush, only a stretch of pressed earth. When the figure moves, it reveals Gayle's corpse: fourteen years old and wearing Sandra's borrowed nightshirt. Her dead eyes flash in mute warning as the figure stands and turns…and is Robby: Sandra's little brother as he was the morning after the suicide, wrapped in a worn quilt, eyes beseeching.

She wakes with a gasp and then lies still, just breathing, until her heart beat slows. She throws off the covers and stands by the window in her long T-shirt, feeling heat radiate away as sweat dries slowly on her skin. The yard is still bright with moonlight and full of shadows, Teague Wood a dark line at its far side.

The sound of whimpering pulls her from the window, and she creeps down the hall to Denny's room. He's asleep but agitated, skin flushed and legs jerking as if he too is being chased by nightmares. She pulls the heavy afghan aside and strokes his hair back from his sweaty forehead until he calms. His breathing slows and deepens.

Sandra kisses Denny's forehead, then returns to her room wide-awake. Her phone says it's 1:13 a.m. She should go back to bed, but she needs to wear herself out. She's searched for Dad's letter to Aunt Phil everywhere in Teague House, but something clicks in her fevered brain. Mom used to wander away from Teague House in the early days. What if she's the one who found it? What if she hid it in the cottage?

She yanks on jeans, a sweatshirt, and running shoes, and

heads toward the cottage, phone in hand in case she needs a flashlight. Thinking back to her aunt's story of discovering Mom at the cottage on that long ago Christmas, Sandra feels as if she's walking in her mother's footsteps.

Maybe there had been things too precious to risk Aunt Phil finding, like the letter Dad had written.

As she leaves the grassy yard and enters the wooded part of the path, she wishes she'd driven. This feels too much like her dreams. Every noise startles her. The trail is rife with brambles pressing inward, catching at her clothing like fingers holding her back. She moves quickly even so, accustomed to trail running on uneven ground. The night air feels good after the stuffiness of the house. At least she's doing something. At least she's moving.

Ahead, a soft light appears through the trees, and in moments, Sandra arrives near the swing set in the cottage's yard. Robby's car is alone in the drive. A single small lamp filters through the living room drapes. Sandra lets herself in with the spare key from under the mat and hurriedly locks the door behind her, still feeling spooked.

It's as clean as if ready for a Realtor's pictures. Even the girls' clutter has been removed from the coffee table, presumably by Christine, and there are no dishes in the sink or on the counters.

Sandra gets her bearings. She doesn't have many memories of living here. She was practically a toddler when Teague

House was complete enough to move into, but the cottage layout is simple, and she knows where she wants to start. She eases the creaky ladder down from the trapdoor in the hallway ceiling, full of dread and a sliver of hope that will not die, although she can't imagine what she could find that would miraculously fix everything.

One of Sandra's worries is laid to rest as soon as she pokes her head through the opening. The dust lies undisturbed. Neither the police nor Robbie's family has been up here recently.

The roof is only five feet above at its highest point. A string dangles from a bare bulb. She pulls until it clicks, and a bluish glow illuminates the area. The rudimentary plywood floor holds a spread of plastic tubs, labeled with masking tape. Winter coats, sports gear, baby gear, all saved in duplicate: "Chelsey" this and "Lottie" that.

She crouches in the middle of the floor, just as Aunt Phil described Mom that long ago night. She twists to examine the shallow areas under the eaves. Empty. Mom had been sitting near the trapdoor, almost as if waiting for her, Aunt Phil had said.

Sandra looks around one last time, hoping for inspiration, although she's starting to think she's wrong. Her mom had come here merely to commune with figments of her imagination. Then Sandra notices the rough plywood flooring isn't nailed down and one piece has a groove along the edge, caused by a crack in the wood not unlike her windowsill. Cracked enough to pull up?

She slides plastic tubs aside to clear the four-by-eight panel. She's dubious. Her mother had never been athletic. But this was decades ago. She would have been able-bodied enough. And there would have been less to move out of the way without all these bins belonging to Robby and Christine.

Setting her feet along the edge of the neighboring piece of plywood, Sandra levers the cracked panel. She sucks in a sharp breath. Nestled in the insulation below is a metal box, almost a twin to the one Denny had found under the porch. Its remaining paint is faded blue.

Awkwardly, she balances the plywood on one knee and reaches to retrieve the box. Like the other, it has a built-in combination lock. She lets the plywood thump down and sits cross-legged with the box in her lap.

Just like the other box, there's a four-digit code. She tries iterations of Mom's birthday and Aunt Phil's, but neither work. She carries the box downstairs, hoping Robby has a junk drawer in his kitchen with a screwdriver inside.

He doesn't. She settles for a sturdy butter knife, shoving it in above the lock mechanism, and twisting hard. The knife bends—and the latch gives way.

Heart in her throat, she sets it on the table. The giddy satisfaction of success drains quickly, leaving only dread.

She lifts the lid. No protective plastic here. A wreath of

caramel-colored braids lies on top, with red beads and silver bells woven in. She feels sick. Sandra reaches as if to touch, then draws back, feeling like a ghoul. How can she justify interfering with what has to be evidence?

But she is hypnotized by horror, contemplating a choice she never thought she'd have. This box was well hidden. No one living knows of its existence and location except maybe Aunt Phil. And Aunt Phil told her to leave the past in the past. Sandra could just put it back. Pretend she never discovered it.

She could even destroy it. The bead in the other box may still have DNA, but maybe not. It's hard, shiny, small, and was stored in a damp plastic bag. Who can say where it came from or who put it there? There's a chance it won't be enough, on its own. Not like this. Not like…hair.

If Sandra destroys the box, Maddie and everyone else tied to the long dead victims may go on living with inexplicable losses. They're used to it, as is Sandra. Sorrow and tragedy are part of life.

Hardly breathing, Sandra lifts the hair out and lays it on the kitchen table. She reveals a blue rabbit's foot key ring with no keys, and a pair of rhinestone-studded reading glasses with most of the rhinestones missing. Taking up the lion's share of space is a packet of thick high-quality paper, folded into thirds and tied up with a ribbon, and under that, torn pieces of her father's staff paper, covered with handwriting. There's also a stack of photographs, which she takes out and flips through: her, Jon, Robby, separately and together, and even the whole family, her parents smiling and wholesome. And a young man in robes, the one Maddie said was Nate Belter, who now owns the junk shop.

Sandra picks out the torn pieces of her father's staff paper and lays them out. She knows where the tape is, on the desk by the hallway, and she fetches it as if in a dream.

As the edges come together, Sandra's mouth goes dry. It's the letter Dad intended for Aunt Phil.

36

RUSS

....

1993

R uss hunched on the couch in the glorified shed he called
a studio, cigarette between his lips, Jacky D in reach like
a security blanket. In the gloom, two wedding bands threaded
on a silver chain flashed on his shaking palm. He tried to
figure out what the hell to do, but his mind kept slipping.

She'd fucked him over again.

The rings on the chain gleamed, flawless against his rough
and ruddy skin. Dim light from a single lamp picked out the
engraved initials: "MC & NC '91." He blinked them into
focus, the tiny letters doubling in front of his eyes, then clearing again. His usual rule was no hard stuff on weeknights. But
tonight it was medicinal. Whatever would get him through.

Nineteen ninety-one was just a couple years ago. What
went wrong, that both bands were on a single chain, instead
of a pair of ring fingers? Russ wanted to find the one who'd

worn it and ask, but he suspected it was too late. He clenched his fist, then forced his fingers open and dropped the chain and rings into the pocket of his flannel shirt.

With a shudder of disgust, he drained the bottle and tossed it toward the overflowing trash can. Glass thudded on the filthy carpet, almost masking the knock. Russ sat up straight, ears straining, and it came again, more clearly. A soft tap at the door.

"Daddy?" The knob twisted back and forth as Russ crushed out his cigarette. The door edged open and a small voice whispered through the crack, voice trembling.

"Dad, are you there?"

Russ pulled the door wide. Robby was shivering in his favorite Ninja Turtles pajamas, but at least he'd pulled on his rain boots to walk over from the house. Russ hugged him hard and smoothed his hair. "What's wrong, big guy? What are you doing way out here? Isn't it past your bedtime?"

Robby mumbled something into Russ's shirt, and Russ loosened his grip and led him to the couch, wishing the place didn't reek of booze and cigarettes. "Now, what'd you say, Rob? Tell me. It's okay."

"No one's there and Mom won't wake up. I got scared." He wouldn't meet Russ's eyes.

Russ winced. Goddammit. The older kids must still be out. Friggin' Val. He swallowed down his fury, the rings burning a hole in his pocket. "Okay, big Rob," he said. "I happen to know Mommy's just fine, only she's extra tired. You look pretty tired too. So how 'bout this? You sleep here tonight, on this extra-comfy couch, and Daddy will keep you safe and sound. I might go check on Mommy real quick though, all right?"

Robby nodded, bleary with exhaustion. "Can you sing me a song first?"

"Course I can." Russ pulled the rain boots off the boy's feet and covered him with an old quilt. He picked up his guitar and crooned a lullaby. Despite the soothing sounds, his sick feeling sharpened to a razor-wire zing of fear and fury, but Robby's eyelids drooped. In a few minutes, he was fast asleep.

Russ set the guitar on its stand and looked down at Robby, who slept like a comatose rock. If he did wake, hopefully he'd remember Daddy would be right back.

Rising, Russ pulled on a knit cap against the autumn night. As he eased the door shut, a breeze wafted through the last of the leaves on the aspens along the path, and he looked up at the clear, star-studded sky. Sucking in a breath of clean air started a coughing fit. He'd taken up smoking again a couple months ago, and his lungs hadn't adjusted to their new reality. He couldn't stand the stench, didn't want his kids around it, but he needed something to keep the top of his head from flying off.

He glanced toward the big house, shaking his head at the thought of Robby picking his way all the way down here in the dark. Brave boy. The edge of the forest obscured Russ's view, but he made out the dim night-light in the kids' bathroom. His and Val's room faced the other direction. He wondered if she'd passed out in the living room. She'd been most of the way through a bottle of cheap red in front of the TV when he crept upstairs earlier to search their bedroom and discovered the rings. He should have checked on Robby then.

He swallowed hard. Even now, the lines of the house filled him with pride. It had been their dream, his and Val's. They'd broken away from the crass lower-middle-class suburbia of their parents and made something more authentic for their own family: a life close to nature, their home a product of his hands, and hers. "We made it," he whispered out loud. He didn't get it. Why wasn't it good enough? What made her listen to that bastard?

Move, he told himself, but his hand sought the flask in his side pocket, which still had some dregs in it. *Dregs of courage. All I've got left.* He took a slug. The burn steadied him and he stepped into the woods. A half moon pooled shadows along the base of the firs that made up most of the forest, camouflaging every root and bramble in his way. The third time he tripped painfully into one of the old-growth trees, he realized despite the clarity of his thoughts, his coordination was off. He resorted to the little flashlight in his jacket pocket, picking his way like an old lady. Dual urgencies burned in his gut: the low-grade wrongness of Robby alone in the studio, and the terrible question of what he would find in the clearing.

He needed to know, or maybe he already knew, although every molecule of his body longed to be mistaken.

The quick-flowing water and slippery rocks of the creek flummoxed him. He'd crossed before, no problem, but high water plus night plus alcohol… He was going to fall on his ass. As he wavered, a branch cracked sharply behind him, and he jumped. Whirling, he strained to see into the shadows. No one could be out here. This was his land, his secret path. Maybe a deer?

He held his breath to listen for anything beyond the constant burbling of the water at his feet, but all was silent.

Must have been a deer, frightened by Russ's clumsy stumble through the wood. He was sweating under his layers, heart pounding, as he picked his way across the creek, his work boots finding purchase on the rocks under the surface, hand bracing the rings in his chest pocket as if he were about to recite the Pledge of Allegiance.

Past the creek, it took ten minutes of bushwhacking to reach the clearing. He hadn't been this way in a while, but there were signs of passage, which constricted his throat, made his breath fast and tight. Way back when they first got the land, he'd stumbled on the dog's old grave because he and Val prided themselves on exploring every inch of their acreage. When that first awful time came to dig, he'd remembered the clearing. Peaceful, like a chapel of green. And so well hidden no one would stumble on it by accident.

He knew even before he ran the flashlight around the clearing, but the fresh disturbance in the earth pulled a deep groan from him. They'd done it, called his bluff. Trapped him between impossible choices. But not really. He knew what he had to do; he just had to find the balls to do it. *What if stepping up to be a man means leaving your children behind?* If he'd done the right thing in the first place, he wouldn't be here now. His love for Val cost so much, in the end.

Spitting into the darkness, he approached the broken earth and knelt. Dampness soaked the knees of his jeans, and the muddy heels of his boots hit the bones of his butt. The flask called him, even with only a drop or two left, and he unscrewed the cap and tipped it down his throat like an offering. *God have mercy.*

He fished out the rings, cradled them in his hands, and felt tears flowing down his face.

"Rest in peace," he murmured. He would leave them here, he decided. Better they be found together. He scooped at the damp earth with both hands.

This time, the snap of a branch came from in front of him, and he jerked up his head. A moment stretched long while his brain unscrambled the impossible. There, where she couldn't possibly be, stood his sixteen-year-old daughter. Sandy, long hair snagged with twigs, face tearstained in the light of the flashlight he'd set upright in the ground. Like a deer poised to run, she hesitated before him, eyes wide.

"Dad? What are you doing?"

"Nothing, honey. Nothing."

Her face hardened. He protested, "I swear, it's not what you think." How long had she been there? What had he said aloud?

He tilted his hand hurriedly to dump the chain into the shallow hole. He pushed earth on top, then clambered to his feet to bundle her away, to paste innocent explanations over whatever she thought she knew. Maybe a bribe, a beer or a joint, would distract her, get her to listen.

But she was gone, her footsteps loud and panicky as she crashed through the woods.

"Fuck," Russ said. He stooped to grab the flashlight, then gazed after her. "Fuck."

Sandy had seen. Sandy had heard. Sandy knew now, and if she didn't, she'd put it together. He wished more than anything that he could turn back time, or even that, somehow, it had been Jon out here. Jon hated him anyway. Sandy was still his little girl.

Oddly, his mind had calmed. He felt steadier than he had in days. No, years. It was a solid calm, the calm of certainty, and it burned away the swirl of alcohol so that he looked down on himself as if from the Milky Way.

He and Val were going to face the music, like they should have with the very first death.

In the studio, Robby slept curled on his side. Russ knelt

to kiss his forehead, inhaling the salty scent rising from the boy's hair. He stumbled getting up, but Robby didn't stir. Russ grabbed his cigarettes and a notebook and went to sit on the front step, door open so dim light fell across the page.

Words were always inadequate without music under them, but he tried to impress his love for Sandy, for all three of the kids, into every line. He tore out the page, folded it carefully, and slid it into his chest pocket. Then he paused. Good old Phil, who would come for the children, thank god for her— she should have the whole truth, just in case. He chewed the pen cap, staring into the darkness.

Phil,

You've been a good sister-in-law and a good aunt through everything. You didn't ask for this and I'm sorry to lay it on you, but you're the closest family we got. Be good to our kids. Don't let them visit us—tell them we love them and we don't want to drag them down more than we already did. Tell them they're nothing like us.

I need you to know what happened, the real story, beyond whatever ends up in the papers. Tell the kids, when they're ready. If they need to know…

Inside the studio, Robby muttered in his sleep. Russ swallowed, looking at what he'd written. He'd never laid it all out, for himself, or for anyone. The opposite. He'd spent the past decade practicing denial. Trying not to think. The surreal moments when he'd had to face the reality of what Val had done, what that monster convinced her to do, were grotesque nightmares to get through and wake from and leave in the rearview mirror.

His hand got sore as he spelled it out. The homeless guy with the little dog. The old lady who lived in her car. The druggie who'd left her baby. Phil needed to know, in case the plan went wrong. In case Val went free. In case that bastard got to her again. Or what if one of the kids turned out to have the same fault lines? He didn't want to believe it could happen, but he thought back to his soul mate, his true love, sweet sixteen-year-old Val with her mischief and her passion for making a good life and doing good in the world, and he never saw it in her either.

He stopped two deaths later and there was more he wanted to say, but if he kept going, he'd never be done. He signed with a scribble, then looked at it dumbly. He couldn't trust this to the mail. Hurriedly, he went back inside and slid it into one of the hundreds of record albums on the studio's shelves, then scrawled a PS on Sandy's note. Sandy would tell Phil where to look. And she was a good girl, respectful. She would leave it for her aunt to read.

He checked Robby again, and once more trusted him to the heavy sleep of the young, closing the studio door carefully behind him. In the big house, he found his little girl snoring softly behind her closed door. He stood with his hand on the knob, wondering if he could steal one more look at her face, but he couldn't risk waking her. He slid the note under her door for her to find in the morning.

It occurred to him that she'd been in the wood awfully late, mascara smeared across her face as if she'd been crying even before she saw him. Protectiveness leapt up, but he beat it down. From this point forward, the kids were better off without him or their mother.

Jon's door was closed too, light showing underneath. He listened closely, hoping his eldest had come home safe. All was quiet, and Russ left him alone, knowing he would wake to a changed world where he'd be the man of the family. He'd leave for college soon, and Russ's heart swelled with pride. His smart boy, his firstborn. He paused and blinked back tears, wishing he could undo their last interaction. Maybe, soon, he would write Jon a letter. Maybe, someday, Jon would forgive him.

In the master bedroom, Val, too, was asleep, or more likely, passed out, since Robby hadn't been able to wake her. Russ shook her shoulder, then gently kissed her cheek. What if she blinked awake, happy to see him, as she used to? But she was too far gone, and he patted her cheek repeatedly, nearing a slap by the time she gasped to consciousness.

"Go 'way," she slurred.

"I love you," he said.

She batted a hand at him. "'M sleepin'"

"I told you it was over, Val, remember? I warned you it was over?"

"Was an accident." She groaned and rolled away. "Promise," she mumbled.

"I'm calling the cops, Val. I'm calling them in the morning, and I'm telling them everything. I just want to tell you I love you, one more time. I'm doing this for you, for us, for the kids."

Gently, he leaned in and planted one more kiss at her temple, then left the room. There was no phone line in the studio, so he'd have to return in the morning. But before he did, he'd spend the remains of the night watching over his baby boy.

37

MADDIE

After going to the junk warehouse, I park downtown. It's a beautiful afternoon, and there's more foot traffic than usual, with kids out of school and families taking a long weekend. The coffee shop is hopping, but I go in for a refill, then walk over to one of the empty benches facing the park.

When I pull out my phone, I find missed texts from Eb and Sandra.

> Eb: Tx for your help & cooperation. Collected evidence
> from Teague House. Arrest made. Dinner this wknd?

I blink. Arrest? He must mean in the Bethested case. But that's huge. Whoever they arrested must have some link to the older bodies in Teague Wood. And his invite may mean there's something he can share. I text back:

Congrats! My treat. You pick the place and time.

Sandra's message is a photo of a printed card with a name, birth, and death dates on it, followed by a text: "Went thru boxes again. Found Catholic prayer card from Dad's grandfather's funeral. Proves he was there?" I try calling her back, but she doesn't pick up. I text:

Give me a call.

Sandra's struggled with the idea of her dad being a killer, and the only saving grace seemed to be that she was able to see her mother as some kind of hero, staying silent to protect the kids from knowing what he was. If Russ was away and Val was part of the killings, Sandra's going to be devastated. It will be better to have that conversation in person.

I get up and stroll a circuit around the small park, thinking. Valerie was an average-sized woman when she was younger, based on the pictures I've seen. It's hard to imagine her luring multiple men and women out into the woods and killing them there or to imagine her killing them in her home or vehicle and manhandling their bodies out to the burial ground. And, not to be sexist, but she was the primary caregiver for three children while Russ, from the sound of it, was away on construction jobs or messing around in his studio. He had a lot more freedom to kill. Where were the kids if Val was doing the killing?

It doesn't feel right. And neither did my foray into the

junk warehouse, although there was nothing blatant about it. I didn't like the Belters' private conversation about burning something down—although that could have been metaphorical, or literal but innocent, rather than as hinky as it seemed.

I make a mental note to run a background check on the two of them when I'm back at my computer.

I also wish I'd gotten a closer look at Nate Belter's pocket watch. It's not such an odd affectation for an older man, especially one who buys and sells antiques. But Davina always wore her grandad's gold pocket watch, with the chain hooked to a belt loop of her jeans or threaded through the buttonhole of a vintage waistcoat she liked to wear. Without a good look at the inscription on the back, there's no way I could tell if it was the same watch, so it's nothing but another niggling maybe, which there are too many of in this case.

Like the Teague House break-in—just kids? Or a family member having a temper tantrum when they couldn't find what they were looking for? I don't like it, any which way, and wish the police hadn't dismissed it so easily. Robby disappeared from the funeral reception early. Is there any way—and any reason—it could have been him?

My phone buzzes: Sandra texting me back:

Sorry, I'm zonked. BTW, Robby arrested for Gayle's murder. Don't want to think re: Mom&Dad right now. Will call tomorrow.

I walk faster for another loop around the park. Robby Rawlins. If Robby killed the schoolteacher, what was his link to the old graves? How old would he have been? I flip backward into my notebook. He would have been about ten when Russ died. A little young to be part of some kind of family serial murder scheme, although if his parents had involved him, it would have traumatized him—enough to do the same himself? On the other hand, if anyone in the world was going to stumble on the clearing by accident, it would be him, considering that he has a legitimate reason to walk Teague Wood regularly.

My ear feels hot, and I realize I've been tugging thoughtfully at Davina's earring as I walk. I force myself to leave it alone.

If Nathan was involved with Valerie Rawlins way back when, might he have a motive to break into her house now that she's gone and her children are going through her things? Might he have a motive to burn something down before evidence was discovered? Might he be wearing a pocket watch that belonged to my foster sister but was too valuable to bury and too special to sell?

I clench my jaw, making up my mind. I'm going to keep an eye on the Belters tonight, just to ensure that no one tries to burn anything down.

38

SANDRA

....

FRIDAY

S andra backs away from the window in the cottage's kitchen.

As she'd read her father's account, wanting to deny every piece even as they slotted into place with what she knew and what she remembered of her parents, an engine rumbled to a stop in the driveway. She'd peeked through the curtain to find an oversized truck outside, a familiar man climbing from the driver's seat. Despite the white hair and the years separating him from Mom's photo, she knows who he is. This is the man her father called a monster, who seduced her mother not only into bed, but into murder.

There's a pause, the firm kerchunk of a truck door closing, and the doorknob jiggles then stops. Sandra strains for any sound, holding her breath. Her cheeks are hot, her muscles twitching. If he tries to break in, if she doesn't hear him return to the truck and start it up in a matter of seconds, she needs to call the police. She reaches for her phone and realizes it's still in the crawl space.

She's pivoting silently toward the hallway when the small metallic sounds of a key in the lock warn her he doesn't need to break in. Her eyes go straight to the box on the table. She stuffs Dad's mended letter into the box and grabs it up, but the door is already opening, revealing the white-haired man carrying a yellow gas can.

Nathan Belter has more than twenty years and no more than an inch of height on her, but he's dense and wiry and might hold his own in a fight. His face blanks with shock when he sees her standing there but only for a millisecond, and then, as he scans her up and down in the same assessing way she'd scanned him, he clocks the box in her arms and his lips stretch in a smile.

"I'm sorry to barge in like this," he says. "I didn't think anyone would be home."

"Nate Belter?" she says. "I was just reading about you."

"Don't believe everything you read. You're Val's girl. Sandy, right?" He smiles, and she thinks for a moment he's going to offer his hand to shake, but he just looks past her, taking in the darkness of the rest of the room and the pool of dim light from the hallway. "You here by yourself? A friend over at the sheriff's told me that brother of yours got himself arrested."

"It's Sandra. I need you to leave the property, right now,"

she says, keeping her voice from shaking by sheer force of will. "The police are on their way."

He sets the gas can down and pulls out one of the kitchen chairs. "Now, I doubt that. Not too many people call the police just because a car pulls up to their house, and this is just a friendly visit. Looks like you've got what I was looking for right there. Very good."

She stands across from him, holding the box in front of her like a shield. "I don't know what you mean," she says, but only to keep him talking. She knows exactly what he means. He came for the items her mother had stashed away, and now he can take them without burning Robby's house down. She supposes it's good for Robby, but it may not be so good for her.

He's an old man. But Gayle is dead, and Nate, as Dad described him in the letter, is ruthless. She must not underestimate him. If he gets his hands on her, she might have a fifty-fifty chance in a physical fight, her relative youth and conditioning against his size and muscle. Her best bet is not being caught. If she were to flee right now, taking him by surprise, she thinks she could make it to her phone in the crawl space, but she'd be trapped. If he uses the gasoline, it's anyone's guess if the smoke would get her before the cops arrived. Her strength is running and endurance. Even with her slow-healing tendon, she should be able to outpace this guy and get away, if she can escape quick enough through a door or window.

He seems in no hurry to try the wrest the box from her,

looking up at her with warmth. "I loved your mother very much. Your brother Robby, he's mine. My son, you know that? I had no desire to hurt any of you."

This confirms something she'd barely begun to suspect. Russ hadn't mentioned it in the letter, but the torn photo Mom saved, the blue of the eyes, the angle of the nose... The resemblance is there, for those who look.

Sandra feels ill. She hugs the box to her. "You're nothing to Robby. And you already hurt us. You killed our father! You killed all those people, didn't you?" It's the truth as she needs it to be. She stares at him, daring him to deny it.

"Sit down," Nate says kindly. Even though her heart is hammering, even though she wants to rage and throw things at him, she reluctantly pulls out the chair and perches on the edge. In his voice is a promise that he will tell her everything.

She's been glued to every shifting expression on his face, and a movement along the edge of the window startles her. Part of her melts in relief because somehow, Maddie is here, peering in from outside. Sandra is not alone with a killer.

"Tell me," she prompts. "Why did you kill them? Why did you bury them on our land?"

"I didn't kill them, and I won't take credit. Your mother did, all but one who wasn't quite gone. They were lost souls. It was a mercy, for them and the community they tainted. I hope you can understand." His expression is open, pleading, but the word sounds twisted on his tongue.

"How could it be a mercy?" she demands.

Nate brushes at his silver mustache. "She and your father, the others—we wanted a better world. Where everybody helped each other, everybody pulled their weight. The others—all hypocrites, all sheep. But your mother understood. A world like that can't happen unless you cut out the rot. When she had the opportunity, she took it."

"A better world? You're saying my mother killed five people because she wanted a better world?"

"It was a mercy. That woman had courage and conviction," he snaps.

Sandra recoils.

His lip curls. "I guess you must take after your father." One of his hands is resting on the table. His fingers begin to tap restlessly.

With a shudder at the disdain in his voice, Sandra says slowly, "But you did kill him, didn't you? He didn't hang himself at all."

"I regret that. But he was about to ruin all our lives with his lack of vision, of faith."

She swallows. "How did you know he was planning to go to the police?"

"How do you think? Your father told Val he was done covering for her, and she managed to call me even though she was pretty messed up. She knew how much was at stake."

Sandra shakes her head. This was it. Her mother had

remained silent for the rest of her life, not because she was weak and self-indulgent as Sandra had always believed, and not because she was protecting her children from knowing their father was a killer. Val hadn't wanted to go to jail herself, and then, perhaps, she'd been destroyed by the resulting death of the man she'd married.

Sandra swallows, wondering what Maddie's doing out there. She must have called the police by now. "And Gayle? What did she have to do with any of this?"

He shakes his head. "That was only an accident. My son DJ has a temper."

"But it benefits you, doesn't it?"

"It benefits my family, in some small ways, although neither of my sons are likely to admit it. I'm very sorry that's she's gone."

Sandra wishes she were clever enough to extract all his sins, prescient enough to have recorded this on her phone, but she's not and she wasn't. She's nauseated with disgust and a physical need to distance herself from this man, this creature. She has no sense anymore that any of the expressions that infuse his voice and cross his face are real; he sat down here, at the table, not to bargain but to toy with her.

He says, "Thank you so much for finding the box for me. I needed to be sure it didn't fall into the wrong hands, and my son couldn't seem to manage it. He checked a favorite hiding spot that Val showed me once at Teague House—yes, she and I used to spend quite a lot of time together there years ago, I guess you didn't know that!—but DJ got scared off. There will be more trouble if I don't stop it here. I'm sorry about you as well, but I'm afraid it's necessary. So much tragedy in the Rawlins family."

In less than a millisecond, he shrugs off the weary old man persona. She senses it even before she parses what he's said. Twisting out of her chair, she scrambles for the hallway in a half crouch before he's moved an inch.

The sound of a gunshot reverberates through her bones. Shock galvanizes her, instinct taking over.

She throws the box at him, hoping to slow him down, and flees unthinking, finding herself suddenly past the master bedroom door, flipping the flimsy lock and lifting the closest window. Two more shots follow as he careens through the hall, and she shudders, anticipating a bullet tearing through the drywall next to her. Something heavy slams into the bedroom door.

She pushes off through the screen, landing awkwardly on damp ground and rolling away. Back on her feet, she runs in a wide arc, casting terrified glances behind her but seeing nothing. Sirens blare in the distance.

She stops, searching desperately. Where did he go? Another gunshot blasts inside the house.

Maddie! But no, Maddie is here, grabbing her arm and dragging her behind Nate's pickup truck. Sandra crumples, breath sawing and eyes wide as she searches the darkness for threats.

Moments later, vehicles with flashing lights crowd Robby's driveway. Sandra allows herself to be wrapped in a blanket. She huddles, shivering, in the back of a police car, light-headed as she hears the confirmation. She makes the officer repeat the words. The shooter is dead.

Nate shot himself.

As the first traces of warmth begin to slow her shivers, her lips turn up, just a little. He's paid for her father's false suicide with a real one.

39

MADDIE

....

MONTHS LATER

We lay Davina's bones to rest in Portland, during a simple ceremony attended only by Davina's family and the daughter of the woman who killed her.

Mama Hempel is here, in her Sunday best, standing tall at the graveside despite the pneumonia that delayed this ceremony until August. Rose holds baby Ivy close, within the encompassing embrace of her husband, Jackson. Sandra stands across from them, bearing witness to one of Val's victims being laid to rest in peace. And I am here, both to say goodbye to Davina and to release an obsession that's shadowed my life.

We all lay flowers on her casket. Rose adds a tiny locket in which I know she's placed a picture of herself and one of new baby Ivy. Davina's father passed away a good decade ago, and Mama Hempel sets in a lock of his hair. I hesitate with my hand at my ear, suddenly uncertain. I was intending to drop my earring in the grave, but no. Better to keep it where it is. Hopefully I'll pull at it less, no longer worrying at her fate, but it will still remind me of Davina's wicked smile and that she always had my back.

Over the past months, Rose and Mama Hempel have drained me of every detail I know about the Rawlins family and how Val Rawlins fell under the sway of Nate Belter, a small town man whose eugenic inclinations were masked by pretty words about mercy and community. They demanded more than I could give them, so I convinced Sandra to talk to them about Val and Russ, the house and family they built and how it all fell apart.

Mama Hempel invited Sandra here today because she's become fond of her and thinks witnessing Davina being laid to rest will be good for her.

None of us will ever know exactly what Davina's last hours were like. I've visited Axel, the boyfriend she'd run away with, and showed him a picture of Nate. Axel admitted that he took Davina's gold pocket watch and sold it to Nate against her wishes. It was the final straw that convinced Davina she was better than him and wanted to go home and mother her baby. It's hard to imagine how she went from throwing a dead crab at Axel on the beach to agreeing to catch a ride home with Nate, but I'm guessing Nate offered her watch back and gained her trust.

A safe in the warehouse office held items of value the

police linked to other victims. Valerie's souvenirs must have had some meaning for her, but not even the wedding rings were worth much. The objects in Nate's safe were different. He may have targeted the victims he brought to Valerie specifically because, despite their current circumstances, they owned treasures that caught his eye. I suspect he didn't want people he thought of as lesser to have them, and in the end, they reminded him of the woman he thought of as his greatest success.

After the ceremony, I hug Rose and Mama Hempel, and kiss little Ivy, and promise I'll see them for Sunday lunch. Then I take Sandra out for dinner in the city before she heads back home.

Over sushi, Sandra catches me up on her brothers. Jon and Denny have moved out of her tiny Bend condo into Teague House. Jon's looking for a low-key eight-to-five job that will let him spend more time with Denny. Robby's living there too, while Christine's staying in the cottage with the girls. Legal charges against Robby were dropped once DJ Belter confessed to killing Gayle, but his marital issues are a little more challenging.

When I ask Sandra about the brooch that got Robby arrested, she rolls her eyes. "Lottie stole the brooch from Gayle's daughter, Liz, who took it without her mother's permission. She was bragging to the whole class about all the jewels she had. Liz was always bragging and picking on other kids, so Lottie stole the brooch to teach her a lesson. That started Liz's 'bullying' campaign against Lottie, which brought Robbie and Gayle together in the first place."

She takes a long drink and continues, "When Lottie understood that the police found the brooch and thought her dad stole it, she went to her mother. But Christine wouldn't listen. Robby's lucky DJ confessed quickly."

If someone had been quicker to link the Belters to the case and I'd run a background check like I'd intended, we would have found a red flag; DJ's lack of self-control was well-documented. He had two assault convictions, one for a bar fight, one for breaking his girlfriend's jaw. In the end, he's been charged with manslaughter rather than murder, as Gayle's death seems to have been unpremeditated and an accident. According to Eb, DJ claims that Nate goaded him about Gayle for months, saying she was using DJ to get dirt on Marcus. He wanted DJ to talk her out of running or, barring that, to break up with her. DJ resisted at first, but he came to doubt her, and eventually demanded that she come clean. According to DJ, they fought, she shouted and pushed him in the chest, and he shoved her back so hard she hit her head on the corner of his slate fireplace and died instantly.

Sandra says, "Jon thinks Nate wanted DJ to force Gayle out of the election. Apparently, he'd been evading fines relating to his junkyard for years, just carrying on business as usual with his cronies in the commissioner seats. A new squeaky-clean commissioner with no family ties would have been a real threat. Considering what we know of his personal philosophy, Gayle's intentions to foster more programs and services for unhoused people in the community probably pissed him off too."

"So when DJ actually killed her, Nate was happy to help bury her at the old secret graveyard? I wonder if DJ knew about its history."

Sandra shrugs, her voice going grim. "I tend to doubt it. I'm betting that monster wasn't much of a father either. All 'hail, fellow, well met' on the outside and entirely self-serving on the inside."

Sandra has seemed a little shaky to me, the times I've seen her since that night. "What about you? How are you doing?"

She smiles. "I met someone. She's a physical therapist. We're taking it slow, but I'm hopeful. Jon says I sabotage my relationships, and maybe it's true. Maybe for some weird reason, I've had trust issues." She opens her eyes wide, and I laugh. "We'll see how this one goes. So far so good."

We continue chatting for a while. I tell her I've gone out with Eb once or twice, just to catch up on the details of the case, of course. And I tell her I've put my house on the market. "Finally got all Mom's stuff cleaned out. I think I'm just going to rent for a while. I need a break before I settle into anything long-term. And I decided to hang on to Mom's ashes. Having them around makes me feel less crazy when I talk to her. But I bought a lovely urn, so she's no longer interred in a cardboard box."

We're paying the bill when I remember to ask, "What about your aunt?"

Sandra's aunt's whereabouts worried the Rawlins siblings for weeks, as she continued to ignore their messages. They'd started to worry that she'd been a victim of misadventure on her cruise, and when they contacted the cruise line, had learned she'd never boarded.

"She left Robby a voicemail," Sandra says, shrugging. "Telling him she heard about the separation and that he should take it in stride and work on himself for a while. The number the message was left from had a Jamaican country code, and is no longer a working number."

"I guess the lady really wants a vacation," I offer.

"We talked about whether to report her missing, but—" She throws up her hands. "She's apparently fine, and keeping a close enough eye on things to know Robby and Christine are living apart. I have a feeling she'll chime in again sooner or later."

"She seemed like a capable woman," I say.

Epilogue

PHIL

....

PRESENT DAY

Phil rests her paperback novel on her lap and sips the fresh rum punch the server left on the little table next to her beach chair. She wiggles her bare toes in the warm sand. A benevolent sun glows in the flawless blue sky, and heat seeps into her bones even in the shade of the palm trees. Years of Oregon dampness are baking out of her, and she sighs in contentment.

High-pitched giggles rouse her as a family with several young children parades past with enough gear for a jungle expedition. Phil watches them, taking another sip. She misses Chelsey and Lottie and Denny and her big kids too. Still, she's glad, at long last, to be away. It wasn't easy acting as chief jailer, nurse, and bottle-washer to a serial killer, even a declawed one, and Phil plans to take it easy for at least a couple years on the proceeds while all the fuss dies down.

She lifts her punch in a secret toast to Nate, the world's most cooperative blackmail victim. When Phil first stumbled across Russ's confession in the *White Album*, her initial horror almost brought her straight to the police. And then she'd thought through the likely consequences: Nate's arrest, yes, but also Val's arrest. More butting in from social services, who might not be satisfied with Phil as a parent without the children's mother around.

She and Nate had a wee tête-à-tête and came to an understanding. Phil kept Val docile with a little of this, a little of that, in quantities and for durations normally frowned upon by the medical establishment. Her nursing degree was put to good use, walking a line so that Val suffered few side effects and had enough clarity to appreciate her surroundings. Meanwhile, Nate gladly made a deposit into her offshore accounts each quarter once he realized she was a pragmatist and charged very reasonable rates for her silence and Val's, which meant security for him and his family.

With a little snort, she thinks of the looks on the kids' faces when she told them she'd invested her alimony wisely. Alimony, hah! Ned would've lived on the streets before paying her one red cent, and Phil had been too proud to accept such a thing anyway. Nate's money was different. She'd worked her butt off for that.

She'd been worried when he almost blew up everything to try and protect his son, but even that had worked out, as things often did. Fitting that the man who had made Val into a monster and painted Russ a suicide had killed himself in the end. Good old Russ would be pleased at that, and at the kids turning out so well, and that the house he built with his own hands would bring joy to another generation of Rawlinses.

She's interrupted in her musings by a hairy hand falling on the back of the chair next to her.

"Is this seat taken, pretty lady?"

The accent makes her smile. She reaches to remove the beach bag she'd used to reserve the chair and smiles up at the charming Aussie gentleman in a wide-brimmed straw hat and baggy blue swim trunks. He kicks off his huaraches and sighs happily as he settles. Phil hands him the drink she'd saved for him.

"Did Katy go down okay?" she asks. She'd met the elderly David and his wife at the bar the same night she'd joined the tour in Bali. In his cups, David had confided that they'd always dreamed of traveling the world, and he'd decided to make it happen despite Katy's Alzheimer's diagnosis. The trip seemed to be hastening her deterioration, he told Phil on the edge of tears. Katy was barely sleeping, irritable and snappish, and uncooperative on outings. Worst of all, she repeatedly asked for their son, who'd passed away years ago. Katy proved the truth of this by narrowing her eyes suspiciously at Phil and demanding, "What've you done with my Oliver, then?"

Now David smiles happily, showing a mouthful of large

square teeth. "Oh my, yes! That tincture is truly remarkable! Katy was almost her old self at the gardens this morning, and now she's napping like a baby."

"Well," Phil said modestly, "I have my talents. By the way, I hope you'll decide to stay on for the next leg of the journey. I'm more than happy to help. Retirement is wonderful, but I miss being of use."

READING GROUP GUIDE

1. The perspectives of the chapters narrated by the siblings are all in third person; however, the chapters that Maddie narrates are in first person. Why do you think that is? Why include Maddie, an outsider, in a story centered around the Rawlins?

2. When Jon discovers Robby's possible involvement in the bones behind Teague House, he contemplates turning him in to the cops. What would your reaction be if your sibling might be involved in a murder case? What would you do in Jon's shoes?

3. What do you make of Val and Phil's relationship? Do you think they loved each other?

4. Does the relationship between Sandra, Jon, and Robby

read as healthy to you? Why or why not? Is there a sibling you relate to the most?

5. Many characters in the novel are parents or parent-like figures. What do you make of their different parenting styles? What kind of effects do each of them (Val, Russ, Jon, Nate, Robby, Davina, and Phil) have on the children around them?

6. Toward the beginning of the novel, Phil seems to resent Val for how much Phil needs to step in to help raise her kids, but she continues to do so throughout their lives. Do you think Phil wanted to be a parent to Val's kids? Do you think being a mother was important to Phil? Why?

7. What do you think of Phil's desires to travel and explore? And how might it relate, or not relate, to her desire to be "of use"?

8. What are your thoughts on Russ, and how complicit he was in the killings? Do you have sympathy for him? Why do you think he wanted to turn himself in?

9. Why do you think Val fell for Nate Belter? Are there any warning signs early on that she might've been susceptible to his views?

10. Compare and contrast the objects Nate and Val saved, respectively. What does their choice in "souvenir" say about their intentions and character?

A CONVERSATION
WITH THE AUTHOR

What inspired you to write *What Remains of Teague House*?

For me, very often the seed of a story is an image or phrase that has an unusual resonance and won't leave me alone. In this case, it was a piece of Sandra's dream about Teague Wood, as if the bones under the surface were calling out to her. It was germinated by statistics on missing persons and unidentified remains amid the hundreds of millions of acres of forests in the United States. The silence of the hidden dead among the silence of the forests haunted me, and the story started to grow to the point where I had to start writing.

This book has many different points of view. What was it like to write in so many voices and timelines?

These characters became so real to me; I *knew* how they fit together, what they would do, and to some extent, what it would be like to be them. Expressing that creatively so the reader can feel it too is the tricky part.

So far as timeline goes: interweaving pieces of the past among the present-day chapters felt very natural in this book, because the secrets of the past were such powerful yet hidden influences on the Rawlins siblings and on Maddie. The past needed its own voice, and Phil was able to offer that viewpoint and tie it to the present events.

For a story so deeply centered around the tragic and bloody history of the Rawlins family, it was interesting to see the importance that Maddie, an outsider, had in the novel. Why include her in a story about the Rawlins?

Murder (like other crimes and traumas) has damaging effects that ripple far beyond the primary victim. Maddie is a catalyst, nudging secrets into the light so that the real story of the past can be revealed. She also stands in for the friends and family who lost each of the victims.

What is your writing process like?

Full of erasing! I delve into ideas and images and characters that are interesting to me, come up with a rough sketch, test it out, throw it out, completely change it, then try again. Sometimes I feel like I'm working with a lump of clay and my pot keeps collapsing until I finally, finally, get the thing to stand up.

After that, I depend on others to tell me if it makes any sense. I'm fortunate to have trusted writing partners and my fabulous agents and editor to give me feedback and help tease out the best possible result.

What characters were your favorite to write? And on the flip side, were there any characters you found difficult to get a handle on?

I know they're fictional so their feelings can't be hurt, but my instinct is not to pick favorites! I will say Maddie was fun, because she's tough and snarky, and who doesn't enjoy a little snark? Robby was also a good time, because I could depend on him to get in trouble, which is what a writer loves best.

Jon was probably the toughest to get a handle on. I resonated with his layers of grief, the loss of his mother following his wife's death so quickly, and his struggle to parent well when he was hurting. However, he'd been happy and successful in his marriage and family, so in my mind, he'd moved furthest past the traumas of childhood. It was a very nuanced place to dial in on.

What do you think happens to these siblings after the novel ends? Robby especially seems to be in a difficult place. Do you think he gets through it?

I was happy for Robby at the end! In my mind, the path most likely to lead to growth was for Christine to leave him.

Without the pain of losing her, he'd slip right back into his old ways, while the possibility of being reunited with the love of his life and their children may be enough to motivate real change and make it stick. Each of the siblings could probably use therapy, but Robby needs it most urgently.

I think Sandra goes home and resumes her coaching business, in some ways lighter of heart without the direct weight of Russ's suicide on her head. She's started dating, and she'll be less likely to keep others at a distance from now on. Of the three siblings, she's most haunted by Val's actions. I imagine her organizing races and running marathons for charities supporting mental health awareness and crime victims.

Jon is on the brink of moving back to Horace and reimagining what single-fatherhood means. I suspect he'll retrain for a job where he can be more present for Denny, and he'll make an effort to keep Sandra and Robby in his life.

There are multiple points in the novel when a character remarks on the experiences specific to life in a small town. What drew you to set the novel in a remote area?

I've spent my life in rural areas—it's what I know best. I love the woods. Plus, I haven't yet figured out where to hide the bodies in a city, unless you own a construction company. Or a crematorium. Hmmm…

What do you want readers to take away from this novel?

My primary goal is to entertain. If the characters and their tribulations resonate after closing the book, all the better.

I do feel compassion toward my characters no matter how much they screw up or have been scarred by past events, and deep down, I suppose I hope spending time with them will allows readers to feel compassion for them as well and to think about the real-world implications of some of the issues raised.

What books are up next on your to-read list?

Mystery is my first love with fantasy and science fiction close behind. Oh, and nonfiction about social science, writing, running, and nutrition. So my to-read list can get pretty long! For fiction at this very moment, I have Erin Kelly's *The Skeleton Key*, Ruth Ware's *Zero Days*, and Kevin Hearne's *Candle & Crow* in my pile, and for nonfiction, I've got *Story* by Robert McKee and *Born to Run 2* by Christopher McDougall and Eric Orton.

ACKNOWLEDGMENTS

This project benefitted greatly from the talent, energy, and time of many people.

Special thanks to the readers who offered feedback in the early stages: Scott Bigger, Laura Rheume, Stephen Nothum, Alesha Orton, Elsie Hayden, and Tamara Mathias.

My agents at Victress Literary, Alisha West and Lizz Nagle, were fabulous and indispensable. I'm incredibly grateful for all their assistance.

My sincere gratitude also to my editor, MJ Johnston; Emily Engwall; and the rest of the Sourcebooks team for their professionalism, patience, knowledge, and talent.

And finally, heartfelt thanks to my family and most of all my husband, Kevin, for his unfailing support and encouragement.

ABOUT THE AUTHOR

Stacy Johns writes fiction that delves into the shadows of lived experience and the delusions and illusions that twist our dreams, our memories, and our relationships. She grew up in small-town New England and transplanted to Oregon for a sociology degree, later adding a master's in information science. A long-time librarian and resident of the coast, she now resides and plots her mysteries in the Willamette Valley.